THE

RANGER OF THE TOMB;

OR,

GIPSY'S PROPHECY.

A Romance.

BY

WILHELMINA JOHNSON.

———— I did hope
For better things! I hoped I should not leave
The earth without a vestige. *Fate* decrees
It shall be otherwise; and I submit.

KIRKE WHITE.

\

LONDON:

PUBLISHED BY E. LLOYD, AT THE OFFICE OF THE "ILLUSTRATED EDITIONS
OF STANDARD WORKS," 12, SALISBURY SQUARE, FLEET STREET.

1847.

PREFACE.

To depict virtue in its true colours, and to give it that meed of approbation which is justly its due, has been the aim of the Authoress; while to show that vice, although it may triumph for a time, is sure to meet with its due reward at last, has not been lost sight of in the delineations of the various characters of the resent work.

The trusting love of the beautiful Lisbia was fully recompensed by being united to the object of her love, in the person of Edwin Mildmay ; and Parrolla Immorf, notwithstanding all his vicious intentions and deep-laid plots, which he had nurtured with such care, and expected to bring to a successful issue, was foiled in his attempt of gaining Lisbia, by fair means or foul ; but far other motives than those of love urged him to the course he had adopted. He courted Lisbia for the sake of her wealth, and when he found himself foiled, he sought revenge. He met a merited doom.

Count Herman, too, after his life of wickedness, was foiled in obtaining a victim, which the ardent love of Ann for him would have prompted her to become, by the wonderful interposition of Providence.

Olando, who our readers will recollect was deprived of that blessing—reason, was taken ample care of by Lisbia.

Peter, the faithful old servant, was rewarded for his fidelity, by being placed at the head of Lisbia's establishment.

Lady Mackenzie, after she had unconsciously rescued Lisbia from dishonour, by murdering Parrolla under the impression that he was her husband, was confined more strictly than she had been previously.

Rose was married to Mr. Manby, and all the minor characters are worked out in a style highly creditable to the talented Authoress.

The Publisher of Miss Wilhelmina Johnson's RANGER OF THE] TOMB, OR GIPSY'S PROPHECY, thinks little apology need be offered to its numerous readers for the reissuing of so justly popular and highly-approved-of a romance.

LONDON,
March, 1847.

THE RANGER OF THE TOMB;

OR,

GIPSY'S PROPHECY.

CHAPTER I.

"Hark! the raven flaps his wing,
In the briery dell below;
Hark! the death-owl loud doth sing,
To the night-mare as she goes."   CHATTERTON.

In Cornwall, near the sea-shore, stood the ancient castle of Ravenswood, a fine old mansion, around whose grey walls the ivy had profusely entwined itself, and formed a shelter not only for the little songsters; but the bat and moping owl also found a habitation beneath its leaves, in the apertures time had made in the rough grey walls.

No. 1.

The former possessor of this castle was Sir Percival Mornington; its present lord was one Parrolla Immorf, a German, who became possessed of this place, in consequence of his marrying Lucy, the only child of the castle's former lord.

Immorf was a man of but little property at that time; he had left his native land, when he was about five-and-twenty years of age; and he, on coming to England, through interest, obtained a place at the court of King James, which situation he held when he first beheld Lucy Mornington at a ball, and selected her for a partner, when an intimacy commenced between them; and Immorf found means to win the heart of the gentle Lucy, who then was but seventeen years of age, and lovely as the opening rose.

Lucy was heiress, at the death of her father, to Ravenswood Castle, and lands of great extent surrounding it.

Although Immorf was at this time full forty years of age, he was still a handsome man; but of course, being of middle age, the splendour of his youth had passed away; but for all this disparity, both in point of age and fortune, Miss Mornington was devotedly attached to Immorf. And her father not wishing to thwart the happiness of his only child, agreed to his daughter's marriage with Immorf; but he settled the greater part of his daughter's fortune on herself, so that her husband had no control over it.

Too soon had the gentle Lucy reason to regret her ill-assorted nuptials; for the partner she had selected—him she preferred to all others—was a sordid and selfish wretch, and one of a vengeful and cruel disposition.

Soon after the death of Lucy's father, which happened some few months after his daughter's marriage, Immorf began to treat his lady very slightingly; in fact, he was tired of the society of his lady, and the sameness of his castle, and was longing to take a journey to London, in order to partake of the gaieties and pleasures he was wont to do whilst about the court, and which his marriage had deprived him of.

Immorf named his intended journey to his lady, who wished to accompany him; but to that her husband objected, as he said, "on account of the situation she was then in."

Lucy was unhappy, on account of her husband's intended journey; but her sorrow was disregarded by her unfeeling lord, who in the course of a few days set out for the metropolis, and on arriving at court, he was knighted by his sovereign.

Immorf now indulged in every kind of dissipation in which the young, the gay, and unmarried lords were wont to do, forgetful of his lady, and the conduct becoming a married and middle-aged gentleman, rioting in scenes ruinous to his circumstances, and debasing to the dignity of man; some time had passed in this way, when Immorf received a letter from Cornwall, begging that he would immediately return home, for that his lady was confined, and had a beautiful little boy to present him with.

Immorf's brows lowered whilst he read this letter; "and I must leave my pleasures," he inly said, "to congratulate my lady and fondle my heir. I would mother and child were both in heaven! I shall not leave London at least for a fortnight; and when I do, I should like to take Corrinna with me to Cornwall, and would, were it not for my wife's aunt—interest will not let me offend her."

A fortnight and some days had passed, and still Immorf was in London; at length another letter arrived from Cornwall. Mrs. Mornington, his wife's aunt, wrote it, desiring Immorf would immediately return to Cornwall, if he had any value for the life of his lady.

Finding he could not with any appearance of decency remain longer in London, on the second day after he had received this letter, he set out for his castle.

When he reached home, he but coolly greeted his lady, and very little notice did he take of his baby. Engrossed by gloom and discontent, he would wander for hours walking by the sea-shore; at other times, he would spend many hours of the day at an inn, situated in an adjacent town, the landlord of that place being not a little proud of his distinguished guest: there Immorf spent some pleasant hours; but when he returned to his castle, his gloom and ill-humour returned with him, and he repelled the modest endearments of his virtuous wife, and sighed for the insidious courtesans he had left behind him in London.

The infant, who now was twelve months' old, was named Parrolla, after his father; and Lady Immorf, in a very short time, expected an increase in her family.

One day, when Immorf was in a very gloomy mood, and so much excited, that he could hardly forbear quarrelling with every one who came in his way, although he knew not for what—to avoid coming in contact with any one, he retired to a turret in the castle, where he sat ruminating on London, and on the pleasures he had experienced there.

It was a very rough day, and the eyes of Immorf were directed to the sea, where he saw a ship dashed about by the foaming billows—and in the bitterness of his heart, he hoped that it would spring a leak, and that every soul on board might perish.

CHAPTER II.

"Dark were his brows, and gloomy to the sight,
Like clouds,—his eyes like meteors of the night."   OSSIAN.

WHILST Immorf was thus engaged, in watching the motion of the turbulent billows, and the fate of the ship, his lady entered the turret.

"Parrolla, I have been seeking for you this hour," she said; "why, my love, do you indulge this melancholy? surely I have not offended you; if I have, it is unintentional."

"Go, Parrolla," she said to her child; "go and kiss your father;" and she placed the little boy standing at the knee of her husband.

"Go, Parrolla," she again said; "go and kiss your father."

"Go to your father," repeated Immorf, with great emphasis; "I don't know that I am his father. Can I not even in this lone turret be at peace? is there not a moment I can call my own? fool that I was to marry, and be thus harassed; have you not servants enough, that you wish me to turn nurse? take away the child," he roared out, "take him away;" and he stamped with his foot, and his eyes glistened with fury.

Lady Immorf was terrified at the violence of her lord, and for a moment she stood, as it were, rooted to the spot.

Immorf, finding he was not immediately obeyed, took up the child, who was still standing at his knee, and dashed it with violence against the wall of the turret, where its little head came with such force, that the forehead of the child was beat in, and the babe's dress and the floor was saturated with its blood.

Lady Immorf stood for a moment, as if petrified to the spot, horror-struck at the cruel deed of her husband; but soon she recovered her presence of mind, sufficiently to enable her to hasten and pick up the disfigured remains of her child.

But as soon as she beheld its forehead beat in, and covered with blood, its innocent and lovely countenance, now horrid to behold, almost a mass of unshapen flesh, she dropped the child from her arms, and fell senseless on the floor.

Immorf now repented that he had given way to his fiery temper, which had caused him to spill the blood of his innocent child, and for which act he might be called to account, and be made to suffer the full penalty of his crime.

Much alarmed by these thoughts, he lifted his lady from the floor, and placed her on his knee until she recovered the use of her senses, but the moment she again caught a glance of her bleeding child, she again sunk into insensibility, and more than two hours passed away before Immorf could in the least pacify his lady, and cause her to listen to his lamentations for the unhappy accident, and to convince her of the necessity of keeping secret the manner in which it happened

"You would not disgrace, and perhaps bring to a violent death your husband," cried Immorf, "that would not restore our child, but leave you a bereft widow, and the babe which will soon see the light, fatherless."

Harkening to the persuasion of her husband, Lady Immorf consented to say that the child met its death, by accidentally falling with great force against the wall of the turret.

The little innocent was buried with great pomp for so young a child, and the accident that caused the babe's death was much lamented by the household of Sir Parrolla.

But how deep and heavy was the affliction of the heart-broken mother, who knew that her child was murdered, and that by its own father!

That very night, the night of the child's funeral, Lady Immorf was taken in labour, and after much suffering, she gave birth to another son, who was named Percival, after his paternal grandfather.

The babe was from its birth but a weak and delicate child, and as he grew, he displayed a disposition most amiable; in short, he was the very counterpart of his mother.

The unhappy fate of her first-born preyed heavily on the mind of Lady Immorf, and she was for some time in a low and desponding state of mind, which caused the unhappy lady to be yet less agreeable to her selfish lord, who now was almost always absent from his castle, and spent much of his time in London.

Fifteen years had passed away since the marriage of Immorf and his lady, which had been to her a series of unhappiness and misery; it being now the season of the year when the courtiers were in town, and Immorf, notwithstanding the objections of his lady, again journeyed to London.

After having been in London about a fortnight, he was one day strolling through Cheapside, when he recognised a gentleman walking near him, with whom in his younger days, before he left Germany, he had been most intimate; and although it was near thirty years since Immorf had beheld Count Herman, yet he knew him, and their old friendship was renewed with pleasure on both sides.

Count Herman, the new-found friend of Immorf, was a profound scholar, a philosopher, and one who studied arts unfit for mortal man to tamper with.

But with that, Immorf was then unacquainted; a strict intimacy subsisted between the two friends, and they passed a great portion of their time together; in every place in which the young and gay resorted, there you would find Immorf, and the Count Herman. On a morning, subsequent to a night spent in riot, Immorf and Herman were strolling along the Strand, near Temple Bar, when they observed a cart coming along the road, followed by a great number of spectators; in the cart sat a criminal, with his arms pinioned behind him; on inquiry, the friends found that the man in the cart was a murderer, he had murdered his own mother, and was then going to pay the penalty of his crime, opposite the house where the murder was committed.

"And where will he be buried?" eagerly demanded Count Herman, of a man who stood by.

"Buried!" cried the man with a sneer, "no, no; they will not bury him; they will gibbet him on high, where the rain may wash the blood from his gore-stained hands, and the raven and eaglet pick out the eyes of the murderer."

"But where will the gibbet be erected?" inquired the count, with impatience.

"Near where he did the murder," replied the man, "in a field, hard by the Mother Red Cap, on the road to Highate."

"Come, Herman," cried Immorf, "what matters it to us where, or whether the fellow is buried or not?—you surely did not know the wretch when living?"

"I did not," replied Count Herman, "but I have my motives, and such motives, that would strike terror into you if you knew them; but no secret dread now withholds me. I have searched into things proscribed to mortality, and ere the moon which is nearly at the full shall hide her beams from the earth, I must visit the corse of that murderer."

"You surprise me," replied Immorf; "did I not know otherwise, I should believe you to be insane, when I hear you express yourself as you do; but what you now say I consider as mere rhodomontade; you mean to have a joke at my expense, and to gull me with the wonderful."

"No, I am serious, serious as the grave," replied Count Herman, "but we ar observed; more of this anon," and Count Herman began talking on other matters.

Immorf turned his head, and saw a person walking close at their heels; he seemed to observe the count with great scrutiny, then turned an angle that led into another street.

"He is still observing us," cried Count Herman; "see, he is now peeping behind that portico."

"There is some mystery in this," replied Immorf; "were it not noonday, I should have my suspicions. Let us cross to the other side of the way."

They did so, and mixed with a crowd of persons, who were pursuing their own avocations.

CHAPTER III.

> "How did you dare
> To trade and traffick with Macbeth,
> In riddles, and affairs of death!"   SHAKSPERE.

SIR PARROLLA IMMORF, having received an invitation to spend a day with a friend, who lived some miles out of town, and which invitation he accepted, in consequence of his so doing, he did not see his friend Count Herman until three days after the morning spoken of, when they saw the murderer going to execution.

It was towards evening when Immorf again visited his friend, whom he found at home, pacing the room in a disordered and agitated manner.

Surprised at seeing the lively and gay, though not young, Count Herman in such a state of mind, so different to what he had ever beheld him, Immorf inquired the cause.

"To you, Immorf, I fear not to impart the secrets of my heart," replied Herman; "I am indeed most unhappy. I told you it was my intention to visit the murderer's corse—I had especial reasons for so doing, and last night, at the hour of midnight, when all was still and lone, I in secret and with stealthy steps drew near to the gibbet; I had the instruments I needed ready, and with the ladder I had provided, I mounted to the corse, which, by the help of it, I was able to reach —again I looked around to see that none were by; for it was light, the moon being at her full height, and her silvery beams fell on all around me—I looked, and that carefully; but no living thing was visible, excepting a large toad that was squatting under the gallows. I listened, but no footstep sounded on the stillness—I thought myself unobserved—and I had my hand on that which I wanted—when in a moment I heard a voice, at but little distance, cry 'Halt, what do you there?'"

"Terrified at the fear of discovery, I dropped from the ladder, and escaped into a green lane hard by; but I heard the person who had watched me, cry, 'You are discovered—I know you.' This adventure, my friend, has given me much uneasiness," continued Count Herman, "and—"

At this moment, some person tapped at the count's door; he started. "Would my project had succeeded!" he inly said; "then I should have no cause for fear."

When the person who had knocked had entered, the count saw it was a particular friend of his, a Mr. Durain.

"Herman," he said, "I hastened here to serve you. I heard it this morning asserted that you are in the habit of studying arts, that mortal man ought not to be acquainted with; and it is also reported, that you was actually seen last night, at the hour of midnight, tearing from the gibbet a murderer's corse."

Count Herman was about to reply, when Mr. Durain said, "I cannot stay to hear you; the authorities are, or will be acquainted with the circumstances; and were the officers of justice to arrive and see me here, they would suspect me of being a conjuror in what you are accused of"—saying this, Mr. Durain hastened down the stairs nor staid to bid Count Herman or Immorf adieu.

Count Herman trembled from head to foot. "What am I to do, my friend?" inquired of Immorf; "this is a most serious accusation, we were watched—the man who walked behind us on the morning of the execution, must have heard our discourse."

"I think," replied Immorf, "it were best to avoid trouble; if possible, I would fly to Germany, and get out of their reach."

"I will secrete myself," said Count Herman, "until the storm has blown over."

"I lament," cried Immorf, "that you ever engaged in such a transaction."

"I was necessitated to do so," replied Count Herman; "I was compelled by necessity—I wanted a murderer's skull to complete my purpose—and where was I to find one, but on the gibbet? perhaps in the churchyard I might have found one who died in undiscovered guilt; one whose hands were hardly cleansed from the blood of the victim, had I supernatural knowledge to particularise such a one; but that knowledge I have not yet; had I disturbed the mouldering remains of the dead, and torn from every grave in the churchyard its loathsome tenant, I could not have distinguished the murderer from the innocent, therefore, on the murderer's gibbet—there and there only—could I for a certainty obtain that which I wanted."

At this moment, heavy footsteps were heard ascending the stairs.

"They are coming," cried Count Herman, "they are coming to take me."

"You unnecessarily alarm yourself," said Immorf; "the persons who have passed your door are merely some, who are come to the hotel; I see the carriage that brought them at the door."

"I cannot bear this," cried Count Herman, "I must begone. Immorf, my friend, take care of the things I have here; if none interrupt you in so doing, remove them from hence; and of that iron box be particularly careful. Lock it and put the key in your pocket—" Again persons were heard ascending the stairs. "They are coming to apprehend me," cried Count Herman, "I dread the flames—which, as one who studied magic, I should be doomed to suffer in."

"Oh, Splatroni! my tutor, why art thou not by me?"

Saying this, he opened a window, that looked in the garden. "Immorf, adieu," he cried, "we shall soon meet again," then dropped from the window on the ground beneath, and by the help of some garden-pots and flower-stands, made his way over the garden wall, and was soon lost to the sight of Sir Parrolla Immorf, who stood some moments lost in thought, and almost petrified by the unexpected occurrences of the morning. Immorf immediately procured porters, who removed the luggage of Count Herman to the lodgings of Immorf.

The luggage only consisted of two portmanteaus, the iron box, and a whole length portrait of Count Herman; the portrait was finely executed—it was as natural as life.

It represented Count Herman, in the dress he usually wore in the winter season —a long black wrapping cloak—a hat, somewhat after the Spanish fashion, large and rather turned up in front, with a long black feather, inclining to his left shoulder.

In person, Count Herman was tall, his face the longest oval; he had very black hair and whiskers, and the penetrating and under-glance of his full black eyes, together with a sneering expression that sat on his curled lip, gave him no very prepossessing appearance.

The particular charge Count Herman had given concerning the iron box, caused Immorf to be very anxious to examine its contents; he thought it might contain gold, and which, in his hurry, the count had not time to provide himself with; but to Immorf's surprise, when he opened the box, he found it contained no more than a crimson velvet bag, embroidered with gold, in which was an old book written in the German language, some pages of which were rendered unintelligible by time, for it was a very ancient book.

Immorf, who was a good German scholar, soon found, by looking into it, that the book treated on the subject, for which his friend was likely to get into trouble for practising. And Immorf feared that he himself would be called to a severe account, if the things of Count Herman, particularly the magic book, was found in his possession.

Immorf, therefore, thought it the wisest way to return to Cornwall with all speed; and he hoped, as neither his name nor quality were known to the persons at the hotel, where Count Herman had resided, that by immediately returning to Cornwall, no unpleasant result would happen, and that the whole affair would be buried in oblivion.

On the following morning, Immorf got all in readiness for his journey, and ordered porters to take his own and the Count Herman's portmanteau to the inn where he intended to start from; the iron box he carried himself, although it was rather cumbersome, and the full-length portrait of Count Herman he covered with a black cloth, lest the countenance should be known, and he placed it well secured between some boards, not only to prevent the face of the portrait from being seen, but also to preserve the massive and richly gilt frame from being broken.

CHAPTER IV.

Oh! take away that portrait, it looks evil,
And much reminds me of, sir, the devil.

WHEN Immorf arrived at his castle, he ordered the portrait of Count Herman, and the iron box, to be placed in the eastern turret of the castle, a place never used by the family.

From the portrait of Count Herman he removed the black cloth, and had the pictures, which for years had been hung in his bed-room, removed, in order to make room for the portrait of his friend, to the no small annoyance of Lady Immorf, who, when she saw it fastened up against the side wall of her chamber, expressed the repugnance she felt when she looked on the portrait, as it resembled the idea she had formed of the prince of darkness; and she thought, that if his infernal majesty was to visit the earth in mortal guise, he would look precisely as the portrait of Count Herman did.

But, as Immorf paid but little attention to the liking, or dislikes of his lady, he insisted that the portrait should not be removed, and there it hung.

Three years passed on, and Immorf had not seen or received any letter, from his friend Count Herman, on which account he was rather uneasy, fearing that his friend was involved in unpleasant circumstances, on account of the accusation under which he laboured.

"He promised that we should soon meet again," thought Immorf, "and three years have passed away, and I have neither seen him, or heard from him, something must be amiss;" to have his doubts satisfied, he wrote a letter to Count Herman's brother in Germany, in which letter he enclosed one for his friend, Count Herman.

To this letter, an answer was returned by Count Herman's brother; it informed Immorf, that Count Herman had returned to Germany, about the time named in Immorf's letter, and that, after remaining there for a few months, he left Germany, and went to Madrid, in Spain, where he remained for nearly two years; he then returned to Germany, and after he had been there some few months, he was seized with an illness, of which he died.

"The proceedings of my unhappy brother was, and still is, a source of grief to his family," continued the writer, "for it is feared they were of such a nature, as rather to retard, than insure his eternal welfare. There were circumstances attending his death, of a very awful and mysterious nature. Those who were standing around his death-bed, heard sounds they had never before witnessed. It was a calm night, not a leaf in the garden quivered in the breeze, but at the moment of the death of my unhappy brother, there was a noise in the room, as if the winds from the four quarters of the earth had united, and with their combined strength, had cleft the roof of the house asunder. You know, I believe, my cousin Pinhorf; he was present at my brother's death, and was so overcome by the strange, unearthly noise, together with the horrific working and writhings of Herman's countenance for some moments after we supposed he had drawn his last breath, that he fell senseless on the floor, and it was some time before we could bring him too.

Soon as he was somewhat recovered, he knelt down by the bedside, and ejaculated a short but fervent prayer. Then rising and looking at the corse, he said, " 'Tis now all over; I cannot bear to look at him; let some one close his eyes," and Pinhorf turned from the bed trembling like a leaf. " I looked at my deceased brother, and was indeed much shocked when I did so; for his features were much distorted, and his large black eyes were wide staring open, and seemed as if starting from their sockets, and fixed on me. This melancholy affair has made a great impression on us all; but we forbear to judge, being all sinners, and hope with Heaven's good pleasure that Herman has found pardon, however great his enormities might have been. With heavy hearts and weeping eyes, we saw him lowered into his earthy bed—fearful—yet, hoping—he rests in peace."

" And is it so?" cried Immorf. " Herman! then I shall see thee no more; the rosy hours we have passed together, no more will return; never more shall I find a companion to suit me like thee, a night-ranger, and ripe for every luxurious pleasure."

Hearing of his friend's demise, and under circumstances of such horror, affected the spirits of Immorf for the moment.

" Herman was somewhat younger than myself," he inly said, and Immorf began to think on the time, when a debt would be called for, which no man can elude or put off.

" What foolery!" he mentally said, arousing himself, " I am getting vapoured, and shall bring on myself that which I would fain avoid:" pouring out a large goblet of wine, he drank off its contents, then putting on his hat, he left his castle, and took his favourite walk along the seabeach. The wine raised his spirits, and he walked along humming—

" To fret about trifles is nonsense and folly,
      The right end of life is to live and be jolly."

Although Immorf appeared cheerful and rallied his spirits, yet all was not right within; nor could he entirely get rid of thoughts not very agreeable or amusing to his mind, namely, the thought of death and the grave.

It was a lovely morning, the sun was shining brilliantly in the heavens, and it being in the month of June, the dog-roses profusely adorned the hedges, and wild flowers in all their varied beauty decked the meadows. Immorf was tired of roaming on the seashore; but he preferred any place to home, and the society of his lady. He turned his steps into the fields, and seated himself on a hillock, over which the wild honeysuckle and rose formed a bower; the linnet and blackbird were gaily singing in a tree near him, and he listened with discontent to their notes.

" Happy birds!" he exclaimed, " ye are chained to no wife, but ramble at large; subject to no control, nor submit to any law, but that of your own pleasure. Then why should man be shackled, subjugated to what is called morality, and strict observance of worldly custom?—why should not man gratify his propensities as do the birds of the air, and beasts of the field? To man is given reason; and that, forsooth, is given him as a make-up for all the privations he undergoes, in consequence of this accounted good, but which I call an evil! Man must forbear, nor indulge in those tantalizing but prohibited pleasures common to the brute creation; their state is better than mine, and gladly would I give my being for theirs."

Whilst engaged in this cogitation, he saw a female crossing the meadow, and coming in the direction to where he was sitting. She held a basket in her hand; but whether she was young or old, handsome or ugly, Immorf could not, until her near approach, discover; for he could not now distinguish distant objects, as he had done in the days of his youth.

CHAPTER V.

"I'll speak to her,
And she shall be my queen."   MILTON.

WHEN the female drew nigh to where Immorf was sitting, he saw she was a girl of about seventeen years of age, of the most surpassing beauty, tall and finely formed, and her clear fair complexion was adorned with the hue of the rose; beneath her polished forehead shone a pair of blue eyes, the most lovely Immorf had ever looked on.

A short petticoat of white dimity showed her well-formed ankle, and a brown bodice laced in front with blue ribbon, confined her full bosom; she wore a round straw hat, and over her temples and shoulders her golden hair fell in rich profusion.

She carefully examined the bank near where Immorf was sitting, and having found some herbs she came in search of, she gathered and put them in her basket.

Immorf approached her, and said, " you are looking for herbs, my pretty maid, permit me to assist you in your search;" and he gathered some of the herbs the girl was in quest of; then said, " for what purpose are you gathering these herbs, fair girl?"

"For my mother, sir," she replied, "who is very ill."

"Come, give me your basket," cried Immorf, "and go and sit on yonder hillock, until I have filled it; with pleasure I will wait on you," and he tried to take her basket.

But she held it tightly : "no, sir," said the girl, "that must not be; what would people think, if they knew a great gentleman like you, gathering herbs for a poor girl like me?"

"And how can you tell I am a great gentleman?" inquired Immorf.

"I am sure you are, sir," replied the girl.

"My name, nor quality, is not written in my forehead," said Immorf, gaily.

"No, sir, but I know you."

"And who am I, my pretty lass?"

"Sir Parrolla Immorf, living at the castle," replied the girl.

"Well, I find you know my name," said Immorf, "and now, now my pretty one, 'tis but fair you should tell me yours."

"My name, sir, is Rose Mildmay," said the girl.

"And where do you live, my pretty Rose?" inquired Immorf.

"I but cross three meadows, and go down the green lane, and there stands my father's cottage," said the girl.

"By Heaven! 'tis too bad, to hide beauty like yours in an obscure cottage; should you not like to go to London, to plays and balls, where you would shine the fariest of the fair—should you not like to be a lady, my charming Rose?"

"Oh, no, I am not fit to be a lady," said the artless girl, "I am unlearned, and unfit for ladies' company."

"Ah, but you could soon learn, my fair Rose," replied Immorf; "should you not like to have silks, and lace, and diamonds, and pearls?"

"I have no wish for such things," cried Rose, "all I wish is that my poor brother William had not gone for a soldier; I fear his going will break mother's heart."

"Then your brother is gone for a soldier," said Immorf; "your mother must not fret about that, I suppose he followed his own inclination?"

"Oh, no, he fell out with Patty the miller's daughter, to whom he was to have been married at Michaelmas, but he saw her talking to another young man, and in a fit of jealousy he went and enlisted for a soldier; poor Patty is almost broken-hearted, and so is mother, for she has but us two, and William severely repents the rash step he has taken ; he always hated the life of a soldier, and says he must have been under the influence of madness when he enlisted, or he never should have done so, but his feelings were hurt, and he did not care what became of

No. 2.

himself. Ah! he was too rash," cried Rose, wiping her eyes. " Patty is very fond of William, and as good a girl as ever lived."

" Love, you see, my fair girl, is a terrible thing," said Immorf, " I hope you have never yet felt the effects of it."

" Oh, no, sir," said Rose blushing, and having gathered the quantity of herbs she wanted, she left the meadow.

" She is a charming girl," said Immorf mentally, " 'tis a pity she's so sh , I will not lose her;" and he at some distance followed her steps through the meadows.

Rose did not observe Immorf behind her, for she went on, without turning her head, or looking behind her.

She entered the green lane she had spoken of, and at length came to her father's dwelling—a neat, white cottage, standing on an eminence ; the jessamine and woodbine ran up, and entwined their fragrant blossoms in front of the house, where encaged a tame jack-daw was hanging, calling " Rose, Rose."

His fair mistress put down her basket, to talk to and fondle her favourite.

" Come, Rose, my darling, have you got the herbs?" said a white-haired respectable old man, who came out of the cottage.

" Yes, plenty, dear father," said Rose, and she tripped into the cottage, followed by her father.

" The old Cerberus !" exclaimed Immorf. " No doubt but the old fellow keeps a sharp look-out after his girl ; she certainly is a beautiful creature, and I, by some means, must get her in my power."

The thought of the charming cottage girl was now never from the mind of Immorf, and scarcely a day elapsed without his walking past her dwelling ; endeavouring to speak a word, or even catch a glance of his rustic divinity.

Sometimes he had the pleasure of seeing the object of his wishes, when a curtsey and smile from Rose would but fan the flame of his evil passion, and the more determine him to effect the innocent girl's ruin.

Time passed on in this way until the summer months had almost disappeared, and Immorf, whose mind was on the rack concerning Rose, could hit on no plan whereby he could get her in his power secretly, and without the affair being known ; for he was not only a villain, but a hypocrite also, and wished to hide his wickedness from the world.

It was now the beginning of October, and still the hoary seducer continued his walks through the meadows, and down the green lane.

Passing near the cottage of his intended victim one morning, he saw Rose, who was sitting on a bank, and calling her jackdaw who had escaped from his cage; tears were in her eyes, and they fast rolled down her cheeks as she called " Jack— Jack."

" What, my pretty lass, are you in such trouble because your bird has escaped ?" said Immorf, advancing to where Rose was sitting.

" I am sorry to lose poor Jack," said Rose, " but it is not that, that so much concerns me."

" And what is it then, that does concern you, my fair Rose ?" inquired Immorf.

" Oh, sir ! my mother is much worse," cried the artless girl, redoubling her tears. "And my brother, poor William, hearing that his mother was so ill, and wishing to see Patty, has come home without leave of absence, and father says he will be taken up for a deserter. Oh, sir ! we are all in such trouble on poor William's account."

A gleam of pleasure brightened the dark visage of Immorf, when he heard the young soldier had deserted from his regiment; but with seeming sympathy he said, " And you fear your brother will be punished as a deserter ?"

" Oh yes !" replied Rose, " every footstep we hear, we fear it is the soldiers coming to take my brother ; I am sure it would quite kill my mother were they to take him—father is like a distracted man, and we have no one to interfere in poor William's behalf."

" I will interfere, my fair lass," said Immorf ; " I go to-morrow to dine with Mr. Nevill the rector, whose son is in the army ; I think he will at my request write to the captain of your brother's regiment, and perhaps we may by some means manage to get his discharge. Meet me to-morrow night at the hour of nine, in the meadow near my castle, on that spot where the large willow droops over the cliff; name what has now passed between us to no one; and I charge you to come alone; I will do all I can to serve your brother, and hope when I see you to-morrow night to assure you of his pardon. Fail not to come at the hour of nine, in secresy and in darkness come—fear not, for I shall be there—remember the hour of nine —be punctual."

"There is no moon, and the spot where the willow droops over the cliff is lone— may not my father come with me?"

"Have I not told you," cried Immorf with impatience, "that none must come with you? I have reasons which I cannot explain to you? if you prefer seeing your brother shot, or to see him fainting, bleeding, and lacerated beneath the lash, be it so; but what a sister you must be, when but a little exertion, merely the walking of two miles, would save him, and you refuse to do it! Why should I feel for the young man, when even his own sister will not stir to serve him; what ingratitude is this for my humanity; but I will interfere no further."

"Oh, sir!" cried Rose, "I entreat your forgiveness, oh! do not abandon poor William; I will come at the time alone, and where you command me."

"Then he shall be saved," cried Immorf exultingly, "but beware of failing in my injunction—name not one word of our conversation to any person whatever; come, I again repeat, at the hour of nine, where the willow droops over the cliff, in darkness and in secresy come—and there await my coming."

"I will, sir," cried the trembling girl, "I will be punctual."

CHAPTER VI.

Nor decked with bridal wreath, the nymph was led,
But girt with sea-weed, in her watery bed. MILTON.

ROSE was unsuccessful in regaining her stray bird; Jack had gained his liberty, and, fearless of famine or the wintry blast, would no more return to his indulgent mistress, but gaily took his flight across the meadow, and was soon to her lost in distance.

When Rose again entered the cottage, she found her brother sitting by the bed-side of his mother, who was lamenting the situation her son's imprudence had placed him in.

"Ah! my child! where can I hide thee?" cried the weeping old woman, "where can I hide my boy from the blood-hounds, who will come in pursuit of him?"

"Do not grieve, mother," cried William, "let them come, I will bear the penalty of my fault with fortitude—I will bear it like a man."

"Bear!" cried his mother, shrieking at the thought. "Shall thy tender flesh be torn and separated by inhuman hands? Ah! little did I think, when I nursed thee in thy infancy, and thou wert nestling in my bosom, that I should ever live to see thee in this thrall. Ah! how mild and tender thou wert in thy childhood!" she continued, "I then little thought, that the strong seeds of rage and jealousy were implanted in thy bosom, and that a day would come, when such seeds would spring forth, and cause us such misery."

William was much affected, not only at the situation he then stood in, but also at the words of his mother, whom he tenderly loved, and in tears he left the room.

"Oh! do not give way to grief, it will kill you, my dear mother, indeed it will," cried Rose; "take comfort, all will be well; yes, I feel assured all will yet be well with William."

"Well!" cried her agonized mother, "well! Oh, Rose! seek not to deceive and soothe me with false hopes; we are poor and without friends—the folly of my poor boy will fall heavily on him."

"Say not so," replied Rose, "we have a friend, and a powerful one, too."

"True," cried her weeping mother, "we have a friend if we seek Him, a powerful, and Almighty Friend," and she turned her tearful eyes to heaven.

"But we have also an earthly friend," cried Rose, "and a powerful one too, one who will do all in his power to serve us."

"Who is he?" cried her mother with impatience, "tell me, Rose, and pour the balm of comfort into my broken heart—tell me, my girl, who is he that will generously befriend the unfortunate, that will be a friend to my poor William?"

"I dare not tell," said Rose, "I have promised secresy."

"This is but trifling with me," said the old woman, "what you have said, is merely to appease me. Oh! that my eyes were closed in eternal night. I would not live to see the dawning of another day, for with day will come trouble, my child will be fettered, and dragged to punishment."

"I have promised—solemnly promised," said Rose, "not to disclose the name of the person who will use his interest on my brother's account, nor to speak of the conversation we have had on that subject. But to you, my dear mother, I will tell all; I will break my promise for your sake, for I know what I have to disclose will cheer and comfort you under your heavy affliction—but you must promise not to drop a word to father, William, or any other person."

"I will not," said the old woman, "Rose, I will not."

"Well, then," said the pleased girl, "this morning when I was looking for poor Jack, Sir Parrolla Immorf went by; he heard me calling the bird, and observing my eyes were red with weeping, he inquired if it was the loss of my bird that caused me such grief?"

"I said I was sorry to lose my bird, but that was not the chief cause of my sorrow." "And what is the cause of your sorrow," he inquired; "I told him what had happened respecting my brother, and he has promised, through his interest, to get William pardoned, and perhaps he will procure his discharge from the army. I am to meet him by the large willow-tree that droops over the cliff to-morrow night at the hour of nine, and then he will tell me all about it; I am sure he will get William's discharge."

"God bless him!" cried the old woman, "how kind and condescending in a great gentleman like him to trouble himself about the affairs of the poor; but thy pretty innocent face, my child, being seen in grief, would intreat any one who possessed human feeling to serve thee. Oh! how my heart is eased by this good news, I long for to-morrow night; and shall think every moment an hour till thy return."

The next day came—evening came—eight o'clock came, and Rose, after kissing her mother, began to prepare for her walk to the willow tree.

"Go, speed thee, my child," cried the old woman, as Rose shut the cottage-door, "mayest thou return with good tidings!"

It was a dark and a starless night, but Rose was well acquainted with the place, and she arrived without difficulty at the willow tree.

How drear and solemn appears this night, thought Rose; what a universal stillness reigns around; but I must keep up my spirits, nor shrink from this meeting for the sake of my poor brother.

Rose stood for some moments, leaning against the willow tree—all was still and silent, except the dashing of the sea against the cliffs; but soon a footstep sounded on the stillness, and in a few moments Rose saw Sir Parrolla Immorf standing before her.

"Rose, my charming Rose," cried Sir Parrolla, "what a shame to keep you here waiting, I ought to have been here first, and in waiting for you."

"Oh, no, sir," said Rose, "you ought not to wait for me, it was proper for me to be here first, and wait your leisure; but say, sir, can you serve my poor brother?"

"Oh, yes, and buy him off too—anything to serve my pretty Rose."

And Immorf caught the affrighted girl in his arms and rudely kissed her; he held her tightly, and almost stifled her with his caresses.

"Oh, let me go, sir," cried Rose, "you frighten, you terrify me."

"Well, I will use no force, I will forbear," cried Immorf, "but it must be on one condition, that condition is, that you promise to leave your parents, and put yourself under my protection; I love you better than they do, and I will indulge you in every wish of your heart; no more shall you return to that odious cottage, but live with me, fair girl, in ease and splendour. A post-chaise shall this night convey you some miles from hence, where, free from restraint, we can enjoy each other's society."

"What! leave my father and mother, and live with a married gentleman?" cried Rose, with indignation. "Oh, never, never."

"Ungrateful girl!" exclaimed Immorf; "is this the return for exerting myself in the behalf of your brother? mere words of thanks will not satisfy me. I have you now in my power, nor shall you escape me. In secresy and in darkness you have met me here—and as you will not consent to leave your parents, in secresy and in darkness shall my purpose be accomplished. Shriek not, for it will be unavailing, and but cause me to be the more firmly bent on the fulfilment of my purpose—nought can save thee: no wandering footstep at this hour and this season of the year is by, and the labouring hinds who live in the straggling cottages across these meadows will not hear thee. Long ere this they have sought their lowly pallets, and, tired with the toil of the day, have sunk into profound sleep. Mine thou art, and mine thou shalt be"—and Immorf stretched out his arms, with the intention of again clasping Rose to his bosom, but by a quick turn she eluded his grasp, and ran on, as fast as her trembling legs would let her, with the thought of gaining the green lane that led to her father's cottage, but soon Immorf overtook the affrighted girl, and catching her by a ringlet of her glossy hair, he stayed her from proceeding.

"Oh, mercy! mercy!" she cried, but the flinty rock was not more deaf to entreaty than was Sir Parrolla Immorf; fainting and unconscious, she sunk on the green sward, extended and pale as statuary marble. The weight of Rose in falling severed the ringlet Immorf still held from her beauteous head, leaving the parted curl twined round the hand of her persecutor.

CHAPTER VII.

"'Tis well thou art unconscious, and at rest;
Or, how this sight would tear my aching breast."

THE spirits of Dame Mildmay were cheered by the words of her daughter, an, after Rose's departure, to meet Sir Parrolla Immorf, the invalid fell into a slumber for she was quite worn out, both by illness and grief.

Old Mildmay had been all the evening by the bed-side of a dying neighbour, so that he knew nothing of the absence of Rose, nor did her brother, who was at the mill, in company with Patty.

William had called for his father, and both father and son came home together. When they had entered the cottage, they found Dame Mildmay still asleep, no supper was prepared, and hardly a glimmer of light could be seen in the dying embers. "How forlorn and neglected everything appears," cried the old man, "no fire! where can Rose be?"

He went up to the bed-side of his wife, who still slept. Eleven o'clock came, and yet Rose was absent. "This is very strange," said the old man to his son, "I never knew the girl to be out so late before."

And he got up, and went to the door of his cottage, to see if she was coming—but Rose was not there; he listened, but no footstep sounded on the stillness of night.

Twelve o'clock came, and Rose had not yet returned; the old man paced the room, uneasy on account of his daughter's absence at so unseasonable an hour; a heavy rain was in torrents pouring down.

"Never has Rose been from home so late before," said the old man, "some evil, I fear, hath befallen her."

" Do not alarm yourself, father," said William, " mother can perhaps account for her absence."

At this moment the old woman started up. " Rose," she cried, " Rose, my child, are you come back?"

" Rose is not come back," cried the old man in a tremulous voice ; " it is past twelve o'clock, and the rain comes down in torrents. Where have you sent her?"

" Twelve o'clock ! and Rose not returned !" cried the old woman, " Oh, God! what can have detained her ?"

" Where have you sent her ?" demanded the old man.

" She is gone to the large willow that overhangs the cliff," cried her trembling mother.

" To the willow that overhangs the cliff!" repeated the old man. " Woman! for what purpose went she there ?"

" Father ! speak not so harshly to my poor mother," said William, " I trust my sister's safe. Mother, where is Rose gone ?"

To meet Sir Parrolla Immorf; he has promised to use his interest to prevent William from being punished, and he will perhaps buy him off from being a soldier."

" Father, do not alarm yourself, but rather rejoice that we have found such a friend," cried William. " Rose is safe enough."

" Safe enough !" repeated the old man, " what in dismal fields, and by the dashing billows, at the hour of midnight, midst storms and darkness? No, boy, she is not safe."

" Not safe !" cried the invalid, " not safe, oh Rose, my child, my child !"

" These lamentations are now useless," cried the old man. " William, light the lantern, we will go and seek her—oh, Alice !" he continued, addressing his wife, " how could you suffer the girl to go; you are ill and in trouble enough about William ; Heaven forbid that I should by unkind words increase your sorrow, but surely it was very wrong to suffer Rose to go. If Sir Parrolla Immorf meant to serve us, why did he not speak to you or me, or William Why was a young girl like Rose to be made the agent? Could he not have made known what he had to say by day-light ; not have lured my poor girl to that lone spot under the cover of darkness ? "

The poor old woman, much alarmed, made no answer to her husband's words, but she sat upright in the bed crying and wringing her hands.

William having lit the lantern, he and his father proceeded down the green lane, and looked carefully around them as they did so ; but nothing could be seen of Rose.

" Call her, William," cried the old man, " thy voice is louder and shriller than mine."

William with all his might called "Rose, Rose !" but no response was made ; all was still, excepting the death owl's discordant song, and the heavy pelting of the raindrops.

They came to the willow that overhung the cliff, but no human being was there.

" This is a sad business" cried the old man, brushing away a tear, "my poor girl, my Rose."

" Father ! do not be so apprehensive," said William; " if Sir Parrolla Immorf is kind enough to interest himself in my behalf, he may have taken Rose to the castle, and the night being so wet, perhaps Lady Immorf wished my sister to stay until morning, and sleep with one of the servants."

" Do not flatter yourself with such hopes," said the old man ; " had Sir Parrolla meant Rose to have gone to the castle, he would have taken her there in the first instance—Rose, I fear, is lost to us."

With heavy hearts the old man and his son returned to their no longer peaceful cottage.

But, to quiet the grief of his broken-hearted mother, William again spoke of the probability of his sister's being at the castle for the night, in consequence of the weather.

"I will go there as soon as morning dawns," cried the old man, "or at least, as soon as any one is stirring in the castle."

Long and heavy passed the hours until day-break ; neither old Mildmay nor his son retired to rest.

Once or twice during the night, the old woman started up, and cried, "Open the door, John, there's Rose—she calls mother !" To satisfy his wife, the old man opened the door, but he knew no one was there, the voice of poor Rose was only in the imagination of her agonised mother.

Soon as morning dawned, the old man and his son waited about the castle of Sir Parrolla Immorf, and at length they saw a servant issuing from thence.

William waited at a distance, whilst old Mildmay went up to the man, and inquired if Rose Mildmay had slept at the castle last night.

"Rose Mildmay sleep at the castle !" said the man, with much surprise, "how came you to think of that ?"

"No matter how I came to think of it," replied Mildmay ; "did she, or did she not ?" for by the man's evasive answer Mildmay thought his son's suspicions, of Rose remaining for the night at the castle, might not be incorrect.

Mildmay again repeated, " Is Rose Mildmay in the castle ?"

" I should say not," replied the man.

" Has your master risen ?" inquired old Mildmay.

"Yes, and at breakfast with my lady," replied the man.

"Then return into the castle, and tell your master that I must instantly speak to him."

" And what name shall I announce you by ?" said the man with a sneer.

" By the name of old Mildmay, who lives in the cottage in the green lane, tell him I demand to see him."

" I shall tell him no such thing," said the man, "you may tell him yourself— do you think I want to lose my place, through taking such an insolent message ?" and the servant went on.

Every moment brought but stronger conviction to the mind of poor Mildmay; he felt certain that some foul play had been used towards Rose, and that by Sir Parrolla Immorf.

He went up to the castle, and rang the bell with violence.

A servant appeared at the gate, and demanded his business.

"My business is with Sir Parrolla Immorf," replied Mildmay ; "tell him, I must speak with him."

The man took in the message, and Sir Parrolla, with much agitation, said, " I am engaged ; tell him he must come again—I cannot now be disturbed."

" But you have disturbed me and mine," cried old Mildmay, raising his voice to its uttermost pitch, as he boldly entered the parlour, where Sir Parrolla and his wife were at breakfast.

"Where's my girl, whom you lured to meet you by the willow tree, that over-hangs the cliff ?—is she here? if so produce her, or tell me where to find her," said the old man.

" Me lure your daughter ! why I don't know the girl, or you either, old fellow— begone, or the stocks shall cure you of these fancies."

" Can you look me in the face and tell me, that you did not appoint Rose to meet you by the willow-tree, and that you would then tell her how you had suc-ceeded in behalf of her unfortunate brother? my wife knows all about it, and saw the poor girl set out between the hours of eight and nine to meet you ; yes, sir, her poor sick mother saw Rose go out for the express purpose of meeting you."

" And am I to be annoyed, insulted in my own house, because of the wild delusions of your sick wife's fevered imagination ? I tell you it is false—some chimera of her own disordered brain ; she did not see the girl go out, at least with any intention of meeting me."

" 'Tis useless to deny it, sir," cried Mildmay, "what have you done with my child—Oh, tell me, where is Rose?"

" Insulting scoundrel !" cried Immorf reddening with rage, and he rang his bell with violence ; when answered, he said to the servant, a strong young man, "turn this madman out."

" Use no violence," cried the heart-broken father, "there's no need of that, I will go ;" then turning and casting on Sir Parrolla Immorf a look which conveyed at once the agony of his feelings, he said—" I go—and may the Almighty deal with you, as you have done with me !"

" What, and so you thought my master had got your daughter ?" said an upstart menial, as he pushed old Mildmay from the gate. " Your daughter, indeed ! why Sir Parrolla would not condescend to notice."

Overcome by grief and resentment, old Mildmay seated himself on the stump of a tree, or he must have fallen, " Oh, Heaven ! preserve me," he cried, " and grant that, in spite of these injuries, I may retain my senses."

Seeing his father had left the castle, William came up to him. " Have you heard of Rose ?" he inquired.

" Oh, no," cried the old man, " Sir Parrolla denies having appointed to meet your sister, and says that she was not even personally known to him."

They now returned to their cottage. Dame Mildmay, as they thought, still sleep. " This torpor is occasioned by grief," said the old man, " I never knew your mother to be so heavy asleep."

The old man with his handkerchief to his eyes, sat leaning his head on the table, whilst William paced the room in extreme uneasiness.

When a loud knocking at the cottage door made them start, and two young men came in, followed by several of the villagers, who said, " Neighbour, we have found your daughter ! see, she is coming yonder."

The old man looked down the green lane, and saw some persons carrying Rose.

" What, cannot she walk ?" cried the old man ? " Oh ! she's dead, dead ! my child is dead !"

" Ah, neighbour, she is, indeed," cried one of the men who supported the body ; " we found her entangled in the sea-weed close to the cliff, over which droops the large willow ; we first saw her hat, then, on looking further, discovered her body."

 " And is it come to this ?" cried the agonized father, " so young, so fair, so good, ah, Rose ! my poor child !" he cried, as he parted back her golden locks, still drip-ping with wet from her fair forehead. " Ah, my girl, a fatal dowry hath thy beauty proved to thee," groaned the heart-broken father."

At this moment the steward of Sir Parrolla Immorf appeared at the cottage-door, and he beckoned Mildmay into the green lane.

" My master," he said, " has heard of the unfortunate death of your daughter, and he feels for your misfortunes ; but, at the same time, the duty he owes himself will not permit him to pass over your abuse of this morning ; nor will he, if you still persist in calumniating him—therefore, my master has desired me to warn you from slandering, or at all mixing up his name in this business, if you do, he will prove your most bitter foe ; he will do all the injury he can to your deserter of a son, and will cause you to be turned out of your cottage ; he will go to law with you for defaming his character, and asserting what you cannot prove ; you are poor and friendless and cannot cope with a rich man—if you do, in a jail you must end your miserable existence." Saying this, the steward departed without waiting for an answer, for he saw Mildmay was too much excited to send back any message that would satisfy Sir Parrolla.

When Mildmay again entered the cottage he went up to the corse of his daughter, which the women had now laid on the pallet on which she usually slept. He kissed her wan cheek as he said, " 'Tis well, my girl, 'tis no worse ; sooner would I see thee lay thus, than living in splendour with the unprincipled seducer, who, sated with thy beauty, would have left thee to want and misery, and thou, step by step, mightest have descended, and sunk to the very lowest grade of society ; but surely thy mother's sleep must be sound," he cried, " that all this noise and my lamentations have not awakened her," for Mildmay addressed his daughter's corse, as if she were yet living.

With a quick step he went to the bed-side of his wife, whose torpor and heavy slumber had ended in the sleep of death.

"And is it so, poor Alice?" cried the old man, "art thou at peace?—Oh! selfish, thou art gone, and staid not to partake of my misery."

"What, is Dame Mildmay dead?" cried one of the women, who stood by.

"Behold!" cried the old man, as he pulled back the curtain, "see the poor old woman, the victim of villany : grief had brought on fits, and there she lies, a cold and pallid corse—I have now no wish to live, and hope, ere morning dawns, to lie beside her."

Not a person in the village, but felt for poor Mildmay, and a subscription was set on foot, to purchase the discharge of William from the army, and the commanding officer being written to for that purpose, his pardon and discharge were sent together

On a Sunday, ten days after these melancholy events, Dame Mildmay and her daughter were buried in the village church-yard ; the mother's corse was borne on first, followed by a long train of mourners, whose sable garments were strongly contrasted with the snow-white apparel of the damsels who held up the pall, and preceded the corse of Rose, strewing flowers as they went.

For although it was October, yet in the green-houses of the gentry in that part, there were still in bloom, myrtles, white roses, and jessamines, a profusion of which was freely given, for the maidens to strew as they went, in allusion to the purity of their deceased companion : that the person of Rose had suffered much violence was undoubted, but by whom none could surmise, excepting her heart-broken father, who felt certain in his own mind, that Sir Parrolla Immorf was the guilty person ; but he had no proof, and therefore hid his suspicions in his own bosom ; for the exposure of Sir Parrolla would not have lessened his grief, nor have again called into existence his departed daughter; it would only have aroused the ire of that bad man, and have most likely caused him to put his threatened vengeance into execution—of harassing Mildmay with law, and ultimately causing him to draw his last breath within the precincts of a jail.

The grave of Rose was annually visited by her young companions, who strewed it with such flowers as the season of the year would allow, and, drooping over it, they planted a willow tree, which is yet flourishing in the village church-yard.—This was done as a memorial of the willow that overhung the cliff, on that fatal spot where perished the unfortunate beauty.

CHAPTER VIII.

"I like the rocking of these battlements.
Rage on, ye winds ; burst clouds, and waters roar."

YOUNG.

It was now December, and Sir Parrolla Immorf had for some time been indisposed, with a severe cold he caught, in consequence of being wet through on the night so fatal to Rose Mildmay.

His indisposition, added to a troubled mind, brought on a severe fit of the gout.

It happened on a very tempestuous night, when the winds, with their broad and invisible pinions, were fast sweeping along the earth, bellowing, and bearing down all that stood in their way.

Sir Parrolla, as he lay on his bed, was amused for a time, by the sound of the rushing winds, as they howling passed over his castle.

But suddenly a dread came over him, that he could by no means account for ; he could not lie in bed, and reaching his crutches, which he was now forced to use, he got up, and seated himself in an easy chair by the fire, which was yet burning.

No. 3.

"I have heard the war of the elements unmoved, and with more pleasure than pain," thought Parrolla; "my nerves cannot be as they were, for the sound of these warring winds affects me; it seems as if the destruction of nature were about to take place, and the earth, and all therein, to be reduced to the original chaos."

The weather was very cold, and a heavy fall of snow was descending. Parrolla stirred up the fire; he then set his watch by a table clock that stood near him, the hand pointing to the hour of twelve; whilst so employed, Parrolla heard the door of his chamber open, he turned his eyes in that direction, and he saw it was his friend, the Count Herman, who had entered; he wore the same large round hat, and black wrapping cloak; he advanced with a stately step to the table at which Parrolla was sitting.

"I said at our last meeting, that we should soon meet again," said the count, "but many circumstances have occurred since that time; I am changed, and very differently situated.—I see, Parrolla, that you are grown grey with years, and afflicted with infirmities common to mortality; from these things I would preserve you, Parrolla; I am come to serve you."

"My dear friend, Count Herman, I rejoice to see you," cried Parrolla, "but really I was so surprised when you first entered the room, that I could not give my words utterance; you said you were changed; indeed you are, why you look even younger than you did before I left Germany. I was surprised to see you enter, for I heard you were dead; but how did you gain admittance here? I thought all the servants were in bed—who let you in?"

"I wanted not letting in," replied the count, "there are beings to whom locks or doors are of no avail."

"Surprised that I had neither seen nor heard from you, I wrote to your brother," said Parrolla," and received for answer, that you had died under circumstances of horror and mystery."

"When I said we should soon meet again, I meant in mortality," replied the count; "and as to the circumstances attending my death being awful and terrific to the living, I do not wonder at it. The mystery attending my death was of a solemn and unearthly nature, and fit only for those to witness, who have courage to step over the bounds prescribed to mortality;—I have dared to step over those bounds;—I was freed from death, and live in a renewed existence, of youth and enjoyment. I have sold my soul, but to a lenient master, all he requires for such service as he does me, is a victim once in seven years, of my procuring; but that's an easy task—very. In tha time, I could find twenty if required; but of course I am diligent, for if I fail, I myself must be that victim. When I so hastily left you at the hotel, for fear of my being apprehended, for what is called the black art, I went back to Germany, and there used all my endeavours to procure a murderer's skull, for that was all I wanted to complete my charm. But I was doomed to be disappointed; no malefactor's corse, that is to say, one who had suffered for murder, was attainable. I was plunged into despair, fearing I should not be able to get that one thing, without which, all my study and labour would fall to the ground;—tired and disgusted with Germany, as I feared that I should never obtain there that which I wanted, I bid adieu to my friends, and went to Spain, hoping to succeed better there. I attended every execution where a murderer was to suffer, but I could not obtain my object; I paid my addresses to several females to whom I proposed marriage, and having obtained their confidence, I tried to worm out of them if any person in their family had ever been guilty of murder—but no; no success for me. One day in a melancholy mood, and quite out of spirits in consequence of my continued disappointments, I strolled into a church-yard that lay in my way to Madrid, there I wandered for some time; reading the tomb-stones, and looking at the graves, imagining which of them was the most likely to contain a murderer. Preparations were being made for a funeral, and I saw a squat old man with a large beard, and full of staring black eyes, and ears of an enormous size; in fact, he appeared more like an Egyptian represented on a mummy than anything I had ever beheld; he was very busy in giving his orders, and I thought by the manner of the old man that he was the sexton of the church; in this conjecture I was not wrong.

" ' Go,' said he, speaking to a poor boy who stood by, ' go and tell Dallabella to bring me the keys of the church, for I have forgotten them.'

" The boy went on his errand, and I waited the coming of Dallabella, for I thought that by forming an acquaintance with the sexton's daughter something might turn up to my advantage, and whether she was young or old I determined to court her, at length the fair Dallabella appeared with the key. She was the very counterpart of her father, a very squat woman, with a limping gait, the same head, eyes, and ears as her father, but with the addition of a most petrifying squint with one of her eyes, and about the age of thirty-seven. Notwithstanding all her imperfections, I determined to make love to the fair Dallabella, for I thought she might be acquainted with the secrets of the grave, or at least, the inhabitants thereof, and through her means, I, perhaps, should be fortunate enough to obtain my object.

" Dallabella having given her father the keys, she left the church-yard ; I followed her, but knew not how to address this amiable fair ; she differed in appearance from any woman I had ever yet beheld, and I thought I must address her differently from what I should have done any other female ; perplexed, I kept following her ; nor for the life of me could I think what to say ; at last a thought struck me. I will tread on her heel,' thought I, ' and when she looks round to see who has done so, I will apologize, and through that incident, we may become acquainted.' I followed her up close, and actually trod on the heel of the sexton's daughter. Oh what a look she gave me ; but I was not turned into stone, and after a short time, found means to soften the offended fair.

" I told her how much she resembled a favourite sister of mine, who had died about two years back. She was the most amiable creature in existence," I continued ; ' and the reason of my not marrying in my youth, and continuing to live single, until now, is because I have never been able to find a female like that amiable girl ; you are like her in person, and I know by your countenance, that you possess the same harmony of temper.'

" ' My temper, Sennor, has never been found fault with,' said Dallabela ; ' and are you a bachelor, Sennor ?' ' Yes,' I replied, but no longer shall I remain so, than I can find an agreeable partner.' She now stopped at her father's house, and I was agreeably surprised by seeing in the window of the lower room, a bill on which was written, a chamber to let furnished ; I looked at the chamber, it was the very thing I wanted, and I took the room, and removed into my new apartment the following day. I paid much attention to Dallabella, we went to public places, the resort of the young and gay, together, and Dallabella was not a little noticed, but it was neither for her youth nor her beauty, but the singularity of her appearance, tawdry to the extreme, and what with her waving feathers, and ill-assorted colours, together with her extreme ugliness, altogether caused her to appear as a rarity, and such a one as you would but seldom meet with. Three months passed on, but I could hear no news of that which I wanted, I had frequent conversations with Dallabella, concerning the dead, and heard the history of several, who had been very great sinners, but still their crimes did not amount to murder. The old sexton appeared very well pleased at the thought of my becoming his son-in-law, and he wished to see me united to his daughter as soon as possible. One day he said, Sennor, I think the affair between you and my daughter has been long enough in agitation, do not put off the wedding, thinking you will have a portionless bride, on the contrary, at my death, Dallabella will have sufficient to keep her in ease and affluence, I have enough Sennor, to keep me, without being a sexton, but 'tis my fancy to be so.' Finding both the old man and his daughter so pressing for the marriage to be completed, I thought it would be best to shift my quarters.

" Sitting one evening alone in my chamber, quite out of temper, cursing my unlucky stars, and wishing the old sexton and his daughter at the devil, Dallabella came limping into the room, ' oh ! Sennor,' she cried, ' I fear my father's dying.' I followed her into her father's chamber, he had been taken with the cramp in his stomach, and was then in great agony, but he did not suffer long, a more violent spasm came on, and the old sexton was no more ; his daughter was in great trouble, not only for the love of her father, but also for his spiritual welfare. She had several conferences with her confessor, I listened, and heard the chink of gold ; a large sum I found was given, that prayers might be said for her deceased father, who, from what I could discover, had in his lifetime committed some deadly sin ; in order to worm out of Dallabella, what sin her father had committed, of such magnitude as to require so large a sum of gold to be paid for prayers and masses, to be said for the repose of his soul, I pretended greater love than ever ; and actually fixed the day for our marriage, in order that she the more freely might open her mind to me ; my scheme had the desired effect.

"Dallabella confessed that her father had committed a murder.

"'A murder !' I replied, in seeming amaze, and with difficulty I concealed the surprise and pleasure I felt at this intelligence.

"'And where did he do the murder?' I inquired.

"'In this very house,' she said, 'Ah ! my father was a bad old man, and I ought not to regret his death, provided I get a good husband, but you know Sennor, bad as he was, I should not wish his immortal part to be praying in sulphur. I did but my duty in giving the priest money for prayers and masses to be read.'

"'And whom did he murder?' I inquired.

"'The old Sennor Jackabo who lodged here,' she replied ; 'the old man had a large sum of money by him, which my father coveted—he was very old and feeble, he had no relations, or any person who troubled themselves about him ; so one night when the old man was in bed, my father entered his chamber, and held him by the throat until he was dead ; it was thought he died in a fit, and that's the way my father got his money—but it shall be all yours.'

"I kissed the murderer's daughter ; yes, Immorf, with ecstacy I kissed her ; I was in spirits, delighted with the information she had given me.

"I beheld the corse of the ugly old sexton with extreme pleasure, and coveted him more than a miser would have done a heap of gold. I longed for his funeral to be over, and found to my satisfaction that he was to be buried in a vault under the church ; that was much more convenient to me, than to have had the toil of raking the mould from his grave ; besides, the risk would have been greater ; in the church-yard there was more likelihood of my being disturbed in my nocturnal visit, and suffering the penalty of so doing.

"At length the day came, when he was to be buried at night by torch-light. I was invited and joined the group of mourners, I saw him placed in the vault, and I marked the spot well.

"That very night I would have gone to the vault for the old man's head, but the company staid late, and I could not with any appearance of decency leave them ; but late as it was, or as I more properly may say early, for it was two o'clock before they departed, I would have gone, but I could not find where Dallabella had put the keys of the church. But on the following day I was more fortunate, I saw where the keys were hung ; I secured them, and as the clock struck the hour of ten, I was at the church door, ready to enter.

"But I was observed ; I turned my head, and saw a man standing watching me, he knew I was not the sexton, and wondered what my business could be there. Confused, I left the church, and turned down a street, to get rid of my observer. I looked back, but he was still watching me ; 'this will not do,' I inwardly said, 'I must come at a later hour, twelve at soonest, and then the streets will be clear.'

"My reason for wishing to have the old man's head early in the evening, was, that the charm might be prepared precisely as the clock sounded the hour of twelve, for otherwise it would not be effective.

"I walked about the church, backwards and forwards, until the chimes went a quarter to twelve, for persons were passing to and fro until that time.

"'I have at least lost this night,' I mentally said, 'if I succeed in getting the old fellow's head I shall not be back in time to make use of it.'

"At length I saw the coast was clear, no person was passing, I unlocked the church door, and entered it, I took out the lantern, which I had brought with me, concealed under my cloak, I passed the gloomy passages in the church, and made my way to the stairs that led to the vaults beneath them.

"I was terrified, a sensation came over me I could not define,—I started, as the wind went rustling along, and shaking the windows of the church; but with a timid and stealthy step, I went on until I came to the place where the sexton's coffin was placed.

"I forced off the lid, and with the instruments I had brought with me, soon severed the head from the shoulders of the corse.

"I again placed the lid on the coffin, and put the head in the bag I had brought with me, I locked the church door, and reached my residence unobserved, and placed the keys where I found them; for having a key that opened the street door, Dallabella was not aware when I returned, and little did she think that her father's head was again in the house."

CHAPTER IX.

Nose of a Turk, and Tartar's lip.
* * * *
 * * * *

For a charm of powerful troub[...]
Like a hell broth, boil, and bubble.

       MACBETH.

I must to Naples ere the matin hour,
And meet fair Lilla in her myrtle bower,
Be not surprised at what such beings can do,
I'd cross the deep before the wild seamew.

       IBID.

"THE following day I was all love and attention to my fair Dallabella, and no subject was talked of but our marriage; as evening advanced I complained of indisposition, and at an early hour took leave of Dallabella for the night.

"All was prepared, I took the old man's head from the bag, and I placed it on the table ready for me to separate his skull from his frightful face, for frightful it was, the face darker than ever, in consequence of the convulsions of death, and his large eyes wide open and yet more projecting. Dallabella I knew was in bed, and I thought all safe—it wanted but one quarter to midnight, the time for preparing the charm.

"I had occasion to go down stairs, I unlocked my room-door, and hastily descended for the purpose I wanted.

"When I returned into my room it wanted precisely ten minutes to twelve, I had no time to lose, I hastened to the table; but in my hurry I forgot to lock the door. Judge of my surprise, Immorf, when I saw Dallabella enter and approach the table.

"'I heard you go down stairs Sennor,' she said, 'and feared you were worse;' she caught sight of the head, which in my consternation at seeing her enter I did not think to remove, the sight of her almost stunned and turned me into stone. She advanced yet closer, 'Oh God! my father's head, torn from the tomb,' and with a piercing shriek she fell to the ground fainting and insensible, so much was she shocked by the terrible sight.

"What to do I did not know, I feared she would give me into the hands of the authorities, for what I had done.

"To destroy the head so that there might be no proof against me I could not think of—after all my toil and waiting; and if I destroyed that, where was I to get another?

"I seized the knife with which I intended to dissect the old man's head, and caught hold of Dallabella as she still lay insensible, with the intention of cutting her throat, lest she should expose me in her fury for my sacrilegious act; but some hidden power seemed to withhold me.

"'No,' I said mentally, 'I will not kill her if there's a possibility of avoiding it; I will try and soothe her, but if I cannot, she must die, and on this very spot if she obstinately will not listen to what I say, but like a headstrong woman, bring on herself her own destruction, she must die ; it is the dead hour of the night, and what's her strength to mine ? but I will see first how I can work upon her.' I put the head again in the bag, and locked it up in my portmanteau, and then I went up to Dallabella, who now began to move ; I took her in my arms, and tenderly kissing her, placed her on my knee.

" ' Oh! how I regret my folly' I cried, in so incautiously suffering you to see the waxen head I have made, in likeness of your father, without first apprising you of it.   Poor Dallabella, have you recovered your fright?'

" ' What, and was that head but an exact representation of my poor father's," she cried, ' made of nothing but wax.'

" ' Nothing more, love,' I said. ' The respect I bore the deceased caused me to take an impression of his features, as he lay in his coffin. I intend to have it placed in a glass case, and to place it on a bracket in the parlour, when we are married ; you don't know, Dalabella,' I continued, ' what a good artist I am.'

" ' Let me see it,' she replied, ' I should like to look on my poor father.'

" I was nonplused by this question, but I soon recovered myself. ' No,' I said, ' no, Dallabella, not to-night, your nerves are already too much affected, consider how solemn the sight of your so lately deceased father would be to you, and that at the dread hour of midnight ; no, love, in the course of a day or two I will get it put in the case, and then you shall see it.' Dallabella was appeased.   I mulled some wine to comfort her, and what with the wine and my flattery, she at length retired to bed, in good spirits, but it was now too late for my charm, and had it not been so, I was too much put out by the unexpected appearance of Dallabella, to think of practising it, and I determined, now I had what I wanted in my power, to leave Spain altogether, and return to Germany, and not put that which I intended to do, in practice, until I reached the home of my relations.

" On the following day, whilst Dallabella was out, I left the house of the sexton's daughter ; I had the old man's head wrapped up in a cloth, and tied up in a silk handkerchief; carefully I carried it under my cloak, more careful was I of it than if it had been pure gold.

" When I reached the home of my friends, I was exceedingly ill, for I had caught a severe cold during my stay in the damp vault of the church ; however, I used the skull and completed my charm.—I had then only to call on the Demon Ziregratta, and all was done ; for what reason, I don't know, but I neglected to do so ; a violent fever came on—I was delirious for some time and near death.

" During this unconsciousness, I thought not of that which I had been so long engaged in, nor, indeed, any thing else, and was totally insensible of everything that passed around me.

" The first sound I recollect hearing after my delirium and unconsciousness, was the voice of my brother —' is he gone?' he said. ' Yes, the last breath hath departed.

" ' No,' said my sister, ' he yet lives; but,' she weeping said, ' it will soon be over.'

" ' What is the time ?' inquired my brother.

" ' The hand now points to the hour of twelve,' she replied."

CHAPTER X.

Near about those viewless agents soar,
All ready to obey the spell.

FAUST.

" ' I WILL not die,' thought I to myself, ' this is the time, the moment for action.'

" I muttered to myself, ' Ziregatta, appear, thy victim awaits thee—all is prepared—I yield me to thy power.' As soon as these words were uttered, with a terribie noise, as if the mighty thunder had crushed the earth and all therein, the roof of the house was rent in twain, and the Demon Ziregratta entered; he was invisible to all but myself.

" ' If you will subscribe to the terms required, tell me thy will, and it shall be done,' he said.

" ' Give me long life, riches, and renewed youth,' I cried, ' and I will agree to thy terms.' He carried me through the roof of the house, which opened, obedient to his bidding, and I, like a butterfly escaped from its chrysalis enclosure, gaily sported in renewed existence and youthful beauty, for my appearance was, and as you see is, the same as when I was but twenty years of age.

" It was but the immortal essence, that Ziregratta bore away ; my body still lay on the bed, surrounded by my weeping relations.

" Unseen to them, I saw my body lowered into the grave, the spirit had escaped ; it was but the dross, the covering, that was returned to its mother earth, whilst the immortal spirit, now freed from the infirmities of age, buoyantly sported in its new existence ;' beauty is in my power and riches are at my command ; and for these benefits there are no other conditions than to procure him as many worshippers as I can, and a victim on a certain day, once in seven years, but if I fail in that, to live in seas of burning sulphur will be my doom—of procuring victims I have no fear, and whilst I do so, my existence will last to the end of time.'

" Parrolla, I come to serve you," continued Count Herman, " wilt thou shake off the trammels of fear, and worship him whom I serve ?'

" Answer me quickly," cried Count Herman, with impatience, " for I must hence, and be in Naples, by the hour of matins."

" ' Impossible,' cried Immorf, " the hand is now on the stroke of one.'

" No matter," cried Count Herman, in a hoarse and unearthly voice, " no matter, I shall be there.—Say, wilt thou be as I am ?"

" I will," cried Immorf, " but I know not how to proceed. Of course a murderer's skull will be necessary, and that I think I can procure—a murderer and suicide was buried but last week in a cross-road, not far from hence, his head will be easily got at.—From what you have said, Herman, I know that that will be one thing necessary," continued Parrolla, " but how to proceed further I know not."

" Search the magic-book," he replied, " and that will inform thee."

Immorf would have asked Count Herman questions for greater information on the dreadful subject, but when he looked towards where the count stood, he was no longer there.

Peter, a youth about sixteen years of age, was one whom Sir Parrolla Immorf had taken into his service to wait on him as a kind of page; Peter had been in the service of Sir Parrolla about three years when this event happened; he was naturally a well-disposed youth and was attached to his master, for Parrolla was partial to Peter, and he treated him with more kindness than he did most other persons.

Peter was not only a well-disposed youth, but he was one of quick parts also; but he had the fault of being very curious ; there was not anything said or done in the castle, but he would peep and pry into it, if there was any possibility of his so doing.

Peter was not only very curious, but very fond of tasting and picking any nice thing that came in his way, to the great annoyance of the cook, who never would permit him to go into the kitchen if she could help it.

However, on the evening of that day when his master received his nocturnal visitor, Peter had been too sharp for the cook, for whilst her back was turned, he got into the kitchen, and indulged himself in eating heartily of a very high-seasoned made dish, intended for the supper of Lady Immorf; but Peter was punished for his greediness—he awoke parched with thirst, in consequence of the high-seasoned food he had eaten; he was very timid, and could not bear the thought of going down stairs by himself at the hour of midnight, when all in the castle were in bed; but tormented with extreme drought, Peter ventured to go down stairs to procure some water, shaking as he did so with the thoughts of ghosts and spectres.

But what was the surprise of Peter, when he saw the door of his master's room standing ajar, and with his usual curiosity peeped in, and saw standing the original of the full length portrait, which had so often interested him, and filled him with wonder and dread; for Peter had listened, and had heard his master tell his lady of the letter he had received, which acquainted him with the death of the original of that portrait—and of the horrible mystery which occurred on the night of his decease.

"There he stands," said Peter mentally, "'tis he, sure enough, the same tall dark figure, black wrapping cloak, and large hat," but thinking the portrait was animated with life, Peter looked to where the massive frame was hanging, but the portrait was still there, and near it stood the original.

Terrified, Peter stood aghast to see the buried Count talking to his master—and when he still listened, and heard them talking of supernatural agency, and the magic-book, he forgot his thirst; and when he saw the count was no longer there, he with noiseless steps again crept up to his bed-room.

But sleep that night no more visited the eyes of Peter, and he rose as soon as it was light in the morning.

Well would it have been for Peter, had he been less curious, nor have troubled his head with that which did not concern him; for now he was terrified, restless, and unhappy, and his thoughts continually reverted to the dread and mysterious Count Herman.

In the midst of Peter's cogitations, Sir Parrolla's bell rung; Peter always answered the summons, but so lost was he in thought, that it thrice sounded before he could answer it; and when he did, he seemed hardly to know what he was about.

The strange manner, and colourless cheek of Peter was noticed by Sir Parrolla, and he inquired if Peter was ill.

"No sir," replied Peter, "I am not ill, but I could not sleep."

"Not sleep, boy," cried Sir Parrolla, "what disturbed you?"

"Oh nothing, sir," replied the youth, "nothing disturbed me," but he trembled as he told the untruth.

"Well, Peter," said Sir Parrolla, "I need a trustworthy person; can I trust you?"

"I hope, sir, you have always found me faithful," said Peter, "and grateful for the favours I have received."

"Well, I will trust you," said his master, "but Peter, you must be secret—yes, secret as the grave—and never to any living soul divulge that, which I am going to confide in you—swear to me that you will be secret."

"Never, sir, will I reveal any confidence you may please to honour me with," said the trembling page; "if I do, may heaven never extend its mercy to me; you placed me near your person, friendless and destitute as I was, and I hope I never shall forget the obligation."

"I believe you are a good boy," said Immorf, "and I may trust you—go up to the eastern turret, and with this key open an iron box you will see standing near the window, take from thence a crimson velvet bag embroidered with gold, and bring it down to me."

Peter obeyed his master, he went up to the turret, unlocked the box, and took the crimson bag.

The curiosity of Peter was aroused by the sight of the richly worked crimson bag, and he wondered what it could contain; he wished to examine it, but he was conscious he ought not to open it.

Peter hesitated, curiosity prevailed, he opened the bag and took from thence the magic book; he read some pages, they filled him with amazement and horror; he read in one part,——

"How to call on supernatural agency, to obtain a lengthened existence."

Peter looked at a few words more, they were such as to make him shudder.

Sir Parrolla's bell rang with violence, it made poor Peter start, and he dropped the book on the floor, he picked it up again and put it in the bag, and then went down to his master.

"Where have you staid so long, Peter?" cried Sir Parrolla.

"I had much difficulty in opening the box," replied Peter, and then blushed, conscious of having told an untruth.

With eagerness Sir Parrolla took the bag from his trembling page, and he took from thence the magic book—but he had not read one page, before he was taken extremely ill, so much so, that though his heart was bent on reading the volume, he could not proceed with another line.

"Oh! I am ill—very ill," he groaned. "Peter, look into that book, and read aloud the page where I left off, the leaf is turned down; be quick, pray be quick; read, read, Peter, the place where it says, how death may be avoided, by applying to the powers of darkness."

Peter obeyed Sir Parrolla; he took up the book, but his faltering tongue could not prenounce the words there written.

No. 4.

"Read aloud," cried Sir Parrolla, "boy, why this delay ?"

"Oh, I cannot, sir, I cannot," cried Peter, " indeed I cannot."

"Dare not to disobey me," cried Sir Parrolla, " boy, I command you to read that page, and read it aloud."

"I dare not, sir," cried the trembling page, "pray do not ask me, it is a wicked book, and for the wealth of worlds, I would not read one single page of that book."

"Wretch ! ungrateful wretch !" cried Sir Parrolla. "Oh ! I feel the hand of death is upon me ; call my wife—call my son."

And for that purpose, Peter with trembling steps left the chamber.

CHAPTER XI.

"If thou thinkst on Heaven's bliss;
Hold up thy hand, make signal of thy hope.
He dies, and makes no sign, oh God forgive him.
*   *   *   *   *   *
" Forbear to judge, for we are sinners all.
Close up his eyes, and draw the curtains close,
And let us all to meditation."

                   SHAKSPERE.

WHEN Peter went by the order of Sir Parrolla, to fetch Lady Immorf and Percival, he found Lady Immorf was in her dressing room, and that Percival was reading in a lower apartment. But when Peter had delivered his message, both mother and son came without delay to the chamber of Sir Parrolla, whom they found sitting upright in bed, he having become much better during the absence of Peter.

The magic book lay before him on the bed, and his hand rested on it.

"Oh, Lucy, I have been so ill," he said, "and am so still, but through this book, this precious book, I over death shall triumph !"

"Yes," said Lady Immorf, "for she thought the magic book she saw lying on the bed, and of which her husband was speaking, was the Holy Scriptures, "yes," she said, "if you follow the dictates of that book, you will live eternally;" and Lady Immorf was glad to hear her husband speak in the way he did, for she thought that he at length would amend his conduct, and find comfort in the performance of his religious duty.

"Swear," cried Parrolla, "that you never will destroy, or cause to be destroyed, one leaf of this precious book ; both you and Percival must swear this."

"By my soul, and hope of happiness, I never will destroy, or cause to be destroyed, that book," cried Lady Immorf, "if I do, may Heaven never show mercy unto me."

"Enough," cried Parrolla, " Percival repeat that oath."

And the oath of his mother was repeated in a solemn voice by Percival.

"There is another thing you must swear," cried Parrolla.

"And what is that," said Lady Immorf.

"That you will never remove, from the place where it now hangs, the portrait of my friend Count Herman—nor either of you in the least injure or deface the said portrait."

"Why do you require such oaths ?" said Lady Immorf : " the sacred volume, your may be sure I should retain in safe-keeping ; and for that hideous likeness, however hateful the countenance there delineated is to me, I would not on any account injure or remove it, if it is your wish that it shall remain where it does."

"These words will not satisfy me," let Percival and yourself again pronounce the oath you repeated concerning the book ; the same oath you must again repeat, on account of the portrait."

Lady Immorf knew her husband was a very strange and overbearing man, and that any thing he said, or did, was not a matter to marvel at.

She again repeated the oath, and so did Percival.

Sir Parrolla was about to address his lady, but before he could do so, his illness again returned, and the hand of death seemed to be upon him.

"I will immediately send John for a physician," cried her ladyship in terror; go, Percival, and tell him to saddle his horse with all speed, and go for Doctor Adams."

"No," cried Sir Parrolla, "send for no physician, read this book, this magic-book; Lucy, read the page turned down—and save me from death."

Surprised at the word magic, and terrified at the manner of her husband, Lady Immorf felt agitated and confused; she hardly knew what she was doing, but the voice of her husband aroused her—"Open the book, and read," he cried.

Lady Immorf opened the book at the turned down page, but when she saw the words "how to call on supernatural agency to procure a lengthened existence," terrified, she let the book fall from her hand, and the colour fled from her cheeks.

Percival saw the change in his mother's countenance, and he hastened to assist her, and held to her nose some volatile salts, that happened to be in the room.

"Mother, this scene is too much for you," cried Percival—"Go to your room, and I will stay with my father."

"Oh, Percival!" cried Lady Immorf, "it is not the bodily illnes of your father that so much affects, me, it is the thought of how he may fare hereafter.—Oh! that book, that horrid book," and the face of Lady Immorf was suffused with tears.

Percival took up the book and opened it. "Oh! dreadful!" he cried as he threw it from him: "mother, send for your confessor; let Peter directly fetch Father Symonds."

As Peter was leaving the room to go on his errand, a low moan from Sir Parrolla, who had lain some short time quiet, made both his wife and son start.

"What, if I did throw her over the cliff," he said, in a moaning voice, "none saw me do it,"

"Then in a kind of whisper," he said, "hush, hush, 'tis your own fault, if i'ts known that I dishonoured you," then deep groans succeeded.

"Alas! alas!" cried lady Immorf, "then is thy soul clogged with that foul murder. Oh! would the priest were here. Percival, let us pray;" and Percival and his mother were in the act of so doing, when Sir Parrolla, who had lain for some moments still as the dead, started up in his bed, and staring wild as a maniac, he cried, "she's over! how she bent the willow in falling—hark! how she gurgles." Then bursting into a laugh, he cried, "Ha, ha, ha, what! not drowned—risen again from the sea. Ah, Rose! were you not pretty enough before, that you must needs take the sea-weed for a scarf, and water lilies to ornament your hair? This is you who wanted not diamonds and pearls, and now to dress yourself so fantastically—Oh! Rose, Rose, you are like your sex— all vanity."

He now fell back in his bed, and lay for some moments without motion.

Percival leant over his dying father; "Oh; I fear he is dead," he cried, "before the arrival of the confessor—father, if you yet live, speak—hold up your hand in sign thereof."

Sir Parrolla opened his eyes, and looked on his son.

"Oh father, tell me, tell me," cried Percival, "that you repent, that you hope for mercy; if you cannot speak, hold up your hand in token thereof."

Again Sir Parrolla opened his dying eyes but he did not move, or give the signal required by his son, and soon over his eyes the dark film of death was seen gathering, and with a deep groan, his soul quitted its mortal tenement.

Just as Sir Parrolla had breathed his last, Doctor Adams entered the apartment, but finding Sir Parrolla, was now beyond the power of medicine, after trying to console Lady Immorf and her son, he left the castle.

When the confessor arrived, Lady Immorf made known to him every particular concerning the magic book, and the promise extorted from her, by her dying husband.

The confessor opened the book, but with abhorrence, he soon threw it from him.

"Oh fatal promise," he cried, "and more praiseworthy in the breaking than in the performance. Let that book be burnt, delay not, put it on the fire."

"Father, it was beyond a promise, it was an oath, a fearful and binding oath, my husband extracted from both me and Percival, and never will my conscience suffer me to injure or destroy it."

"Then we'll secure it," said the confessor, "and place it where none can be influenced by its diabolical counsel. Let it be placed in some disused part of the castle."

"When or where Sir Parrolla obtained this accursed book I am not aware," said Lady Immorf.

"Perhaps Peter, the page, knows something of it," said Percival, "he was much with my father," and he rung the bell for Peter.

Peter came trembling into the chamber.

"Know you anything of this book-boy?" demanded the confessor.

Peter fell on his knees; "oh indeed I am not to blame," he cried, "my master gave me the key of the iron box in the eastern turret, and commanded me to bring down to him the crimson velvet bag that contained this book—I know 'tis a wicked book, and I could not read it to my master when he desired me. I'm sorry my master's dead," continued Peter, weeping, "and if he has been struck dead through reading that wicked book, it is no fault of mine."

"Rise, Peter," cried Lady Immorf, "no blame is attached to you.—Take up the book, and again put it in the velvet bag, and take it up to the disused eastern turret, and again place it in the iron box you spoke of."

"I am sorry, Peter," continued her ladyship, "that you know there is such a book in existence, it is most unfortunate; but, Peter, you must obliterate it from your memory, nor never name it to any one, for if you do, it may excite curiosity, and cause the perdition of the reader; therefore, Peter, I solemnly enjoin you to be secret respecting that book, and never from this hour even to think or speak of it."

Peter bowed his head in silence, and having taken up the book he put it in the velvet-bag, and took it up to the eastern turret, and locked it in the iron-box, and brought his lady down the key.

But Lady Immorf drew back her hand from touching the key, and she desired Peter to hang it on one of the nails that supported the portrait of Count Herman.

That portrait was now more than ever an object of hatred to Lady Immorf, for she believed it to be not unlikely, from what she had heard of that mysterious man, that he had been the original possessor of the magic-book.

And though bound by her oath not to remove or destroy it, she determined no more to behold a countenance which always inspired her with dread, and Lady Immorf, without delay, ordered a curtain of black cloth to be placed before the portrait, whose ample drapery descended from the ceiling of the room to the floor.

The shock of Sir Parrolla's death, and the circumstances attending it, greatly appalled both Lady Immorf and her son; particularly the words he used in his dying hour concerning the death of Rose Mildmay.

CHAPTER XII.

> "'Tis well that sorrow hath not made me wild.
> Will gold restore to me my wife and child?"   SHAKSPERE.

AT the expiration of ten days, the corse of Sir Parrolla Immorf was interred, and as the sable group left Ravenswood Castle, to follow the corse of Sir Parrolla to its last habitation, a great number of the villagers were assembled to view the pompous funeral, but no tears were shed in memory of the deceased, for he was not a man beloved by any.

As the mournful procession slowly descended the eminence in front of the castle, and wound round the tall trees, that lay to the left on its way to the church, Lady Immorf breathed a prayer for the soul of the departed, then seated herself, ruminating and alone in her chamber. The youthful Percival now drooped, and appeared the picture of melancholy, as he sat mournfully pondering on recent circumstances.

"Oh, that was a dreadful affair of poor Rose Mildmay," thought Percival, "I will go to poor old Mildmay and discover if I can assist him, under his heavy affliction." On the following day, Percival named his intention to his mother, and Lady Immorf highly approved of her son's intention.

Many days had not passed away, before Percival sought the cottage of old Mildmay; it was on a Sunday, for Percival thought he should on that day be more likely to find the old man at home during the hours not appointed for public worship. Mildmay had but just returned from church with his son, when Percival entered the cottage, and Patty, who was there, was laying the cloth for their dinner.

When old Mildmay saw that it was Percival Immorf who had entered, he withdrew his eyes, and a shuddering ran through his frame, but he tried to repress this feeling, and he looked on Percival with a composed but melancholy countenance. "The son could not help the fiend-like conduct of his father," he mentally said; "of the poor girl's death he is innocent."

Then with courtesy he arose, and bid his honor walk in.

The tears were in the eyes of Percival, when he seated himself in the chair the old man had placed for him, he looked with sorrow on the sable apparel of both old Mildmay, his son, and Patty, and again called to his mind the expressions his father had let fall concerning Rose, on the night of his death. Soon as Percival had somewhat recovered himself, and could command his voice to an equal tone, sufficient to explain the nature of his visit, he said—

"Mildmay, I have heard of your misfortunes, and I pity you—yes, from my inmost soul I pity you," said Percival, "and I am come to alleviate your sorrow, if I possibly can; that money will not bring back the dead, I am well aware, nor can you forget that such things were, and were most dear. But yet, my friend, we must reflect that no sorrow will bring them back, and that we all must submit to the wise dispensations of providence, not refuse, whilst we sojourn here, to receive consolation, nor any kindness which the hand of friendship and sympathy may offer.

"The miller of the fly-mill, I understand is lately dead; the mill, and the house belonging to it, are my mother's property. Patty, no doubt understands that business. I will give you, Mildmay, one hundred pounds to commence business with, and take no rent of you for three years. I have heard the whole of your misfortunes, and I pity you from my heart.—Are Patty and your son married?"

"No, sir, we are not," said William, "our grief will not permit us to think of mirthful occasions."

"Mirthful! oh, no," replied Percival, "there is now no room for mirth, but 'tis fit that you should be united; you have been used to the comfort of female society and need a female to render your home comfortable; of course, under the present circumstances, yours will not be a wedding celebrated with mirth and festivity— but a marriage rendered holy by a union of hearts and minds, humbled and bowed down to the will of Heaven."

The offer of Percival was thankfully accepted by old Mildmay; but more on account of his son than himself, for all comfort was now wrested from him—and his only consolation was in the hope of another and a better world. He forbore to mention the name of Sir Parrolla, as by so doing, he knew he must wound the feelings of his good and generous son.

Lady Immorf highly approved of the manner in which Percival had acted towards old Mildmay; but she was grieved to see the grief that preyed on her only child, on account of his deceased father; two months passed on, but still the melancholy of Percival was not lessened, and his mother proposed, nay, she absolutely insisted, that Percival should go for a short time into Devonshisre, to visit a distant relation who resided there, and from whom both Lady Immorf and her son had received a very pressing invitation.

At the repeated solicitations of his mother, who, herself, at that time declined the journey, Percival at length consented, but he had no wish to go ; in fact, it was highly disagreeable to him to quit home in the state of mind he was then in; but he wished to oblige his widowed mother, to whom he intended to act with the most filial respect, and supply to her as much as lay in his power the place of both husband and son.

Percival would not be persuaded to go his journey by any other conveyance than by horseback, although the distance he was going was upwards of fifty miles ; but the weather was then fine for the time of year, and after taking an affectionate leave of Lady Immorf, he departed, attended by Richard, an old and favourite servant.

Lady Immorf watched the horsemen as long as her strained eyes could view them in the distance, and when an angle in the road hid them from her view, she uttered many a prayer, and hoped every blessing would fall on the head of her beloved son.

CHAPTER XIII.

"Straight mine eyes have caught new pleasures,
    Whilst the landscape round it measures,
    Russet lawns and fallows grey,
    Where the nibbling flocks do stray."

                                                    MILTON.

PERCIVAL, who was a great admirer of fine scenery, finding his ride greatly tend to amuse his mind, did not hurry himself on his journey, but stopped at each place he came to, to see anything worthy of observation.

When he reached the house of Mr. Rosemont, the gentleman whose family he came to visit, he found Catherine and Julia, the daughters of Mr. Rosemont, whom he had not seen for upwards of two years ; they had now left for some time the boarding-school at which their mother had placed them, and where they were when Percival was last in Devonshire.

The charms of Julia, whose person was much improved in beauty since Percival last beheld her, although she was then a very pretty girl—now filled him with admiration ; and Percival not only admired her beauty, but he was also charmed with the sweetness and simplicity of manner, and the amiability of temper, which he discovered in the lovely Julia ; nor was Julia less taken with Percival than he was with her—and very loath were the lovers to part ; but after a fortnight's stay at the house of Mr. Rosemont, Percival prepared to return to Cornwall, not wishing to stay longer from the home of his widowed mother, who he knew would feel very lone without his society, and who he knew had persuaded him to take the journey into Devonshire, to shake off in some measure his melancholy ; but Percival knew it was greately against her own comfort, for he was now all to her, and without him, the world was as a wilderness.

Mr. Rosemont saw with pleasure the attachment that existed between Percival and his daughter ; and having no fear of his mother disapproving of his union with Miss Rosemont, Percival parted with the fair Julia, after mutual vows of eternal truth, and promising often to correspond with each other.

Just as Percival had mounted his horse, and was making his adieu to Mr. Rosemont's family, a letter was put in his hand—it came from his mother.

After the most respectful remembrances to Mr. Rosemont's family, she informed her son, that since his absence, she had been nearly at the point of death, but was now much better, but still very much indisposed ; the letter concluded, by desiring Percival would return back to Ravenswood Castle as soon as convenient to himself, "as the presence of my son," continued the writer, "will be more beneficial to me, than all the medicine in the world."

It was a fine morning, when Percival and his servant left the house of Mr. Rosemont, but it proved to be but a very gloomy day, and before Percival could reach the inn where he had before rested, a heavy storm came on, and Percival and his servant were obliged to take shelter in a cottage, that stood by the road-side.

The storm at length subsided, but Percival had yet three miles to go before he reached the inn, and the shades of night were fast advancing.

"I would advise you to stay here, sir, for the night," said the cottager's wife, "and I will accommodate you and your servant, in the best way I can. It will soon be dark, and to persons unacquainted with it, the road is extremely dangerous; there are several very deep pitfalls, at but a short distance from here, in which many persons have lost their lives. And not only that, but the road is much infested by robbers; it was but last Friday se'nnight that poor old Dame Brown was knocked down and robbed of all the money, for which she had sold her butter and poultry."

"My good woman, don't think to alarm me with poor Dame Brown's mishap," replied Percival, "both myself and servant; are strong young fellows, and not easily intimidated; and we are mounted on the best horses England can produce —robbers would find it difficult to keep up with us—pitfalls I, by all means, wish to avoid—on which side of the road do they lie?"

"To the left," replied the good woman, "just beyond where the road turns."

"Oh, we shall do well enough," replied Percival; "we found our way here, and I have not the least doubt, but that we shall find our way back again; 'tis now a fine evening, and see, we have a new moon to light us on our way." But Percival had not rode more than one mile, before he severely repented of not taking the cottager's advice; for the moon became hid by clouds of sable, and a heavy rain again began to pour down.

"I think, sir, we had better take shelter under those trees," said Richard to his master, "if we go on we must be wet through."

"I wish I had taken the old dame's advice and remained at the cottage," said Percival, as, in pursuance of Richard's advice, he turned his horse's head from the road, and took shelter under the trees that grew thereby.

The heavy pattering of the rain at length abated, but it was still extremely dark, and with some dread, and in silence, the travellers pursued their way.

Soon a loud whistle sounded on the stillness; it was answered by a respondent sound, which seemed to proceed from no great distance.

"There are ruffians abroad," cried Percival; "Richard, spur on your horse, spur him to his uttermost speed—hark! we are pursued, I hear the tramp of their horses' hoofs."

They were now precisely at that part of the road of which the cottager had warned them.

Here Richard, unthinkingly, and in haste, turned the angle in the road to avoid his pursuers, who were now fast gaining ground upon them, and he fell with his horse into the deep and marshy pitfall. Knowing by the cry of his unhappy servant, together with the noise the horse made in falling, and the splashing it made in the mire, at the bottom of the pit-fall, what had happened, Percival stopped his horse, and was for some moments almost petrified and chained to the spot; but the thought of his own danger aroused him; for the persons following, he could hear, were not now many paces behind him.

With as little noise as possible, Percival got off his horse, and softly crept into a copse which adjoined the road, leaving his horse to stand still, or go on, as it pleased.

As if aware of danger, and fearing to share the fate of its companion, the horse stood still, until the men came up to it.

Percival could not distinguish their persons or number; but he heard their dreadful vociferations when they discovered what had happened.

Seeing Percival's horse standing without a rider, and hearing the cries of

Richard and the dreadful writhings of the poor horse, they concluded that both riders had fallen into the pit-fall, and by that means disappointed them of their expected booty.

"Curse the blundering fools," cried one of the men, we cannot get at them to-night; "we must not lose the swag, however, but endeavour to come at it, when 'tis day-light."

"But our labour is not entirely lost," he continued, catching hold of the bridle of Percival's horse, "this will fetch us something."

The groans of Richard had not yet ceased, and the poor horse still struggled with the agony of suffocation, when the ruffians, as they rode away, cried with a horse-laugh——

"That's right, old boy, flounder away, and we will come at a more convenient time and help you out."

Percival stood for some moments, hardly daring to breathe, but as the sound of the horsemen died away, he became more assured, and he looked around him and listened, hoping to discover some light, or hear some sound, which might guide him to an habitation, where he might pass the night.

To be better enabled to make such discovery, he emerged from the copse, and after some time looking around him, he at length saw a light faintly glimmering through a window at no great distance.

The rain still poured down, and the darkness was intense : with cautious steps Percival walked on, until he came to the house, where from the window the light still glimmered ; it was but little he could see of the house, on account of the darkness of the night, but that little was sufficient to awaken his suspicions, and fill him with unpleasant apprehensions.

CHAPTER XIV.

"Some ruling fiend hangs in the dusky air,
And scatters ruin, death, and wild destruction."   ROWE.

FROM what Percival could discern, the building in which the light still faintly shone, was of large extent, of desolate and dilapidated aspect—a place in which robbers might be supposed to congregate.

"Surely some evil power must rule this eventful night," thought Percival; "poor Richard is no more, and Heaven knows what misery is in store for me."

"I will not knock," he inwardly said, "murder seems written here ;" and he withdrew his hand from the ponderous knocker, "yet, if I stay unhoused until morning, exposed to the pitiless peltings of the storm, my death will be inevitable; if I knock and solicit admittance, the chance may be in my favour, for notwithstanding the appearance of the place, honest people may dwell here."

Percival let the knocker fall from his hand, but none answered—again he knocked more loudly; at length he heard footsteps approaching, and as they did so, his heart palpitated with extreme terror.

The door opened, and the tall, gaunt figure of an aged man stood before him.

"What is your business here?" he gruffly inquired.

"I have lost my way, owing to the darkness of the night," said Percival; he did not think it prudent to mention his servant, or the robbers. "I am wet through, and would beg shelter for the night."

"Begone!" cried the old man; "serpent, begone! I will not shelter thee—I have been stung enough by thee ; I know no pity—begone!"

"Oh! hear how the storm pours down," cried Percival; "in pity give me shelter for the night; if you drive me hence, you will be my murderer—too late will you repent the cruel deed; if so, when you are at the judgment-seat, the Almighty will no more listen to your petition, than you now do to mine, nor extend more mercy to you, than you now show to me."

The old man seemed somewhat affected at the entreating words of Percival, whose proud spirit was much brought down in consequence of what he had suffered, and the thought of what he might yet endure, if exposed to the inclemency of the weather, he therefore condescended again to request shelter for the night.

"Oh! suffer me to remain," he cried, "shut not your hospitable door against me."

"Hospitable!" said the old man, with a bitter smile, "it once was hospitable, but now none enter it."

"Oh! man, man;" he cried, "more destructive, and more to be dreaded, than the tiger of the deserts!"

"I have vowed no more to feel pity—no more to let the sufferings of my own species affect me; but you—you have prevailed—you have caused feelings long banished to arise in my bosom; come in, I will shelter you for the night."

Percival followed the old man into a large and gloomy apartment on the ground floor, a fire was burning on the hearth, and some pottage was smoking on a table near it.

No. 5.

"You are wet," said the old man, "pull off your upper garments, and dry them, if you like, you are welcome to partake of this pottage."

Percival declined the old man's offer, "I am extremely chilly," he said, "from the effect of the rain, and ill from the dread I felt, at the thought of remaining un-housed. I thank you, but I feel no inclination for food—this is a lonely spot," continued Percival; "do you live here alone?"

"Why that inquiry?" replied the old man. "Have I not given you shelter? give me not reason to repent having done so. When morning dawns, as soon as it is light enough for you to see your way, you must depart. I have no better accom-modation to offer you, than what you now possess, but a seat by a fire is preferable to remaining unhoused in the open air, exposed to the pelting storm."

Percival fully acceded to the old man's opinion, who, having wished Percival a good night, departed.

Several times during the night, Percival went to the widow of his apartment, to ascertain if the storm had yet abated; but the rain still poured down, and black darkness o'erspread the horizon.

"This has been to me a night of dread and awfulness," thought Percival, "and glad shall I be, when I again reach my home."

A low moan broke on his ear; he listened, and could distinguish the voice of some one who appeared to be suffering under mental or bodily anguish.

"Surely the old man is not connected with the banditti who infest these wilds," thought Percival. "Murder may be doing."

The moan became more audible—'twas nearer—footsteps approached, and an effort was made to open the door of Percival's room; the effort was repeated.

"Who is there?" cried Percival.

"'Tis I, your entertainer," replied a feeble voice, which he knew to be the old man's. When admitted, he said—

"Stranger, I need your assistance." He tottered to a chair, and when seated, he said, "I feel the hand of death upon me—Providence, I believe, directed you here; for your coming has saved the life of a fellow-creature, for on my death the destiny of another depends. I intended never to forgive, but I will be merciful; your words to-night penetrated my soul—I feel that if no mercy is shown, none can be expected. Give this paper to Alfred Montford—here are the keys," and he held out his hand to Percival, with the keys and paper. "Alfred is—in," —he could utter no more, the words died on his lips, and in a moment he fell a lifeless corse on the floor.

Percival lifted up the old man, and endeavoured to place him on a chair, for he flattered himself that the old man was not yet dead, but the pulsation of his heart had ceased—life had fled for ever. Finding such was the case, Percival laid the corse on the floor, and examined the paper the old man had desired might be given to Alfred Montford. The paper ran thus :—

"I give and bequeath to Alfred Montford, all my right and title in Oat Farm, to John Grub, at the yearly rent of forty pounds per year.

"As witness to my hand,
"THOMAS ROCKINGHAM."

Neither the place, parish, or shire, in which Oat Farm was situated, was named, nor was the date of the year, or month specified. It was evidently written with some difficulty and in haste, by a hand tremulous and unsteady.

Percival stood for some moments observing the countenance of the corpse as it lay extended on the floor. "That old man could not die in peace," he said.

"What a frown is on that brow; what an unrelenting disposition is expressed in the lineaments of that countenance. He said my coming was directed by Providence, and by my appeal to his feelings I had altered his mind, and directed his thoughts from vengeance to mercy. How strange, that words spoken at random and unfelt by me, used merely to interest him, and cause him to give me shelter for the night, should have so deeply affected him, but 'tis evident they did so."

Morning now began to dawn, but the rain in torrents yet poured down, "I will look over the house," thought Percival ; "the old man said 'there are the keys,' he must have had some meaning in giving me them, which his sudden demise prevented him from expressing."

Percival ascended the stairs. They were covered with dust, and seemed as if it were long since any foot had passed them ; some of the apartments appeared to be in a very dilapidated state, while others seemed to have been more lately repaired and beautified, but dust, damp, and mildew had defaced their beauty.

In some of these rooms were chairs, tables, and glasses of most expensive workmanship ; in others, bedsteads, whose lofty testers were covered with dust, and from whose massive posts, the spiders with great industry had spead their web of death.

One of the rooms was particularly noticed by Percival for the expensive furniture with which it abounded : richly inlaid Indian cabinets stood there, on which were placed vases of the finest china ; the window curtains and bed-hangings were of rich blue silk, but the summer sun and winter damps had rendered them colourless ; the room that adjoined the bed-room was fitted up as a library ; there was a couch in it, it appeared in disorder, as if some persons had slept therein, and on the floor there were several spots of blood—one part of the room in particular appeared deluged in blood.

Percival turned from this appalling sight : he looked through the window of the apartment, all around was drear and desolate ; no house was within sight ; nought was to be seen but the distant forest trees, the heavy rain-drops, and long grass waving with the wind in the fore-court of this mansion of desolation and death.

CHAPTER XV.

Oh ! she was lovely as the summer rose,
Sweet as the violet when it opening blows,
Her lips were of the coral's richest red,
Her eyes were azure, as the sun's blue bed.

ROWE.

PERCIVAL again descended the stairs ; he opened a door which was in the passage at the bottom of them, and there saw another flight of stairs. Here all appeared involved in gloom and darkness, for these stairs led to some under-ground apartments.

In order to find his way into this subterraneous place, in which he thought, from the strange manner of the old man, that some human being was perhaps confined ; he went into the room where he had passed the night, and having looked about it, at length found a lamp, which he lighted, and descended the stairs.

As he descended these stairs, he saw several particles of blood lying on them, as if dropped by some person who was carrying a larger quantity down them. At the bottom of the stairs was a door, which Percival opened, and he stood terrified at the sight that presented itself.

A young woman, seemingly about twenty years of age, and of most interesting appearance, stood inside the door ; she had a frightful gash in her bosom, from which the blood appeared to be profusely flowing.

"Rash girl ! what have you done ?" cried Percival, and he hastened to the assistance of one who, he believed, had that moment committed suicide, for the gloom of the under-ground apartment had deceived him, and prevented him discovering, until nearer inspection, that the suppposed female was but a waxen representation. Whilst viewing it, he was startled by hearing a voice exclaim—

"Great God ! for what am I reserved ? Stranger, art thou come to destroy me ?"

Percival looked towards the upper end of the apartment, where he saw standing the tall, spectre-like figure of a man, one who looked more like a shade, a being who had passed the confines of the grave, than a mortal man.

Almost petrified by fear and amazement, Percival did not reply, for the events of the night were too much for his nerves, and his tongue as it were clave to his mouth.

"Art thou come to destroy me?" again demanded the man, "if so, strike and end my miseries."

"Fear not, I intend you no harm," replied Pervical, "who art thou, and what means that figure?"

"She was my bane, my temptress, my ruin," replied the man, "but where is Mr. Rockingham?"

"If you mean the old man, he is no more," replied Percival; "but come up stairs, I wish to have an elucidation of these mysteries."

"I cannot leave this place," said the man. "Do you not perceive the chain that encircles me?"

Percival had still the keys the old man had given him in his hand, and with one of them he unlocked the padlock which confined the chain round the waist of the unfortunate man; who, when released from his confinement, followed Percival up stairs, but it was slowly, and with difficulty that he did so; for he was extremely weak in consequence of long confinement, and his limbs were numbed and stiffened, by reason of the dampness of his underground dwelling-place.

When Percival again entered the apartment in which he had passed the night, he pointed to the old man's corse, and said, "Is this Mr. Rockingham, the man you inquired for?"

"'Tis he," cried the man, "but the sight of those ghastly features shocks and affects me with sorrow, and bring to my memory scenes I would fain forget. There was a time when, if I had seen him lay thus, it would have filled my heart with anguish; but he punished my crime with too great severity; he made no allowance for my youth, nor the temptation that assailed me, nor would he take into consideration the fallibility of human nature, though often petitioned by me to do so."

"You have at length escaped his tyranny," said Percival, "and can now rejoice."

"And wherefore should I rejoice?" replied the man; "'tis true that I may now view the green fields, and hear the melody of the birds, and behold the glorious firmament, the moon, and stars, and see the bright luminary of day, shining in radiance above me. Yet though I have my liberty, I cannot my food like unto the birds of the air, or beasts of the field, nor I labour to earn my bread; the relations of Mr Rockingham will take possession of all that belonged to him, and hating me for the misery I caused the deceased, they will show me no kindness, but send me forth a vagabond on the face of the earth."

"Not so," said Percival, "a better fate awaits you, as I suppose your name is Alfred Montford."

"I am that unfortunate," replied the man.

"Then read that," said Percival, and he gave him the bequest of Mr. Rockingham to read

"Oh! God be thanked," cried Alfred, "who but the Almighty could have softened the stern resentment of Mr. Rockingham's heart, and have caused him to pity and provide for my destitute and friendless condition."

Seeing the agitation of the man, Percival begged he would compose himself, "for joy may be as detrimental as sorrow," remarked Percival, "and now you have wherewithal to support yourself, life is worth your care. Sit down, and I will look amongst the old man's stores, and see if I can find any wine, for I, as well as yourself, require something to cheer me."

Having succeeded in finding some wine, Percival gave a large glass to Alfred, and having taken another himself, he said, "I am in great haste to depart, but cannot until I have heard some particulars concerning Mr. Rockingham, yourself, and the female, whose likeness I saw below."

"You have been my preserver," said Alfred, "and it would be ungrateful in me to refuse your request, however harrowing to my feelings the recital may be." He then began as follows :—

CHAPTER XVI.

Woman, thou art true copy of the first,
In whom the race of all mankind was curst,
Nature took care to dress you up in sin,
Adorned without, unfinished left behind.   ALWAY.

"THE corse you there behold," said Alfred, "in whose countenance is wanting the blessed composure of those who die resigned to their fate, and in peace with mankind, is he who brought me up from my childhood, and was to me a second father ; he was a man of a kind heart, and the most benevolent principles, but a man of the strongest resentment when injured ; from my long knowledge of his disposition, and from the expression of his countenance even in death, it convinces me that his last sigh was more on account of the injuries he had received, than the loss of life."

"'I am hated by earth and Heaven,' he would cry. 'Is there one whom I have loved, served or confided in, but serpent-like, hath stung the hand that fostered it ? the Supreme hath given me a heart to feel and to suffer."

"With deep regret, I acknowledge that I, amongst others, heaped misery upon him—upon him, my friend and benefactor. My parents were respectable, but unfortunate persons, who died when I was little more than six years of age, leaving me a destitute and friendless orphan ; when my helpless situation became known to Mr. Rockingham, he took me into his house and became a father to me ; he placed me at school, provided me with books of amusement as well as instruction, toys, and every indulgence the fondest father could bestow on a petted child, he bestowed on me.

"There was a cousin of Mr. Rockingham, named Reuben Randal, they had been school-fellows, and in manhood they were extremely intimate ; although they agreed so well, they were quite different dispositions. Thomas Rockingham was liberal, generous, benevolent, unsuspecting, and humane, until the tenderness of his heart was turned into bitterness, and he then, according to his own wish, would have become a misanthropist, but his heart would not permit him to be so.

"The wretch who first caused this change in the noble minded Rockingham was Reuben Randal, his cousin, his selfish, scheming, perfidious cousin.

"They had an uncle, from whom they both had great expectations ; Reuben tried, by every artful means he could devise, to set his uncle against Thomas Rockingham, but what he said against his cousin was only given in hints and inuendos, for he feared to speak in too plain terms of circumstances, the falsity of which, if discovered, must turn to his own confusion ; but his art was of no avail with the old gentleman ; he saw through the design of the deceptive Reuben, and at his death left Thomas double the sum he bequeathed Reuben.

"Enraged at the preference shown Thomas by his uncle, Reuben, though under the mask of friendship, hated his cousin with a deadly animosity, which was only increased by the death of another relation, who left Thomas Rockingham Oat Farm, and several other houses ; but in case Rockingham died without an heir, the whole was to devolve to Reuben Randal. Every day Thomas lived, Reuben thought it a day too long, and ardently hoped that some illness or accident would deprive him of life; often, when they have been on the most seeming friendly discourse, Reuben hath turned his head aside, lest his cousin should see the vengeful expression that glared in his eyes, whose ireful glances he could not control ; however, he pretended more friendship for Rockingham than ever, and almost every day he went out a riding with him, an exercise Mr. Rockingham was very fond of. He had a very fine bay horse he was in the habit of riding ; this horse Reuben contrived to lame privily, and when the servant went to fetch it from the stable by the order of his master, he returned with the news that the horse was quite lame and disabled.

"Surprised at this account, Mr. Rockingham and Reuben went to the stable to view the horse, which they found lame, and indeed, almost unable to stand.

" ' I have a nice little horse at home,' said Reuben, 'one I have lately purchased; he is not so handsome as yours, but he may serve until your horse is recovered of his lameness, or until you have got another: don't let us be disappointed of our ride ; I will go home and fetch him.'   This he did, and both gentlemen set off together.

" The horse Reuben Randal lent Mr. Rockingham had a very ugly trick of setting off at full gallop, and if reined tightly would kick up behind and lower his head in front, over which he was almost sure to throw his rider, if he was not aware of his tricks, and prepared to manage him ; one person met his death in consequence of having his skull fractured through being thrown from this horse, and another had his collar-bone broken.

" For this propensity, Reuben bought him, fully anticipating that mischief would happen ; nor was he mistaken, for they had not rode more than a quarter of a mile, when the horse set off at full gallop, and when curbed by Mr. Rockingham, he kicked up behind, as was his usual practice, and endeavoured to throw his rider over his head, which he at length effected.

" With pleasure Reuben saw Rockingham fall, and he hoped to find him a mangled corse, but, to his sorrow and surprise, he found that Rockingham was still alive and with no bones broken, but almost stunned, and much bruised by the fall.

" With affected sorrow Reuben assisted his cousin to rise, and when somewhat recovered from the shock he had received in falling, Reuben would have persuaded his cousin to mount his horse, whose mad career was stopped by a labouring man then passing.

" But Mr. Rockingham would not agree to that, he had had quite enough of the nice little horse, and he got home, as well as the bruises he had received would allow him to do.

" In consequence of the liberality of Mr. Rockingham's temper, he became rather straightened for ready money, when a circumstance happened that put him in possession of a very large sum of money.

" Mr. Rockingham was very fond of flowers, and would nurse and mould them up himself ; during such employment he one day turned up with the small spade he was in the habit of using, a piece of gold ; this induced him to search deeper into the earth, where he found placed beneath where he had been digging, a large earthen pot full of the same coin.   According to law, Mr. Rockingham knew the hidden treasure belonged to the king ; however, his conscience was not troubled by keeping it, as it was not found on his majesty's ground, neither was he present at the finding thereof.

" ' It was on my own ground,' thought Mr. Rockingham, ' I therefore consider it to be my own property, and shall make no scruple in using it.'

" None knew of this affair but Reuben Randal, to whose keeping Mr. Rockingham confided every secret of his heart.

" Reuben seemed delighted with his cousin's good fortune ; he wished to see the coin, which was produced by Mr. Rockingham ; Reuben then counted it, to ascertain to what sum it amounted.

" Scarcely a week had passed away after this occurrence, when Reuben called on Mr. Rockingham, and said ' that he was, through disappointments, much drove for a large sum of money;' the sum he named was precisely half the amount of the coin Mr. Rockingham found in his garden ; this sum was lent with pleasure by Mr. Rockingham, who was pleased that he had it in his power to serve his perfidious cousin.''

CHAPTER XVII.

Fatally fair they are, and in their smiles,
The graces, little loves, and young desire inhabit. ROWE.

"At the time of Mr. Rockingham's finding the hidden treasure, I had been under his protection about fifteen years; he was at that time about forty years of age, and unmarried, but Mr. Randal was married, and had a family.

"Mr. Rockingham was returning home one evening, and on his way, he saw a young woman walking before him; there was something so attractive in the figure of this young person, that it impelled Mr. Rockingham to follow her; this he did, and was struck with the singular beauty of her countenance.

"After several attempts to draw this lovely girl into conversation, he at length succeeded, and found her name was Phillis Vivian, the daughter of a tradesman, who had become bankrupt, and that she was living with her parents, who were in very reduced circumstances.

"Phillis was the first woman who had ever made an impression on the heart of Mr. Rockingham, and he determined to marry her, if she was agreeable to have him, and her character answered his expectations.

"After having inquired in her neighbourhood, and not having heard anything to her disadvantage, he sought an interview with her father, to whom he made known the love he bore Phillis, and declared, if all parties were agreeable, his intention of making her his wife.

"Neither the consent of Phillis nor her parents was wanting, and in a very short time the marriage took place; this was a most fortunate circumstance for Miss Vivian, for, had she not become Mrs. Rockingham, she must have laboured to support herself, in consequence of the insolvency of her father, but rather than do that, she gave her hand where her heart was not, and to a man old enough to be her father; for Phillis was but eighteen.

"As if fortune was never tired of showering her favours on Mr. Rockingham, another relation died, and left him ten thousand pounds in the stocks, besides this house and the land adjoining it.

"This handsome addition to the fortune of Mr. Rockingham was a fresh source of mortification to his covetous and envious cousin, and he now, if it were possible, hated Rockingham worse than ever.

"I was at that time at college studying divinity, for it was my benefactor's wish that I should be a clergyman; I had but three months more to remain at college, when I received a letter from my father, as I was in the habit of calling Mr. Rockingham; in this letter, he informed me that he was now married to a very amiable young woman, and one who he knew would do all in her power to promote my welfare and happiness.

"I was rather surprised at this intelligence, for as Mr. Rockingham had lived so long single, I little expected he, at his time of life, would get married.

"I longed to see my mother, for such of course I was to call her, little expecting how fatal that sight would be to me.

"Mrs. Rockingham was the guest of the gay, the star of every company she went into, and admired and idolized by her adoring husband, whose love since his marriage had rather increased than diminished.

"But at length Mr. Rockingham began to be rather uneasy in consequence of the great attention paid his bride, by almost every gentleman they were in company with; men, whose years were more suitable to the charming Phillis than his own, and from whose lips he saw she rather courted than shunned adulation.

"Amongst the admirers of Mrs. Rockingham was Mr. Randal, the yet friend of her husband; he was older than Rockingham, but yet a beau, and as great an admirer of beauty as when he was but twenty-five. Although a married man, he was generally in the train of the beautiful Phillis, extolled her to the sky, and declaring that to possess her was a felicity too great for mortal man.

" On one occasion, when he happened to be alone with her, and after paying the vain, unthinking girl the most fulsome compliment, he, kneeling, caught her hand, and imprinted on it a fervent kiss.

" At this moment Mr. Rockingham entered the room followed by Mrs. Randal, who had called to pay a morning visit to Phillis.

" Enraged at the sight he beheld, Mr. Rockingham collared Randal, 'what mean you, sir?' he cried ; 'what am I to conclude by seeing you in that posture?'

" ' You may conclude what you please,' said Randal, ' I can only say I acted involuntarily, fascinated and bewitched by the beauty of your wife, whose presence I shall for the future avoid.'

" Irritated and inflamed by jealousy, Mrs. Randal cried, ' Don't believe him, Mr. Rockingham, he is continually following Mrs. Rockingham about, flattering her, and trying to win her affections from you; 'tis well we came in, for Randal is the wickedest man on earth, and would have insinuated himself so much in the favour of Mrs. Rockingham, that an elopement might have taken place. The horse he lent you he bought on purpose to break your neck, and he borrowed part of the treasure you found, without any intention of repaying it.'

" ' I own it,' exclaimed Randal, ' I hate you with a deadly hatred; through your art you wormed yourself into my uncle's favour, and by that means, enjoy what I ought to have received.'

" ' Wretch, hypocrite, begone !' cried Mr. Rockingham, ' nor no more presume to darken these doors ; and for the money you borrowed, I will compel you to repay it.'

" ' I had as much right to it as yourself,' replied Randal ; ' dare to ask me for it again, and I will acquaint the authorities, and they will make you refund what you still retain.' He walked towards the door, followed by his wife, but before he departed, he turned his head, and said, ' I see I have vexed you, and I glory in having done so ; however, I'll give you a word of advice before we part, and that advice is, to look well to your Phillis, your gentle, complying Phillis, too tender-hearted to refuse any favour required of her.'

" ' I will not bear this,' cried Mr. Rockingham ; ' he shall fall by my sword, or I by his,' and he snatched up his hat to follow Randal. when Phillis, clinging to him, cried, ' Oh ! do not go, for my sake— don't go, I beg, I entreat you will not.'

" ' I will grant you anything but this,' said Mr. Rockingham, ' my own injuries I could put up with, but your character, my Phillis, shall not be sported with.'

" Rockingham and Randal met, with their seconds, the following morning, when Mr. Rockingham was severely wounded, but after much suffering, he slowly amended.

" But the confinement Phillis endured, as she wished to preserve an appearance of concern for her husband during the precarious state he was in, from the effects of his wounds, mortified her extremely ; however, she concealed her chagrin beneath winning smiles, and affected solicitude for his recovery.

" For by such behaviour she hoped, in the event of his death, that he, out of gratitude for her love and attention, would leave her the whole of his property without restriction.

" Phillis was one of those females, who, if her vanity was not continually fed by flattery and praise, became vapoured and unhappy ; her thoughts were continually occupied by the thought of the admiration she obtained, and how she could look and dress the more to set off her charms. Even when her husband was in the greatest danger, she consoled herself, by thinking how very lovely she would look in widow's weeds, should Rockingham's death take place.

" And she consulted her milliner, as to what shaped mourning cap would best become her features, and if she did not think the fairness of her complexion would not be improved by wearing black apparel.

" But Phillis was not fated to become a widow, the wounds of Mr. Rockingham healed, but the treachery of his cousin Reuben, him he had loved as a brother, dwelt heavily on his mind, and much retarded the recovery of the noble-minded Rockingham.

"He reflected too, on the remarks made on Phillis, by Randal, and calling to mind her behaviour on some occasions, he concluded that she was rather too fond of admiration, too unsuspecting and pliant, to mix much with the world; and he resolved to leave London with his young wife, and reside entirely in this place.

"Phillis was dull and unhappy at the thought of leaving London, where she was fairest of the fair; in order to please her, and cause her to be satisfied with her new abode, he ordered workmen to alter and beautify some of the rooms, although the house was then in most excellent repair; he bought some of the most beautiful and expensive furniture that could be procured, and the bed-hangings and window-curtains in Phillis's room were of rich blue silk.

"The time was now arrived for me to leave college, and I, as directed in the letter of my benefactor, came to this house; Mr. Rockingham and his wife were from home when I arrived, but they soon after returned; I saw my father as I had ever called him alight from his horse, and he assisted from her horse his companion, the most beautiful young creature I had ever beheld.

"'Can that be his wife,' thought I; 'am I to call that fair girl, mother, whose years but little exceed my own?'

No. 6.

CHAPTER XVIII.

" But if she smiled ;
A darting glory seemed to blaze abroad :
That men's desiring eyes were never wearied,
But hung upon the object."
                                                    DRYDEN.

" IN person Mrs. Rockingham was remarkably fair, and the hue of the damask rose was on her finely rounded cheek ; her forehead, mouth and nose, were most beautifully formed, and dimpled smiles gave an inexpressible charm to her lovely countenance.

"She was rather above the middle size, and her green riding habit, showed to advantage her slender form, and a cambric habit-shirt, of the finest material, covered her full bosom ; she wore a small black velvet hat, rather turned up in front, displaying her fair high forehead, and her hair of the lightest brown, fell in ringlets over her shoulders.

" Mr. Rockingham presented his wife to me,

" ' Alfred, this is Mrs. Rockingham,' he said, ' she will act as a mother to you.

" Mrs. Rockingham, smiling, said, ' I hope so.'

"Oh ! what a smile was that, showing two rows of pearl between opening coral, to this hour I remember that smile, and the impression it made upon me. I became melancholy and reserved, and passed great part of my time in the library, or walking in the fields or gardens, for I could not rest ; I loved with a guilty passion, the wife of my benefactor ; I knew the guilt, the enormity of such a passion, and I avoided Mrs. Rockingham as much as I possibly could, whilst she, as if conscious of my feeling towards her, continually threw herself in my way, and by the most marked attention, fanned the flame that consumed me.

"There was at about ten miles distant from this place, an estate to be sold in consequence of the death of its owner ; this estate Mr. Rockingham agreed to purchase, and for that purpose, he intended going to London to sell out the ten thousand pounds he had left him in the stocks.

"On the day of his departure, Mrs. Rockingham fondly hung on the neck of her husband, and embracing him, said, ' Oh ! what an eternity will this short absence be to me.'

" ' Foolish Phillis,' said Mr. Rockingham, as he pressed her to his bosom, " I shall soon be back again ; I would not leave you behind, but in your state, travelling may be attended with unpleasant consequences ; Alfred, will, I know, do all in his power to amuse you, and make the time pass as pleasantly as possible during my absence.'

" Oh, Heaven ! what did I at that moment feel ; I loved my kind unsuspecting benefactor, of whom, I now feared his beautiful, his fascinating wife, was unworthy ; I felt the danger I should be exposed to in her society, and would have given worlds, had I possessed them, to have been spared this trial of my integrity.

" I wished to propose accompanying Mr. Rockingham, but that was not now to be thought of, he had, as it were, left his wife in my charge.

" When in company with Phillis at meal times, I preserved an appearance of great gravity, and as soon as my meal was finished, I retired to the library, as an excuse for which, I spoke of the necessity there was for me to prosecute my studies with great diligence, as I shortly must appear before an audience, where a greater study of divinity and elocution than I possessed would be necessary.

" It happened on an afternoon, when Phillis, in consequence of the state of the weather, was confined to the house, that she came into the library where I was sitting, dejectedly poring over a volume.

" Come, now, Alfred, I insist that you spend a few hours with me,' she said ; ' leave those dull prosing books, at least for one afternoon, or I will tell Rocking-ham when he comes back, that instead of amusing me, and trying to keep up my spirits during his absence, you have shunned me as you would a pestilence.—

Come, you must go with me into the drawing-room, and I will sing a song to amuse you—I am thought a tolerable singer, though you never heard me sing.'

" Politeness, and I am sorry to say, my own inclination, would not suffer me to refuse the request of the charming Phillis, although I was aware of my own danger in so doing, but who could resist such beauty?—she sang several songs, all of which touched on the passion of love, the soft pathos of her voice ran thrilling through my heart—I was affected even to tears.

" I felt that every moment I was in company with Phillis, I loved her more and more, that greater was her power over me, and the more incapable was I of mastering feelings I had resolved to subdue.

" Phillis observed the melancholy of my countenance and the starting tear which she saw, I endeavoured hastily to brush away, when she said—

"' Alfred, are you too in grief? I thought I only was unhappy.'

"' You unhappy !' I replied, ' you, so lovely, so loving and beloved, and blessed with every good that heaven can give ; I surely misunderstand you.'

"' Oh, no,' she replied, ' have I not sacrificed myself at the shrine of Mammon, through the insolvency of my father, and a fear of coming to want. For a subsistence I married a man I could not love ; had I not seen you, I might have been contented, but now I feel the wretchedness of my lot; I love you, but you shun and hate me.'

" ' Hate you !' I replied, ' 'tis not in nature to do so; no, I love you to distraction, but you are a wife, the wife, of my benefactor, the wife of more than father ; not for the universe, would I have him know of my guilty passion, confessed in a moment of rapture and excitement ;—but I will leave you, madam, or I shall no longer be master of myself.' Having said this, I was quitting the apartment, but Phillis detained me.

" Oh ! where was my resolution, my honour, the self-denial with which I meant to have acted ? all vanished like the dew of morn at the approach of day.

" Beauty triumphed ; I forgot all but the fascinating Phillis, and became the slave of an unprincipled woman.

" For years past, in the elysium of her smiles, I then would have signed my own perdition."

CHAPTER XIX.

"I know
Thou hast a tongue to charm the wildest tempers;
Herds would forget to graze, and savage beasts
Stand still and loose their fierceness, but to
Hear thee."   ROWE.

" WHEN Mr. Rockingham returned, Phillis took occasion to pout and find fault with him for his long absence, though indeed, he returned sooner than she wished or could have expected ; the money which he had obtained by selling out in the stock, was in bank notes, which he placed in his desk in the library, where they remained ; the deeds which were to convey to him his intended purchase not being yet ready.

" Mr. Rockingham had, during his journey, caught a severe cold, which caused him to be restless in consequence of a troublesome cough, on that account Mrs. Rockingham proposed sleeping in another bed, as he disturbed her.

" And as there was no other bed-room on that floor, she insisted on having a couch placed in the library, that she might be near her husband.

" Before Mr. Rockingham was up on the following morning ; Phillis came to me into the garden, where I was walking in a very disturbed state of mind.

" It was a cold, cheerless morning, the latter end of October, the flowers had long since departed, and yellow leaves, shook by the autumnal blasts, bestrewed the garden walks ; but Phillis chose an harbour at the most remote part of the garden to converse in, as there we were less likely to be overheard or disturbed.

" ' Alfred,' she said, ' I am come to the determination of leaving Rockingham; will you be the partner of my flight ?'

" ' Impossible !' I replied, ' for myself I should not care ; but you know I am entirely dependant on Mr. Rockingham, and privation and poverty must not reach my Phillis.

" ' Neither shall it,' she replied, ' come to me in the library at midnight ; I shall not undress, but employ myself in packing up what will be needful of my wardrobe, and the jewels Rockingham has presented me with. You must contrive and force his desk, the ten thousand pounds there, will secure us from want.'

" ' I cannot,' I replied, ' I cannot do so vile an act ; have I not wronged him enough ? and shall I by robbing him of his wealth, add to the injury he has already sustained from me ?'

" ' If such is your determination, I will no longer exist,' she cried ; ' these eyes shall never more behold the light of another day ; here I cannot abide, my husband is hateful, loathsome ; and you, for whom I have sacrificed so much, would rather see me a lifeless corse at your feet, than take from Rockingham what he does not want, but what could ensure our felicity !'

" Every objection I made, Phillis removed, and so overcome was I by her tears and carresses, that my resolution gave way ; I agreed to meet her at midnight in the library, to plunder Mr. Rockingham, and to do all she required of me.

" The clock had some time sounded the hour of midnight, when I left my chamber to join Mrs. Rockingham, who was impatiently waiting for my coming; there was a good fire blazing in the library, and a decanter and some wine glasses were on the table.

" Phillis had packed some clothes in a bundle together with some rings, earrings, and necklaces of great value; ' this miniature of Rockingham I shall leave behind me,' she said, as she threw the picture on the floor.

" ' But I will not leave these pretty scissors behind me,' she continued, whilst she looked on a pair of scissors of exquisite workmanship, ' they were given me by Rockingham before I was married,' and she handed them to me to look at.

" The scissors were, indeed, very beautiful, extremely pointed, with golden bows and sheath exquisitely chased, and riveted with a diamond, set round with small rubies ; after I had admired them, I gave them back to Phillis, who put them in her pocket.

" We each of us drank several glasses of wine, Phillis appeared to be quite elevated with the thought of her removal, whilst I was low-spirited and heart-smitten with the thoughts of the base act I was about to perpetrate.

" ' We must be far from hence before five,' said Phillis, or the servants will be stirring.—Come 'tis time you forced the desk,' with some trouble I did so— the notes lay exposed to my view—' take them,' said Phillis, and place them safely in your pocket.'

" But my hand trembled so that I could not touch them.

" ' Coward,' cried Phillis, laughing, and having rolled up the notes she put them in her own pocket.—' I fear I have put too many things in that bundle,' said Phillis, ' lift it, Alfred, and feel if it is not too heavy for you to carry.'

" I took the bundle in my hand, ' oh no,' I replied, I can carry it with ease.— At this moment, the door of the room opened, and in came Mr. Rockingham ; surprise, horror and grief were pictured in his countenance."

CHAPTER XX.

"In a damp dungeon will I place thee;
  Where thou may'st reflect at leisure, on thy crime:
  And the misery to which thou hast reduced me."
  BY THE AUTHORESS OF EVA; OR, THE BRIDAL SPECTRE.

"WHEN Mr. Rockingham first entered the room, he stood for a moment as if rooted to the spot.

"'Oh! my desk broken open,' he cried, and he hastily crossed the room to his desk and saw that his notes were missing.

"'Wretch! for this you shall suffer,' cried Mr. Rockingham, 'your life shall pay the forfeit of your crime.'

"He rang the library-bell with great violence.

"Alarmed, a man servant ran up stairs half undressed, and several other servants were soon in the room, for hearing the library bell ring with such violence and at so early an hour, filled them with the utmost consternation.

"'Richard, fetch an officer, that I may give this wretch into custody,' said Mr. Rockingham.

"The servant went out to obey the orders of his master; when Mr. Rockingham said, addressing Phillis,—

"'Woman! who I have raised from poverty to affluence, think not the love I once bore you shall now soften my heart towards you. No!' and he stamped his foot with rage, 'I swear by the Great Eternal, that you shall pay the full penalty of your crime; I have fixed on a punishment for you more dreadful than you can imagine. And you, pauper boy,' he continued, addressing me, 'you, who I have treated and loved as my own child; you monster of ingratitude; you, who have poisoned the mind of my wife, and plundered me of my property, but for this baseness you shall die, the evidence of your guilt will be found upon you.' ''Tis false,' cried Mrs. Rockingham, 'there are no proofs against him, both Alfred and myself defy you.'

"I looked towards Phillis, whose unabashed manner surprised me; but what was the astonishment of Mr. Rockingham, when he beheld consuming beneath the fire-grate, the last remnant of the stolen notes.

"'Base, remorseless woman,' exclaimed Mr. Rockingham, 'this but aggravates your guilt;—there are your prisoners,' he said to the officers, who now had entered the apartment.—'I will not be a prisoner,' cried Phillis, 'these will set me free;' and she held in her hand the scissors, that her husband, before their marriage, had presented her with. 'Rockingham! I despise you; in death I despise you!' and in a moment, before any one could prevent her, she plunged the point of her scissors into her left side, groaning heavily, she expiring, fell deluged in blood. Petrified with horror, at this dreadful and unexpected event, all seemed to be rooted to the spot, none broke the dread silence, until the officer said, 'is it your wish, sir, that I take this man into custody?'

"'Not now,' replied Mr. Rockingham; 'that ghastly sight has unnerved me, I shall see you hereafter. Go to your chamber, sir,' he said, turning to me, 'and there remain until you know my intention respecting yourself; dare not to meditate escape, if you do, your punishment shall be greater than I now intend it to be. To escape me long would be impossible, for to the very verge of eternity would I follow you.'

"'Slowly, and in tears I left the library, and retired to my chamber, where I sat pondering on the occurrences of the night.

"There was nothing in the conduct of Phillis that caused me to remember her with love or esteem; the infatuation caused by her beauty was gone by, and I, too late reflected on her vile conduct, and the arts she had used to ensnare me.

"No person came near me until the evening, when one of the servants brought me some food.

" I wished to have asked him some questions; but the look the man gave me convinced me of the abhorrence he held me in.

" His look seemed to say, through you has this tragedy happened; through you has this blood been spilled."

" On the second day, towards evening, I was again brought food.

" And the following morning before I was up, Mr. Rockingham entered my chamber, he was much altered in appearance, the paleness of death was in his countenance, and his dress, in which he used to be very particular, hung on him loose and disordered.

" With a commanding air he said, ' Alfred, arise and follow me.'

" With tremulous steps I followed the man I had so deeply injured, determined in my own mind not to resist any penalty he might think proper to lay upon me.

" With a lamp in his hand, Mr. Rockingham descended the stairs; in terror I followed him into the under-ground apartment where you found me; there was a staple drove into the wall, to which a chain was suspended.

" Having placed the chain round my waist, he confined it together with a padlock, which having locked, he put the key in his pocket.

" ' I have precluded all possibility of your escape,' said Mr. Rockingham, ' this shall be your everlasting abiding place, here shall you stay till death calls you hence; it was my intention to have had you brought to the bar of justice for forcing open my desk, and robbing me of the ten thousand pounds contained therein—in that case, thou must have expiated thy crime on a gibbet amidst the clamour and execrations of the surrounding multitude, who would have reprobated thy perfidy and black ingratitude. But I will not shorten thy days by causing thee to undergo a violent death; no, here shalt thou linger, and drink with me of the cup of sorrow to the very dregs. No triumph shalt thou have over me, for you, though young in years, will soon follow after me; none shall know thou dwellest here, therefore none can liberate or sustain thee; here will famine end thee.

" ' Oh! revoke thy dread sentence,' I cried, ' fix a limited time for me to suffer; deaden not the last ray of hope in my bosom, my protector, my more than father! you felt for my destitute and friendless state, fostered and reared me to manhood. Oh! do not be to hard upon me, and cause me to curse the day you took me from my poverty, for your kindness has turned to cruelty. Oh! that I were now some wandering beggar !'

" Would I had suffered you to have been so,' said Mr. Rockingham, ' but the wish is now too late, you might have been happy, but your crimes have brought misery upon you.'

" ' Think not that I will revoke, or alter your sentence; no power on earth shall ever induce me to vary, or in the least swerve from my fixed determination.'

" ' Oh! that I had ended my days as Phillis did,' I cried; ' what misery should I have been spared.'

" ' What misery you would have been spared,' cried Mr. Rockingham, ' but rather say, what punishment, what everlasting perdition, you by such an act would have drawn down on yourself, by entering the presence of your Maker, your own destroyer, with all your unrepented sins to answer for; rash man, no more let me hear such words fall from your lips, what you now enjoy is more than you merit; and for thy Phillis, her representation shall be placed here to comfort thee; if comfort it will be—when thou lookest on her figure it will remind thee of the pernicious effect of her beauty; it will bring to thy mind, that through her thou hast lost thy liberty; through her no enlivening sun's beam will cheer thy loneliness; no blooming flowerets ever assure thee of the approach of summer; nor the hoar frost indictate to thee that the season of desolation is drawing nigh; wretched man, that season hast thou brought upon me; the summer of my days thy viper-like conduct hath withered; and the spring of thy youth shall wither also.'

" Saying this, he left me, fastening the door after him. When I thought on the eternal punishment I was to undergo I became almost frantic, I blamed myself for so tamely suffering him to chain me to the staple; and cursed him for passing on me the dreadful fiat he had done; I longed for death, and more than once begged he would release me from my confinement, and place me at the bar of that tribunal, who in mercy would end my sufferings by dooming me to a violent death.

"After some time he brought down and placed in my dungeon an exact resemblance of the once beautiful Phillis.

"How often have I begged he would take pity on me, and release me from my confinement, but he would not hearken; nor from the first day of my confinement until now, have I beheld the light of heaven.

"About one month back I was informed by Mr. Rockingham that Robert, the only servant he kept, was dead, and to prevent strangers coming to the house, he had himself dug a grave, and buried his servant in the garden.

"Your coming here I must believe was ordained by Providence, that you might witness the death of Mr. Rockingham, and receive his dying directions respecting myself and the property he has bequeathed me."

The rain had now abated, and Percival arose to depart, "I shall not proceed on my journey," he said, "but return to the cottage I left last night, and send from thence for a chaise to carry me to the next town. If you wish it, I will desire the good woman at the cottage to send some person to attend you."

Alfred thanked Percival, and said "he should be extremely glad of some person to be with him, for he felt very debilitated in conesquence of his long confinement."

When Percival had reached the cottage, he told the cottager what had happened to his servant, and of the jeopardy he himself had been placed in; he desired the woman to go to the first place where a chaise might be procured to carry him on his road to the nearest town, where he would seek a further conveyance; he desired her to look out a nurse for poor Alfred, and described the situation the house stood in.

Of the house she was perfectly aware, having often observed it when she was wandering to gather fuel, and felt a dread when she gazed upon its dreary and dilapidated aspect.

Percival having rewarded the woman for the trouble he had given her, stepped into the chaise, and when he came near the pit-fall, where poor Richard lost his life, he saw the driver of the chaise was aware of danger, for he guided his horses with great caution, lest they might turn in the direction in which the pit-fall lay.

As Percival passed it, he could perceive one foot of the horse sticking up above the mire, and some part of the hat of his unfortunate servant; "poor fellow," mentally said Percival, "it is no small thing that I would have sacrificed to have spared thy life."

CHAPTER XXI.

"And wet my cheeks with artificial tears,
And frame my face to all occasions."   SHAKSPEARE.

WHEN Percival reached home, he found his mother was still indisposed, and, but a few days after his return, he was himself confined to his bed, in consequence of getting a severe cold during his journey.

A violent fever came on, and Lady Immorf was much alarmed for the life of her son; amongst other incoherent expressions, used by Percival, as he lay on his sick-bed, was the name of Julia Rosemont, that name he often called on, indeed, she, even in his moments of delirium, seemed above all things, to be uppermost in his thoughts.

From this circumstance, Lady Immorf discovered the state of her son's heart.

For Percival talked much of the love he bore Miss Rosemont, and spoke of the engagement into which he had entered with that young lady.

At length the disorder of Percival took a favourable turn, and he rapidly amended. Willing to agreeably surprise her son, Lady Immorf wrote to Mr and Mrs. Rosemont, she acquainted them with the illness Percival had had, a said, that during that illness, he had of his love raved for Julia, and La Rosemont continued, I am happy that Percival has made so good a choice.

She concluded by hoping that Mr. Rosemont and his family would favour with their company, to spend some months at Ravenswood Castle.

Percival was now recovered, and happy in the company of Julia, who with parents and sisters, was now on a visit at Ravenswood Castle.

Both Percival and his intended bride were but young to settle in life, howev it was agreed, that the young people should be united the ensuing June twel month.

Lady Immorf did not wish her son's marriage to be concluded in privacy, intended, when that event did happen, that it should be celebrated with splend and old English hospitality.

On the day of her son's wedding, she meant to give an entertainment to who chose to partake of her bounty; but Lady Immorf did not think it prop to have rejoicings and festivity at the Castle, until at least twelvemonths shot have elapsed since the death of her husband.

Mr. Rosemont highly approved of the intention of Lady Immorf, and it arranged that Percival should go into Devonshire to visit Miss Rosemont, once every ensuing three months, until she became his bride. Lady Immorf was mu pleased with Julia, and Percival was in high spirits, full of love, hope and j

Percival was extremely fond of both angling and shooting, and as the season shooting was not entirely over, there was seldom a day passed, without Perci ranging the fields with his gun.

One day when he had had but bad sport, he was passing hastily through a bre in an hedge, when his gun got entangled in some briars, in extricating it, the g went off and severely wounded Percival in the shoulder.

A young man, who happened to be nigh, and who was shooting in the field, ca running to the assistance of Percival, for he saw the gun drop from Percival's ha and he knew he had received an hurt.

He inquired where Percival resided, in order that he might accompany h home, but when he found that Percival lived at the castle, two miles from t place, he begged that Percival would accompany him home, as his residence but across the field,

Percival accepted the young man's offer, and went across the field with his co ductor, to a house called White Farm, a place Percival knew had been late repaired by its new tenant, and whose improved and pleasing exterior he had of noticed—but he never before had seen any of its inmates.

When they had reached the enclosure before the house, they were met by most respectable looking man, about fifty years of age, who, when he found wh had happened, conducted Percival into the house, and immediately sent a serva for a surgeon, who lived but at a short distance.

The wound was not considered to be of a dangerous nature, and when it w dressed by the skilful surgeon, Percival was comparitively easy.

Percival was most grateful to the strangers for the attention they had shown him he found Frederic Manby, the young man who was shooting in the field at the tin of the accident, an agreeable and gentlemanly sort of person—he had nothing of t farmer about him, and his father appeared to be a scholar and a polish gentleman.

A young female came into the room to speak with her father, and Percival thoug her the most interesting girl he had ever seen; she like her father and brother, w in deep mourning, and had not Percival's heart been irrecoverably fixed on Mi Rosemont, the charms of Celeste Manby would have made a great impression o the heart of Percival.

Percival was now in the habit of calling to see the good folks at White Farm.

He found by Mr. Manby's discourse, that himself and a sister who were lel orphans, were brought up by an uncle, who was a widower with no family; "fron this uncle, who is immensely rich, I had great expectations," said Mr. Manby, "but i consequence of my marrying a young woman without fortune, my uncle never forgave me ; and I am sorry to say," continued Mr. Manby, " that my sister, for her own advantage, made all the mischief that lay in her power, and kept my uncle's anger alive against me—he forbade me his house, and made an oath never to leave me a shilling—' your sister,' said he, ' shall be my heiress.'

"Never shall I forget the look Gertrude gave me when she heard my uncle say so—it was a look in which malice and triumph was blended ; unnatural sister ! who only disliked my wife for her superior attainments."

"And has she not since repented of her conduct?" inquired Percival.

"No," said Mr. Manby, 'I am sure she has not, for I have several times written to both my uncle and sister but never received any answer to my letters Heaven knows I should be most happy to see, and be reconciled to either my uncle or sister ; the sight of them would gladden my heart, and cause me to forget all the unkindness and neglect I have suffered at their hands.

"The fortune I had, independent of my uncle, was but small, and to increase my income, I studied the fine arts ; for some time I was very successful in

No. 7.

portrait painting. I succeeded beyond what I could expect, and realised a very considerable sum of money, but new artists started up, and through patronage obtained great public favour.

"In consequence of these people I lost much of my fame, and my business rapidly decreased; my wife, who is lately dead, had been for some time in a very declining state of health, I thought the country might be serviceable to her, and being myself fond of farming, I determined to leave town, and turn my thoughts to the study of agriculture.

"I flattered myself my son would enter into my views, and prefer a country life—but there I am disappointed, Frederick does not like a humble state; he has a friend in India, and he is bent on going there to mend his fortune: I was almost broken-hearted when I lost my wife," continued Mr. Manby, "and now the thought of my son leaving me to go to India, gives me much concern."

"Oh, riches, riches," cried Frederick ; "who would not go to India to get riches? I shall make my fortune there in a few years, and then come back to England, and bring my carriage to fetch you and my sister to live with me in a large house that I shall take at the court end of the town."

Mr. Manby was vexed to hear his son still persist in his intention of going to India, from which he found it was useless to endeavour to dissuade him.

Celeste saw by her father's manner that he was in very low spirits on account of her brother; "Pray, Frederick, don't persevere in the intention of going to India," she said, "you know even the mention of it gives my father pain ; but six months back he hoped to live here in peace and comfort with his family; my mother is dead, and now you talk of going to India ; pray, brother, for your father's sake relinquish such a design."

"I cannot," cried Frederick ; "Celeste, how can you ask me? it will be the making of all our fortunes, I have given my word to go, and have a most lucrative situation promised me."

The more Percival saw of the Manbys, the more he saw to admire in that family.

Lady Immorf called one day at White Farm with her son, and she gave Miss Manby a very pressing invitation to spend a day at the castle, for her ladyship was much pleased with Celeste, and thought how happy she should be, if Heaven had blessed her with such a daughter ; time wore away, and Percival set off for Devonshire to visit Miss Rosemont, as agreed on ; meantime, Celeste was much at the castle as company for Lady Immorf.

One morning, when Mr. Manby was seated at breakfast, he said, "who do you think I was dreaming of, Celeste ?" Celeste said " she could not imagine, unless it was her mother."

"No," said Mr. Manby, "it was not your mother, but a very particular friend of hers that I was dreaming of—it was Amelia Montague ; I thought she called here with Mr. Monteagle, and I thought your mother was there too, and she looked serious, and vexed to hear Mrs. Montague say, this devil Monteagle would come with me ; and I thought Mrs. Montague looked so well and seemed in such high spirits," continued Mr. Manby ; "is it not strange, Celeste, that I should dream of a person I have not seen or heard of for more than six years?"

"Oh, no, there is no accounting for dreams," said Celeste ; " I well remember Mrs. Montague, I think I see her now, dressed in blue silk ; she was tall, and had flaxen hair hanging in ringlets over her shoulders."

"Yes," said Mr. Manby, "Amelia was a very handsome young woman, but unfortunately she had too much levity of conduct ; it used to grieve your mother to see her so much in the company of Mr. Monteagle; your mother would often say, surely if Mr. Montague knew, Amelia, that you were so much in the company of Mr. Monteagle, he would not like it.'

" 'Oh!' she would say, ' whether he likes it or not, he must put up with it; and if he is saucy I'll run away ; you know I have seven thousand pounds to receive when I come of age, independent of him.'

" ' Your mother always spoke her mind freely,'she did not like Mr. Monteagle;

he was a very gay young man, and one, who no one that I knew could tell his circumstances or pretensions. Amelia took offence at your mother's interference respecting Mr. Monteagle, and she kept away ; about five years back, I heard she was in Scotland with her husband.'

"'I have still the wax doll she gave me,' said Celeste, 'she was very good -natured, and so was Mr. Monteagle, I remember him as well as Mrs. Montague ; he was a thin, dark-haired gentleman, with very laughing eyes.'

Frederick now came into the room. "Here's a letter I have just received from he post-office," he said, "it is from India, Thompson is impatient for my coming; he tells me the Cerberus will leave England for India on the first of next month, which wants but fifteen days ; I must be ready to start then." Finding it was useless to oppose the inclinations of his son, all things were prepared for his voyage, and on the appointed day he set sail, leaving his father and sister in grief.

CHAPTER XXI.

"The time is so tender for lovers to meet
Alone by the light of the moon."

PERCIVAL, whose arm was now healed, was returning home one evening, when by the light of the moon he saw two persons discoursing on a spot that lay rather out of the road ; being rather curious, he stopped to observe them, and to his surprise saw it was Osmond, the only son of Sir James Durant, and Miss Manby.

"You are, no doubt, surprised, my friend," cried Osmond, "to see me here talking to Miss Manby, but in her you see my intended bride ; circumstances oblige me to meet her with privacy ; I fear being sent abroad by my father from interested and ambitious motives, but in twelve months I shall be of age, and no longer under parental control. I shall to-morrow set out with my father for Ireland, where we shall remain six months, and I meet Celeste here, to acquaint her with the circumstance."

Percival was pleased with what he had heard respecting Miss Manby ; he rejoiced to hear she was likely to become the wife of an accomplished and rich man, "for Celeste will grace any society, however elevated that society may be," Percival mentally said.

But poor Celeste was in very low spirits ; the thought of not seeing her lover for six long months quite depressed her, and the departure of her brother much added to her uneasiness ; she was in very low spirits all the evening, and when she sought the solitude of her chamber, she expressed her feelings in singing the following song :—

Changed are the hills and flowery meads,
  Where late I loved to rove,
For then I trod with buoyant step
  And heart untouched by love.

Well pleased I roved, in hawthorn break,
  To hear the linnets sing,
And from the gay, sweet smelling banks,
  The blooming flowers would bring.

And round my temples would I twine
  A wreath of varied hue ;
The daffodil and the wild rose,
  And bells of lovely blue.

But now Durant is far away,
  For me no flowers bloom,
And one to me, is morning's ray,
  Or evening's deepest gloom.

The next day was Sunday, and she feared her father would have more time to observe her want of spirits, and feared he might question her respecting the cause, which would have been unpleasant to the feelings of Celeste to explain, for Durant did not wish, until he became of age, the engagement between himself and Miss Manby to reach the ears of his father, therefore Durant had begged Celeste at present would not speak of their attachment, not even to her nearest friend.

Celeste forced a smile on her countenance, when she went into the breakfast-room, where her father was already seated.

But notwithstanding the smiling countenance and forced gaiety of Celeste, her father saw that something had disturbed the tranquillity of his daughter; tenderly taking her hand, he said, "Come, come, my child, I will not have you give way to low spirits—has anything happened more than I know of?"

"Oh, no," said Celeste, "I don't know what possesses me, but I will endeavour to be cheerful—I know it is wrong to indulge in lowness of spirits;" then to change the conversation, she said "'tis time to prepare for church, hark! is it not the first bell sounding?"

"There is no sound, Celeste, but in your imagination," said Mr. Manby; "it is not yet nine o'clock," and he opened his prayer-book, and read the lessons for the day, which being finished, they separated to dress for church.

During service, the thoughts of Celeste wandered from the clergyman's discourse to her lover, and when the service was ended, and her father arose to depart, she did not for some moments perceive that he had left the pew.

When Mr. Manby had nearly reached home, he saw standing a chariot, in which sat an elderly lady and two young ladies.

The elder lady put her head out of the chariot window, and for a moment regarded Mr. Manby with great earnestness, and then she beckoned him to the chariot window, when the exclamation of "brother," burst from her lips.

And "gracious God, Gertrude!" was uttered in surprise by Mr. Manby.

"I with great trouble discovered you had removed to Cornwall," said the lady, "and my footman was inquiring for your house, when I saw you."—"And you knew me, notwithstanding time, and the alteration sorrow has made in me," said Mr. Manby; "and have you, brother, been in sorrow?" inquired the lady.

"I have," said Mr. Manby, "and who may I thank for much of that sorrow but yourself?"

"You wrong me," said the lady, "deeply wrong me, if I sided with my uncle, against you, brother, in respect of your marriage, it was what I considered to your advantage; when I did so, I thought you might have done better, but let us not talk of those disagreeables of twenty years' standing. I assure you, if you did not think of me, I often thought of you, and longed to see you."

"Say, brother, are we friends, if so, I am come to visit you, and pass a happy hour in your company," and she held out her hand to Mr. Manby. "God forbid that I should bear any malice towards you, sister," replied Mr. Manby, and he held out his hand towards her.

The chariot now drew up to White Farm, and Mr. Manby handed out the lady and her daughters, Miss Maria and Miss Juliana, who amused themselves as they walked up the avenue before White Farm, with making silly remarks on their country cousin, as they termed Celeste.

When the ladies were seated, and had some wine and cake set before them, Gertrude said, "I suppose, brother, you heard I married Sir Nicholas Nettleby, the greatest fox-hunter this country ever produced."

"No, I did not, indeed," replied Mr. Manby; "all I heard was, that you were gone to live with my uncle, in Yorkshire, on an estate he had purchased there. I wrote several letters to him, but none of them were answered, I therefore was too much offended at the treatment I received to inquire about anybody."

"You had no reason to be offended with me," replied Lady Nettleby, "but uncle, he certainly behaved like a complete brute to you; often have I wept for hours on your account when I have heard him say, if ever that villain, Augustus, dare approach my dwelling, I would have him whipped like a strange dog from my threshold."

"Good God!" cried Mr. Manby, "could he say that? my uncle, the man who brought me up, and was my second father, and who I revered as if he really had been such."

"Oh, that was once on a time," cried Lady Nettleby, "since then, you have hated each other."

"'Tis false," cried Mr. Manby, in a passionate tone of voice, "I never hated my uncle."

"Good Heaven, brother, don't strike me," cried Lady Nettleby; "really your behaviour is quite intemperate, if you don't hate uncle, I am sure he hates you, and no concession on your part will ever induce him to see or forgive you."

"I am the injured party," replied Mr. Manby; "was there any crime in my marrying a lovely and amiable young woman, in concordance with the affection of my own heart? if she had no fortune, that was to my loss; what wrong in so doing did I do my uncle, that he should disclaim me?"

"Certainly, no reason whatever," replied Lady Nettleby; "you had a right to please yourself, in what concerned none but yourself, and so I always said; I told uncle plainly, that he had used you most shamefully, and when I heard that he had forbid you his house, I thought I should have fainted, but I will speak no more of the old brute, who has used me not much better than he did you; you may believe me, brother, that when I think on his unnatural conduct it almost throws me into hysterics."

"But where is my sister, Mrs. Manby, your wife, I mean?"

"My wife," said Mr. Manby, brushing away a tear, "can no longer be an object of discord in my family, she is gone where all is peace and blessedness."

"Oh, then, Mrs. Manby is dead," said Lady Nettleby; "I see you are in mourning, Heaven grant that I could speak of my deceased husband as you do of your deceased wife; I believe that I did not tell you before, brother, but I am now, and have been a widow, these three years."

"'My husband, poor fellow, unfortunately both for himself and me, was a complete sportsman, and what with the bruises, contusions, and broken bones, he got whilst hunting, and the ardent spirits he drank with his jovial companions after the chase, brought on a complication of disorders from which he no more recovered.'

"I cannot say," continued Lady Nettleby, "that I deeply regretted the loss of Sir Nicholas, for, through his sporting propensities, he began to mortgage his estates, and there was not a night passed but he went to bed in a beastly state of intoxication, and his rude and brutal behaviour was such as no woman could endure.'

"If I waited dinner for him an hour or even two, when he was following the chase, he would say, 'zounds, why didn't thee get thy dinner, what didst wait for?' and if I did not wait, he would say, 'methinks you was in a woundy hurry.'

"Are these young ladies the whole of your family, sister?" inquired Mr. Manby.

"Oh, no; I have a son, as fine a youth as you ever beheld," replied Lady Nettleby, "he must come to White Farm, and pay his uncle a visit.

"I have been living in Yorkshire, near the dwelling of my uncle ever since my marriage, until about three months back, when I went to town in consequence of a law-suit my husband got involved in, some short time before his death.

"I intend to return into Yorkshire again in the course of twelve or eighteen months; it is astonishing, the delay of law, particularly when it is in the Court of Chancery.

"Since my coming to town, I have formed an acquaintance with some of the first families in the kingdom; you know, brother, when one has girls, it will not do to shut them up in a band-box, to let them blush unseen, and waste their sweetness in the desert air.

" You must promise to visit me if it is only for a week or two, and my niece must come and spend a month with Maria and Juliana ; here is my card," continued the lady, and she handed Mr. Manby a richly embossed card on which was written,

LADY NETTLEBY, KENSINGTON.

" Everybody of any note is acquainted with my residence," said her ladyship.

" For myself, I must decline leaving home," said Mr. Manby, " but Celeste will accept your invitation ; the poor girl has been in low spirits ever since the death of her mother, so much so, that I fear it will affect her health ; change of scene I think would be of service to her."

" I am certain it would," replied Lady Nettleby ; " I am now going about ten miles from this place to pay a visit ; I shall remain there a month, and when I come back I shall call for Celeste, and she must remain with me five or six months."

Lady Nettleby now rose to depart ; Mr. Manby would have persuaded her ladyship to stay dinner, but she would not be persuaded.

After many professions of love to her brother and niece, she left the house.

As Mr. Manby was attending his sister and her daughters down the avenue before White Farm, Lady Nettleby said, " who would have thought my once elegant brother would have ever turned farmer ?—You seem to have a large stock of poultry," continued her ladyship, as she looked over a gate in the fence that separated the farm-yard from the avenue.

" Hark ! what hideous voice is that?" cried her ladyship.

" I hear nothing but the snoring of the sleeping pigs, whose styes are under that shed near the gate," said Mr. Manby.

" Oh! what a nuisance," cried Lady Nettleby : " I protest I would not live here, to be annoyed by those odious sounds, for the universe ; they put me so in mind of my poor dear Sir Nicholas ; I at first was really startled, for 'tis the very sound of his hard breathing after hunting, when a midnight carousal had concluded the sport of the day.

" Let us go, ma," said Miss Marie, " perhaps the odious animals may come out and terrify us."

" Oh what fun that would be," cried the romp, Juliana, " I should like to see the whole troop, pursuing you round the farm-yard, then if you happened to slip down near their habitation, with what pleasure you'd look at your dress when you got up again. A Yorkshire young lady, and be frightened at a pig !—Ha, ha !"

Maria turned up her nose, and much scorn was expressed in her countenance. " I blush for you," she said, " Juliana, I really blush for you. Let us get into the chariot, ma."

———

CHAPTER XXII.

" So he serve my purpose, let him hang or drown, I care not,
Friendship is but a word."　　　A NEW WAY TO PAY OLD DEBTS.

" WELL," said Mr. Manby to Celeste, after the departure of his sister, " that Gertrude should have so remembered me, and have taken so much trouble to discover my residence, is to me really surprising. She, I really believe it was, who misrepresented your mother to my uncle, and caused all the mischief between us. Yes, Celeste, it certainly was through my sister, that I lost the favour and affection of my uncle, she set him against me for her own advantage.

" You know, Celeste, I am not of the most forgiving temper, but on your account I wish to be on good terms with my sister ; your mother is dead, and should any thing happen to me, you would be left friendless in the world, with none to protect or advise you ; it is therefore your interest to endeavour to gain the love of your aunts and cousins, who are the only relations you have, excepting my uncle, but he has done with us.

"I beg, Celeste, you will have everything in readiness against my sister calls for you."

"I cannot go to London with my aunt, indeed I cannot," replied Celeste; "do not ask me to leave you, my dear father?"

"You must go," said Mr. Manby; "Celeste, I insist that in this you oblige me."

Finding her father had made up his mind respecting her going to town with her aunt, Celeste made no further objection; but the thought of the journey was to her most disagreeable, the thought of leaving her home and residing with strangers, who, until that day, she had never before beheld, and, indeed, had seldom heard spoken of.

"Lord, measter," said Jenny, as she entered the room, "I thought as how the grand lady would never ha' gone; the dinner's all spoilt, there it has been, frizzling and coddling by the fire these two hours."

"Never mind, my good girl," said Mr. Manby, "the lady and her daughters would not be prevailed on to take a bit with us; she dines late herself, and has no consideration for those who take their meals early."

"Celeste had now enough to do in preparing for her intended journey; she had many things to buy, for Mr. Manby laid strict injunctions on his daughter, "not to be sparing, nor by any means disgrace by her appearance the ladies with whom she was going to sojourn with."

Poor Lady Immorf was but in very ill health; the thought that her husband, even in his dying moments, should wish to have intercourse with the powers of darkness, dwelt heavily on her mind, and greatly injured her health.

The family of the Morningtons were all Catholics, and Lady Immorf, as a good member of that faith, prayed herself, and ordered masses to be read for the soul of her departed husband, and though a considerable time had elapsed since the death of Sir Parrolla, yet that pious lady was unremitting in her prayers for the soul of the deceased, and masses were yet read.

But when Lady Immorf watched the receding group, who followed the corse of her husband, winding their funeral way round the angle in the road, in the way to the last cold bed of the deceased, she inwardly said, "those who are not aware of what has transpired in my family, will, I fear, blame me, and think it a mark of disrespect in me, towards my husband, in not having him buried in the same tomb with my honoured father; but under these circumstances that is not to be thought of, nor must I sleep in death beside him."

But although Lady Immorf had not permitted her husband to be buried in her family vault, yet she was willing to pay him all possible respect.

She had, as soon as Sir Parrolla was interred, sent for a sculptor from London, to whom she gave orders for a large and magnificent monument of black marble, to be made and placed over her husband's grave.

Sir Parrolla's grave was in the church, but not near the tomb of the Morningtons, which was in the chancel; Sir Parrolla's grave lay at the opposite side of the church, at the eastern end of a row of pillars, that supported the gallery.

The monument was now arrived from London, and fixed up over the remains of the deceased Sir Parrolla.

It was in the shape of a very large urn, standing on a high pedestal of the same dark stone. No sculptured figures of angels or cherubs ornamented the monument; the only emblems engraven thereon were an hour-glass, a death's head and cross bones; and no other inscription than the name, age, and date, when the deceased had departed this life.

Lady Immorf had been out visiting, and as she returned on her way to the castle, she saw the workmen who had been fixing up the tomb of her husband, were leaving the church.

Wishing to see the monument, and as the church-door was yet open, Lady Immorf entered it.

But a solemnity and dread came over her as she passed along the lone aisle, for the shades of evening were fast advancing, and ghostly and indistinct figures seemed flirting in the distant obscurity.

Though terrified, Lady Immorf would not turn back, but proceeded until she came to the row of pillars, at the end of which the monument of her husband was situated.

As she drew nigh to the tomb, she saw some person standing near it, but who the person was she could not, until her nearer approach, distinguish; but she concluded that it was one of the workmen who had not yet left the church.

Rather glad than otherwise, to find some living being near; but what was the terror and affright of Lady Immorf, when close to the monument, to see that a person there standing, and who was deeply engaged in tracing with his finger; the inscription on the tomb, which the dim light hardly rendered discernible, was no other than the original of the hated portrait, which yet hung in the chamber of her late husband—veiled with a black curtain.

She had never seen the original before, but the likeness between the portrait and the original was so strong that none could mistake, besides, he still wore the costume he was first drawn in; the long black wrapping cloak, large turned-up hat and long feather, inclining towards the left shoulder.

Hearing footsteps behind him, Count Herman, for him it was, looked towards where Lady Immorf was standing, his glance met hers—but she shrank appalled from those glowing eyes that beamed with more than mortal lustre.

Almost fainting with terror, Lady Immorf clung to a pillar for support.

But with pleasure she in a moment saw him leave the monument, and she listened to his receding steps, until the sound was lost in the distance.

Recovered by the absence of this terrified personage, Lady Immorf prepared to leave the church as speedily as possible, nor did she stop to look at the monument of her departed husband.

She hastened down the church-yard as quickly as she possibly could, lest she should encounter the fearful Count Herman—but as she passed the clustering cypresses, whose entwining branches formed a gloomy grove, she beheld the tall outline of Count Herman yet lingering there.

As quickly as possible Lady Immorf hastened on, nor stopped until she reached the castle.

That this man, who, according to his brother's letter, had been long dead, and whom his brother had actually seen depart this life, should be now living, and roaming in the receptacles of the dead, to her was astonishing.

" He must have called on the powers of darkness to prolong his existence, as my husband would have done," thought Lady Immorf.

" Oh, that I was not bound down by that fatal vow, I would burn that accursed book, and destroy that doomed man's portrait. I shall now never know peace, that fatal vow has brought misery upon me."

" But should this Count Herman call, and demand his portrait and the iron box that contains the magic book, I, of course, must deliver them up to him, and very glad I shall be to do so," thought Lady Immorf; " my husband extorted an oath from me and his son, not to destroy, or cause to be destroyed, either the book or the portrait, but if the owner of these things demand them, then shall I be rid of the fearful charge."

Lady Immorf hoped that the portrait and the iron box would be demanded, but week after week passed away, and yet nothing more was seen of Count Herman, who, gloomy and restless, had returned to Naples; there he wandered along the bay, and looked with envy and hatred on some fishermen, who were mending their nets, and singing with blithe and merry hearts, as they did so—

> " Hear the lark tune his merry lay,
> Whistling, singing, through the day,
> So shall we when labour's o'er,
> Gaily sing at the tapster's door,
> Joking, laughing, singing, quaffing,
> Merry fishermen, when labour's o'er,
> Gaily sing at the tapster's door."

" Curse on their happiness, I have it not," Count Herman inwardly said, "yet I can range the globe, and riot in all it possesses ; I have all, all but peace, and that is denied me."

" In the midst of gratified wishes, misery is my portion, and the vultures seem continually to gnaw my heart."

He stood for some moments viewing the sea, then turned his eyes to the lofty and sublime Vesuvius, down whose sides were then flowing torrents of burning lava.

Count Herman sighed, as he viewed the terrific scene, " I must be industrious," he mentally said, " not fail to procure my victims, for by such failure, to lave in those seas of liquid sulphur, must be my doom."

Still Count Herman strolled along the bay, discontented and restless in mind ; at length feeling weary, he made up to a plot of ground, of an inviting appearance, being shaded by trees, it stood in front of a small inn, there were benches, on which a number of persons were seated, and the trees formed in one part of the ground an arbour.

No. 8.

Here Count Herman seated himself, and he called for a measure of wine, but it was not the heat of the sun that caused Count Herman to seek the cooling shade, for it was now near the close of day.

He seated himself there to be private, for no other person beside himself was in the arbour, there he thought to enjoy uninterrupted his own reflections, and likewise to observe the conduct of some drunken shepherds who were there, some of them sitting, and others were lying on the benches.

Count Herman was a keen observer, he was fond of watching the conduct and frailties of human nature, and he sat observing the scene before him with much interest.

" I was thinking of offering mine host, the old ram," said one of the shepherds, winking his eye at his companion.

" I killed the old ewe last week, and a rare tough, strong morsel she was. But the ram I should not like to eat, nor could I sell part of him, to my neighbours as I did the ewe—they would not buy it—'tis time he was killed—I thought he was dead this morning—but he will do for mine host to make some ragout for travellers who may stop here and need refreshment; I'll speak to him about it," he continued, hiccuping.

" What, oh, Signor Jacques," he bawled out, " bring us another measure of wine."

" Have you the money to pay for it, good signor?" inquired the host.

" As to money, that's of no consequence," I have a bargain to sell you, as fine a sheep as ever was butchered."

" And where is it?"

" Where, why grazing before my cottage, to be sure."

" Grazing before your cottage?" said the host, bursting into a loud laugh; " what, the lame old beast I for some time have observed there, hobbling about, without a bit of flesh on his bones?"

" I say he's a fine beast," said the man, " and would make fine ragouts for your guests."

" Villain!" cried the enraged host, " don't think to bring a disgrace on my house, by insinuating that I feed my guests on rotten rams; begone all of ye, ye drunken crew, you have spent all your money, and now 'tis time that you go home to your wives and children!"

" Begone, ye drunken, idle fellows,
 Ragged rascals go away;
All your money's gone, I know it,
 Think not longer here to stay.

" Muddling, fuddling, gegling geeses,
 Drunken rascals go away;
All your money's gone, I know it,
 Think not longer here to stay.

" Think not that I pay house and duty,
 For who, without coin, come here in flocks?
Begone, or I'll make one amongst ye,
 Soon I'll put you in the stocks."

Whilst singing these words he drove the shepherds out before him, and then, after putting the benches in their right positions, and wiping down the tables, he went, with napkin under his arm, bowing up to Count Herman, and begged to know if he chose to have his measure replenished? this the count declined; he left the arbour, feeling contempt for both the landlord and his guests.

Count Herman was in a contemplative mood; he strolled along the bay until he reached Naples, and there saw a gentleman about forty years of age, handing a lady of great beauty and high deportment into a carriage that stood in waiting, they came out of a very noble house, and were attended by a number of servants in rich liveries.

Count Herman followed the carriage—the gentleman and lady were set down at the theatre, into which Count Herman went also.

The lady and gentleman were seated in a superb box, where Count Herman could well observe them; he inquired of a person who sat near him, and found the gentleman was the Marchese De Gusman, a nobleman of very high family and fortune, but of a very melancholy and reserved disposition.

"When the great, who have everything to make them happy, are miserable, there must be a reason for it," said the man shrugging up his shoulders, "God keep us—and grant us all a clear conscience."

"What!" inquired the count, "do you say that?"

"I say nothing—I know nothing" replied the man, "who are you, signor? I should really take you for an inquisitor."

Count Herman said no more, but he closely observed the marchese, who, he observed, was under the influence of great melancholy.

The bay of Naples was a favourite spot with Count Herman, thither he often wandered—it was past the vesper hour—the evening was still and serene, and Count Herman flung his wearied length beneath some tall trees that grew in the avenue before the monastiey of the "Contrite Heart."

Footsteps approached, and two knocks at the low, gothic door of the convent was given, when, by the light brought out by a monk, Count Herman saw the visitor was the Marchese De Gusman.

"He has come here to do an act of penance," said the count mentally. "I must search into this—murder may have been done; if so, I must accuse—then save, if he will pay the penalty I have done."

It was now the time that Percival had promised to visit his intended bride, and he left Ravenswood Castle for that purpose.

Poor Lady Immorf severely felt the loss of her son's society, but she took great pleasure in calling on old Mildmay and his son, who were now comfortably settled in the fly-mill, through the bounty of Percival and her ladyship. Mildmay's son had married Patty, in pursuance of the advice he had received; and that worthy girl, remembering the kindness of Lady Immorf and her son, always behaved to her ladyship in the most grateful and respectful manner.

CHAPTER XXIII.

" False face must hide
What the false heart doth know,"   SHAKSPERE.

WITH a heavy heart, Celeste beheld the carriage of her aunt drawn up in front of the farm.

"Come, Celeste," said her ladyship, "step into the carriage,—your things of course are all packed."

"Oh, yes," said Mr. Manby, "Celeste has all in readiness to depart, she will not keep you waiting; but will you not alight, and take some refreshment?"

"Oh no, I am in great haste to get to town," replied her ladyship, "remember Celeste is to stay with me for two months, I will not part with her one day sooner."

The luggage of Celeste was arranged by the footman, and after taking an affectionate leave of her father, and promising to write to him in a day or two, the carriage drove on.

It may be now necessary to give some account, as very little hath yet been said of Gertrude Manby, now Lady Nettleby—the widow of Sir Nicholas Nettleby, of hunting notoriety.

Sir Nicholas had departed from the noise and tumult of this sublunary world about three years previous to his lady's visit to White Farm.

Sir Nicholas left his lady one son and two daughters; Miss Nettleby at this time was about the age of twenty-two years, Mr. Barnaby Nettleby, her son, was nearly twenty, and Miss Juliana was about eighteen.

Lady Nettleby, according to her own account, was but thirty-nine; however, truth obliges us to say, that she might with the greatest veracity have added sixteen years thereunto.

But that was a profound secret, for such a fact being known, might, her ladyship thought, injure and counteract her scheme of again entering into the bands of wedlock, which she intended again to do.

And every widower and bachelor, whom she thought were suitable matches either for herself or her daughters, were invited to her house on their first acquaintance, and treated with great attention, not only by Lady Nettleby, but by the young ladies also; who hoped to find, as well as their mamma, in London, that great mart for all kinds of wares, husbands both rich and handsome.

Lady Nettleby was in person very short and very stout, of a fair complexion, much freckled, light hair, and very full grey eyes.

Miss Nettleby was a tall, slim, fair-complexioned girl, and Juliana was also tall, fair, and of a very ruddy complexion, with red hair, as was her father's.

Mr. Barnaby Nettleby took after his mamma in stature, being very short and stout for so young a man; he had large light-coloured eyes, and hair like his sister Juliana.

"There is our house," said Lady Nettleby to Celeste, as she pointed to a house of elegant appearance, at which the carriage stopped.

When the party had entered the house, Miss Nettleby threw herself languidly on a sofa.

"Dear ma," she cried, "I really am so fatigued that I cannot change my dress; if company comes, let us be denied."

"What can have fatigued you so, Maria?" said Lady Nettleby, "it is not more than fifteen miles from hence to the inn where we slept last night."

"Well, no matter," replied Maria, frowning, "to-morrow, Celeste can be made fitter to be seen."

"Fromong had better arrange her hair."

Celeste was much mortified at the words of Miss Nettleby, "what she says about fatigue," thought Celeste, "is merely an excuse to be denied on my account, she fears my appearance will disgrace them, it seems I am to have my hair dressed by this Fromong, whether I like it or not. I wish I had not come to London with them, it may be from motives of kindness, but it is treating me like a child, and as if I was not allowed to have a will of my own."

Celeste slept but little that night; she thought on her father and on her absent lover, and longed for the time to arrive when she should again meet him.

When the party met at breakfast the following morning, Lady Nettleby inquired for her son of the servant who attended them. "Mr. Nettleby has not been at home all night, madam," replied the man; "he went out with Mr. Ashton to look at some horses, and he has not been home since."

"Faugh! those nasty horses," cried her ladyship; "I detest the very name of horses and hounds; I had quite enough of them, when my poor dear dead Sir Nicholas was alive."

The hair of Celeste was arranged by Fromong, and Lady Nettleby presented her with an elegant necklace and ear-rings of jet, and some ornaments for her hair of the same materials, for Celeste was still in deep mourning.

In the afternoon a party of gentlemen came in with Mr. Barnaby Nettleby, amongst whom was a Mr. Ashton, a young gentleman intended for a physician, and a Mr. Cubby, his uncle; to the heart of this gentleman, Lady Nettleby intended laying *siege!* not that he was either a widower, or a bachelor, but his lady was every day expected to give up the ghost, being in the last stage of dropsy.

After the first compliments had passed, Lady Nettleby said, "permit me, Mr. Cubby and Mr. Ashton, to introduce to you my niece, Miss Manby;" then taking

Celeste's hand, she gave it to Barnaby, and said, "this, Barnaby, is Celeste Manby, your cousin."

Barnaby took the offered hand of Celeste, and at the same time snatched a kiss, which he would have repeated, had not Celeste, covered with confusion, escaped his grasp, and took refuge behind Lady Nettleby, who appeared to be extremely angry with her son."

"Barnaby! this rudeness to your cousin is unpardonable," she said; "this boisterous behaviour will cause you to be disliked and avoided by every woman of delicacy, and I am very angry with you for staying out all night; you did not do so in the country."

"In the country!" cried Barnaby, laughing, "what we do in the country, and what we do in London is quite a different thing altogether: I met my friend the Count Le Mar, and I spent the night with him; not that I think it necessary to be accountable; a young fellow of my age cannot always be tied to his mother's apron-strings;" turning to Celeste, he said, "you are not offended, are you, my pretty one; if I take another kiss you will not avoid me for that, will you?"

Celeste did not reply, but blushing, turned from the rude Barnaby.

"Poor little dear, she seems to be quite put out," said Mr. Cubby, "she's not fond of these rackety sparks."

"No," replied Lady Nettleby, "it is impossible to like any thing so bearish; the rudeness of Barnaby is enough to make my niece faint."

"Faint, indeed," cried Juliana, bursting into a horse-laugh.

"Indeed, Miss Hoyden," cried Maria, turning up her nose, "I would advise ma, to provide you with a pair of unmentionables for the next fox chase; you will make a good compeer for Barnaby, nor can I tell which of the two would call tantivy loudest."

The colour rose in Juliana's face, and she was about to answer in no very pleasant key, when Mr. Ashton put his hand before her mouth, and at the same time giving her a most languishing glance, unperceived by Maria, he said, "never let me hear the graces disagree, I must plead pardon for Mr. Barnaby on account of the greatness of the temptation; the beauty of Miss Manby might make any man forget himself."

Miss Nettleby frowned at this remark of Mr. Ashton's, then turning to Celeste, she said, "don't think any thing of what Mr. Ashton says, he flatters every body."

Juliana took an opportunity, whilst the rest of the company were engaged in discourse, to request Celeste would walk in the garden with her; whilst they we e walking Juliana said, "you must pardon me, cousin, for what I said about your fainting, in consequence of Banaby's rudeness; I did it to tease my sister, who pretends to such extreme delicacy, and always acts the invalid, when I really believe that she is quite as strong as my brother Barnaby."

"I have a secret to tell you, Celeste," continued Juliana, "but you must on no account mention it,—ma intends Barnaby shall marry you; I tell you this to put you on your guard, for I really like you, Celeste, and I should be sorry to see you unhappy; which I am sure you'd be, if you were to marry Barnaby, he has such a bad temper—gentle as you are, he'd break your heart."

"Dear Juliana, don't think of such a thing as that," said Celeste, "my aunt would not like her son to marry a girl without a fortune, and that she knows I have not got,—you certainly must be mistaken."

"Oh no, I am not," replied Juliana, "what the reason is I am not aware, but I know she wishes it."

Both the person and manner of her cousin Barnaby was any thing but agreeable to Celeste, and had not her affection been otherwise engaged, he was the last person she would have chosen for a husband; she doubted the information of Juliana; yet, thought Celeste, if such should be the case, how very miserable I shall be—for by my refusal, I most likely should bring on myself not only the displeasure of my aunt but of my father also.

Celeste was now very unhappy, on account of the communication from Juliana, and when she retired to her chamber, although the hour was late, instead of going to bed, she sat up to write to her father; in her letter she begged that he would by some means, find an excuse to send for her home, for that she was already tired of a town life, and longed again to be with him in his rural abode.

"Tired of a town life in three days!" said Mr. Manby in the immediate answer to his daughter's letter; "how is it possible in so short a time that you can tell whether you like it or not? No, Celeste, I cannot consent to your leaving London until the three months your aunt invited you to remain with her are expired."

Barnaby was out evening after evening, and day after day, to the great mortification of his mother, "who feared," she said, "a town life would entirely ruin her son."

"I wish he was married to a girl like you, Celeste," said her ladyship, "he would stay at home,—how should you like Barnaby for a husband?"

Celeste changed countenance at the question of Lady Nettleby. "I do not intend to marry," she replied; "indeed, madam, I should be so glad to return into Cornwall to my father."

"Oh, you little hypocrite, not marry," said Lady Nettleby, "and because I proposed a husband to you, you want to go into Cornwall to your father; pardon me Celeste, but really a baby at nurse could not answer more simply.

"Talk of going home to your father;—no, my love, I will not part with you until the three months are expired, for that time your father said you should remain with me,"

A walk was proposed by Lady Nettleby, which was agreed to by Miss Nettleby, and Julianna; but just as the party were setting out, Mr. Jordan, Lady Nettleby's solicitor was announced; Lady Nettleby therefore did not accompany the young ladies, but went into the parlour with her solicitor, who called on her to take instructions respecting the Chancery suit.

After Mr. Jordan had taken those instructions, he said, "I received a letter yesterday from my brother in the north, which informs me that your uncle is given over by his physicians, and it is not expected that he can long survive.

"I told your ladyship some weeks back in confidence the news I had received from my brother, who made your uncle's will, how he had disposed of his property; and I must say I think it very unnatural of him, to leave the whole of his property between the children of your brother, and nothing to you or yours, who are quite as nearly related to him."

"Oh! the old brute," exclaimed Lady Nettleby; "he always loved my brother better than he did me, and I have no doubt but he would yet be friends with him, if my brother went to see him; but I have done all I could to keep him away; for the event of their being friends, my uncle might again alter his will and leave his property to my brother, instead of his children; but that would not do for me; the old man's property, at least half of it, must come to my son, through his marriage with Celeste."

"I am under a great obligation to you, Mr. Jordan, for inquiring of your brother, and informing me. My uncle is worth, I should think, at least fifty thousand pounds in money and estates."

"More than that, madam, more than that," said Mr. Jordan, "my brother, who has been solicitor to, and in the confidence of Mr. Russell these thirty years, says he is at least worth in money, land, and houses, full eighty thousand pounds."

"Celeste is certainly a most desirable match for Barnaby," cried her ladyship. "It will be wise to forward the marriage with all speed—before she hears of her good fortune."

Soon as Mr. Jordan had taken his leave, Lady Nettleby burst into a hysterical flood of tears; "the spiteful old hunks," she exclaimed, "not to leave me anyng; he vowed he would not, but I thought that before his death, he would ve relented, and have left me at least a few thousands."

"Well, never mind," she said, drying her tears, "Celeste shall be Barnaby's wife. Yes, old miser, in spite of your teeth, my son shall have the spending of your money; and instead of wearing black, and lamenting your death, I'll give a ball and banquet on the joyful occasion."

CHAPTER XXIV.

"But why grieve I
At this, it makes for me, if she prove his?
All that is her's is mine, as I will work him."
A NEW WAY TO PAY OLD DEBTS.

ON the following morning, whilst Miss Nettleby, Juliana, and Celeste were out taking a ride, Lady Nettleby sent her maid to Barnaby, desiring he should come to her in her dressing-room, as soon as he had taken breakfast; for that she wished to speak with him on very particular business.

It was then past noon, but Barnaby had not yet finished his breakfast.

At length he entered his mother's dressing-room; but with a very disconsolate countenance, and whistling a doleful tune, which he sometimes was in the habit of doing when troubled with the blue devils; and that he often was, when his expenses over ran his prudence; and that was now precisely the case with Barnaby; for he had spent even his last shilling, and he wanted of his mother a fresh supply, which he sadly feared she would not grant him, on account of the large sums he in a very short time had expended; and, moreover, he expected a very severe lecture from his mother on account of the very late hours he kept, and his eternal absence from home.

He would have sung, "Away with Melancholy," but that was impossible, and with a long face he stood before his mother, expecting a storm was brewing.

Instead of which he was agreeably surprised, by seeing a smile on his mother's countenance; and she greeted him by saying "good morning to you, Barnaby; I sent for you, my dear, to impart some very pleasing information, by which, if you take my advice, you will receive great advantage."

"Nay, don't look so peevish and fretful," she continued, "is it so unpleasant a task to you, to grant me one hour's conversation?"

"I made no objection," said Barnaby, "you are always finding fault."

"No, no, I do not wish to find fault," replied his mother, "but you must look pleased, you must be very particular in your appearance, and make yourself as agreeable as you possibly can, for good fortune awaits you;—a handsome girl and forty thousand pounds."

"Forty thousand pounds!" cried Barnaby; "forty thousand pounds is not to be laughed at; but who is she?—what fine bets I could make with it at the races;—five thousand to one,—go along Miss Slough."

"Oh, Barnaby, don't talk so," said Lady Nettleby; "you must leave off this sporting propensity, or else you will do as your father did; get broken bones, shortened days, and mortgaged estates."

"Nonsense," cried Barnaby, "the pleasure of sporting, will prolong instead of shortening my days; and the bets I shall win will redeem, instead of causing me to mortgage my estates;—but who is the handsome incumbrance?"

"Incumbrance, indeed! cried his mother, "I really think you are determind to provoke me; the girl you are to take with the forty thousand is worth herself double the money; where will you find a girl so beautiful and amiable as your cousin Celeste?"

"Celeste, Celeste!" cried Barnaby, "I thought her father was poor; how, for Heaven's sake can she have so much money?"

"She has not yet got it, but she will be sure to have it," said Lady Nettleby.

"You shall hear; you know your great uncle Russell, and you must have heard that he is extremely rich, and you also know that we are not on good terms. The first thing I ever seriously displeased my uncle in, was my marrying your father, though it was a good match for me; yet my uncle took it into his head to dislike Sir Nicholas, poor man, because he was fond of the chase and his glass; and he heard of his enormous betting, and how he had mortgaged some of his estates.

"On these accounts they had quite a quarrel, and your father did not go into my uncle's house for more than two years before his death.

"I too unfortunately offended him, and through the most simple thing in the world; a thing, that no other person would have taken notice of.

"You must know, Barnaby," continued her ladyship, "that my uncle had a very ancient and valuable gold watch, a repeater of most exquisite workmanship which he sent to his jeweller's to get regulated; the very day he sent it, he was taken ill of a fever, and so violent was his disorder, that in less than a week he was given over by his physicians. I knew the repeater was sent to be regulated for I used to visit my uncle although my husband did not.

"Feeling fully assured that my uncle could not survive, I determined to get possession of the repeater; I thought he would leave it to me, for I heard that he was going to alter a will he had formerly made, but as there was no certainty to whom he might leave it, I determined to secure the repeater myself; I ordered my carriage to the jeweller, who had the repeater to regulate.

"The man knew me, and made great apologies for not having sent it home before, and said he would that moment send it.

"Oh no," said I, "you need not give yourself that trouble, I will take it with me;" he gave me the repeater and I paid him for repairing it; unfortunately for me my uncle's disorder took a favourable turn.

"Unfortunately, I say, for I heard at that time I was named in his will.

"I called at my uncle's house two days after my visit to the jeweller's, and to my great surprise found that my uncle was better.

"I will candidly own to you, Barnaby," continued Lady Nettleby, that the change in his disorder was more a matter of grief than consolation to me, for who, though possessed of the most feeling heart, could regret the sordid wretch?

"For appearance sake, I put on a feeling and anxious look, put on, I need not say, for in truth, I was anxious enough to know the precise state he was in.

"I went into his chamber, and gently drawing back the curtain nearest his face, I took his hand and tenderly prest it between my own,

"He started up, for he was not asleep; I think I see the disagreeable old wretch now, with his large black eyes widly staring at me.

"Where's my repeater?" he bawled out, loud as his weakness would allow him; "where's my repeater? I'll have you hanged, if you do not this moment bring it back; I'll make you pay the full penalty for the crime you have committed; to be thus talked to, and before the servant threw me into hysterics; soon as came to myself again, I expressed to my uncle the grief I felt on account of the bad opinion he entertained of me respecting the watch, which I took but to keep in safety, until his wished recovery.

"My wished recovery!" he gnashed between his teeth. "Traitress! you wished my death, and watched me as the carrion crow does the dying sheep that you might prey upon me, and pluck me to the bone.

' I now know you, and heard, though you were not aware of it, the unnatural expression used by you and your imp, Maria, when I laid, as you thought, in a dying state; you then little thought that I was capable of hearing and understanding your consulting and contriving how to dispose of my property.

"Did not Maria say those paintings will look well when they are cleaned, and the frames new gilt; and what sweet china jars, they will look pretty on the cabinet in my room! And you can't think, ma, how I long to go into mourning black gives one such an interesting appearance; I should like a black silk slip, and a crape frock, and a nice black satin sash;—I wonder if he's dead, peep ma, for I can't, I am so nervous.'

"Pretty conversation, indeed, over a dying relation, and one who brought you up with the tenderness of a father; but go, madam," he continued, "and never let me see your face again— send my repeater by your footman.'

"I would have excused myself, but he would not hear a word I had to say in my defence.

"Show Lady Nettleby the door," he said to'his servant; "talking so much has fatigued me," and he sunk down exhausted on his pillow.

"I sent the repeater, and with it a letter, begging that my uncle would not for amoment suppose I meant to keep the watch, for that he should entertain such an tpinion of me was agonising to my feelings; and in regard to the words spoken by Maria, they did not allude to the pictures, or china jars in his room, though certainly

such things were there, but she was speaking of other pictures, and other jars; and her observations respecting mourning were not, my dear uncle, in contemplation of your death, for which I am sure she would be most heartily sorry, but merely expressing her partiality for that colour.

"I begged that I might be permitted to see him, and to hear my pardon pronounced by his own lips; but no, the obstinate old man would not pardon me, but sent a letter written by a friend, for he himself was yet too weak to write; in this letter, he desired that I would not write to him any more, he concluded by saying,

No. 9.

' that he considered he had now no relations, and intended to leave the whole of his property to some public charity ; this happened about five years back, when you were at school, how he made his will then I don't know, but it seems that he repented of what he had done, for not long before I went into Cornwall, I was told by Mr. Jordan, my solicitor, who had the intelligence from his brother at York, who altered my uncle's will, that the whole of his property was to be divided between the children of my brother; the old man's death is every day expected, and you, Barnaby, will come into his property, if it is not your own fault, perhaps the whole of it, for it is an hundred to one if ever that foolish youth, Celeste's brother, ever comes to England again ; the yellow fever, or some other Indian disease, most likely will carry him off, and then the whole of the property must come to Celeste.   I was determined to secure her, and hope you will prevail on her to fix an early day for your marriage ; neither you, nor any of mine, has he left one shilling ; but we shall be too many for him, and have the pleasure of spending the unnatural brute's money yet."

"But she is so shy and so squeamish," said Barnaby, "she'll not be touched, by Jupiter, from what I have seen of her ; I might as well get a wife made by the confectioner."

Lady Nettleby laughed at her son ; "no," she said, " Celeste is not so brittle as that comes to, but, as I said before, you must be more particular in your behaviour and conversation, it won't do to be continually talking to a lady about horses and dogs, five-barred gates, and break-neck ditches."

"I hate a fop, and will not be one to please anybody," said Barnaby, " and as to talking of horses and dogs, I shall not deprive myself of that pleasure."

"You surely will not be foolish enough to let forty thousand pounds slip through your fingers," said Lady Nettleby.

"I must be foolish indeed, to do that," said Barnaby ; "but I think, shy as she is, I shall be able to bring her to ; but I must have some cash, mother ; for I assure you I can no longer sing to the tune of money in both pockets."

"Why you certainly cannot have expended all," said Lady Nettleby.

"But I certainly have," cried Barnaby, interrupting his mother, " and I must have a further supply ; come, you must advance handsomely on the forty thousand in expectation."

"Well I suppose I must let you have another check for fifty pounds," said Lady Nettleby, "provided you do all in your power to win the heart of your cousin, so that the marriage may be concluded before she knows anything of her good fortune; —suppose you give Celeste an airing in the carriage this morning, she is now gone out with your sisters, but I expect them back soon."

"No," said Barnaby, as he put the check into his purse, " I must get this cashed ; and I have this morning an appointment with my friend, the Count Le Mar, but I shall be back again in a few hours."

"I shall depend on you," said his mother ; " remember our agreement."

"I will fulfil it to a tittle," replied Barnaby, "and then in a few days I shall expect another fifty."   Humming a merry tune, he left the apartment.

"Another fifty !" muttered Lady Nettleby ; "extravagant boy, you'd spend the riches of Crœsus.

CHAPTER XXV.

Come, and trip it as you go,
On the light, fantastic toe.   COLEMAN.

As tickets of invitation had been issued by Lady Nettleby for a ball she intended giving in the course of a few days, in celebration of Juliana's birth day, the ladies were busily employed in preparing and arranging their dresses.

This subject caused great consultation between the Miss Nettlebys and their mamma.

"Blue, I think, best becomes a fair complexion," said Miss Nettleby, as she with a languishing air spread a blue crape dress on the sofa, "this colour," she continued, "best becomes me, don't it ma?"

"Yes, my love," answered Lady Nettleby; "but pink I should say for Juliana."

And I should say the reverse," cried Juliana, "blue will suit me and my sister being rather pale, will look best in pink."

At this moment, Barnaby and the Count Le Mar entered the room. "Give me leave to introduce my friend the Count Le Mar," said Barnaby. "This, sir, is my mother, my sister Maria and Juliana, and this young lady is my cousin, Miss Manby."

"I have often heard you speak of your friend, the Count Le Mar, Barnaby," said Lady Nettleby, "but never before had the pleasure of seeing him; I hope sir," she continued, addressing the count, "that you will be a frequent visitor."

I think, sir, I have had the pleasure of seeing you before," said Celeste; "do you not know a lady of the name of Montague?"

"Montague—Montague," replied the count, appearing as if endeavouring to recollect himself; "no, I know no such person—was she an English or foreign lady?"

"Oh! English," said Celeste, "I certainly remember you, sir, coming with Mrs. Montague to see my mother; it is now some years back, but I recollect how you used to tease her, you would pull her ringlets and untie her sash; and then mother used to look serious, and say, 'how is it, Amelia, that Mr. Montague is not with you?'"

"You mistake, madam," replied the count, colouring up to his ears, "I have not long been in England, and I am by birth a foreigner; if you persevere in this statement, madam my friend must think me an impostor."

"Oh by no means," cried Lady Nettleby, "my niece must be mistaken; and I hope she'll acknowledge it"

"If I have offended you, sir, I am sorry for it," said Celeste; "I may be deceived; one person may greatly resemble another."

"I am glad you are convinced of your error, madam," replied the count, who yet looked rather embarrassed, but he soon recovered himself.

Barnaby, who it was evident had taken a glass too much, stood ogling Celeste, with a look he intended should convey to her the violence of his love.

Then he said, "well, charmer, how are you to day? I heard your conversation as I came in about blue and pink, the colours worn last by Miss Slouch, and Euphemia, but none of your pink and blues for me; this is the little mare for my money," and he patted Celeste on the shoulder.

Miss Nettleby turned up her eyes. "Disgraceful," she cried, "compare a lady to a mare! really, brother, I am ashamed of you; I am quite shocked at the odious comparison."

"Come, none of your fantastic tricks, Maria," said Barnaby, "I have certainly made a blunder, which I hope my cousin's goodness will excuse, but there is no reason for you to faint, or to go into hysterics on account of it; I have brought my friend the Count Le Mar, to spend an hour, but if you behave as you have done, I shall wish you a good day."

"Barnaby, do not leave us," cried Lady Nettleby, "I fully depended on an hour or two of your company; I must certainly say you behaved with rudeness to your cousin, but Maria and you must settle your own differences."

"Nothing was further from my thoughts than offending my cousin," said Barnaby, offend her, indeed, who I intend to make it the whole study of my life to please!"

Deeply sighing, he laid his hand on his heart, and at the same time, cast a very loving glance at Celeste.

At this moment, the footman being out, Susan, the housemaid, brought to her lady a set of new novels that had but just been issued from the press, and were sent to Lady Nettleby from the circulating library where her ladyship dealt, with the respects of the proprietress, and "that she had that moment received some new works from her bookseller, and had sent them for the inspection of her ladyship before any other person had seen them."

The ladies were employed in looking over the books, and the Count Le Mar was looking through a window in the apartment; when Barnaby, who thought himself unobserved, pulled hold of Susan's hand as she was leaving the room, and Celeste saw a smile pass between them, expressive of the greatest familiarity.

There were some beautiful flowers placed in a stand at one of the windows of the apartment, to them Celeste walked, and was enjoying their beauty and fragrance, when Mr. Barnaby came up to where she was standing, and plucking a rose from its parent stem, and placing it in his bosom, said in a whisper—"

"Here is an emblem of your lovely self, but not so sweet." He then began in a low voice to sing a song, the burden of which was, " I love thee night and day, my love."

Having received a letter for her mistress, Susan again entered the apartment, and Celeste again saw the significant looks pass between the girl and Barnaby.

Susan was a black-eyed, cherry-cheeked girl of eighteen, short and very lusty, so much so, that she was almost as much in breadth as length.

Lady Nettleby opened the letter; and saw it was an invitation for herself and family to dine with a Mrs. Popham, a widowed lady residing at Chelsea.

"Mrs. Popham declares she will not forgive the absence of one of my family," said Lady Nettleby; "we must all go, for it will be quite a select party; there will be there, the letter says, ' Doctor Langdon, Mr. Cubby, and Mr. Ashton, and Miss Hagilston ; you, Barnaby, of course, will go with us," continued his mother.

"If you'll give me leave of absence to-day, I will promise to attend you to-morrow," said Barnaby; " on my honour, both the Count Le Mar and myself have a particular engagement.

"And I particularly wish your company," said Lady Nettleby. " I know the count will make some handsome excuse for you—will you not, sir ?"

"Certainly, madam," replied the count, bowing, "it is but for you to order, and me to obey: it is always a pleasure to me," he continued, "to see Venus in the ascendant."

But Barnaby would not be persuaded to remain at home that day; but after promising to be punctual the next morning in attending his mother, sisters, and Celeste to Mrs. Popham's, after making his adieus, the Count Le Mar and Barnaby sallied out together."

"Well, really, the Count Le Mar is the most polite man I ever was in company with," said Lady Nettleby, " so complaisant and gallant."

"Do you not intend to invite him to the ball, ma ?" said Miss Maria.

"I would have invited him this morning, if I had thought of it," said Lady Nettleby, "but Barnaby can take him a card of invitation ; the count is certainly a handsome man, though not young, and he looks more like an Englishman than most foreigners do."

"I never was so mistaken in anybody in my life," said Celeste, " I really took the Count Le Mar to be a Mr. Monteagle I knew some years back, before my mother died; the Count Le Mar is exactly like Mr. Monteagle, and he has the same voice ; the only difference is, the count looks older than Mr. Monteagle did, and he is more corpulent and high coloured, yet for all that, I can hardly believe but that the Count Le Mar and Mr. Monteagle are one and the same person."

"Good Heaven, what an idea !" cried Lady Nettleby, "how positive you are, Celeste; that you think him Mr. Monteagle is to me really surprising ; I tell you, child, the count is a foreigner, and a man of great property, and very high connections in his own country ;—I think him a great acquisition to any company he may go into, he is so very polite and agreeable."

Celeste would have excused herself from going to Mrs. Popham's party with Lady Nettleby, for she wished to devote an hour or two in writing a long letter to her father, but Lady Nettleby would not hear of Celeste's staying at home, the four ladies therefore contrived to sit in the chariot, and Mr. Nettleby followed on horseback.

CHAPTER XXVI.

I tell you again these are the idle,
Flashy young dogs, but when you have to
Do with a staid, sober man — LOVE IN A VILLAGE.

MRS. POPHAM received Lady Nettleby and her party with great respect, and in the drawing-room was seated Mr. Ashton, Mr. Cubby, and Miss Hagleston, a relative of Mrs. Popham.

When Mr. Ashton had made his bows to Lady Nettleby, her daughters, and Celeste, he introduced a gentleman named Leon to their notice, as his particular friend.

The conversation of Mr. Leon was directed to Lady Nettleby; but his glances wandered to Celeste, whose risible faculties were much excited by the appearance of Mr. Leon, who, in his appearance, looked like the monkey who had seen the world—all grimace, affectation and ugliness.

Mr. Leon had a low, but projecting forehead, a pug nose, lank cheeks, and a wide mouth, which he generally distened to its utmost stretch, in order to show his teeth, which were certainly very white and even.

Mr. Leon finding his ogling had no effect on Celeste, he tried the artillery of his charms on Miss Nettleby, whom he handed to the dinner-table, and he paid her the most marked attention.

Although Mr. Leon helped Miss Nettleby to the greatest niceties on the table, he could not prevail on her to eat more than a small custard.

"I do not eat an ounce of solid food in a day," she said, " a slice of pine, or a small confection, is quite a sufficient meal for me."

"Sweet ethereal being," cried Mr. Leon, looking languishing into the eyes of Miss Nettleby, " no dross, no earth about you, all pure and seraph-like."

Celeste was listening with extreme attention to the panegyric of Mr. Leon, when her attention was arrested by an exclamation from Lady Nettleby, of "Good Heavens! Barnaby, what are you about, how can you be so careless, you have spoilt your cousin's dress."

Celeste looked round, and saw Barnaby had overturned a glass of jelly into her lap, and whilst trying to save it from falling with one hand, he knocked down a glass of red wine over her with the other.

"Poor Miss Manby, I quite feel for her," said Mr. Leon, shrugging up his shoulders, " and I would advise her, and every other lady whilst at dinner to be cased in oil-skin; egad, it would be well adapted to repel the disagreeable effects that might arise from sitting too near an awkward gentleman."

Lady Nettleby's face was the colour of a full blown piony, when she heard Mr. Leon's impertinent remarks, whilst Barnaby apologized as well as he could for the mischief he had done, although in reality he was ready to burst into a laugh at what he considered a good joke.

Celeste retired, and with the aid of Mrs. Popham's maid, cleaned and dried her dress; but the stain still remained.

Celeste, when she returned, found the drawing-room vacant, she therefore went into the garden, where she saw Miss Nettleby and Mr. Leon, sitting in an alcove.

Mr. Leon was entertaining his fair hearer with the most fulsome flattery, whilst several of the company were admiring the green-house plants, of which Mrs. Popham had a large collection.

Glad to get a moment to herself, Celeste turned round a remote walk in the gardens in which their were several statues placed on pedestals, turning down an angle in the walk, she unexpectedly, and to her mortification came in contact with Mr. Cubby, who was staring through his spectacles, at a model of Venus placed there.

Celeste endeavoured to pass him unperceived; but Mr. Cubby heard a footstep, and turning his head, saw it was Celeste, he caught her hand and detained her.

" What, popsy," he said, " have I caught you, you sly rogue, did you see me come into this walk?"

" I did not indeed, sir," said Celeste.

" Well wife's not dead yet, but she's not expected to live another day," he continued, ashe drew Celeste nearer towards him, and he would have kissed her, had she not with some difficulty prevented him."

" Don't be so prudish, popsy," he said, "it will be all right bye-and-by; wife can't live much longer,—never had a family—married a rich widow twenty years older than myself—but I have got a present for popsy; but, mum, dont say a word to Lady Nettleby, she knows I am rich, and she would like me herself, but no widows for me, I married one old woman, and that's quite sufficient."

Seeing Juliana coming into the walk, Mr. Cubby no longer detained Celeste.

" I have been looking for you, Celeste, this half hour," said Juliana, "and so has William."

" William," repeated Celeste, " who is that?"

" William Popham, who is dying in love for you," replied Juliana, "but here he is, and as I live he has brought the great monkey with him."

" I have brought Jacko to amuse you, ladies," said Mr. Popham. "he is the drollest animal alive; come, sir, go through your exercises," but the disobedient monkey, instead of obeying the commands of his master, threw down the stick, and in a moment ran up Celeste's dress, and seated himself on her shoulder, where he sat grinning at his master.

Terrified at the unwelcome intruder, Celeste screamed aloud, and before Mr. Popham could release her from the mischieveous animal, her cousin Barnaby, was by her side.

" This is very unhandsome behaviour of you, sir, to frighten my cousin in this way," said Barnaby; "indeed Mr. Popham, I could not have thought it of you, d——n the ugly brute, if I had my gun, by gad I'd shoot him; if you had brought a pack of hounds to have shown her, I should not have been surprised, but this ugly brute, why you deserve to be horse-whipped."

" You talk very large, sir," replied Mr. Popham, "but this I assure you, that shooting my mother's monkey would have made work for the lawyers, and to bring a pack of hounds into a flower garden to show the ladies, I think none but a madman would do that; to terrify or displease your cousin, I had not the least intention, I love her too well for that. I intend to lay myself and fortune at her feet, whether my mother likes it or not.

Saying this, he dragged away Jacko, who grinned and chattered as he went, as if unwilling to quit his ground.

" Ha, ha, look how he drags the obstinate brute," cried Barnaby; "by gad I don't know which is the greatest monkey of the two. And he intends, it seems, to offer you his hand, Celeste, but there will be two words to that bargain."

" Come, Celeste, let us join my sister and Mr. Leon," said Juliana.

Mr. Ashton came up at this moment, and taking Barnaby's arm, they turned into another walk.

Tea and coffee was served, and Mr. Popham, who had seated himself next to Celeste, was most assiduous in paying her every attention in his power, but unfortunately for poor Mr. Popham, in his hurry and endeavour to be beforehand with Barnaby, he spilt great part of a cup of coffee over Celeste's shoulder, as he was handing it to her.

" I beg, sir, you will not trouble yourself to wait on my cousin, said Barnaby, "it is a pleasure I will allow none but myself."

However, Mr. Popham would not be said nay, and both Mr. Popham and Barnaby were most troublesomely attentive to Celeste, to the no small mortification of Mr. Cubby, who kept watching them; and he seemed as it were to sit on thorns, whilst beholding the devotion of the rival lovers.

He sat looking at them for some time, but at last he could bear it no longer; complaining of heat, he arose from his seat, and seated himself in a recess window at the further end of the room.

Tea being finished, Miss Hagleston arose from her seat, and amused herself by looking at some pictures that were hanging in the room; she then walked up to where Mr. Cubby was sitting, and having seated herself near him, she said, "'tis very warm, sir."

Mr. Cubby did not reply, for he was so lost in thought concerning Celeste, Mr. Popham, and Mr. Nettleby, that he neither saw Miss Hagleston approach, nor heard her voice until she again repeated—"'Tis very warm, sir."

"It is warm, madam," at length replied Mr. Cubby, "the tea was warm; the room's warm; the weather's warm; and in short 'tis all warm together. There's Mr. Popham and Mr. Nettleby,—only observe them,—how they are tormenting poor Miss Manby; their hearts she seems to have warmed with a vengeance; but I'll lay my life she disappoints them both."

"I am not of your opinion, sir," replied the lady, "I have been told that Miss Manby has no fortune, and if so, she certainly will not be foolish enough to refuse an offer so much above what she could reasonably expect."

"She'd be a fool to accept either of them," replied Mr. Cubby, "I say, she may do better."

"'Tis no business of mine," replied Miss Hagleston, "whether she does or not, I did not mean to offend you."

"Offend me!" said Mr. Cubby, "what have I to do with it?"

"Certainly, what I said did not meet your approbation," replied Miss Hagleston, "or you would not have taken it up so warmly; it appears to me, that you have an interest in Miss Manby."

"Me an interest in Miss Manby!" said Mr. Cubby, vexed that he had expressed himself so unguardedly, in the hearing of Miss Hagleston.

"Me have an interest in Miss Manby! he again repeated; "no, indeed you know, my dear madam, that I am neither a widower nor a bachelor, nor have I a son who might think of her for a wife, why then should I feel an interest in Miss Manby?"

"Certainly not, my dear sir, certainly not," replied Miss Hagleston, "but you know, my dear sir, that beauty has sometimes great power over, not only single persons, but married also; and Miss Manby, I know is thought handsome. Now for my part, I was never reckoned a beauty, and I am very glad I was not, for beauties are generally so vain, and study their persons so much, that they have no time to adorn the mind; permit me, my dear sir, to say, although in my own praise, that though I was not handsome, I was always very discreet. I managed my father's house with the greatest ability—prevented his servants from robbing him. I well looked after them; nor would I suffer them to waste, or give away a crumb of bread, or a mug of ale. I permitted them to have no junkiting with the fellows. I routed out all their slut-holes, so that you could not find a grain of dust in the whole house. I assure you, sir," continued Miss Hagleston, "that I might several times have been married, and that most advantageously, in respect of money matters; but no, none of your fly-abouts for me; I made up my mind to wait, until I should have the good fortune, to meet with an elderly discreet gentleman, like yourself, Mr. Cubby; that is to say, were you a bachelor, or a widower."

"Very flattering, madam, very flattering," said Mr. Cubby, bowing, and wiping the perspiration from his fat cheeks.

"But, unfortunately," he continued, "I am neither a bachelor nor a widower."

"No, sir, of that I am well aware," replied Miss Hagleston, "but I was only speaking, sir, only saying, that I am convinced of your merit."

Mr. Cubby felt himself in a very awkward situation, for he feared Miss Hagleston was going to pop a question he was by no means inclined to answer, to the satisfaction of that lady.

Therefore, to end any hopes, Miss Hagleston might entertain of ever being Mrs. Cubby, Mr. Cubby replied.

"If it pleases Heaven to call my wife, I don't know that I should marry again; and if I did, it should be to a young woman; for I have had my house like an hospital, these ten years; full of doctors, nurses, and physic, through marrying one old woman; and you may believe me, madam, when I tell you, that I will never venture on another."

Rage sparkled in the eyes of Miss Hagleston, at this very unpolite speech of Mr. Cubby's, and her face changed to a colour to which vermillion, or the darkest damask rose was, comparatively speaking, snow. She took up a fan that lay on a table near where she was sitting, and having flirted it with great violence, she began to fan herself, and cast a look expressive of great disdain at Mr. Cubby; then arose, and joined Lady Nettleby and her party, who were engaged in an argument on philosophy and astronomy.

"As to an earthquake at present happening here is not the least of my thoughts," said an old gentleman, a relation of Mrs. Popham's, "but that an inundation will take place on the 23rd of next May, I feel certain, it will happen at ten minutes past one in the morning of that day; the sun and moon will then be in conjunction, and cause the tides to rise to a surprising height, so much so, that they will overflow the land for at least thirty miles round London Bridge."

"Really, sir, you quite alarm me," said Mrs. Popham.

"Oh! horrible," cried Miss Nettleby.

"The gentleman is only joking," said Juliana.

"Joking, madam! it is no theme to joke about," cried the old gentleman, "for the inundation will certainly happen. I have discovered this, through the labour of many nights spent in studying the planetary system, and have by the most abstruse study, found that a great flood will happen precisely at the time I mentioned.

"Houses will be washed down, and persons of all ranks, both great and small, will be washed from their beds, and carried by the tide to where its fury may hurry them."

"For my part, in order to be out of the way of this dreadful calamity, I intend to go to Halifax, there I shall be safe, for the inundation will not extend so far."

"Oh, what a scene that will be," cried Mr. Cubby, who had joined the company, and did not believe one word of the threatened calamity; "what a scene," he repeated, laughing as he did so. "In fancy I see them awakened from their midnight slumbers, ladies and gentlemen divested of their apparel, that is to say, with only their night clothing on, swimming down the flood—then what an assemblage of hats, bonnets, coats, petticoats, and unmentionables, we should see swimming with the tide."

"Sir, the gross indelicacy of your speech, is an insult to every lady present," cried Miss Hagleston; "to talk of ladies and gentlemen, divested of their clothing, swimming together—and the very idea of male and female apparel being huddled promiscuously together, even though accidental, in consequence of their being carried away by the tide, to me, is really shocking!"

"Lord, madam!" cried Mr. Cubby, "if this gentleman's prophecy comes to pass, you, even you, immaculate as you are, if awakened by the gushing waters, and I was near you, you would cling to me for support, whether dressed or not."

"No, sir: sooner would I lose my life," replied Miss Hagleston. "Sooner should you hear me gurgling in all the agony of suffocation, than I would save my life by such indelicacy.

"Lady Nettleby, may I trouble your servant to order my carriage; and I beg that when Mr. Cubby is of the party, your ladyship will never more invite me."

Saying this, Miss Hagleston left the drawing-room, and as she went, she turned her head, and cast on Mr. Cubby a look of great indignation.

"I am sorry I have offended the delicacy of Miss Hagleston," said Mr. Cubby, "I am sure I had not the least intention of so doing, and as I find she has made up her mind to avoid me, I shall for the future avoid her, and depart immediately from any company she may chance to be in. Yes, my Lady Nettleby, the moment I see the shrivelled face of that disagreeable lank-starched spinster of fifty-five, I shall immediately make my exit."

"Sir, Mr. Cubby, you are really too personal," cried Lady Nettleby, " I beg, sir, you will wave the unpleasant subject."

Nothing more was said of Miss Hagleston, earthquakes, nor inundations, and the evening passed off very agreeably to all the company; excepting poor Mr. Cubby, who anxiously watched for an opportunity to speak in private with Celeste.

But she, as if penetrating his thoughts, as anxiously avoided giving him an opportunity to do so.

When Celeste returned home, she found a letter from her father, and after taking

leave of Lady Nettleby and her daughters for the night, she retired to her chamber, impatient to read the contents.

The words in her father's letter were most affectionately expressed; he hoped " she would recover her spirits through her visit to town," and begged that Celeste " would do all in her power to please and merit the approbation of Lady Nettleby;" and desired, " that should Lady Nettleby wish her to extend her stay, she would not refuse to do so; things do not exactly run pleasant with me, my dear girl,"

No. 10.

continued her father, "but to-day I have passed a pleasant day, that is to say, a pleasant day as regards my feelings and tone of mind ; and what do you think, Celeste, has caused this pleasurable sensation—why a dream, a mere dream; but so like the reality,—I thought you came home, and brought with you your brother well and rich. I put no faith in dreams, but something persuades me that he will return, as in my dream."

Celeste was grieved to hear that things did not go pleasantly with her father; but to extend her stay beyond the three months agreed on, she could by no means consent to do, and she ardently hoped that her father's dream would prove prophetic in regard to her brother.

CHAPTER XXVII.

Oh, what joys there would abound !
Was my wife laid under ground,
The earth should cover her, I'd dance over her.   MIDAS.

THE uneasiness of Celeste was every day more increased by the troublesome attentions of Barnaby, which she plainly saw his mother encouraged, and that the words of Juliana were but too well founded, she had no doubt.

She dreaded lest Barnaby should in plain terms offer her his hand, and wish to fix a day for their wedding; if such should be the case, she feared her father would second the views of Barnaby, and wish her to become the wife of her cousin.

The thought made her miserable : "what excuse can I make ?—what reason can I assign for refusing the hand of Mr. Nettleby ?" thought Celeste.

" My father knows not that my heart is already engaged, nor can I have courage to tell him !" Unhappy in her mind, in consequence of these thoughts, Celeste could not sleep, and she arose at an early hour, thinking to answer her father's letter; but Celeste could not sufficiently collect her thoughts to do so.

She seated herself near the window of her chamber, and read until her spirits were quite depressed by the tale she was reading ; she looked at her watch, and saw that it was but eight o'clock, and she knew that it would at least be an hour before either Lady Nettleby or her daughters were visible. To wile away time, until the family were risen, Celeste put on her bonnet and shawl, and took a stroll into Kensington Gardens, which were near the house of Lady Nettleby; but Kensington Gardens did not that morning please or enliven Celeste; the beautiful walks there did but increase her melancholy, and caused her to think on the green lanes in Cornwall, where she had so often roved with her lover.

She left the gardens, and whilst knocking at the door of Lady Nettleby's, a stranger put a letter into her hand, and immediately disappeared.

Celeste hastened to her chamber, and having divested herself of her bonnet and shawl, she hastily tore open the letter, and read as follows :—

" DEAR CELESTE,

" Meet me to-morrow morning, at the hour of seven, in Kensington Gardens, just within the gate near the Serpentine River ; excuse my naming so early an hour, I have done so to avoid observation—fail not to come, I have something of the greatest importance to communicate."

Celeste was much surprised at this note; she thought that Osmond had by some means been prevented from going to Ireland, and that he had discovered her residence, and wished a private interview.

Celeste did not name having received this note to any one, but she intended to keep the appointment therein named.

On the following morning, Celeste, at the hour named, was in Kensington Gardens, where she fondly hoped to meet her lover.

She waited some short time, but no person was visible ; hardly knowing what to think, or who the person could be, that had sent her the letter, and which, on again inspecting, she did not believe to be the hand-writing of Osmond; much disappointed, she was going to leave the gardens, when she saw sitting on one of the seats, a corpulent gentleman, and to her great mortification and surprise, saw it was Mr. Cubby; without noticing him, she was hastening on, when Mr. Cubby caught her arm, and detained her.

"Stop, popsy," he said, "didn't you see me—you had my note?"

"Gracious Heaven!" exclaimed Celeste, "did that note come from you, sir? I expected it came from a very different person—I little thought it came from you."

"And why not from me?" said Mr. Cubby, "you are single, and I very soon shall be so; then what is there so very surprising in my sending you a note? The fact is, you prefer that leap-gate, break-neck, fox-hunting spark—or, that poor, simple, milk-sop, Billy Popham.

"You think me old, but I am not old in constitution; don't be afraid, popsy; I can yet dance and jig with the best of them.—I wanted to see you, to give you the present I told you of—I could not get an opportunity to give them to you, at my Lady Nettleby's. Here they are," he continued, as he opened a box, which contained a superb pair of diamond ear-rings and bracelets to match; "there, popsy," he said, "there's sparklers—cost a great deal of money—fit for popsy to wear—wife can't wear them now."

Shocked at the vile conduct of the infatuated old man, and much disappointed at not seeing Osmond, who she fully expected to see, was altogether too much for the spirits of Celeste; with a tremulous hand she pushed the bracelets, which Mr. Cubby was then exhibiting, from her; and had she not reclined against a tree for support, she must have fallen. The seat Mr. Cubby had risen from was near, and, for a moment, Celeste sat down to recover herself.

Mr. Cubby sat down beside her: "Poor popsy!" he said, "shall I call a coach to convey you home?"

"By no means; I shall soon be better," replied Celeste.

"Oh, you can't think how I'll wait on you, when you are Mrs. Cubby;" he continued, "I think I now see myself standing before you, with a basin of caudle, and nurse, with the little chubby, fat-faced boy in her arms. 'Is he not a charming child?' I think I hear the old woman say, 'Oh, he's the very picture of the Cubbys.'"

Celeste could bear no more: she started up, and in her haste to be gone she pushed against Mr. Cubby, who was sitting on the extreme end of the seat; he fell on the ground, and not being very active, on account of his corpulence, when he fell, he rolled from the side he fell on, and turned on his back, lying for some moments in that posture before he could recover himself, but with some difficulty he at length gained his equilibrium, but to his mortification he found Celeste had fled.

When Celeste reached the house of Lady Nettleby she found the family had not yet assembled at the breakfast-table.

But Lady Nettleby had risen before her usual time, and had gone to her son's bed-room, with whom she then was in deep conference.

The cause of Lady Nettleby's early rising was in consequence of a dream that made her very uneasy.

She dreamed that her uncle Russel was dead, and that he had left the children of her brother the whole of his property; she thought that the children of her brother were advertised for, to come forward and receive their bequest.

In consequence of coming into so much money, Lady Nettleby thought that Celeste refused to become the wife of Barnaby, but was united to a lover she had left in Cornwall.

Uneasy on account of this dream, Lady Nettleby arose, and went to the bed-room of her son, who she awoke from a very agreeable dream; for at that moment his mother came into his room, and awoke him by so doing; he thought he was receiving a won wager of some hundred pounds, for which he had backed his favourite mare, Miss Slouch.

Vexed at finding the won wager imaginary, Barnaby, rubbing his eyes, cried, "Lord, mother, you ferret one out everywhere!"

"I am sorry to disturb you, my dear," said Lady Nettleby, "but it is for your own good that I have done so. Dreams have always proved most ominous to me, and last night or rather this morning, I dreamed that Celeste had come into a great deal of money, and would not marry you.

"Now, as I every day expect to hear of my uncle's death, when that happens, then my dream will be realised, as far as Celeste having a large fortune; but to prevent its further fulfilment, you must lose no time in making her your wife; I will propose to her that the day after to-morrow the marriage between you shall take place."

" The sooner the better," replied Barnaby, "provided old uncle soon dies; I want money, you keep me so short. If I had now ten thousand pounds in ready money, in betting, I'd make twenty thousand of it."

" Oh, odious !" cried Lady Nettleby, " pray let me hear no more of betting, you must turn all your thoughts now to win the heart of your cousin. I came before you were up to advise you, lest you should slip through my fingers, and have gone out before I saw you; then perhaps I should not have seen you all day."

" You don't think I can be always tied to your apron-strings," said Barnaby, " and my courting cousin Celeste. It is more to oblige you than myself; I think I have paid her attention enough—she need not be so coy and squeamish. I can tell you, mother, she is not the girl of my choice, but her money will enable me to sport with the best of them."

Lady Nettleby left her son's room, after giving him some further instructions respecting his behaviour to Celeste, to whom, when they met at breakfast, Barnaby was all attention, according to the advice of his mother.

After breakfast was ended, Maria and Juliana retired to practise some new music, and Barnaby went to the stable to see that the horses were well taken care of; meantime, Lady Nettleby desired Celeste would attend her in her dressing-room.

When there, Lady Nettleby closed the door, and desired Celeste to be seated, "I have brought this piece of figured satin for you, my love," she said, as she unfolded a piece of beautiful gray satin to the view of Celeste; "there's enough for a dress and hat," she said, "in which I think you would look most lovely; but why," continued Lady Nettleby, "should I endeavour to make you look more charming than you already are; perhaps it would be well for many that you had never quitted Cornwall; in London, the gentlemen are such admirers of beauty."

" You are pleased to be jocular at my expense," said Celeste.

"No, indeed, child, I am serious," replied Lady Nettleby; "for instance, what a hole you have made in the heart of poor Barnaby, the preference shown you by Mr. Popham almost drove him mad; he wishes me to break the matter to you, which he has not courage to do himself, for fear of a refusal; he dreads the thought of losing you, nor can he rest until you are his own. I hope, if you have feeling, and wish to save my son from doing a deed of desperation, you'll consent to an early and private wedding. This evening, we celebrate Juliana's birth day—to-morrow, no, not to-morrow, we may feel rather fatigued then, in consequence of dancing, and keeping late hours to-night. What think you of being married the day after to-morrow? a license shall be procured, and when you have once given your word, it will put poor Barnaby out of his pain—he will be no longer on the rack of doubt and despair. There is no occasion for the delay of consulting your father, he will be proud to see you so advantageously settled. Some mothers would object to their son's marrying a girl without fortune; but I was always very disinterested; money had never any weight with me; I wish to see my son happy, and that I am sure he'll be with you, Celeste."

Celeste seemed quite stunned by the words of Lady Nettleby.

"Well, Celeste," said her ladyship, "then I'm to tell Barnaby that you agree to make him happy, and that the day after to-morrow the ceremony is to be performed?"

Celeste's colour went and came; she felt confused, agitated, and dismayed, at this most pressing and unwelcome proposal, nor could she for some moments find courage to answer her aunt.

Finding Celeste did not answer, "well, silence gives consent," said her ladyship, "of course it is all settled, Barnaby will be in raptures; as soon as he comes in, I shall acquaint him with the pleasing intelligence."

"Stop, madam," cried the trembling Celeste, "do pray not misunderstand me; I thank my cousin for the regard he has expressed for me, but do not let him think I ever can be his wife. I don't mean to marry, indeed I do not."

"Not marry!" cried Lady Nettleby, frowning and tossing up her head with indignation, "not marry—then I suppose you hate the male sex, and intend to retire to some nunnery; really, Celeste, it is quite ridiculous to express yourself in this way; if you persevere in this whim, I must write to your father, and hear what he says about it. But I'd have you well consider of what you are about, and not drive Barnaby to despair by your coolness; I shall tell him you want a few days for consideration, and in that time I shall expect a more favourable answer for my son. 'I never mean to marry,' said you. Oh, Celeste, can you for a moment think I suppose you are sincere in such a declaration? no, certainly not; perhaps you have left your heart in Cornwall, with some rustic swain, and that is the reason why you refuse my son; if so, you must forget the low-bred object of your choice; your own advantage, and the peace and honour of your friends, demand that you should do so. A fine thing, indeed! I invite you here, treat you as my own child, and what's the consequence? why, through your perverseness, the misery, nay, perhaps the suicide of my only son—for Heaven's sake, Celeste, if not for love, for pity's sake, accept the hand of poor Barnaby— oh! think, what would be the grief, the misery of his family, should the unhappy boy take poison, or plunge into the water to end his sorrows!" Lady Nettleby wiped her eyes, as she continued—"You, you, Celeste, are the first female who ever touched his heart; females were his aversion until he saw you; tell me, Celeste, what message must I take my son—it must be favourable—dare not to send him a refusal!"

Celeste burst into tears, hurt beyond measure at the almost bullying manner of her aunt, who seeing the grief she had caused, and fearing Celeste might insist on returing home, she, Lady Nettleby, in the most tender tone said,—"Forgive me, my love, if I have spoken harshly; you must excuse the feelings of a mother when she fears the peace of her only son may be broken for ever. I know the steadiness of Barnaby's temper; where his love once fixes, there it will remain, and dreadful will be the consequence of a disappointment. Think, my love," continued Lady Nettleby, "on the advantages offered you,—a doating husband, a carriage and independence; all, everything your heart can wish; reverse it, should you lose your father's dependence, privation and poverty must follow."

The picture drawn by Lady Nettleby was too much for the feelings of Celeste to endure with calmness; she again burst into a flood of tears.—"Oh, permit me to return home, madam," she said; "I thank you for the kindness you have shown me; but you have greatly hurt my feelings, particularly by naming an event, which I hope for many, many years will not happen—I mean the death of my father," and her tears redoubled.

"How foolish to distress yourself in this way," said Lady Nettleby; "I hope, as you do, that your father will live many, many years; and believe me, Celeste, nothing was further from my thoughts than to give you pain. Come, my dear girl," she continued, kissing the cheek of Celeste, "dry up those pearly drops; you are not angry with me, I hope, for pointing out the advantages you may receive, and the disagreeables you may avoid."

"I thank you, madam, for your advice and good wishes," replied Celeste, drying up her tears, "but pray let me return to my father."

"Oh, no, that I cannot," said Lady Nettleby; "your father, I know, wishes you to stay with me, at least the time agreed on when you left Cornwall, nor will I part with you one day sooner; surely, Celeste, you are not such a baby as to cry after your father, because I have been talking to you about a husband; turn what I have been saying to you in your own mind, and let me have your answer to-morrow evening; until that time I will not write to your father, and I beg you will consider that the life or death of my son depends on your answer. I am really sorry, Celeste, that I have vexed you, but you will, I know, forgive me," and she took the hand of Celeste. "I wish, my love," she continued, "that your gray satin had been made up for you to appear in to-night, but you shall wear my pearls, they will enliven your black silk: 'tis time, Celeste, you left off your mourning, and for a bride, black will never do. I will go and look out the pearls."

"I beg I may be excused appearing in company to-night," said Celeste, "I am not in spirits, and unfit for company.

"But you were not unfit for company when you were talking to a gentleman at an early hour this morning in Kensington Gardens—who was that gentleman?— Your father, Celeste, has trusted you with me, and 'tis fit I should know—was it a lover?"

"No," said Celeste, "it was Mr. Cubby; he sent this note for me to meet him there, but there being no name to the note, I was deceived, and thought it came from another person, and when I went, according to the appointment, I found the writer was Mr. Cubby," and Celeste handed Lady Nettleby the note.

"And you was imprudent enough to meet the writer?"

"I was," replied Celeste, "and blush for myself that I did so; but it was in the expectation of meeting a very different person."

"I really did not think you'd have been so imprudent, Celeste," said Lady Nettleby, "however, I will not say anything to vex or disturb you, we had enough of that this morning; but I'll read the old man's note.—And what was the very important communication," inquired Lady Netleby, when she had finished reading the note.

"To make me an offer of marriage," replied Celeste, "and to present me with his wife's diamond bracelets and earrings,"

"Oh! the foolish, the wicked old man," cried Lady Nettleby, her face crimsoning with rage, "to write, and make such an offer to a mere child, a baby to him; really I am quite fluttered, Celeste; shocked at the old dotard's folly and wickedness. Unfeeling man, before Mrs. Cubby has breathed her last to endeavour to bespeak another wife, and that a young creature like you. Knowing I am a widow, and fearing least some other gentleman might engage me; if he, rather to prematurely on that account had offered me his hand, and he had gained my promise to accept it when circumstances would permit of my so doing, that would have been, more excusable than his making you such an offer—a young creature like you indeed—do not name the foolish affair to Maria or Juliana. All you have to do, Celeste, is to treat old Cubby with coolness when he comes again. No wonder, my love, Barnaby is impatient to call you his own; until you are married to him, he will always be in fear of losing you."

Poor Celeste was plunged into a dilemma, from which she knew not how to extricate herself; her father she knew, wished to see her settled in life, and she feared her father would urge her to marry her cousin.

But Barnaby was her aversion, and that aversion every day increased. "How unlike Osmond Durant," she mentally said, and tears stole into her eyes, when she thought on her absent lover.

Lady Nettleby's maid now came into the room, and begged Celeste would go to her mistress, who wished Miss Manby to assist her taste in the arrangement of some exotics, and the placing of some festoons of flowers in the room appropriated for dancing.

"Celeste, my love, what think you of this—or what think you of that?" said her ladyship.

At length the dinner hour arrived, when Barnaby, who that day dined at home, was most tiresomely attentive to Celeste.

CHAPTER XXVIII.

'Tis not her beauty that I prize,
Give me gold's glitter, *that* before bright eyes.
Let her be wrinkled, with a monkey face,
But gold in plenty, she'd be quite a grace.

BY THE AUTHORESS OF EVA.

"I REALLY can't think, ma, how you could give in to Juliana's whim," said Maria, "in having a ball the very beginning of September, and so warm too, it is quite absurd."

"You need not dance, Maria," said Juliana; "I wish to dance, and ma has indulged me."

"The first invited guest who arrived, was the Count Le Mar, who brought with him a gentleman he wished to introduce to Lady Nettleby and the young ladies; the gentleman's name was Synegall.

"He is a very particular friend of mine," said the count, "a young man of very great merit, and only son of Mr. Synegall, the richest man in Derby."

Mr. Synegall was very kindly received by Lady Nettleby, although he certainly had not the most pleasing exterior, for Mr. Synegall had rather a disagreeable cast with one of his eyes; he was a tall sandy-haired young man, with a large head, and a look that seemed to shun observation.

His reverse, the Count Le Mar, was a short thick-set man, about forty years of age, of a very dark complexion and assured countenance; his wide, open, full black eyes, were quite an annoyance to Celeste, when he gazed upon her, as he often did, and not only on her, but on Lady Nettleby, and her daughters also, who rather considered his ardent gaze a compliment, than otherwise.

To Lady Nettleby, the count was particularly attentive, as was his friend Mr. Synegall to Maria, who he appeared to be quite struck with; and he ogled her unceasingly, in proof of his admiration, whenever he happened to be in her company.

The Count Le Mar lamented that himself and Mr. Synegall must leave the company assembled at Lady Nettleby's at ten o'clock, as both himself and Mr. Synegall had a previous engagement, before he, the Count Le Mar, had the honour of receiving her ladyship's card of invitation.

It was Juliana's birth-day, but Maria was the presiding deity of the ball-room; in fact, Maria was a person of more importance than Juliana in the eyes of her mother, in consequence of Maria having seven thousand pounds more than her sister, left her by her god-mother, which sum she had obtained possession of when she became of age.

The house of Lady Nettleby was most elegantly furnished, for it was not only on account of the law-suit that her ladyship came to town about; but she came on a matrimonial speculation also, on her own account, as well as her daughters; she intended keeping the best company, displaying all the pomp in her power, in order to promote her design.

In the apartment intended for the ball, all was splendour and brightness.

At the upper end of the room, on a sofa of white satin with gold mouldings, sat Maria, beneath festoons of roses and water-lilies, dressed in the heretofore mentioned blue crape dress, with a white lace scarf, and the top of her long ostrich feathers, drooping over her left shoulder, as she sat reclining against the arm of the sofa, picking to pieces a white rose, and strewing the leaves around her.

Whilst sittiting in this attitude, Mr. Synegall approached her.

"Will you not dance?" he said, "permit me to lead you out."

"Oh, no," replied Maria, "'tis too warm to dance."

"How happy am I," said Mr. Synegall, "to hear that you do not intend to dance, it will give me an opportunity of passing some moments of delight in your company."

Mr. Synegall made the best use of his time in winning the heart of Maria, who, when the Count Le Mar came to inform his friend, that the hand of his whate pointed to the hour of ten, and it was full time for their departure; she, Maria felt vexed and disappointed at his going.

Mr. Synegall loitered, and seemed loth to leave fair Maria, until he was again reminded by the Count Le Mar, of the promise they had given to Sir Henry, Haverton.

With extreme reluctance, Mr. Synegall at length departed, execrating his folly for making the appointment he had done, as it deprived him of the supreme pleasure of Miss Nettleby's company.

Miss Hagleston, who was of the party, had the pleasure of finding that she was not entirely overlooked that evening. For the Count Le Mar paid her many compliments and much attention, as was his way to elderly ladies who possessed good fortunes.

But the count took especial care that his attention to Miss Hagleston should not be noticed by Lady Nettleby, not that the count had made any overtures to Lady Nettleby, but he particularly avoided letting one lady hear the compliments he bestowed on another.

"Well, really, that Count Le Mar is the most pleasant gentleman I ever was in company with," said Miss Hagleston to Maria, who happened to go into the card-room, "I have spent a most agreeable evening."

"I am glad of it," said Maria; "it happens fortunate that you are not annoyed by the presence of Mr. Cubby."

"I assure you, my dear Miss Nettleby, if Mr. Cubby had been here, I should not have staid. But I knew he would not be here; for I heard, and that from good authority, that he was sent for this morning to Finchley, in consequence of the death of Mrs. Cubby, who died last night; his nephew has gone with him. However inattentive as he was to the poor old lady during her life, he surely will not be indecorous enough to call here if he returns to town to night," cried Miss Hagleston.

"Oh no, there's no fear of that," said Maria.

"It is now, more than eleven o'clock, and after the solemn scene of a death-bed, I should think he would be in no mood to come into a ball, or card-room; if he does, I shall immediately depart," cried Miss Hagleston.

Poor Mr. Popham, who was there with his mother, could not obtain Celeste's hand for one single dance.

Barnaby engrossed her the whole night to her no small mortification; she was, as it were, compelled by Lady Nettleby to join the company, and could not do otherwise than accept Barnaby for a partner, whose flattery and attentions were to Celeste, worse than disagreeable. At length the gay party separated, and Celeste, with pleasure retired to her chamber.

The following morning, the Count Le Mar and Mr. Synegall waited on Lady Nettleby and her daughters; when some other gentlemen, who were at the ball on the preceding evening, likewise called in, to inquire after the health of the ladies.

"Have you heard, Lady Nettleby, how poor Mr. Cubby is after his fright last night?" said one of the gentlemen.

"What alarmed him?" inquired Lady Nettleby, "I have heard nothing about it."

Before the gentleman could reply, Mr. Ashton, Mr. Cubby's nephew came into the room; and after the usual compliments were over, he said, "have you heard of the unpleasant adventure we met with last night, ladies."

On being answered in the negative; he said, "my poor aunt died at a very early hour yesterday morning at Finchley, and a messenger arrived by post to inform my uncle of the event. I accompanied my uncle there, and after he had put his seal on the valuables, and given orders for the funeral, we were returning home in his chariot; it was then somewhat more than eleven o'clock, it might have been half-past—it was as you know, ladies, a fine night.

"Well, when we were just on this side of Finchley Common, and I was lamenting to myself the privation, the most mortifying privation of being absent from your ball, and uncle was enjoying a little doze.

"A whistle sounded on the stillness of that lone spot, and it being almost midnight no travellers were passing, nor was any human being visible.

"Uncle started, the whistle aroused him from his doze. 'I fear there are robbers abroad,' he cried, 'I wish I had not asked that toping old person to take dinner', he said, 'when once over his wine, there was no getting rid of him; 'tis too late, much too late to travel a road like this;—hark!' said my uncle, 'there are horsemen coming this way.'

"In a moment, two men rode up to the heads of the horses and stopped them; whilst a third, with a pistol in his hand, and with horrid imprecations demanded our money.

No. 11.

"Uncle first gave the ruffian his money and watch, and whilst I was delivering up mine, my uncle, in order to get as far as he could from the fellow and his pistols, leaned back against the door which his weight forced open, and he fell out, and unfortunately rolled into a ditch by the road-side,—there was not much water in it, but plenty of mud.

"As soon as the fellows rode off, the footman and myself helped my uncle out of the ditch, where he had remained quiet enough, and when we had taken him out he declared, 'that he had rather have staid where he was, imbedded in mud, than risk his existence by remaining in the presence of his bloody-minded assailants.'

"I was certainly much alarmed myself," continued Mr. Ashton, "although I possess as much courage as most men, certainly, having a pistol clapped close to one's ear has a most disagreeable and startling effect."

"The footman and myself would have wiped the mud off uncle's clothes with our handkerchiefs, but he would not permit us."

"'No, said he, as he hurried into the chariot, ' never mind the mud; let's be off, lest some other bloody-minded villain overtake us.'"

"The coachman tore with all possible speed until we reached town. When we got home I prescribed a draught for my uncle, whose nervous system was a great deal deranged by the fright he had received, and he likewise is somewhat bruised in consequence of his fall from the chariot into the ditch; however, though not up yet, he is much better this morning, and he intends, if he possibly can, in the course of the day to call on your ladyship; whom, I don't know how it is, but he seems most anxious to see," added Mr. Ashton, with a smile that seemed to insinuate more than his words expressed.

The quick perception of Lady Nettleby was not at a loss to interpret the meaning look of Mr. Ashton.

"Surely the vanity of Celeste must have deceived her," thought Lady Nettleby, "Mr. Cubby, I dare say wanted her to intercede with me on his account, she must labour under a mistake altogether."

"And your uncle Mr. Ashton, is anxious to see me?" said her ladyship. "Poor dear Mr. Cubby, I must advise him to be more careful, and on no account to travel such lonely roads at so late an hour; I have heard of a great many robberies, and even murders that have been committed on Finchley Common."

"Yes, 'tis a dangerous place," said Mr. Ashton, "but I have the pleasure to say, that I think I shall have the pleasure of bringing the villain to justice, who held the pistol to my ear, for at the moment that he was so doing, the crape that he wore over his face, to hide his features, slipped down, and I plainly saw his countenance; of which I mean to give a description to the police. I beg pardon, sir," continued Mr. Ashton, bowing to the Count Le Mar, "but did not I know you to be a gentleman, and the thing altogether impossible, I could have sworn that you were the very man—and your voice too, resembles his, when he demanded our money."

Mr. Synegall, who at this moment was in discourse with Miss Nettleby, and seemingly by paying great attention to what she was say, yet his ear caught the words of Mr. Ashton, and he turned of a death-like paleness, his eyes were cast on the ground, and seemed even more than usual to shun observation.

The Count Le Mar advanced to Mr. Ashton bursting with rage :—

"How dare you, sir, insult a gentleman of my pretensions with your infamous comparisons?" he exclaimed,—" me like the fellow who robbed you?—Sir, by Heaven, 'tis only respect for the ladies that withholds me—I fear to terrify them, otherwise I'd wring the nose from your face, for insulting me with the insolent comparison.—But think not that I mean to put up with the affront; no, sir, name your own time and place, and either with sword or pistol, I'm your man ;—and then, sir, you to your sorrow will find such wounds in your person, that though you are a practitioner in physic, neither your salves, ointments, nor lotions will heal."

Terrified, the ladies interfered, and begged that the Count Le Mar would be pacified. They declared their full conviction of Mr. Ashton's meaning no offence to the count, and merely spoke of the resemblance—and it was a well-known fact, that one person sometimes very greatly resembled another.

Rather alarmed at the menacing manner of the count, and hearing the name of sword, and pistol, weapons to which Mr. Ashton had a most decided aversion, he, as well as the ladies, began to conciliate.

"I am sure, sir," said Mr. Ashton, "I meant not the least offence; can it be supposed any person would take you for a highwayman, a person of your property and appearance?—could any one suspect you of being a highwayman, a genleman who is honoured with the friendship of Mr. Barnaby Nettleby, and his amiable mother and sisters; I only spoke of the very great resemblance. Permit me to say, my dear sir," continued Mr. Ashton, "that however strong my likeness might be to the King of England, and he died without an heir, I don't suppose that they would crown me, neither would an honest man be hung, because he chanced to resemble a thief; that would be fine law indeed. Were you like me, sir, to study anatomy, and to dissect, sir, as many bodies as I have done, you would not be surprised at one man's resembling another.

"I declare to you, sir, as a matter of fact, that I was called on by the friends of a foreign prince to open him in order to ascertain what had caused his death, for he died suddenly, without any previous illness, and the cause of his death was a matter of doubt. The following week I assisted in opening a vagrant, merely for practice; and I could have sworn, had I not been convinced to the contrary, that the foreign prince and the vagrant were one and the same person; the same stature, age, feature, and complexion. Consider, my dear sir, the millions and millions of faces that have appeared since the beginning of the world; think you they can be all different? No, 'tis quite a mistake; for instance, in our coinage; if it was all to come from the mint with a different head, what endless work that would be;—no, we have the same impression, the same face over and over again; and so it is with the human species. No wonder then, my dear sir, that one man may be mistaken for another;" saying this Mr. Ashton held out his hand in token of friendship to the Count Le Mar.

The count gave his hand to Mr. Ashton, but it was with a very ill-grace, and he at the same time rather sullenly remarked.—

"You must be careful, my good sir, of making such mistakes; the taking one man for another may lead to very awkward consequences; and as to swearing against an innocent man, as you were but now talking of, might send you a longer journey beyond sea than you might like to go."

Harmony being at length restored, the party entered into some pleasant conversation on fashionable subjects, amongst the rest of a masquerade that was to take place the following week, and at which Lady Nettleby and her daughters intended being.

Miss Nettleby inquired of Mr. Synegall if he would be there, and his friend, the agreeable Count Le Mar.

"I am most unfortunate in having such a multiplicity of engagements," said Mr. Synegall, "and so is the Count Le Mar, but I will break my engagement to be in the company of my fair friend, to whom I have a few words to say on an affair that I trust will not meet with a refusal."

Whilst saying this, Mr. Synegall pressed the hand of Maria, and gave her a most languishing glance.

Neither the Count Le Mar, nor Mr. Ashton appeared to be perfectly at ease in the company of each other; the count at times threw an under glance at Mr. Ashton, expressive of both dislike, suspicion, and menace, and although peace was restored, yet the violent words used by the count were not forgotten by Mr. Ashton, who soon made his adieus and departed.

CHAPTER XXIX.

Think me too old, I am but sixty-three,
And quite as brisk as any man can be ;
Ladies are whimsical, and have odd ways,
An hundred years was boyhood, in Methuselah's days.
　　　By the Authoress of Eva, or the Bridal Spectre.

As evening approached, and Celeste was to give a decided answer respecting her marriage with Barnaby, her spirits drooped ; she felt awed and unhappy, when she thought on the last conversation she had had with Lady Nettleby on that subject.

Celeste plainly saw that Lady Nettleby had fully made up her mind to Celeste's union with her son ; and Celeste feared, from what she had observed on a former occasion, that her ladyship, who she knew to be of a very violent temper, when put out of her way, would be much exasperated by a refusal.

Celeste had thought of acquainting Lady Nettleby with the state of her heart, respecting the love she entertained for Osmond Durant, as a reason for her refusing Barnaby.

" But if I do so," thought Celeste, her ladyship may inform my father of my secret, and he would be both grieved and angry with me for concealing my sentiments in favour of Osmond from him. No, I will not tell her," thought Celeste, " surely I have a right to refuse an offer, if it does not meet my approbation, an offer on which the happiness or misery of my life must depend."

Tea was over, and Miss Nettleby and Juliana had stepped into the carriage to go to the theatre, to which place Mr. Synegall escorted them.

Soon as they had departed Lady Nettleby, who was anxious for Celeste's answer, began the subject and said, " well, my love I suppose you have made up your mind to become the wife of Barnaby."

But before Celeste could answer, Mr. Cubby was announced ; and Celeste immediately withdrew, before Mr. Cubby entered the room.

Lady Nettleby received Mr. Cubby's visit with pleasure, and expressed the satisfaction she felt in seeing him safe, after the disagreeable affair he had met with, and said, " she hoped he felt no ill consequences, arising from his last night's adventure."

" It has certainly caused me to be rather indisposed," replied Mr. Cubby. " Indeed I should not have come out, but I much wished to see your ladyship."

" And did you come out on my account sooner than you would otherwise have done ?—how kind ; indeed, Mr. Cubby, you lay me [quite under an obligation," said Lady Nettleby.

" Then, madam, you have it in your power to repay the obligation," replied Mr. Cubby.

" Sir, I am quite willing to do so," said Lady Nettleby ; " how can I serve you ?"

" You can, madam, and infinitely two," replied Mr. Cubby ; " you know my Lady Nettleby, my wife, for years before her death, was very ill ; in short, madam, I had a wife and no wife ; I have, as one may say, been a widower for years, and can you now blame me, for wishing for the comfort of a married life, in the society of an amiable partner ?"

" Certainly not, sir ; certainly not, Mr. Cubby, there are but few ladies who would refuse you.'"

" Do you think not, madam," replied Mr. Cubby ; " you really put me in spirits ; quite give me new life in the thought of not being refused."

" Oh ! sir, don't think of a refusal," cried Lady Nettleby.

" I know it is rather indecorous—rather too soon—the very day after Mrs. Cubby's death to talk of another wife," said Mr. Cubby, " but I fear to be superseded ; it is best to speak in time."

" Of course, sir," replied Lady Nettleby, " but although you make the proposal, the wedding need not take place for some time; the world would be apt to talk, and I can't bear to give room for scandal; to be sure, we may be married, and keep the affair secret for twelve months or so."

"Madam, you misunderstand me;—of what are you talking?" said Mr. Cubby.

Mortified and disappointed, the truth now flashed on Lady Nettleby, and she replied with much haughtiness, ' Sir, I would ask, what you are talking about?"

"Talking about? why of marrying your niece, to be sure," said Mr. Cubby.

"Then sir, you will not have my niece," replied Lady Nettleby, "she would not think of having a man at your time of life; besides, she's engaged to my son, to whom I expect in a few days she will be united;—and if that, sir, is all you have to say to me, I beg to wish you a good morning."

Had Lady Nettleby given way to her enraged feelings, she would have given Mr. Cubby such a lecture, that he would not soon have forgotten, but she checked her ire, thinking that when Mr. Cubby found Celeste was the wife of another, the marrying old man might yet make her, (Lady Nettleby) proposals.

As soon as Mr. Cubby had left the house, Lady Nettleby rang her bell, and desired the servant who answered it, to tell Miss Manby that she (Lady Nettleby) wished to speak to her.

When Celeste entered the presence of Lady Nettleby, the subject of her marriage with Barnaby was renewed, and when her ladyship found Celeste was determined to refuse her son, the ire Mr. Cubby had raised in her bosom flamed yet higher; but she hid her anger, being unwilling to offend Celeste.

"It is no easy thing for me," observed her ladyship, " to see my only son break his heart, or commit some deed of desperation; this very night, Celeste, I'll write to your father, he has more influence over you than I have, I think he will coincide with me, and rejoice at the good fortune that awaits your acceptance."

Celeste was about to reply, but her ladyship stopped her by saying, "say no more, child, I shall write to your father."

This, Lady Nettleby immediately did; she wrote a very kind letter to Mr. Manby, and told him in it, of the very great love her son bore Celeste, who he wished to make his wife; she spoke highly of Barnaby's temper and good disposition, and of the very excellent husband, she felt assured, he would make Celeste; and she rather exaggerated the property left Barnaby by his father. Lady Nettleby observed, " that such an offer might not again occur to Celeste, and it ought not to be treated with indifference, nor to be lightly thrown away."

Lady Nettleby begged that Mr. Manby would interfere, as Celeste did not appear willing to accept the hand of Barnaby; " she is but young," continued her ladyship, "and must be ruled by parental authority, nor be foolishly suffered to ruin her prospects for ever: perhaps, brother, you will come to London, and be present at the celebration of the nuptials of my son, and your daughter," concluded her ladyship.

Celeste too, wrote to her father, she said in her letter, "that she could not think of marrying her cousin; she begged that her father would send for her home, and declared that with every coming day her hatred toward London, increased, and the greater was her desire to return to Cornwall."

After Celeste had finished her letter, she remained in her chamber, nor was her company desired by Lady Nettleby, who was vexed and disappointed, both on account of Mr. Cubby's explanation, and Celeste's firm refusal of Barnaby.

Much chagrined, she retired to rest, or rather to consult her pillow, in respect of ways and means, for the high style her ladyship lived in, whilst in London, together with the extravagance of Barnaby, who had formed an acquaintance with several sharpers, who pretended to be men of high consideration and property, and to keep pace, in high betting, and other vices of these gentry, he not being of age, frequently borrowed large sums of his mother, who granted him whatever sums he required, intending amply to repay herself, when her son should receive the fortune of Celeste; on this account, she, well knowing the temper of her son, indulged him in whatever he thought fit to do, fearing if she crossed him, that he would be sullen, and though to his own loss, would not press for a speedy marriage with Celeste, and by that means disappoint her of her expected booty.

She knew Barnaby was good natured, if he had all his own way; and her ladyship meant to have at least five thousand pounds out of the fortune bequeathed Celeste by her great uncle, merely by way of a present, a grateful remuneration, for having been at some trouble and expense, in bringing the affair about.

But Mr. Russell was not yet dead that her ladyship knew of, and though the property was certain, yet it might be some time before it fell into the hands of Barnaby and herself.

Lady Nettleby was in want of money. "I will ask Maria," she mentally said, "to assist me with one thousand pounds for twelve months or so, in that time, Barnaby, no doubt, will be in possession of the old man's money."

On the following day, Lady Nettleby informed her son of her ill success with Celeste, and she begged Barnaby would not be discouraged by her, Celeste's, refusal, but do all in his power to please her, and gain her affection.

"I shall give myself but little more trouble about her," replied Barnaby, "before I could make her behave to my mind, she'd want as much training as a horse. She's so coy, so proud, so squeamish; give me a free-hearted girl, I hate such flummery; I should like the money, you say she'll have well enough," continued Barnaby, "I certainly could make some capital bets with it, but for my cousin, I'm sure she's not the girl to my mind, then why should I sell myself—my estates will maintain me."

"What!" cried Lady Nettleby in great alarm, "do you not mean to marry Celeste?"

"I don't say that," replied Barnaby, "but if she don't soon come to, I shan't follow the chase much longer, she has almost run me down."

"She must be your wife," said Lady Nettleby, "I have written to her father, who, no doubt, will urge her to a step that appears so much to her advantage. I place great dependance on that."

The entrance of Mr. Ashton and Mr. Leon prevented the subject of Celeste's union with Barnaby from being at that time further discussed; the former of these gentlemen had brought tickets for Lady Nettleby and family for a masquerade that that was to take place in a few days.

"Let me see," said Lady Nettleby, reading one of the tickets, "to-day is the seventh, and this is for the eleventh of September, that is next Tuesday; we will certainly be there."

At this moment a moaning noise was heard as of some person in extreme pain, and Lady Nettleby, who had been some moments listening, now rang her bell, and she inquired of the servant who answered it, "who was ill; and the cause of the running up and down stairs, and the reason of the bustle there appeared to be in the house.

"Susan is still ill, madam," replied the man.

"What is the matter with her," said Lady Nettleby.

"Don't know madam," replied the man, "Martha can inform your ladyship."

"Send in Martha directly," said her ladyship.

Martha came blushing and curtseying into the room.

"What is the matter with Susan?" inquired her ladyship.

"She is very bad, madam," said Martha.

"Bad, so I was before informed," cried Lady Nettleby with impatience, "I did not send for you to know if she was bad or not, I wish to know the cause of her ailment—what is the matter with her?"

"Madam, she is—she is in labour," said Martha, "I am afraid she will die?"

"Afraid she will die! the wretch, and what matters if she does," cried Lady Nettleby; in labour, the vile creature; do Mr. Ashton step up, and tell the servants who are with her, that it is my desire for her to be instantly removed; let some conveyance be procured, and away she shall go pack and package."

Mr. Ashton ran up to Susan's chamber, but soon came down again into the room where Lady Nettleby was sitting.

"The girl cannot be removed," he said, "a removal will cause her death—I will do what I can for her—humanity demands it," and Mr. Ashton again went up to Susan's chamber.

"What a fuss there is with such creatures," said Miss Maria, " if I was ma, out she should go, live or die."

"Madam, you are wrong, decidedly wrong," replied Mr. Leon, "I, who have studied the law, am fully aware of the danger of such a proceeding ; my Lady Nettleby, in case of the young woman's death, might be arraigned for man-slaughter, or woman-slaughter, which is one and the same thing, and the expense, trouble, and disgrace, and perhaps punishment such a proceeding would be liable to, would be most unpleasant, vexatious, and harassing to her ladyship. I assure you, my dear Miss, no persons have a greater dislike to law on their own accounts than the lawyers themselves and you will find I advise you for the best."

"I think, ma, you had better be advised by Mr. Leon," said Maria, " I'd let the wretch remain here for the present ; but I would make her confess who has caused her disgrace."

Barnaby, who had been looking through the window, whistling a dismal tune, turned sharply round to where Maria was standing, and he exclaimed with some warmth—"and pray, miss, what is it to you; why do you wish to know who has caused the poor girl's trouble ?"

"And pray, sir, why do you take the liberty of speaking so rudely to your sister, she has a right to inquire, and so have I ?—I will go up to the girl's chamber, and insist on knowing the name of her paramour," said Lady Nettleby, and she went up to Susan's chamber.

The poor girl had just given birth to a still born child, when her ladyship entered the room, and she was then in almost a dying state—but regardless of her situation, Lady Nettleby, with menace, demanded who was the father of the infant ?

"Oh do not ask me, madam," Susan faintly replied, "I cannot, indeed I cannot tell you."

"I will know," cried Lady Nettleby, " instantly tell me, base wretch, who is the father of your child? I have no doubt it is some married gentleman who visits here, and who your wanton arts have seduced; tell me, or it shall be the worse for you."

"Consider, madam said Mr. Ashton, "I beg you will consider."

"I will consider nothing," cried Lady Nettleby, "tell me, I again command you, who is the father of your child ?"

"I beg, lady Nettleby, you will leave this matter to me," said Mr. Ashton, "if you will go down stairs I will endeavour to find out what you wish to know ! but gentle means must be used, for she's in great danger."

Repeatedly Susan fainted after Lady Nettleby left the room ; but Mr. Ashton having ordered her a reviving cordial she became somewhat better; and she, to the repeated questions of Mr. Ashton, at length confessed that her young master was the father of her child, and that he, under a promise of marriage, had seduced her, and by that means caused her disgrace and shame.

"Oh! sir, let a messenger be sent to my poor father," she cried, " he lives but at Brentford, Martha knows the direction ; oh, let me see him before I die, for I know my time is fast approaching."

A shivering fit came on, convulsions followed, and before Mr. Ashton left the room, Susan was no more.

"She's dead," said Mr. Ashton, as he entered the room in which Lad Nettleby and her family were sitting. "She's dead; the poor girl is no more !"

"Susan dead," said Barnaby, "poor girl; poor girl; who would have thought it Oh, how suddenly she's cut off.—I love the girl, as I shall never love another: if I had thought she would have been taken ill so soon, I would have removed her.

"This sad affair is all owing to mother, who wishes me to marry my cousin who I have no fancy for; oh! how unfeeling, to want to turn the poor dying, creature out of doors.—Oh, you bitter, bitter woman," said Barnaby, casting a fierce look at his mother, as he snatched up his hat, and hurried out of the house.

"Mr. Nettleby is certainly the father of the babe," said Mr. Ashton, "Susan declared that before her death;—I must beg, madam, that you will, for humanity sake, govern your temper in future, before women in the situation of Susan, whose premature death, I verily believe, was hastened through the terror she had of your ladyship."

"You had better say at once I murdered the girl," cried Lady Nettleby. "Oh! was ever woman so ill-treated?" and Lady Nettleby fell into violent hysterics; this scene was too much for the feeling heart of Celeste, soon as she could with decency leave Lady Nettleby, whose fits continued some time, she retired to her chamber; ill, shocked, and harassed in mind.

"What deceit in Barnaby," thought Celeste, "to pretend love to me, when he himself, and that in my hearing, declared he loved Susan, and has no fancy for me."

"I am very sorry for poor Susan," she mentally said, "but glad on my own account; my father, I feel certain, when he is acquainted with what has passed, will not wish me to marry Barnaby, nor stay longer than I choose in London."

Barnaby, when he left home, hastened to his friend the Count Le Mar, to whom he related his grief respecting the death of Susan, and complaining of the avarice of his mother, who wished him to marry Celeste against his own inclination, because she would have a fortune of forty thousand pounds.

"Forty thousand pounds!" cried the Count Le Mar, " why I thought Miss Manby had no fortune—I understood her father was a man reduced in circum-stances."

"So he is," said Barnaby, "but it is old uncle Russell who has left her the money—he is not yet dead that I know of, but he is expected to die every day; he has made his will, and she's sure to have the money; but she's not herself aware of it, and my mother wished it at present kept sacred."

"And you will not have her," said the count.

"I will not," replied Barnaby, "and if I would, I don't think she'd have me, after this affair of Susan's."

"She's a devilish fine girl," said the count, "can't you speak a good word for me?"

"Not I;" replied Barnaby, "I mean to keep out of her way, for I suppose she'll look on me now like dirt; she's such a squeamish, coy, precise thing—in fact, I'm glad I'm rid of her. I have a good estate, then why should I sell myself for money? I am sure she'd not suit me, as I told mother. I might as well get a wife from the confectioners made of sugar and almonds.

"If you have a fancy for her, you can speak to mother about it, but for my part, I shan't interfere."

Lady Nettleby passed a most wretched night ; the exposure of her son to Celeste dwelt on her mind, and the money belonging to her uncle she now feared she never should have the pleasure of handling ; her host of duns too stood in terrible array before her.

"I will ask Maria for the loan of a thousand pounds," thought her ladyship, and that the first thing in the morning—she has it in her power to oblige me, and cannot refuse."

After the family had left the breakfast-table the next morning, Lady Nettleby begged to have a little conversation with Maria in her dressing-room.

Maria's colour rose to crimson at her mother's request, for Maria thought that her mother had by some means discovered a secret she did not wish known.

But when both ladies were seated in the dressing-room, Maria found that what her mother had to say was on a very different subject to what she at first had imagined.

"My dear Maria," said Lady Nettleby, " you know I have been at a very great expense since I have been in London ; I wished to keep high company, in order to form splendid and wealthy establishments for you and your sister—in short, I have gone far beyond my income.

"What I wish to say to you, Maria, is, that you will lend me the loan of one thousand pounds, for which I will pay you interest, the same as you now receive; the money may as well lay in my hands as Government's, and it will be doing me a service."

"La! ma, you are always short of money," cried Maria, "there is nothing on earth I so much hate as talking on money matters,—to-day I have a very particular

engagement; to-morrow is Sunday; Monday we go to the masquerade, so that I can say or do nothing in regard of your request until Tuesday."

"Then on Tuesday I may expect it," said Lady Nettleby.

"Oh, yes, yes, yes," said Maria, and she left the room.

Lady Nettleby's heart was now somewhat lightened, by the acquiescence of No. 12.

Maria, for with the sum she expected to receive from her daughter she intended to settle with some very troublesome creditors, who very much annoyed her.

Having procured the direction of Susan's father, she wrote the following letter, which was immediately sent off to Brentford.

To John Mayfield, Gosling Green.

"Mr. Mayfield.

"Your daughter Susan, who, I am very sorry I ever took into my service, is dead, in consequence of having given birth to a illegitimate child; she has by her base conduct rendered me most unhappy, and prevented the marriage of my son with a very amiable young lady of large fortune. I desire you will immediately come with a shell, and fetch away her corse, which hardly deserves Christian burial, and I must tell you, that you yourself deserves punishment for palming that lewd girl into a respectable family.

"G. Nettleby."

When Old Mayfield had received and read this letter, he fell back in his chair, and remained for some moments petrified with grief and surprise, when somewhat recovered—

"Susan dead!" he cried, "my child, the darling of my heart, no more—dead —in giving birth to an illegitimate child—impossible; I'll not believe it; was she not the most modest girl in the neighbourhood? My Lady Nettleby's the first place she ever had. Who dare call my child lewd?" and he banged his hand down on a table that stood near him, then tore his white locks, whilst the big tear rolled down his sun-burnt cheeks, no longer ruddy, but bleached with grief and agony."

"Susan, dead!" fell upon his quivering lips, in words rendered almost inarticulate by grief. "Susan, dead—all I had left to comfort me. Lewd; Susan, lewd; no, no, she has been basely betrayed. Oh! that I had not suffered her to leave Brentford; poor Susan, how pretty she looked when sitting at my cottage-door knitting. I think I see her now, feeding the blackbird of a summer's morning, modest and lovely as the snow-droop, and sweet as the opening rose; but her mistress says she was lewd, and does not deserve Christian burial. Oh! Susan, Susan! can it be a woman, and a mother, who so speaks of thee? The sabbath bells are chiming; and I was agoing to the House of God, which I never yet omitted on a sabbath-day. But my child's dead, and I must fetch her home; she shall lie by her mother, if I sell my little all to enable me to place her there." Mayfield again yielded to a flood of tears, then taking in his hand the stick he usually carried, when going a journey, with a grief-stricken heart, he fastened up his cottage-door, and set forward on his mournful journey to Kensington.

CHAPTER XXX.

"Her modest look the cottage might adorn,
Sweet as the primrose peeps beneath the thorn."   Goldsmith.

Heart-broken, old Mayfield wept over the corse of his late blooming daughter, "can this be my Susan," he said, "she, who was the comfort and the support of my age? Can this pale, colourless face, be my Susan's, her, whose cheeks were blooming as roses; poor girl, how pinched are thy features, and sunken are thy beauteous eyes; no more my child, wilt thou smile on thy poor father, nor greet him with endearing words, the heaviness of death is upon thee. Who brought this misery on thee, my child, who hath caused thy desolation and downfall?"

Mayfield was very urgent to see Lady Nettleby, but her ladyship would not see him; "I have had trouble enough with his girl," said her ladyship, "and I cannot be bored with the old man; there is what's coming to the old man of his daughter's wages," said her ladyship, as she gave Martha money. "Tell the old man," she continued, " to fetch away the girl's corse to-morrow morning, by six o'clock, and desire he will come with as much privacy, and as little noise as possible."

Without consolation, refreshment or being offered even to sit down, the poor broken-hearted father departed; and at an early hour, on the following morning, he caused to be borne from the house of Lady Nettleby, all that remained of the once blooming Susan.

The Count Le Mar, lost no time in seeing Lady Nettleby, with whom he begged to be indulged with half-an-hour's private conversation.

He told her ladyship of the love he bore her charming niece; declared that he was not at all swayed by interest, he himself having an immense fortune, so that fortune was with him by no means a consideration.

" 'Tis true," said the count, " that Mr. Nettleby told me in confidence, that Miss Manby will have forty thousand pounds; but to convince your ladyship," continued the count, " of the purity and disinterestedness of my love, of the charming Celeste, I am willing to give up one quarter-part of her fortune to your ladyship, for your good offices in promoting the match."

"Indeed, I made up my mind for my son to marry Miss Manby," replied Lady Nettleby, " but there has been an awkward affair happened, of which, perhaps, he has told you.

" 'Tis most unfortunate; for Celeste has such refined and delicate notions, that I am sure she will never be induced to look over it; and in that case, count, as I am sure you will make my niece a good husband, and on account of the generous offer you have made me, I shall certainly do all in my power to promote your interest with my niece. But how am I to be secure? perhaps when you are married, you will forget your promise."

" Do you doubt my honour, madam ?" said the count.

" Oh, by no means," cried Lady Nettleby, " you might not recollect—many things might occur."

" My Lady Nettleby, so great is my love for your niece, that I think no sacrifice too great so that I can obtain her ; to prove the sincerity of what I say, I will immediately secure to you the sum of five thousand pounds, in any way you please ; I will even give you my bill at three months ; and if more satisfactory to your ladyship, my friend, Mr. Synegall, who is the son of the richest man in the country, will endorse the bill, or bills; perhaps they might be more negotiable.',

" Celeste will have forty thousand pounds," replied Lady Nettleby, " you offered me one quarter of that sum."

" 'Tis not money I value," said the count, " the bills shall be given for ten thousand, how would you like them drawn ?"

" But you are sure she'll have you," said Lady Nettleby.

" Oh, I have no fear of that," said the count, " if your ladyship will but second my views, and allow me to carry on the seige in my own way, it is all I require. I must use a little management, for Celeste, I know, has got it into her head, that I am no other than some Mr. Monteagle, with whom she was formerly acquainted ; and the obstinate little puss will not relinquish her opinion, notwithstanding every person who knows any thing, knows that I am a foreigner; through this foolish idea, I know the lovely Celeste is prejudiced against me; but when once a lady has got a crotchet in her head, it is in vain to try to get it out ; as this is the case, I must act on my own plans. Therefore, madam, if you will get the stamps ready to-morrow morning, I will sign, and I know Mr. Synegall will endorse them.

Both the Count Le Mar and Lady Nettleby parted in high spirits ; " I shall be now quite comfortable in money-matters," thought her ladyship, " what with the thousand pounds I shall get from Maria, and the ten thousand I shall have from the count, those sums will enable me to get rid of those odious duns, and pass another winter in town with élite."

The following morning Lady Nettleby was much engaged with the Count Le Mar, and Mr. Synegall in drawing, singing, and endorsing the bills that were to be given to her ladyship.

So busy were the parties, that the absence of Celeste was unnoticed, who that day sat two whole hours in her room undisturbed, a thing which had never before happened since Celeste had resided with her aunt.

Maria and Juliana had gone to the masquerade warehouse to order dresses for the following evening.

Lady Nettleby wished the Count Le Mar to attend Celeste to the masquerade, but the count declined doing so.

"You must leave me to my own operations," he said, "and I beg your ladyship will not name me as a lover to your charming niece;—by so doing you would ruin my designs."

"Well, count, I shall not interfere," replied Lady Nettleby, "you, no doubt are a skilful general in love affairs, and know how to act better than I can direct you."

The conversation was all now concerning the masquerade.

"I shall go dressed as the Goddess Diana," said Juliana, "and would you believe it, ma, that Maria is going in only a plain domino; what dress do you go in, ma?"

"I shall go in the dress of a sultana," said Lady Nettleby.

"And what dress have you fixed on, Celeste?" inquired Juliana.

"I'd much rather remain at home, if you will excuse my going," said Celeste

"That we certainly will not," said Juliana, "what dress will you go in?"

"Oh, the dress of Venus, to be sure; that is the most appropriate dress for Celeste," said Lady Nettleby.

"Your ladyship's pleased to banter me," said Celeste, "but if I do go, I will go in a plain domino."

The party now separated for the night.

But the thoughts of Celeste was too much disturbed to permit of her sleeping she thought on the deceit of Mr. Nettleby, the unhappy fate of poor Susan, her father, and her lover. It was a lovely night, and recalled to the mind of Celeste the last meeting she had had with Durant, who, although the hour was near midnight, had left his father's house, and come across the heath, near where the dwelling of Celeste was situated, to take a second farewell of her he so loved.

And Celeste had, unperceived, left her father's house at that late hour; secure in the innocency of her own heart, to take one more fond farewell of Durant, whom she now thought on more than ever.—In a low and plaintive voice, she sung the following words :—

> "I think on thee at midnight hour,
> When all around are sunk in sleep;
> To my lone chamber then I go,
> To think upon thee love and weep.
>
> "For it was that hour when last we met,
> When glittering moon-beams fell around,
> In lengthened shadows o'er our path,
> And on the yellow furze crown'd ground.
>
> "When e'er I wander near the rill,
> Across the field, or near the tree,
> Where you and I so oft have sat,
> Oh then, my love I think on thee."

"How different is this situation from Cornwall," thought Celeste; "how limited and confined are the views, no distant mountain tops, nor forest trees waving with the wind are here to be seen."

She thought she heard a sound beneath her window as if some persons were discoursing in whispers.

Celeste listened, and to her surprise distinguished the voice of Maria and Mr. Synegall. Love, from what Celeste could hear was the subject of their discourse and the masquerade she heard mentioned—"this private meeting is surely un known to Lady Nettleby," thought Celeste, "how strange for Mr. Synegall to be in the house at this late hour, when every other visitor has left it; there certainly must be some clandstine correspondence between him and Maria; but it is not for me to interfere or name the subject."

CHAPTER XXXI.

"Hence vain deluding joys,
The brood of folly." MILTON.

THE masquerade was numerously attended; there were Jews and Gentiles, sultans and sailors, and, in short, almost every character that can be mentioned; Lady Nettleby waddled a fat sultana, and Juliana looked a very sprightly Diana.

There were two persons there who much anoyed Celeste; for they followed her wherever she went; one of these persons was a short, corpulent man, in the dress of a Jewish rabbi, the other was also a stout man, muffled up in a domino.

The manner of these persons perplexed Celeste extremely, nor could she conjecture who they were, when the rabbi was at her elbow, and just going to speak to her, the domino would start from behind a column and prevent him; but at length to the joy of Celeste, the domino disappeared, and she had reason to think he had left the room.

But the rabbi still followed her; at length, when Lady Nettleby was much engaged in talking to a Spaniard, who, it appeared, had discovered her ladyship; the rabbi took the opportunity of speaking to Celeste.

"What, popsy!" he said, "have I found you out?—Ah, you little sly rogue. But you served me a sad trick in Kensington Gardens—you pushed me down, and then ran away. Oh, fie, popsy, you are a wag, but I forgive you;—asked Lady Nettleby's consent to court you, but she refused—she wants me herself, but it won't do;—come give me that pretty hand."

Celeste turned away.

"Oh, cruel popsy!" cried Mr. Cubby, "you ought to love me; see what trouble I take on your account—come here like a rabbi, and all to please you— but you don't like the dress of a rabbi, popsy, I know you don't—and no wonder. —Oh, if I had but hired the dress of an Apollo, I should have pleased you, I know I should—although my knees are somewhat stiff, I would have contrived to have knelt before you, and have sung in character—

"Oh! lovely nymph, assuage my anguish."

That would have been the thing, popsy—the very thing to have made an impression on your heart; I should have looked well in that dress."

"Indeed, sir, I think the dress you now wear, much more suitable," said Celeste.

"You think me too stout, and too old, for an Apollo I suppose," said Mr. Cubby; "but let me tell you, Celeste, stout as I may be, you will never get a truer lover; however, I am glad that it is all up between you and that fox-hunting spark.'"

"And who told you that, sir?" said Celeste.

"Who? why the same person that told me how to find you out;—a piece of gold will buy secrets, popsy."

At this moment, the Count Le Mar entered the room; he went up to Celeste, and told her he had something of importance to communicate; he led Celeste to a recess in the room—

When he said, "I was with Mr. Nettleby, at the house of his mother, when a man came on horseback to fetch you;—your father is very much indisposed, at the house of some person at Highgate;—the moment I heard this intelligence, I came to acquaint you, being told some particulars in your dress by which I might discover you, by my Lady Nettleby's maid."

"Oh! Heaven protect me!" cried Celeste, "my father must be ill, indeed, or he would not have sent for me at this hour;—Oh Heaven!" she cried, as she looked at her watch ; "it is nearly eleven o'clock.—Oh ! he is very ill—perhaps dead."

"Oh, no, no," cried the Count Le Mar, "do not think that. I have brought a coach to the door, and will myself attend you to Highgate, as it is too late; —sit down, my dear miss, whilst I inform Lady Nettleby of what has happened —let me see, she's in the dress of a sultana, I think."

"There she is talking to that gentleman," said Celeste, "near Juliana, who is dressed as Diana."

Lady Nettleby, seemed to be quite shocked, when she heard of the sudden illness of Mr. Manby, and said, "she was extremely glad that the count would accompany Celeste, as the hour was late, and the road lonely."

"With a heavy heart, Celeste put on her silk wrapping cloak, to hide her domino, and the bonnet Lady Nettlebys thoughtful servant had sent her, she then stepped into the coach, accompanied by the Count Le Mar.

CHAPTER XXXII.

By a lone wall, a lonelier column rears,
A grey and grief-worn aspect of old days,
'Tis the last remnant, of the wreck of years,
And looks as with a wild bewildered gaze,
Of one to stone converted, by amaze,
Yet with consciousness, and there it stands,
Making a marvel, that it not decays.   BYRON.

THE horses tore on with great speed, in a direction for Saint Giles-in-the-Fields nor stopped until they came to the rise of the hill, near Highgate, and was close to the (at that time famed.) Holly Hedge, which extended about a quarter of a mile in length, growing against a high wall, on which the top of these holly tree rested ; but at the bottom of these tree, that is to say near the roots, there was a vacancy between them and the wall, and there robbers used to lurk, and spring on the unwary traveller.

About an hundred yards distant from this place, and yet more on the steep o the hill, stood a public-house, know by the sign of the Fox ; not far from tha place, to the right of the road, stood the ancient mansion to which the count wa hastening; he alighted, and pulled with violence the ponderous bell-handle.

Again he rang, when the sonorous sound vibrated fearfully on the stillness of th night.

An old woman in her night-cap, and with no other covering than an old cloak answered the summons ; as she unlocked the massive gate, she cried in a voice, t which the croaking of a raven was melody.

"Oh, Denish ! and is it you, and who in the devil's name have ye brough wid ye ?

Celeste clung to the arm of the count. alarmed at the fiend-like appearance o the old woman, and terrified at the look of the old building whose high enclosur of wall in front of the mansion, and the thickly-set embowered trees gave it most gloomy appearance.

It was a place, the fanciful and superstitious mind might imagine was deserte by mortality, and left to the possession of demons and unquiet spirits.

And what surprised Celeste was, that her father should be at this place, as sh never heard him speak of being acquainted with any person at Highgate.

Terrified, she faintly said in a hurried but tremulous voice—"how is Mi Manby ?—how is my father ?"

"Your father, honey," replied the old woman, "and how should I know any thing about him."

"I beg you will not speak to her, Miss Manby," said the Count Le Mar, "she can give you no information; go in," he said, speaking to the old woman, "and send the old man with more lights."

As he said this, he snatched the candle the old woman held in her hand, and himself fastened up the cumberous iron gate in front of the enclosure.

The Count Le Mar handed Celeste into a spacious parlour, wainscoted with dark oak, ornamented with heavy carved work, in flowers and figures, illustrative of many parts of Scripture.

He drew forward a seat for Celeste to sit down by an ancient table, on which he placed the candle, the legs of this table were carved in the form of monks in the act of prayer, bearing on their heads the heavy top of dark-coloured marble.

Celeste would not sit down; "where is my father, sir?" she said, "pray lead me to him.—Wherefore is this delay."

The Count Le Mar drew forward another chair, and he placed it near the one he had placed by the table for Celeste.

He seated himself, and taking the hand of Celeste, said, "pray let me intreat you to be seated; do not put yourself out of the way, it will be of no avail."

"Oh! pray let me see my father!" cried Celeste. "In which room shall I find him?"

"Not in this house," said the count.

"Why then was I brought here?" cried Celeste. "Oh! tell me; in pity tell me, where is my father?"

"Safe, and in Cornwall I trust," answered the count. "Forgive me, my dear Celeste, for having deceived you; but the deception was caused by love. I madly love you, but I feared my suit would be denied. I would not risk a disappointment, and by stratagem I have gained your lovely person; but think not I mean to act dishonourably by you; no, to-morrow morning a clergyman shall unite us, and when we are married, we will go into Cornwall to visit your father, who ,I know will congratulate you on the occasion, and be proud to see his darling child, the Countess Le Mar."

"That I never shall be," replied Celeste. "I beg, I intreat, that when morning dawns, you will suffer me to depart."

"What! that you may expose me, and bring the vengeance of your father upon me. No, no, I again repeat, never shall you quit these walls, but as my wife"

Celeste could no longer bear up; she sunk fainting in the chair, beside the Count Le Mar, who was rather alarmed at Celeste's livid and death-like countenance. She several times fainted, for when she recovered her consciousness and looked around her, she again relapsed into insensibility.

After some time she became composed, and the first object beheld when she recovered, was the old woman who opened the gate on her first arrival standing before her, and holding burnt feathers to her nose in order to revive her.

The old woman now appeared more like a human being, having divested herself of her old red cloak; she now stood before Celeste decently attired.

"And are ye now better me liddy?" said the old woman, "don't be frightened honey, you are in good hands; the count, my master, is a gentleman, and he has a power of estates in Killarney, and he will make you happy as the day is long."

The Count Le Mar was at this time pacing the room in evident uneasiness.

Coming up to Celeste, he said, "compose yourself Miss Manby, I beg you will compose yourself, 'tis useless struggling against your fate, mine you must be; never shall you quit these walls until you are my bride. Come, Judith," continued the count, "prepare the supper you will find in the parcel I brought with me in the coach; a chicken ready dressed, and a bottle of wine."

Celeste could not be prevailed on by the count to taste the chicken, or drink a glass of the wine; she felt as if her heart was dying within her, and she could scarcely support herself in the chair in which she was sitting.

But hope whispered "you will escape—sink not under your injuries."

"God will protect me," she inwardly said, "I will not give way to despai
she now wetted her parched lips with the wine the count had poured out
her.

Celeste begged the count would suffer her to retire, as she felt both fatig
and ill.

The room to which Celeste was shown to pass the night in, was hung with an
representing Herod's cruelty; but so old and faded by time, that the figures co
be but imperfectly traced.

The furniture of the bedstead was of dark purple silk velvet; and from
lofty tester drooped an enormous plume of black ostrich feathers, causing the
to appear more like a bier for the dead, than a resting place for the living.

The gloomy appearance of the apartment caused a shuddering sensation
awe to run through the frame of Celeste; she requested the old woman wo
place the lamp on the hearth, and leave it there for the night.

Tired, and harassed both in body and mind, yet unable to close her eyes
sleep, she seated herself near the window, and opened it—all was still dark
drear, the moon had sunk beneath clouds of sable;—but by the light of a
twinkling stars she could perceive that the back part of the house lay open to
fields and copses whose towering tops she could see waving in the breeze, wh
the swept over their heads in loud gusts, threatening a coming storm.

All was dark, lone and silent, except at intervals; the barking of some fox
whose dens were not far off and whose deep toned voices sounded most dism
on the stillness of the night and the moaning of the wind which was rush
with violence through the branches of the trees, but added to the dreariness of
scene.

Celeste still sat at the window, and tears of bitter anguish, traced each ot
down her pale cheek, she thought on her lover, her father, and the thrall and mis
into which the villany of the Count Le Mar had brought her.

Overcome by her feelings, she could hardly support herself, and she arose fr
her seat at the window, with the intention of lying down; but when she looked
the bier like appearance of the bed, she felt an awe steal over her, and she ag
seated herself at the window.

The few stars that before were visible, had now disappeared, and dark gather
clouds overspread the sky, emitting flashes of vivid lightning, and loudly rolled
thunder in long and reiterated peals, threatening as it were to beat down, a
crumble creation into its original nothingness.

The rays of her lamp now gleamed but with a faint and uncertain light, leavi
her at times in almost utter darkness, but the lightning's glare at times illumin
apartment.

Celeste could no longer witness the war of elements, she arose, and approach
the bed, thinking she would lie down.

Fearing to encounter the sight of the dark plumes over the bedstead, she sh
her eyes, and felt her way along the room, until she had reached the bedstea
where she knelt down.

"Oh! God deliver me," she cried, "protect me from the storm, and from t
hands into which I have fallen." Somewhat more comforted and encouraged, s
arose and laid down on the bed.

Her lamp had now gone out, but Celeste hoped to get some sleep, and she kne
it could not now want many hours to day-light; soon she heard the church clo
heavily sound the time,

Half-past two; at that moment a more vivid flash than any she had yet see
illumined the chamber, and she perceived the form of a tall female, standing ne
her bed.

The momentary view she had of this person, only enabled her to perceive th
she was of a tall figure, and dressed in white, with a very pale complexion an
flaxen hair.

This person, Celeste thought she had seen before, but who she was, or where sh had seen her, Celeste could not recollect, and how she had gained admittance into her chamber, was a mystery to Celeste, for she had locked the door ; but Celeste hoped again to see her, for she flattered herself, that the lady might be induced by entreaty to aid the escape of her, Celeste.

At length the storm died away, and nature again resumed her unruffled quietude.

The sun arose beautifully, shining amidst clouds of burnished gold, and vegetation, freshened by the rain that had fallen during the night, appeared in yet more verdant beauty.

Celeste for a moment forgot her troubles ; for a moment forgot her fears, as she looked from her chamber window on the surrounding scenery.

In consequence of the very elevated situation of the house, there was a very fine view of the country for many miles round ; and in the valleys nigh, the lambkins were sporting round their dams, whilst in the copses, the blackbird and linnet were singing their jocund lay.

No. 13.

The terrace walks, beneath her window, were edged with the most beautiful shrubs, and flowers of luxuriant growth, whose charming variety of hues were intermingled with each other, unchecked by the hand of man, growing wild and profuse in the bounty of nature, forming a wilderness of sweets, like another Eden.

A tap at Celeste's door caused her to start; she left the window, and when she had opened the door of her chamber, she saw the old woman standing before her.

"Breakfast is ready, and my master is waiting your coming, my lady," said the old woman; "shall I show you into the breakfast-room?"

Celeste hesitated; "yes, I will go down," thought she, "whilst the count behaves with respect to me, it were best not to offend him; if I do, I shall have less chance of escaping."

Celeste followed the old woman into a very antique chamber; the compartments, as well as the floor, were of dark cedar, exquisite, but heavily carved; here the Count Le Mar was sitting, awaiting the coming of Celeste.

The count arose when Celeste entered the room, and he handed her to the breakfast-table; but few words during this meal passed between them; the count seemed in deep thought and rather in low spirits, although he assumed a cheerful air.

Celeste did not name the subject nearest her heart—namely, to beg that the count would let her return into Cornwall, for she feared the mention of that subject might lead to some unpleasant discussion, and that she most wished to avoid.

But Celeste intended most diligently to watch for an opportunity to make her escape, and such opportunity she trusted the Almighty would give her.

After breakfast was ended, the count proposed showing Celeste over the grounds at the back of the house; fearing to offend him she did not object, and she suffered the count to lead her down the high flight of steps at the back of the house; these steps led from the house to the terrace, edged with the most beautiful shrubs and flowers.

Crossing this terrace, there was another flight of steps that led into a beautiful lawn—after crossing the lawn they descended another flight of steps, which led into a grove of high and thickly planted trees.

For when at the extreme rise of Highgate Hill, on which this house stood, the descent is so very steep that the owner had an opportunity of indulging his taste, in the laying out of his ground.

From the grove, a gate led into the garden which was on more level ground; here, too, as well as on the terrace, bloomed every flower beautiful to the eye, and sweet to the sense; and there were trees cut in the most grotesque and fantastic forms and figures, according to the fashion of the time in which the mansion was erected.

"What think you of the mansion of my forefathers, my lovely Celeste?" said the count, "is it not most delightfully situated? that hill," he said, pointing to an eminence, "not far distant, is called Traitors' Hill, it was there that some good Catholics stood, on account of the survey they could there take of London, and expected to see the daring exploit of Guido Vaux crowned with success—and that the Parliament House and the members thereof, would have been blown as high as yon silvery clouds. On that height they could well have viewed them; but through too much humanity their scheme was frustrated;—Guido was taken—and those good Catholics who stood on that hill to survey the destruction of the heretics were followed; but they would not be taken—they defended themselves like men, and were left bleeding corses on the green sward."

"There are certainly some very fine views here," said Celeste, "and the garden walks being of such steep descent, causes them to be most interestingly beautiful."

"And none other but yourself shall be mistress here," replied the count, "when we are married, I will have the house beautified and new furnished. In the bed in which you slept last night, royalty hath reposed on—yes, beneath that plume of black feathers, hath Queen Mary often lain. My ancestor was a man most zealous in his religion and an agent of Queen Mary's, and him she often visited here. He was a mild and charitable man to those of his own persuasion, but for heretics, he felt no pity. Many for the crime of heresy have been brought here and confined in dungeons that are beneath this house. There hath the cry of pain and the groan of anguish issued, there hath the flesh been torn from the quivering bone with red-hot pincers, there hath a heavy stone been laid on the bosom of the contumacious, when the sufferer hath cried out,—

'Oh! suffer me to breathe; stop not the respiration God hath given me; remove the stone—I faint—I die.'

Celeste turned pale as a corse at the horrid recital; "and was not the stone removed?" she faintly inquired, "was not mercy shown them?"

"But in a few instances, I believe," replied the count, "they would not recant, they died in their heresy, their blood was on their own heads; but we will not talk on circumstances that occured so long back; we will now talk of what is to come, when you are my bride. Say, Celeste, shall a clergyman this morning unite us?"

"Oh, no," cried Celeste, "I must see my father, I beg and entreat Count Le Mar, that you will first let me go to Cornwall, and hear what my father says to your request; indeed, it is useless for you to mention the subject of marriage to me, whilst I am here detained a prisoner."

"And a prisoner you will be, until you are my bride," exclaimed the count, "remember madam, you are in my power."

"I do not wish to be hurried into an act that is to end but with life," said Celeste.

"You shall not be hurried, name your own day, but let it be an early one, say this day week, will you promise me then."

"I cannot promise anything until I have seen my father," replied Celeste.

Rage now sparkled in the eyes of the Count Le Mar, "you think to deceive and escape me?" he with vehemence exclaimed, "but mark me well, madam, never shall you quit these walls, until you are my wife. I swear by all the host of Heaven, by all I most value on earth, and by the hope of salvation, never to suffer you to quit these walls until you are my wife. No, Celeste, mine thou art and mine thou shalt be. Was the whole artillery of Heaven levelled against me, and the earth convulsed was to open beneath my feet, I would sink down the yawning gulf with thee, Celeste, rather than escape without thee. I lay my hand and fortune at your feet, then do not perversely thwart my wishes, if so, I warn you, you'll repent it and cause me to lay the hands of violence upon you."

"In the grave you cannot persecute me," cried Celeste, "nor lay hands of violence upon me." Then falling on her knees, she cried, "Oh Heaven, forgive me! nor impute to me as a sin, the act which this man's cruelty may force me to commit."

At these words, the Count Le Mar turned of a deadly paleness; "contemplate suicide," he cried, "and that for no other reason than a wish to avoid becoming the wife of a gentleman of birth and fortune who adores you—but mark me well, madam," he said, whilst his eyes flashed fire, "if you dare harm yourself my disappointment shall not go unavenged. Here, would I bring your father, and he should suffer for your fault, what others have done for their heresy; beneath this house, as I before told you, are dungeons, where reigns eternal night in those dark shades would I place your father—where no footstep could approach—no human sound meet his ear; there, where to him, even the howling of the winds and the beating of the waves would be melody, for their sound would give him hope that he had not yet passed from the earth as the gloom of his subterraneous abode and the bones and the corses there left rotting in putridity, would intimate; and when he had been there a time new horrors should await him—the heavy torturing stone is yet here, the press, the skull-cap, and the thumb-screws."

"Oh, sir! talk not thus," replied Celeste, "unless you wish to see me expire at your feet,—my father suffer, oh, no! God will protect him," and Celeste turned of a death-like paleness.

"And if not your fault, I will protect him," replied the Count, "my fortune he shall share with me ; but of you I will not by any means be defrauded. When I hear you talk of the grave, you irritate me to madness, and cause me to say things that none but a madman would utter.   Come, my gentle love," continued the count, " you must forgive, what I in my passion have said ; come, let me lead you to yonder wood-bine bower," and he pointed to an arbour which stood at the end of the terrace most delightfully situated, and overlooking a great extent of country.

But Celeste had nearly fainted.

Seeing the state she was in, the Count took her in his arms, carried her into the house, and left her in care of the old woman, and she soon recovered:

At dinner they again met, when the count was all submission and kindness; after the cloth was removed and he was taking his wine, he said,

"You, no doubt, are surprised at my owning this mansion Celeste, as I am a foreigner ; but this house belonged to my great-grandfather, who, as I before said, was a great favourite with Queen Mary.   Adela, that gentleman's daughter and grandmother, went to France, and there married my grandfather, who was a Frenchman.   My father was born in France ; I have great estates there left me by my father,—of course, I can do no other than consider myself a foreigner.   But what is country, what is fortune to love, were you poor without friend or home, you would be the same to me, Celeste.   Oh ! how often have I wished you here; I had penned you an invitation, but was afraid to send it, knowing you were so loved and admired, I feared a refusal—by your leave I will sing you the invitation."

Celeste bowed her head, and the count, who had a fine voice, sung the following words :—

> " Meet me in the woodbine bower,
> And there we'll pass the sultry hour,
> And roses sweet, and lilies there,
> Shall all combine to please my fair.
>> Roses fade and lilies wither,
>> Summer's bloom won't last for ever,
>> Flowery wreaths will soon decay,
>> Haste, Celeste, haste away.
>
> For thee, a table have 1 spread,
> With sweet grapes and nectarines red ;
> Then come, Celeste, come away,
> Nor mar my hopes by cold delay.
>> Roses fade, and lilies wither,
>> Summer's bloom won't last for ever,
>> Flowery wreaths will soon decay,
>> Haste, Celeste, haste away."

"Had I made known the love I bear you," said the count, "you would have been on your guard, and most likely would not have accompanied me here.   I much lament, Celeste," he continued, that business of great importance calls me into the city this evening ; before I go, I will bring you some books to amuse you during my absence ; there is a fine library in an adjoining apartment ;" so saying, the count fetched in a number of books, they were mostly on religious subjects, but amongst them she found one or two romances.

"I am sorry, I cannot do otherwise than confine you to your chamber during my absence," said the count ; " I fear by some cross accident, to lose you—and until you are my wife you must submit to be a prisoner ;—say but the word, and this moment you are free."

"I will remain in my chamber," said Celeste, to which she went ; the old woman locked the door, and took the key ; and very soon Celeste heard the trampling of a horse's hoofs and she knew that the count had left the house.

Celeste sat at her chamber window, and she watched the setting sun, then the gathering clouds deepening into night ; a dread and heaviness was on her spirits, and in despair she threw herself on her bed, and in a flood of tears she bewailed her misery.

"Oh, God! be merciful to me," she cried, and deliver me from this thrall;—I cannot marry this man—this Count Le Mar, he is my aversion, my detestation. Oh! Durant, can I ever forget thee? were I in my grave, and beyond the reach of this man, happy would it be for me;—but then he has threatened to bring my poor father here and make him suffer;—1 must not die, I must bear my load of affliction. "Oh!" continued Celeste, "had I but the wings of a bird, how would I wing my gladsome way into Cornwall, and leave this place for ever.'"

Restless, she arose from her bed; her face was deluged in tears which she had long suppressed in the presence of the count, but now in the privacy of her chamber, they flowed without restraint.

With extreme uneasiness of mind, Celeste paced her apartment; and she earnestly hoped that the lady she had seen on the preceding night, would again enter her chamber; for from a momentary glance she had of the countenance of the lady, she thought her of a mild and melancholy character, and a person likely to be moved by the affliction of another.

But where, or by what means she had entered, Celeste could not imagine; she had searched her chamber, but could perceive no outlet by which the lady could have entered.

She looked from her window, but it was again a dark and moonless night; she heard the church clock heavily sound the hour of eleven, and at that moment, the report of a pistol sounded as if let off at no great distance; and soon she heard the sound of feet crossing from the grove to the lawn, and from the lawn to the terrace, and then into the house.

The persons then came up stairs and entered the room on the same floor as the chamber Celeste occupied.

Terrified, Celeste heard their noisy bawling for Judith, which was the name of the old woman.

"Have patience," cried the old man, whose voice Celeste knew; "have patience —you may call the old woman long enough—she is in her cups, as usual, and you might as well attempt to wake the dead, as wake her."

"Then you must get up yourself, old boy," said one of the men. "Get us a light, and bring in the brandy and horns with you."

When the old man came into the room where the men were sitting, they inquired what he had got in the house; and they were told by the old man that he had nothing but some bacon.

"Well, be quick and fry some of that," said one of the men.

"And how long will it be before Denish comes home?" inquired the old man.

"That's more than I can tell," answered one of them; "we left him going to the gambling-house, where he expects to make a good booty."

Celeste continued to listen; she heard the old man quit the apartment, as she supposed, to dress the supper.

Soon as the old man had left the apartment one of the men emptied the contents of a purse on the table, and then counted out the pieces of gold; "there's five for you, Tom, and five for me," said the counter; "I thought the old fellow had more— I run a pretty good risk for it, and thought once he'd have been too many for me ; but when you came up, your pop soon settled him; he's quiet enough now, and lies still like a good boy, where we have placed him;" he then began singing—

"Now, deep, deep, he sleeps in his watery bed,
Surrounded by osier, grass, nettles, and sedge,
And the willow, the willow doth droop o'er his head."

And, responded his companion in a voice, gruff and unearthly—

"And the frogs croak his requiem
Amongst the green sedge."

The old man now brought in the supper, and when the meal was finished the ruffians again resumed their discourse.

" Have you heard what luck Jack Leary has had ?" said one of the men.

" I heard something about it," said the other, " but I don't know the particulars."

" Well, then, I will tell you," said the first speaker, " you must know he fell in company with a farmer at an inn at Reading, who had sold a large quantity of hay and grain ; of the cash he had received for these things Jack meant to ease him ; but the farmer went home in company with several of his neighbours who had been to the market to dispose of their stock also.

" The odds was too great. Jack found it would not do, but the gold made his mouth water, as I may say," continued the man, " and he determined if possible to be possessed of it.

" He watched the farmer home and lurked about the neighbourhood for some time, considering how he should act to get the booty.

" After long waiting about he saw an old lame beggar hobbling along ; a thought struck Jack, he followed the old man, and offered to exchange his clothes for the beggar's.

" ' I wish to have a frolic, father,' said Jack, ' it will be a profitable exchange for you.'

' Glad to exchange his tatters for a good suit of clothes, the beggar struck the bargain, and he hobbled off as soon as the exchange was made, fearing lest Jack should alter his mind.

' Jack, who is, you know, a smart fellow, must have cut a queer figure in the beggar's clothes ; for the old man was very short, and Jack you know is very tall: he had an old hat with the crown beat in, and a patch over one eye, and the beggar's wallet at his back, without shoes or stockings, he went up quivering and quaking to the farm-house door ; singing with a very pitiful face,—

' Famished with hunger, and fainting with thirst,
Bare-footed 1 wander through rain and through dust,
With my wallet hanging empty behind me.

' Seeing his pitable figure, the farmer's daughters were melted by compassion, wretched as he looked, they took him into the house, and sat victuals and drink before him. Jack's eyes were more employed in looking about him, than on the victuals before him ; he was eating his meal in the kitchen, adjoining it was a parlour, the door was open, and there Jack saw a desk, the key was in it, and there the farmer had hastily thrown his cash, for he was in haste to be gone to his club, held at the sign of the Jolly Beggar, nor did he in his hurry stop to take the key with him. The farmer's daughters, who were thoughtless young girls, and not expecting that the beggar was a thief, went up stairs, where the eldest was busily employed in writing a letter to her lover, in the wording of which, she was assisted by her sister. Soon as Jack saw all safe, he made himself master of the cash, then ran down a lane, by the side of the house, and after jumping over several ditches, and crossed two or three fields, he found himself in a lane, that led to Dorchester.

' Out of breath he sat down for a moment, but soon he took to his heels again, for he well knew, that if the money was missed, there would be a hue and cry raised against him ; and he thought his safest way would be, to walk on as fast as he could towards London. Jack kept walking on in by-ways and green lanes, for he feared to walk the public road.

' And hard would he have been put to it for food, had he not have taken the precaution to put in his pocket some of the bread and fat pork given by the farmer's daughters.

' Jack intended when he reached London, to hide himself in some bye place until night, when, under the cover of darkness, he meant to go to Westminster to Bill Turner's and get some clothes.

' But a lucky incident turned up for Jack ; a tailor was hurrying down the lane through which Jack was passing, with a suit of clothes tied up in a bundle.

'The tailor seeing a man of no very prepossessing appearance crouched down in an angle of the road, became much alarmed, and quaking with fear, cried, 'halloo! who are you?'"

"Who am I, you vagabond," cried Jack, 'what do you mean by that? I'll soon let you know who I am; what bundle have you got there; something you have stolen I suppose? Deliver it up to me; what! do you hesitate?' and Jack gave the tailor such a drive on the head, that it stunned him, and down he fell flat as a flounder,

' Jack took the bundle, and ran on with it for some miles without stopping; at length he sat down, for he thought himself safe, nor in danger of pursuit.—When Jack opened the bundle, he found it contained a complete suit of clothes, he put them on, and they fitted him to a nicety, and in safety he got home with his booty.' "

"Well, he was a lucky dog," said the other voice, " I think begging is a good introduction, I mean to adopt it myself."

"Did you hear of the quantity of plate May got the other day at Henley on Thames; and how he managed to get it?"

"No," replied the other, " I heard nothing of that."

"I will tell you then," said his companion, " May, you know has a handsome face, and such a mild countenance, that he would pre-possess any one in his favour,—well, he heard that there was a great deal of family plate at the house of Sir Thomas Willoby, and he heard likewise that the family were from home; what does May do, but as soon as the thunderstorm was over, which happened on the very night that he went to Henley, for the express purpose of doing the robbery."

"What, as I said before, does May do, but begin singing in a plaintive voice the following words,—right before the house of Sir Thomas Willoby :—

" Though the thunder is hushed, and lightning no longer
Illumeth the river with its rays of light,
And Nature seems slumbering in peaceful serenity,
Nor wild rising storms doth the traveller affright.
But chill blows the wind on the mountains;
I am faint, and my garments soaked through,
Then refuse not to shelter a traveller,
Whose prayers shall be offered for you."

' The servants of Sir Thomas Willoby were much taken with May, and they let him come into the kitchen to refresh himself, where they were much pleased with his discourse, and felt so much for the misfortunes of the gentleman, as he styled himself; for May pretended that he had been plundered of a large sum of money which he had received at Oxford for the sale of a house.

' Indeed, sir, we pity you,' said the servants, 'and if agreeable to you to stay to-night, we will make you up a bed, for the family are from home; you can set out as soon in the morning as you please; and if you will accept it, we will contribute to raise a small sum to bear your expenses home.' "

'May thanked them, and said, he would ' gladly accept their kind offer, and stay till morning.' The evening was spent in jollity; for the butler furnished the servants with wine, and requisites to make a good bowl of punch into the bargain.

' May has a good voice, and he greatly contributed to the harmony of the evening. After supper, he was shown to a good bed, but he would not close his eyes, fearing that if he once fell asleep, he should not awake until morning. Well, soon as all the house was quiet, May arose, and forced the butler's pantry; he found a large bag, in which he put the plate, then safely opened a door that led to the lawn, and escaped safe with his booty.

The potent effect of the brandy now began to operate on the spirits of the men, they began singing the most obscene songs, swearing and using expressions that made Celeste tremble. At length she heard them stagger into another apartment, where she supposed they slept, but no sleep visited the eyes of Celeste; she thought not of going to bed, but remained sitting at her window.

She heard the church clock strike four, and soon, to her joy, she beheld some streaks of light, announcing the coming of morn.

Again the church clock sounded—it struck the hour of five. About an hour afterwards, she heard the old man awaken the men. " Come," she said, " arouse yourselves, 'tis time we were off."

Presently, Celeste heard them go down stairs, she saw them cross the terrace with the old man, then the lawn, she then saw them go down into the grove, where she lost them.

That these men were robbers—nay murderers, Celeste from their own conversation could not doubt, and that the Count Le Mar was of the same stamp, she had now every reason to believe ; she called to her mind how Mr. Ashton had said, that the Count Le Mar resembled one of the men who had robbed Mr. Cubby, and she had now no doubt but the Count Le Mar was the man.

It was eleven o'clock, before the old woman brought Celeste her breakfast, and when she did, she was hardly able to walk, not only from the effect of the liquor she had taken overnight, but that morning also ; staggering, she came into Celeste's chamber.

" I have brought your breakfast, lady," she said, " and sure enough, 'tis lonely for you to be here by yourself, honey ; you shall come and sit with me a bit, but the old man, nor Danish, must not know it. Bad luck to the old man, he has taken the keys with him, and I can't get out, even for a bit of bacca; but one good job is, he didn't think of taking the key of the cellar, where there's a good keg of brandy—I have brought up a pint ;—come, honey, take a drop," and she poured out Celeste a large cup full.

Celeste excused herself from drinking it, but she accepted the old woman's offer of leaving her chamber, and she followed the old woman into the room she occupied.

" Come, sit ye down at the table," said the staggering old woman, " and drink that, honey," she said, again offering Celeste brandy ; " it will do ye good, and don't fret because you are locked up for a short time ; sure Denish will make ye happy as the day is long ; and as soon as ye are married, he will buy you a power of fine clothes. Oh! by my faith, and I always said, Denish would be a jontle-man ; when he was but an urchin, he took to his learning with the best on um, at the charity school at Killarney ; and then he wint for a foot-boy to Mr. More the clergy, and then he got a place with Squire O'Hara, and come to London with his master ; and thin, by my soul, Dneish set up jontleman on his own account. And this house I know, will be his own, for Mr. Montagle, the owner of it, left the country when Queen Mary died, and Elizabeth came to the crown, bad luck to her ; and my great uncle was left in the care of the house, and here we have been, childer after childer, until all the family are dead, now the old man's got it, and it will come to Danish after him, for there's none left now, honey, to say nay to it."

" And was not your son's name Monteagle ?" inquired Celeste.

"Monteagle ! no, his name is Denish Brian —O'Brian I mean ; for he descended from the kings of Ireland, in a straight line ;—Oh, by my soul, he came of a great and noble family."

" Is there not a lady in this house, tall, and of a fair complexion, with flaxen hair ?" said Celeste.

" And why do you ask such questions ?" said the old woman.

" Because I saw such a person in my bed-room, the first night I slept here," said Celeste, " and I have taken a great fancy to the lady, and should like to be in her company."

" Hurrah ! and wid ye be in company wid the dead ?" cried the old woman, crossing herself, " and is it a ghost ye want to keep ye company ?"

" A ghost !" cried Celeste in terror, " who was the lady ?"

"Who—but the wife of Denish to be sure;—who else should she be? she was sick and bad a long time, and very cross she was—and she provoked Danish, and he jist gave her a little wipe with his fist on her temple, and she took a fit and died, honey."

"Was not her name once Montague?" inquired Celeste.

"Oh, by the powers, and 'tis more than I can tell," said the old woman; "Denish used to call her Milly—she was here more than a year, and did nothing but fret and fume all the time."

Overcome by the liquor she had been drinking, the old woman dropped her pipe; she laid her head upon the table, which upset, and the old woman and the table fell on the floor together.

"Poor unfortunate Amelia!" sighed Celeste, "then thou art no more, it was thou who appeared to me. I too may feel the murderer's hand, as thou hast done. Heaven give me strength and fortitude," she inwardly said, "that I may bear up, nor sink under the misery that this monster hath brought upon me."

No. 14.

CHAPTER XXXIII.

Did you never see that pale blue light
Steer its course at the dead of night?
Follow its track, if thou art bold,
It will lead to the dead in unhallowed mould.
BY THE AUTHORESS OF EVA, OR THE BRIDAL SPECTRE.

THE old woman being in no condition to offer any opposition to the wishes of Celeste, she hastened out of the apartment, and tried to open several doors, but they were all locked; she then went down stairs, and tried the street door, but that was fastened, as was every door in the house, excepting the back door, and that was unfastened.

She descended the steps and crossed the terrace, passed the lawn, and went into the grove, there she saw a low door situated in the high wall which surrounded the whole of the premises. Celeste tried this door, but that was fastened also; she saw the high holly hedge hanging in some places over the wall, particularly in that part where the door was placed; she knew from this circumstance, that the door must open behind the hedge, and the entrance into the grove must be concealed thereby; by this door she knew the men must have left the house.

Celeste surveyed the wall all round, hoping that in consequence of its age, it might be in some part decayed, and that she might be able to pull away the loosened bricks and make an aperture, through which she might pass and make her escape, but to the grief of Celeste, the wall was all sound, and there was nothing on which she could stand to enable her to climb the wall; dispirited, she was returning into the house, when at the end of the terrace, she saw through a grove of thickly planted yews, a building she had not before observed; hope again inspired her heart, and Celeste passed through the trees, and came up to the building, which she found to be a chapel of a very ancient and dilapidated appearance.

She entered the porch, and proceded down the aisle, where darnel and long grass were growing in rank luxuriance. Celeste saw a door, it was near the altar, she hastened to it, but what was her terror when she had opened it; for in this room there were several figures, both male and female, of a very white and ghastly appearance, but whether they were material, or immaterial beings, she at first, nor until her nearer approach, could distinguish, for the storied windows of painted glass emitted but a dull and uncertain light, being not very lightsome of themselves, and now covered as they were with dust, objects without very close inspection could not be distinguished.

Celeste was not in a state of mind to hesitate at trifles; she advanced close to the objects of her terror, and saw that they were merely a group of figures in white marble. There was the Virgin Mary and the Saviour, Saint Paul, the Pope, and an effigy of Queen Mary of the same stone.

Celeste found there was no escape for her through the dilapidated wall of the chapel, it being surrounded by the same high wall as enclosed the whole of the premises.

Dispirited, Celeste returned into the house; the old woman still slept, and did so till evening, when Celeste lighted her lamp, and went into her own chamber, and there she sat at the window, bemoaning her fate, and thinking what would be the result of her stay there.

The church clock had some time struck the hour of eleven, when Celeste from her window saw the two men who had left the house that morning, and the old man, come from the grove cross the terrace, and then enter the house; but the Count Le Marwas not with them.

She heard them bestow many oaths on the drunken old woman, and after they had sat drinking for some time, the two men left the house.

In about two hours she saw them return, for Celeste's mind was too much agitated to permit her to sleep; she saw the men had brought something heavy with them, and they passed with it through the grove of yews that led to the chapel.

"I hate these jobs," said one of the men, as he came up the stairs, "Highgate church-yard is too public, if Doctor Finch had not come down handsomly, I would not have done it, and I now fear we shall repent it, I have reason to think we were watched."

"Pooh!" said the other, "I won't believe it, thou hast always got some fancy in thy fool's head; let's get to bed, for I am tired out."

Celeste heard them ascend the stairs, and very glad she was to hear them do so, for when these men were in the house, she was in continual fear of being molested.

Tired, and harassed in mind, she laid down in the bed, but she did not pull her clothes off, neither had she done so, since she had been in the custody of the count.

Celeste had not been long on the bed, before she saw a pale blue light, gliding before her; it appeared to come from the door, then wound its way round her bed, and stood there stationary for some moments.

Alarmed, Celeste sat upright in her bed, and she gazed with amaze, not unmixed with terror, on the pale blue light.

"Oh, Amelia," she cried, "is it thou who, with this pale corse light, wouldst lead me from this mansion of iniquity and death?"

Soon as Celeste had uttered these words, the pale blue light moved slowly towards the door of her chamber, and she thought she saw Amelia Montague's pale and sepulchral form beckon her to follow the light.

"Oh, I will go," cried Celeste, "blessed spirit, I will follow thy bidding, no fear shall deter me, when my all; my life; my honour is at stake."

And she snatched up her lamp, and followed the light which preceded her down the stairs, being not a prisoner this night in her room, in consequence of the old woman being too drunk to think of locking Celeste's door, or indeed anything else.

The light wound its way down the stairs, and out of the back door, it then went slowly on along the terrace, and into the yew-tree grove; with a determined mind, but trembling steps, Celeste followed her supernatural guide.

The light glided on down the aisle, and Celeste followed it, through the long grass and darnel, until she came to what had formerly been the altar, she there saw a sack lying.

And there the light stood stationary; the sack was tied at the mouth, Celeste put her lamp down, and untied the string, and opened the sack, when to her surprise and horror, she saw it contained a dead body.

"Oh! it may be my father," she franticly cried, "the wretch has murdered and brought him here."

Fainting, she reeled against the dilapidated altar, and for some moments she remained unconscious of her misery; but she determined, when she recovered her recollection, to ascertain if her fears were really true, and whether the corse in the sack, was her father or not; suspense was terrible, her feelings were worked on to madness.

Hastily, she tore open the mouth of the sack, she looked at the face of the corse, and saw it was a man, but not her father; she had borne up with fortitude —borne up beyond her strength; but she now could hold out no longer; fear and dread overpowered her spirits, and strange and unearthly beings seemed 'flitting in the gloomy aisle,' illumined by no other light than the lamp she carried.

Thinking she heard a low moan, she turned her head, and fancied she saw Mrs. Montague standing near her; Celeste started, her lamp fell from her hand, and in a moment, she was in total darkness.

Affrighted, she groped her way along the dark walls, with the intention of returning to her chamber, and she succeeded in getting out of the chapel, but not without some difficulty.

Celeste had passed some trees, in the yew-tree grove, when she heard voices, then a loud noise; it appeared to come from the grove.

Terrified, Celeste stopped to listen—the noise increased; it appeared as if some persons were hammering at a door, with the intention of breaking it down.

" What can this mean ?" thought Celeste, " perhaps the officers of justice are coming to apprehend the wretched inmates of this place. I will not enter the house," she mentally said; "for if such be the case, they will apprehend me with the rest, and I should be dragged to prison as a felon. I will not go into the house, I will conceal myself here."

Trembling, Celeste stood concealed behind the yew-trees, and soon she heard the door give way, and a number of persons rushed into the grove; some of them carried lights in their hands, and they rushed forward towards the house, which, as they entered, they cried to their companions, " Come on ; I told you we were right, here dwell the wretches, who tear the dead from their graves; at that very gate, behind the holly trees, we saw them enter, with poor Teddy Leary, in a sack, after they had pulled him from his grave."

" Oh ! and why did he let the spalpeens rob him of his coffin, and the bran new shroud I bought him ?" cried an old man in the crowd, " why didn't he put up his good looking fist, and knock them down ? Oh ! Teddy my boy, I never knew you to be a coward before."

They had all now entered the house, and Celeste, with the speed of a fawn, left her station behind the yew-trees, and ran along the lawn, and quitted the grove through the door by which the men entered.

With joy, she once more found herself at liberty, and she ran on for a considerable distance, but the road was lone ; on each side of the way were fields and hedges, and not a light glimmered from a window, nor was there a traveller passing.

What to do, Celeste did not know ; she feared to proceed, for fear of meeting some lawless murderer, and to stay where she was, she feared to do ; again she hurried on, and saw a light glimmer in a cottage that lay by the road side,—Celeste stood down under the window of the cottage, she heard a low moan as of one in pain, then heard a voice, as if some person was in prayer for the recovery of the afflicted.

"These are persons who will not harm me," mentally said Celeste, " I will knock, and request shelter for the night."

An elderly woman opened the door and to her. Celeste related her distresses and requested shelter for the night.

" Poor child, come in," said the woman, " I have drank deep of the cup of affliction myself, and I can feel for the woes of others;—my husband now lays on the bed of death, and every earthly hope has long since withered in my heart."

Celeste with thankfulness followed the good woman to the chamber of death, and it was not more than an hour after Celeste had entered the chamber, before the sick man in peace resigned his last breath.

The poor woman made Celeste take some refreshment before she left the cottage, and behaved to her with the greatest kindness.

" You, no doubt, are surprised, my dear young lady," said the old woman, " to see me part with the aged partner of my days with so little sorrow ; but better is it for him to lay as he does, than live, to have his heart torn by the ingratitude and disrespect of those he loved, and once climbed his knee, and called him by the endearing name of father.—He had a loved and favourite son, whose disposition he thought angelic: he grew rich, and as his riches increased, his avarice increased also. This darling son told his father, some days back, not to come to his house, as his wife thought the meanness of his father's apparel disgraced her; my poor husband felt this, and what made it worse, my son said,

" ' I think, father, when people get old and past labour, if they have no property, it were best that they should go and drown themselves ; I would do so, rather than be burdensome to my children ; when old people come to that, it is time they were gone.'

"This cruel speech from his favourite child, cut my husband to the heart, how he came to use such expressions I can't think, for we wanted nothing from him. Certainly he lent us a pound towards paying our rent; but my husband always returned it to him; it will be but a mockery to ask my son to follow his father's corse to the grave, as such was his advice; he, perhaps would do, as I have heard they do among the savages, were it not for the laws of the country, rather than give parents a meal, knock them on the head, or throw them in the river to be food for fishes. He himself has a family, and he should recollect these words, 'as thou measurest to others, the same shall be meted to you again.' But God forbid that that should be the case, I love my son, and wish him every blessing that can possibly attend him, well knowing that nothing could affect him without my deeply feeling it."

The words of this good woman made a great impression on the feeling heart of Celeste, and she left with her her father's direction in Cornwall; and begged if she was ever in distress, and able to reach Cornwall, to come to her father, and she knew he would not let her want. "You have shown me much kindness," said Celeste, "I shall never forget it."

The good woman, when it was light in the morning, directed Celeste the best way to Kensington, for it was the intention of Celeste to return to Lady Nettleby's, and to immediately write to her father, and tell him of what she had suffered, and request that he would directly, on the receipt of her letter, send for her home, for that if he did not, he would not again see her alive."

When Celeste reached the house of Lady Nettleby and was let in, she inquired of the servant for her aunt, but she had hardly uttered the words, when overcome by the fatigue she had undergone she sunk fainting to the floor.

Alarmed and surprised, the footman went up to his lady.

"Miss Manby has returned, madam," he said, "and has fell down in a fit on the floor."

"Good Heavens! Celeste returned," cried Lady Nettleby, and her ladyship hastened down stairs, followed by Juliana.

Restoratives were used, and Celeste after some little time recovered.

"Celeste, I hope you are married," were the first words spoken by Lady Nettleby.

"Married!" cried Celeste, "God forbid!—to whom did you ladyship hope I was married?"

"To whom? why to the man you eloped with so be sure," said Lady Nettleby, "the Count Le Mar."

"What! to a robber and a murderer," said Celeste. "I did not elope, but was deceived, and taken away by that bad man."

"What! and is not the count a man of property?" cried Lady Nettleby, evident dismay.

"Oh, no," cried Celeste, "his right name is Brian, he is an Irishman of poor parents, and the person I took him for; I was positive I knew him, he once went by the name of Monteagle, as I told your ladyship."

"Oh! then I am ruined," cried Lady Nettleby, "his bills are worth nothing, I have got part of them cashed, and paid away the money; was ever woman so ill-treated." Lady Nettleby left the room in which Celeste and Juliana were seated, and retired to her dressing-room, and there gave way to a passionate flood of tears.

Celeste related to Juliana all she had undergone, and the kind-hearted Juliana sympathised in her sufferings.

CHAPTER XXXIV.

"Leave her to Heaven,
And to these thorns, that in her bosom lodge,
To prick and sting her."

" 'TIS strange that ma should have any concerns with the Count Le Mar in money matters," said Juliana. " I am surprised, and sorry to see her so vexed. She is troubled too on account of Maria, who eloped on the night of the masquerade with Mr. Synegall ; and ma has inquired, and heard that Mr. Synegall bears but a very equivocal character ; Maria, ma has found, received her fortune two days before she eloped, and she has heard, that Maria and her husband are gone on the continent. And this information we think correct, for Maria, sent a letter to ma, two days after she left home, and in her letter, she said she was going abroad and perhaps might not again return to England. Ma had requested the loan of a thousand pounds of Maria, and Maria agreed to let her have it, but she disappointed her and sent ma word, that she had no more money than she wanted for herself—and concluded her letter by saying, that extravagant people generally came to want."

Being much fatigued, Celeste retired to lie down ; and was agreeably surprised when she arose and entered the drawing-room, to see her father seated there, with Lady Nettleby.

Lady Nettleby had informed Mr. Manby, before Celeste entered the apartment, of the extreme uneasiness she had suffered, on account of her niece having been runaway with by a Count Le Mar. "I did not inform you of it," said her ladyship, " as I well know how very miserable such information would make you ; and I hoped to recover my niece, in consequence of the incessant inquiries I made after her."

" Oh, I am so thankful she is come back," said her ladyship, " and I hope now she will take pity on poor Barnaby ; we must have the wedding concluded at once."

" I know, brother, you will give your daughter to her adoring Barnaby."

" I should be happy to do so, if it is with the consent of Celeste," said Mr. Manby. " What say you Celeste, will you become the wife of your cousin, who my sister says loves you with such affection ?"

" I have already told my aunt my determination on that subject," said Celeste.

" I never will marry any one, unless I preferred him to all on earth beside, that preference I do not feel for my cousin—I love him as a relation, as the son of my her's sister, but nothing further."

" Nonsense !" cried Lady Nettleby, " I did not think, Celeste, you had such foolish romantic notions. Love in a hovel, is quite out of fashion now-a-days; your father, I trust, has more sense, and will enjoin you to accept a rich man, who can keep a carriage for you to ride in, not suffer you to wed some poor and unworthy object, who perhaps you are under promises to, in Cornwall."

" 'Tis strange you should put forward a supposition like that," said Celeste with spirit, for she felt her feelings wounded by the words of her aunt; " and, indeed, I wonder, madam," she continued, " how you can talk to me of marrying my cousin, when he declared in my own hearing, that he loved the unfortunate Susan, and had no fancy for me. I dare say Barnaby himself, if appealed to, would be candid enough to acknowledge that he did say so."

" I shall not appeal to him, I assure you," cried Lady Nettleby. " Barnaby, I am sorry to say, is a very foolish young man—and all I can say, Celeste, is, that if you will not be his wife, he must get another. You are sure my wishing you to be his wife, is purely from disinterested motives. But how is it, brother, that you came to the resolution of coming to London, when I have so often tried to persuade you to come, and you so often have refused me ?"

" It is a very strange circumstance I assure you, said Mr. Manby, " ten days back, on two successive nights, I dreamt I saw Celeste in an old chapel, soon a man of a ferocious aspect, started from behind a pillar, and was forcibly dragging her, towards the altar, when I thought, a pale and sepulchral form stood before me, and said, 'hasten hence, and save your child!' for two successive nights I dreamed the same dream, and saw the same shadowing figure stand before me. In the figure I recognized the features of Amelia Montague."

"Oh, Heaven! how inscrutable are thy ways," cried Celeste, "poor Amelia! even in death has her friendship continued. She appeared to me," said Celeste, "when I was in the house of her murderer. Poor Amelia was murdered by that wretch, Monteagle, and he it was who stole me away from my friends, pretending that you were ill at Highgate, and wished to see me—oh, what a tale of horror I have to tell you, my dear father," continued Celeste. "And was it through your dream and the cause of Amelia, that caused you to come to London?"

"I had no thought of coming before," said Mr. Manby, "but a dread and a heavy foreboding on your account dwelt on my mind, and I could not rest until I saw you."

Celeste related all she had undergone, since the night of the masquerade; her father could not help shedding tears at the dreadful recital.

"The wretches! they will no doubt be all taken," cried Lady Nettleby, "Count Le Mar, as he called himself, has robbed me of several thousand pounds,—and my daughter Maria has left her home and treated me with the greatest unkindness. I intend in the course of a few weeks to return to Yorkshire; Heaven grant that I had never come to London."

"There is nothing like submitting to our lot with patience," said Mr. Manby, "I lately have been most unfortunate; my cattle have died, and I have been robbed by a friend, to whom I lent a large sum of money."

"If you are in difficulties," said Lady Nettleby, "and I can help you out, I will do it with pleasure,—I know you would do so by me if you had it in your power; there are but us two, brother, and we ought to serve one another as much as we can."

Very glad was Celeste when she returned to Cornwall. She visited the garden, the green-house, and wandered over her favourite walks where she and Durant had so often strolled together.

The winter wore away, and yet Mr. Russell was not dead; he was kept alive, as it were, by every nourishing thing that could be procured, and the skill of his eminent physicians.

Celeste had entreated her father not to call the Count Le Mar to account for his treatment to her; nor to interfere about the unfortunate Mrs. Montague. "The count's villainy will not go unpunished," said Celeste, "but let him not be brought to justice through our means."

Mr. Manby's wrath burnt against the wretched Count Le Mar, but to satisfy his daughter he let the affair drop.

It was now May; but Durant and his father had not yet returned from Ireland, and Celeste began to think his absence long.

Mr. Manby received a very kind letter from Lady Nettleby, in which she informed her brother that she had not yet returned into Yorkshire, nor did she think of doing so for some months; the letter ended with great professions of regard, and a promise to visit Mr. Manby in a very short time.

In a few days after Mr. Manby had received his sister's letter, he read an advertisement in the paper, which stated, "that if Augustus Manby or the children of the said Augustus Manby, nephew of the late James Manby, of Skipton, Yorkshire, would apply to Mr. Jordan, attorney of Skipton, they would hear of something very much to their advantage."

"Gracious Heaven!" cried Mr. Manby, when he had read the advertisement; "then my poor uncle is dead, and has at length relented of his cruelty to me."

He immediately wrote to Mr. Jordan, and received for answer, that his uncle had left the whole of his property to himself and children; twenty thousand pounds he left to Mr. Manby, and the house he lived in, and estate contiguous; and to the children of Mr. Manby, he left forty thousand pounds and several houses.

Mr. Russel's affection for his nephew returned; and he altered his will during almost the last moments of his existence.

Mr. Manby and Celeste immediately set off for Skipton, and were put in possession of the bequest of Mr. Russel.

But as Mr. Manby did not intend living in Yorkshire but to remain in Cornwall, he wished to dispose of the estate left him by his uncle, and he remained in Yorkshire for some time, as he was in treaty with a neighbouring gentleman for the sale of the Russel estate.

The time was now arrived for the union of Percival Immorf and Julia Rosemont to take place, and a magnificent entertainment was given by Lady Immorf on the occasion.

Tables were spread in a field adjoining the castle, where roast beef and plum-pudding was placed in abundance, and a number of barrels of ale, and mugs to drink it out of, were also placed there; her ladyship's gift was given in the true spirit of old English hospitality, all who chose to come and partake of the good things were welcome.

It happened on that very day that a party of gipsies who had for some days encamped themselves in a hollow at but a short distance from Ravenswood Castle, had a wedding celebrated among their own people, and they were allowed to fetch plenty of provision and ale from the castle.

The hollow they had made choice of to celebrate their wedding festivities in, was a lovely place surrounded by trees and flowers. It was the gipsy king's daughter, who was married after the custom of their people.

Many of the neighbouring gentry as well as others, went to visit the ceremony used by the gipsies, and see their antic dances, amongst the rest there were assembled the two Misses Devels; Miss Mary Devel was a lady about thirty-five, and Miss Jane, her sister, was twenty-two. The ladies were seated on a bank viewing the gipsies dance, when Osmond Durant entered the hollow.

He had returned from Ireland with his father, and had at an early hour that morning reached home; he had walked past the dwelling of Celeste several times, but not seeing any of the family he was much surprised, and on inquiry found that Mr. Manby and his daughter had left Cornwall some weeks. Surprised, and uneasy at this intelligence, Osmond could not rest; for as several months had elapsed since he had seen Celeste, he did not know what might have transpired;—and full of those fears so commonly felt by true lovers he became truly miserable; he seated himself on the same bank as the Miss Devels were sitting on; but so perfectly lost in thought was Osmond, that he was not aware of the presence of the ladies who sat near him, and he turned his back towards where they were sitting; perplexed, and ruminating on what could have caused the absence of Celeste.

Miss Jane very much admired Osmond Durant; she had once or twice been in his company, and Miss Jane thought Osmond the next handsomest man to Frederick Manby she had ever seen.

But now seeing the position he had placed himself in, she was quite provoked at his unpoliteness, and she began to talk aloud to her sister, and threw herself into the most affected and ridiculous attitudes to obtain his notice.

At length Osmond turned his head, and seeing the Misses Devel sitting there, he begged pardon for his rudeness, and made up by his complacent behaviour, a full recompense for his former rudeness.

"The gipsey bride is a very pretty girl," said Durant, "and the bridegroom, though of a tawny complexion, is a good-looking fellow."

"But of course they are nothing, when compared to the bride and bridegroom at the castle," said Miss Devel. "I have seen the lady, and she is a most interesting and lovely young creature; but she is pale, and looks as if she had but delicate health."

Miss Devel was right; for Julia Rosemont that was, but now the bride of Percival, had been for some time before her marriage in but delicate health.

CHAPTER XXXV.

I met a wrinkled hag, with age grown double,
Picking up dry sticks, and mumbling to herself.   OTWAY.

ALL was mirth and happiness in Ravenswood Castle. Mr. Rosemont, who was proud to see his daughter united to Percival, went down the dance as agile as the youngest person there.

"And may prosperity and happiness attend the bride and bridegroom," issued from the lips of those who were partaking of the good cheer in the meadow.

Julia was tired with dancing, and she retired with Percival to a window that overlooked the lawn in front of the castle; it was a beautiful evening, and a full moon shed her lustre on all around. "The heat of the room is oppressive," said Julia, "let us walk on the lawn."

They left the ball-room, and were enjoying the lovely scene, before them, and

No. 15.

inhaling the scene of the violet and eglantine that was borne on the breeze. When suddenly, a tall, gaunt figure of an aged gipsy stood before them.

" Hail ! lord of the ancient hall !" she cried. " I have eat of thy bread, and drank of thy cup, and for which I will make known to thee thy fate. The volume of thy destiny is now open before me, and I see what shall hereafter come to pass."

She then in a harsh, and almost unearthly voice, sung the following words—

> " Sing, sing a merry lay,
> The lord of the castle's wed to-day,
> To a bride as fair as the flowers in May.
>
> " Let the goblets o'erflow,
> And the tapers be lit—
> But in destiny's dark record
> Thy name is writ.
>
> " For know, lord of the ancient hall,
> The murderer's hand on thee shall fall,
> And the blood shall flow, and the bell shall go,
> And the death-owl shriek in the dell below."

Julia appeared terrified at the words and the wild figure of the woman.

" Let us go !" she said ; " Percival, let us go into the house !"

" Woman, begone !" cried Percival, " you say you have eat of my bread, and drank of my cup, and now out of gratitude, you are come to utter your accursed prognostics, and cast your evil spells on me and mine."

" I have but spoken the truth—have but told thee what will assuredly come to pass !" said the woman.

" Begone ! impostor, begone !" cried Percival ; instantly quit my grounds ;" and he hastened into the castle with Julia, who now was very unhappy, on account of the gipsy's prediction.

Percival did all in his power to raise the spirits of his bride, and reason her out of her fear respecting the fulfilment of the gipsy's prophecy. " These wandering vagrants have no skill in futurity, as they pretend to have," said Percival ; " what the say, are words merely spoken at random to extort money from the credulous. These gipsies have had as much meat and drink as they wanted to make them comfortable in the celebration of their marriage; and now the ungrateful old crone, to come with her horrific prediction, to terrify and make you unhappy. I have a great mind to compel them to leave my grounds, nor suffer them to remain in the neighbourhood."

" Oh, no," said Mrs. Immorf, " take no notice of them, perhaps the old woman had been taking more ale than did her good, and she did not know what she was about.   Pray, Percival, take no notice—do not send the gipsies away—I dare say they will soon go—they seldom stay long in one place."

" Well, Julia, to please you, I will not ;" said Percival, " but I assure you, I feel much provoked at the audacity of the old woman."

Mr. and Mrs. Rosemont passed a month at Ravenswood Castle, and then returned into Devonshire with Catharine, who would not be prevailed on to stay behind them, and pass another month with Julia ; for Catharine had left her lover in Devonshire, and she thought the time long until her return.

As soon as Lady Nettteby heard of her uncle's death, and that he had altered his will in favour of her brother, she went post to Yorkshire, as she said, " to congratulate her brother on his good fortune, which gave her," she said, " great pleasure, although it was to her own loss. For you know my dear brother," continued her ladyship, " that whether I had my uncle's property left me, or it is left to you, is the same thing—as you have it, I dare say you will act as liberal to me, as I should do to you, were I in your place."

" Gertrude, in no instance, you ever found me act with selfishness toward you," said Mr. Manby, " and I should be sorry to do so now."

"Well then," said Lady Nettleby, "I am very much pressed for a thousand pounds; which sum I am minus, in consequence of my having such a loss, through that wretch who ran away with Celeste."

"You shall have the thousand pounds, sister," said Mr. Manby, "with pleasure, I will give it you."

"Now, brother, you act precisely as I should have done," said Lady Nettleby, "where was a greater proof of the disinterestedness of my temper, than I showed in wishing my son to marry Celeste, when I thought you could not give her a shilling?"

"True," said Mr. Manby, "you behaved very kind to Celeste, and I shall ever remember it."

Mr. Manby soon settled his affairs in Yorkshire, and returned to Cornwall. When Sir James Durant heard from his son, the attachment he had to Celeste, and was told of the fortune she was come to, he was quite agreeable to the match, as was Mr. Manby, to his daughter being united to Osmond.

And in a few months Celeste and Osmond were married, and the dwelling of Sir James Durant being a large mansion, it was agreed, that the two families should reside together. All Mr. Manby now wanted to make him happy, was the presence of his son, to whom he meant to write without delay, to acquaint him with his good fortune, and beg he would return home as soon as he possibly could.

In the course of twelve months, Mrs. Immorf presented her husband with a little son, who was named Percival after his father; and in two years afterwards, Mrs. Immorf was again confined with another son. Some few days before the confinement of his lady, Percival was seized with a fever; he became delirious, and his life was considered in great danger; the situation of her husband greatly affected his lady, and she was extremely ill, as well as the infant; who it was deemed necessary to have baptized, lest it should die without that ceremony being performed.

Mrs. Immorf was at a loss what name to give her child, her husband was in no state to be consulted on the subject. Percival, their first-born, bore the name of his father; "and who in the family shall I name my second child after," thought Mrs. Immorf, "I should like to name him after my own father, but I will not do so without the consent of my husband, and such consent he cannot now give me I will name him Parrolla, after my husband's father." And the infant was baptized Parrolla.

When Percival recovered his illness, and found his child was named Parrolla, he was extremely grieved.

"Oh! why did you give him that name?" cried Percival, "Julia, on no account would I have had him named Parrolla."

"What! not after your own father?" said Mrs. Immorf, "I could not think you would have been displeased at that."

"Oh! I have reasons," cried Percival; "and such reasons—if you knew them——"

"Tell me?" cried Julia, "tell me what those reasons are?"

"No, not at this time," said Percival, "you are but lately recovered from your confinement; and I am but yet weak, and unable to enter into the unpleasant recital.'"

Mrs. Immorf tenderly loved her husband; and seeing that the subject was painful to his feelings, however great her curiosity was to know his reason for not wishing his child to be named after its grandfather, she forbore to question him any more on the subject.

The little Percival was a mild and compliable child, of a very affectionate and tender disposition; but the infant Parrolla showed, when even not more than twelve months old, symptoms of a very morose and turbulent disposition.

It was in the month of May, when the white thorn and day roses were in full bloom, that Mrs. Immorf with her nurse maid, and two children walked in the beautiful valley, some short distance from Ravenswood Castle, the place before mentioned, where the gipsies celebrated their wedding festivities.

Little Percival was running on before its mother, and the infant Parrolla was sitting in the arms of his nurse, when a bee came out of the hedge and settled on his hand, and stung it in a terrible manner, The child screamed with pain ; and when the tender mother saw how the child's hand was swelled with the envenomed sting, she felt as much pain by sympathy, as her child did by the sting. " Oh! what shall we do to ease his pain," cried Mrs. Immorf to the nurse, " it will take at least half an hour before we can get medical advice, the child will scream himself into fits."

At this moment, a gipsy, who was sitting under the hedge, though unperceived by Mrs. Immorf, stood suddenly before her.

The gipsy took an ointment from out of her wallet, and applied it to where the bee had stung the child, whose loud cry was silenced as soon as the ointment was applied.

" Our people," said the gipsy, "always carry this ointment about them, in case of being stung by venomous reptiles or insects, to which by sleeping in the air, in fields, and under hedges, they are liable to. The infant hath felt the sting of the bee," said the gipsy, "and many will feel the sting of him. The volume of his fate is open to my view, and the scenes of his manhood are before me ; he will be a parricide, a homicide, and tamperer in the black art ; and I here predict, woe unto the babe !"

" Woman ! or fiend ! which ever thou art," cried Mrs. Immorf, " hast thou no human feeling, to use words like these to a mother ?" she looked at the woman, who she, in her anxiety for her child, had not before noticed, and she saw she was the same prophetess of evil who had so terrified her on her wedding-day.

" What malice—what wickedness is this ?" cried Mrs. Immorf. " Woman ! what is your motive for so annoying me ? you know you are but an impostor, and have no knowledge of what is to come."

" Think so !" replied the gipsy, "but when the things which I have foretold shall come to pass, then remember me ! that your husband shall fall beneath the assassin's blow is most certain; but the child is not yet born who shall do the deed; but the flax is being spun, and the loom is ready to weave the fine linen which shall swaddle the babe who is to be the murderer."

Saying this she went through a gap in the hedge, and was in a moment out of sight.

" My husband to be murdered, and my child to be such a demon !—I'll not believe it," cried Mrs. Immorf, kissing the face of the little Parrolla, " can thy innocence ever ripen into such guilt as that vile woman foretels? no, never, never. Who could he take after?" she said, speaking to her maid, "I never heard that any in the family of my husband were wicked people,—and, never did I hear of any in my own family, but who were upright and good persons,—to foretel that this innocent child will be a parricide, a homicide, and a tamperer in the black art.—That woman must have the heart of a fiend, or never could have entered her head such dire imagination. Margaret," said Mrs. Immorf to her maid, " did you ever hear anything to the disadvantage of any of my husband's family ?"

Margaret was silent.

Mrs. Immorf again repeated the question.

" It is not for me, madam, a poor servant like me, to repeat what I hear of my betters."

" Speak, I command you to speak, and tell me all you know," said Mrs. Immorf.

Margaret with much hesitation at last said :—

" I believe, madam, Sir Parrolla, who is dead and gone, was a very bad man."

" A bad man !" said Mrs. Immorf with surprise, " I never heard anything to his disadvantage ; in what respect was he bad ?—Speak, don't be afraid."

" Well, madam, if I must speak," said Margaret, " it is said he threw a young woman over the cliff,—and——"

"Oh! we must not believe all we hear," said Mrs. Immorf, "some false report I dare say."

"No, madam, it is no false report," said Margaret, "he owned it on his death-bed.—And then, madam, have you not observed the large long portrait that hangs in your bed-room covered with a black cloth? Well, madam, that gentleman is the devil himself, and he paid Sir Parrolla a visit in his own proper person, only the night before Sir Parrolla died."

"What romantic legend is this you tell me?" said Mrs. Immorf, "who has imposed on your credulity by telling you such a tale?"

"I am not imposed on, madam, it is a truth," replied Margaret, "I had it from good authority."

"And who was the person who told you?" inquired Mrs. Immorf.

"I am not at liberty to tell that," said Margaret, "I have promised secresy."

"That is the way with all slanderers," said Mrs. Immorf, "they always bind those who hear their falsehoods down to secresy, and every one but the injured party bears the false accusation, and those most interested have no opportunity of clearing themselves from the unjust aspersion. I insist on knowing who told you this tale, or I shall think that you are yourself the author.—Who was it told you?"

"I am sorry I spoke of it at all," said Margaret, "but rather than you should think me capable of raising false reports, I will tell you, Peter told me in confidence, he heard Sir Parrolla, when on his death-bed talk, and when he was delirious, say, 'what if I did throw her over the cliff, none saw me do it!'—then, he said, 'how she has bent the willow in falling; hark! how she gurgles!' And then, madam, Peter saw with his own eyes the original of that portrait talking to Sir Parrolla the very night before he died, and there was such a sulphureous smell, that Peter was almost suffocated; and terrified, he went up to bed as fast as he could; and how the dark gentleman got in or got out, Peter could not think, for the doors were all locked, and nobody let him in or out."

When Mrs. Immorf reached home, she sought her husband. She told him how she had again encountered that fearful gipsy, who had so alarmed her on the night of her marriage.

"And she uttered a yet more fearful prophecy," said Mrs. Immorf, "she has predicted that Parrolla shall be a parricide, a homicide, and a tamperer in the black art. And the predestined to be thy murderer," she said, "has not yet seen the light—but the flax is being spun, and the loom is ready to weave the fine linen which shall swaddle the babe who is to be thy murderer."

"I will immediately send and have the impostor taken into custody," said Mr. Immorf, "not another gipsy will I suffer to come on my ground, I will have the whole tribe punished for that woman's audacity. Those wandering vagrants shall all be taken up and sent to prison for rogues and vagabonds; Cornwall shall be cleared of them," and he rang his bell for a servant, to whom he meant to give orders to go after the old woman, and take her into custody; and not only her, but any other gipsy he might find in the neighbourhood.

But Mrs. Immorf prevailed on her husband not to interfere with the gipsies. "I have always found them very well conducted," she said, "excepting that old woman, who perhaps is deranged, and if so, she is to be excused, and her wild ravings forgiven. But I have heard that which has given me more pain than even the gipsy's prophecy. What portrait is it that hangs in my bed-room, Percival, covered with a black cloth?—of that portrait I have heard a strange account."

"And who has alarmed you by speaking of that portrait, Julia?" inquired Percival, "surely not my mother."

"No," said Mrs. Immorf, "your mother never has named the subject to me."

"Who then has told you of that mysterious person, which that portrait represents? it must have been told you merely to make you unhappy; tell me, Julia, who is the person?"

"I was told by my own request; nay, command," said Mrs. Immorf. "Margaret inadvertently let a word drop, which she would have recalled, but I insisted on hearing all she knew."

"And what more did she tell you?" inquired Mr. Immorf, "anything about my father?"

She did, but that I could never have named to you; it was about a dying acknowledgment."

"And how could Margaret have heard anything of that?" said Mr. Immorf, "she did not live here then; besides, what you have spoken of, none knew but my mother and myself; you may suppose such circumstances we did not wish to make the world acquainted with, nor did we wish you to know the errors of my unhappy father. But who could have told the secrets of my family to Margaret? —surely not my mother?"

"Your mother!" said Mrs. Immorf, " no; it was Peter who told Margaret."

"Then he must have listened," said Mr. Immorf, "for he was not in the room; Peter is a worthy lad, and a good servant; but he has the fault of peeping and prying about and listening to everything that passes; I must put a stop to this, or it will be the talk of the neighbourhood."

Mr. Immorf, rang the bell, and Peter answered the summons.

"Peter," said Mr. Immorf, "I am surprised that you should take the liberty to talk of my family affairs, the knowledge of which you must have obtained by the mean practice of listening, a fault of which you are very guilty; had I caught you in the act, I should certainly have made you suffer; and after listening, to expose what you heard, and that to a woman is unpardonable."

Peter, who was now about nineteen years of age, had never trusted any person with the discovery he had made of secret matters in Sir Parrolla's family, excepting Margaret, who he one day intended should be flesh of his flesh, and bone of his bone.

Surprised and grieved that what he had told his intended in confidence, and as a secret never to be spoken of should have reached his master's ears, Peter felt abashed and could hardly face his master.

"What I said to Margaret," replied Peter, " I will not deny, but I told her in confidence, and intended at a future day to make her my wife;—but now I'll have no more to do with her; I'll never marry a woman who can't keep a secret—and I now before you, sir, renounce the sex for ever, and swear to live and die a bachelor, for I now would as soon marry a magpie as a woman."

Some few days had passed, when Mrs. Immorf received a letter from her sister who was going to be married to a Mr. Phillimore in a very short time, and Catherine begged that Mrs. Immorf and her husband would not disappoint her of their company on her wedding day.

But what with the gipsy's predictions, and what she had heard respecting her husband's father, so weighed on the spirits of Mrs. Immorf, that she could not bear the thoughts of leaving home; and she in the most affectionate terms, worded a letter in which she begged to be excused from her sister's invitation.

Mr. Phillimore was a man of large property, but by no means a fit husband for the gentle Catherine, for she was meek as a lamb, whilst he was turbulent and fierce as a fire-brand; and through the violence of her husband's temper, Mrs. Phillimore nearly lost her life.

She was confined three months before she expected to be so, and gave birth to twins, a boy and a girl; the girl died, being but seven months' children, they were very weak; but the boy, who was named Olando, after some relations of his father's survived; but he was of a very weak intellect, indeed, he was almost an idiot, yet very artful, abounding with that cunning people of weak understanding generally possess.

Two years after Olando was born, Mrs. Phillimore gave birth to a daughter, who her mother named Lisbia. She was in every respect the reverse of her brother, for Olando was not only of weak intellect, but very plain in his person; he was very thin and tall, and had a long face, wide mouth, high cheek-bones, and a nose of peculiar flatness ; whilst Lisbia was very beautiful, graceful, and light as a wood-nymph.

Her son being of weak intellect, gave Mrs. Phillimore much concern, as did the disagreeable temper of her husband, who though of a bad temper, had feeling for his lady, who he saw was in a declining state of health, and to oblige her, he removed to Cornwall, that she might be near her sister.

Percival and Parrolla Immorf grew two very fine boys ; but they were entirely different in person as well as temper ; Percival was very fair, like his mother, and of a soft, mild, and tender disposition ; Parrolla was a handsome, dark boy, but of a very turbulent, obstinate and revengeful temper, and his unkind and morose manner often caused his mother to be in tears.

CHAPTER XXXVI.

So farewell hope, and with hope farewell fear,
Farewell remorse, all good to me is lost,
Evil be thou my good.   MILTON.

AFTER Count Herman had remained some time in Naples, he again visited Spain, and he began anxiously to look out for a victim, as the time was now fast approaching, when the Demon Zinegratta would demand his due.

Count Herman paid his addresses to several females, but he feared that all he then knew were too cunning for him, and would not be so easily ensnared as was the gentle Dollabella.

Passing some vineyards, he saw sitting on benches before their cottage-doors, several persons ; they were men and women who got their living by their labour, and the produce of their vineyards.

"By your leave, my friends, I will sit down and rest myself," said the Count ; "I am tired, and need refreshment. Can you accommodate me with a bowl of milk ?"

An old woman, of mild and prepossessing countenance, placed the milk before Count Herman, and requested to know if he would not choose to have one of her home-made cakes, to which he should be heartily welcome.

The Count declined the good woman's offer respecting the cake ; but he kept his seat on the bench, and drank the milk at his leisure, and he listened to the conversation of two men, who appeared to be engaged in an argument.

"I tell you, Lopes, it is very wicked to be so discontented," said an old man about sixty years of age, to his but a few years younger companion ; "you are but poor it is true, but you were always so—so was your father, your grandfather, and all your family—then why should you expect to be rich?"

"Ah! old Peres, talk away till you are dumb, and your words will make no impression on me," cried Lopes, "you foolish old goatherd ; 'tis well for you to be minding a few goats, and your old dame, and this youth, to be labouring in the vineyard from sunrise to sunset, and what is it for ?—why a morsel of bread. Look at the dons, they have nothing to do but eat, drink, sleep, and take their pleasure, whilst we poor labourers, who do all the drudgery, who make the corn grow for their support, and feed our kine for their use, and by our management cause the purple cluster to yield the nectar-like draught—and what for all these benefits are our wages ? a hard pallet, a half-starved life, and the contempt, and perhaps, whip of the great."

"Oh, no, I will not hear this," cried Peres, "there are different stations in life certainly, and God, for wise ends, hath willed it so ; we are paid by the rich for our labour, and what more can we expect ? Here is Julian, I fear he has taken a leaf out of your book ; he was contented before I let him go to Madrid to see my wife's sister, who lives servant in a great family there, and since his return, he has done nothing but talk of the dons, how grand they were drest, and how noble they looked when they sat on their horses; he has become quite discontented, and despises the life of a goatherd, neither does he like to work in the vineyard, nothing will now serve his turn but being a don himself."

"Well!" replied a youth of about twenty years of age, who was sitting near the door of the cottage, and who Count Herman had not before noticed, "well, if I do wish to be a don, my father was a don, and why should I not be a don too?—I know he would despise a goatherd, or a vineyard dresser's life, then why should not I?"

"I tell thee what, Julian," said old Peres, "thou hast too much pride; thou ought to be glad that I took care of thee, and that thou art as well off as thou art. When I found thee, thou wert in a high fever, and what thou said about thy parents, I believe to be but a delusion of thy fevered brain. The portrait thou wearest might not have been thy father's, as thou fondly thinkest, but perhaps dropped there by some one, a stranger, and by no means related to thee."

"Oh no," said the youth, deeply sighing, "what I told thee was the truth, it happened before I was ill—it was no delusion of a fevered imagination, but a real fact."

Count Herman now noticed the youth, who he had not before particularly observed; he was of a dark complexion, but had very handsome features, and very fine dark eyes, they were expressive of melancholy and of a languishing and downcast apperance; the youth was tall and finely formed, and from the natural stateliness and grandeur of his deportment, but few persons would have believed him to have been born of peasant parents.

"What! and is not that youth your son?" inquired Count Herman, of old Peres.

"He is but my foster-son," said the old man, "I have brought him up from when he was about six years old."

"And does he not know his father?" inquired Count Herman.

"He does not," replied the old man.

"But he wears his portrait," said Count Herman.

"So he believes," replied the old man.

"I have a very extensive acquaintance," said Count Herman, "and may very probably know the original, was I to see the portrait—I should like to look at it."

The youth arose, and going up to Count Herman, took a portrait, suspended by a ribbon from his bosom, and held it up to the view of the Count.

The portrait was that of a gentleman, who appeared to be about twenty years of age, handsome and elegantly attired; from the dress and features of the person represented, Count Herman believed him to be an Italian, and he thought it was a countenance he had before seen.

"Who would not almost risk their salvation, to be such a don as that," cried the discontented old Lopes, "I should not care what I did, so I enjoyed myself in luxury. To see such fine raiment, such fine palaces, such fine wine, and fine women, as we all do, and yet are debarred the use of them; by Saint Jenuarius, I can hardly blame the banditti, or even the assassins, for doing as they do to get money—to be so debarred, of what ought to be common to all men, is enough to make a man do what he would not do. The other day when I saw a couple of fat capons, fish, and ragouts, going up to the cardinal's table, methought I could have eat until I burst—then for wine, I'd not be one moment without a glass to my lips, and for women, I'd have as many as the grand signor."

Count Herman was glad to hear the old man express himself in this way.

"You seem a hearty fellow," said the Count, "I should have no objection to spending an hour with you—another opportunity, when, perhaps, I may be able to put something in your way. I will see you here to-morrow evening, when we will walk down by the vineyards, and I will speak to you on the subject, that will be greatly to your advantage."

"Happy should I be, signor, if you can put Lopes into some more money getting employment, than he has at present; for poverty don't suit him, not but he can get as much as I can; he has no children, none but his wife and himself, and yet he is always a grumbling."

"I must say for a man like him to want capons, fish, and ragouts is quite ridiculous, and then to talk of always having the wine glass to his lips, and having as many women as the grand signor, and at his time of life too."

"At my time of life," repeated Lopes, "I tell thee, Peres; old as you may think

me, I am as young in constitution as ever I was; and if thou art of such a saintly disposition, and like a foolish old monk, likest to mortify thyself, think not that I will do so."

"Well, well," said Count Herman, "don't quarrel, meet me here, Lopes, to-morrow evening at this hour, and at this place, and we will confer upon this subject."

No. 16.

CHAPTER XXXVII.

He, like the tenant,
Of some night-haunted ruin, bore an aspect
Of horror worn to habitude.   MYSTERIOUS MOTHER.

COUNT HERMAN met the discontented man as he had appointed; they strolled along the wine-grounds, and then into a bye place, obscured by trees, where none could hear their conversation.—The terms were proposed by Count Herman, and agreed to by Lopes; who being introduced to the Demon Zinegratta by Count Herman, he (Lopes) made known that which he required, to which the demon gave his assent.

Count Herman having procured Zinegratta a victim, his term was again renewed for seven years, and he now returned to Naples, and much frequented his favourite spot, the bay.

He often strolled by the mansion of the Marchese De Gusman, but although Count Herman so often passed and re-passed, he could not see him; and at length, by inquiring, he found that the Marchese De Gusman had been laid up with a severe illness; but that he was now getting better.

"I shall yet see him," the count mentally said, "and I will discover the cause of his melancholy," for this purpose he watched incessantly.

After many days' watching, Count Herman saw the Marchese De Gusman leave his palace, he looked very thin and emaciated, and a yet deeper shade of melancholy sat on his countenance. Count Herman fixed his eyes on the Marchese, who shrunk with awe from his scrutiny.

"I will watch him," thought Count Herman, and for that purpose he lingered behind; the marchese went on in a direction for the monastery of the Contrite Heart, and again entered the low gothic door of that building.

It was now about the hour of three in the afternoon, but twilight darkened the earth before the Marchese De Gusman left the monastery. Count Herman had awaited his coming; he hid himself behind some trees that grew there, and as the marchese passed, he groaned in a voice scarcely human—

"Thy iniquity is remembered!—where is Julian thy son?"

Thinking the voice of Count Herman was a voice from Heaven, the Marchese De Gusman fell on his knees.

"Oh, forgive me—forgive me!" he cried, "nor suffer the shade of Rachel to haunt and embitter my existence. That I slew her, it is true, but I greatly repent of my misdeed, and I have done many, many acts of great penance; and for Julian my son, if possible, I will yet do him justice."

"Julian!" mentally repeated Count Herman, "the youth at the vine-dresser's cottage. And the Marchese De Gusman acknowledged the murder of Rachel. I must bring the son acquainted with his sire, whom I must work to my purpose."

After a short prayer the marchese arose, and with a slow and tremulous step departed.

On the following day, Count Herman again watched the palace of the marchese, but he did not leave the palace—again he watched, and again, and again, until his patience was exhausted; he at length inquired, and found the marchese and marchesa were gone to Sweden, where it was expected they would remain some time.

It was now the time of the carnival at Venice, and Count Herman was too much engaged with those festivities to think at that time any more of either Julian or the Marchese De Gusman. But although he did not interfere with them for the present, he determined not to lose sight of them, as the marchese, he considered, must ultimately fall into his power

CHAPTER XXXVIII.

These shall the fury passions tear
The vultures of thy mind.

GRAY.

WE must now for the present leave Count Herman enjoying himself at the carnival, at least, enjoying himself as well as a man in his circumstances could do ; that is to say, where there is no peace within, there can be no real enjoyment, and return to England, where we left Celeste the bride of Osmond Durant, and her aunt, Lady Nettleby, smarting under the unkindness of her favourite daughter Maria, and the disappointment she met with respecting the Count Le Mar. The thousand pounds she obtained of her brother was soon swallowed up, and she determined soon to make another application ; whilst she was thinking of doing so, Mr. Manby received a letter from the pretended Count Le Mar—it ran thus :—

"SIR,

"Being convicted for house-breaking, and sentenced to die, I think it but an act of justice, to inform you of the art and duplicity of that base woman, Lady Nettleby. Your sister being fully aware of the property your daughter would come into, she invited her up to London, and endeavoured to get Miss Manby married to her son, Mr. Barnaby Nettleby, on account of the fortune she would have ; finding her scheme failed there, she sold Miss Manby to me for ten thousand pounds, with full liberty to gain her niece as I could ; but her wickedness will be of no advantage to her, the ten thousand pounds being given in bills which never will be paid. I write this out of good will towards you, to put you on your guard against the arts of her ladyship.

"I remain, yours respectfully,

"DENNIS BRIAN,

(Commonly called the Count Le Mar)."

Had a thunder-bolt fallen at the feet of Mr. Manby, he could not have been more shocked and surprised than he was, when he read this letter.

"Then Gertrude must have been aware of my uncle's intention, respecting the disposal of his property," said Mr. Manby, to Celeste. "I could not have thought my sister could have been so base. I know, when a girl, she was very artful and deceptive, but I thought a complete change had taken place in her sentiments."

"It certainly was very odd," said Celeste, "if my aunt had certainly known nothing of the intention of the Count Le Mar, as he was called, that she made no inquiry after me, nor did she write to you, to inform you of my absence. I think she must have known that the Count Le Mar had taken me from the masquerade."

"Anything but this I would have forgiven her for," said Mr. Manby, "but to be the instrument of your ruin is unpardonable—this Judas-like trick of selling you to that ruffian, the pretended Count Le Mar, was most inhuman ;—I never more will own her for my sister. Poor Amelia," continued Mr. Manby, "the ruffian who took thy life, will now pay the forfeit of his own."

It may be recollected, that Lady Nettleby was deeply engaged in talking to a tall Spaniard at the masquerade, that gentleman had commenced the lover of Lady Nettleby, and their marriage was soon to take place. His name was Mackenzie, a Scotchman by birth, and an attorney by profession, he had chambers in he Temple.

Finding herself again put to it for money, she, with her intended, took a journey to Cornwall ; but when she reached the house of her brother, her reception was very different from what she had anticipated. When Mr. Manby heard that Lady Nettleby was waiting to see him, he said, loud enough for her to hear—

"Tell her no more to darken my doors, until the pretended Count Le Mar has honoured the bills he gave my Lady Nettleby for the sale of her niece."

These words were quite sufficient for Lady Nettleby, she perfectly understood their meaning, and not daring to face her brother, crest-fallen she quitted his house, and entered her carriage, telling her coachman to drive back on his way to Kensington with all speed.

The mind of Lady Nettleby was now torn by conflicting passions; anger, malice, disappointment, and shame alternately filled her bosom. How her brother could have discovered her negotiation with the pretended Count Le Mar, she could not surmise. "There must be treachery in my own family," thought Lady Nettleby, "perhaps Mr. Synegall has told Maria, and she has written to Celeste, and acquainted her with the circumstance. Ungrateful girl, to disappoint me of the thousand pounds and then to expose me."

Lady Nettleby was ready to burst with vexation, and could she have indulged herself by giving vent to her tears, it would have much relieved her; but she could not do that before Mr. Mackenzie, it would have let her down, and she wished to be high in his estimation; she therefore bore up, and said, "I don't see why I should be vexed at the ill-treatment of my brother, I want no favours of him."

"Favours! I think not, whilst you have your adoring Mackenzie," said her companion. But when, my dear Lady Nettleby, shall our marriage take place? this is Friday—suppose we say on this day week; you are not well treated, and need a protector."

Lady Nettleby did not object.

When her ladyship reached her own habitation, she was surprised by Martha's crying, soon as her mistress set her foot in the passage, "Lord, madam, the house has been turned inside out since you have been gone; Mr. Mansfield came up to London, and has taken Miss Juliana down into Yorkshire with him, and Mr. Barnaby has married the cook!"

"Oh! dreadful!" cried her ladyship, "I am the most unfortunate and ill-treated woman breathing," and, almost choked with passion, she went into an hysteric fit.

Mr. Mackenzie did all in his power to comfort her. "Never mind your brother, nor your children," he said, "I will supply the place of every body. You shall go with me, love, to Scotland, where I have a fine castle and grounds; I mean to give up the law, for people it seems now settle their differences without applying to a solicitor, 'tis not worth while to keep chambers, when not a single soul comes for a week together. I certainly had one lady call about business some days back, and a bad customer she was! I was called from dinner to answer her. She asked me a question which I resolved her, she thanked me and was going, when I said—

"Stay, madam, there is my fee."

"'Your fee! I did not suppose you would charge me anything for merely asking a question," said the lady.

"What, madam! do you take me for a quack doctor—do I write up 'advice given here gratis,' that I am to be called up from my dinner to answer your questions?"

"Tired of such customers, I intend to give up the profession; I have property sufficient, then why should I be pestered?"

"Why, indeed," replied Lady Nettleby.

At this moment Barnaby came into the room.

"Mother!" he said, "I don't know whether you will like it or not, but I am married; I have married your cook, and Kitty I know will make a good wife. I shall set out for Yorkshire to-morrow, and live on my own ground. Sister Juliana has married young Farmer Mansfield and they are gone down before us."

"Since your children have run away from you, I would advise you to run away from them," said Mr. Mackenzie, "I would sell my furniture off, and we will be married, and go to my castle in Scotland."

Lady Nettleby was married to Mr. Mackenzie; her furniture was turned into money, and in little more than a month she was on her road to Scotland with her husband; and in her haste to set forward on her journey, she forgot to settle with some very heavy and troublesome creditors.

CHAPTER XXXIX.

One rude water all around us,
All above us one black sky,
Different deaths at once surround us,
Hark! what means that dreadful cry?

Still the leak is gaining on us,
Both chained pumps are choked below,
Heaven have mercy, here upon us,
Only that can save us now.

DIBDIN'S STORM.

It happened on a stormy evening and on the same evening, that Lady Nettleby set out for Scotland, that a cotter and his son, who lived at Margate, stood on a cliff, watching the motion of the turbulent billows, when they saw a gallant ship advancing; it was not more than half a mile from land, when the fury of the storm increased, and the ship was borne up aloft, then dashed with violence into the bosom of the deep. The cotter and his son stood looking at the awful sight, and their feeling hearts trembled for those in peril. At length the ship sprung a leak, the long boat was hoisted, all were eager to leave the ship, when owing to the rush, the boat was upset, and in their too hurried endeavours to preserve life, great part of the crew perished. From this agonising sight, the cotter and his son turned their eyes to the ship, where some they saw still clinging to the shrouds, but they could not long retain their hold; soon they were washed from their station, and engulphed with their companions in the deep; their eyes yet followed one man, he was a good swimmer, and he buffeted the angry waves until he was near the shore, with exhaustion he fainted; but he was borne up by the water, and washed on the beach, near the cliff.

"Come along, boy, come along, Anthony," said the cotter, "let us hasten to the poor souls' relief."

They ran to the spot, where the waves had washed the body, and there saw a young man lying apparently lifeless. The cotter drew the young man further on the beach, then opened the bosom of his dress, and found that though feeble, there was still a pulsation of the heart.

"Is he dead, father?" inquired the boy.

"No—no—Anthony, he is not dead," said the cotter; "come, boy, and help me up with him on my back."

"Stop father, the wind has blown away my cap," cried Anthony.

"Never mind thy cap, boy," said the old man, "the thought of saving the life of a fellow-creature, will do thee more good than twenty caps."

The good man hastened home with his burden, calling,—"come along, boy, come along, Anthony."

The cotter had the pleasure of seeing the young man revive; and on the following morning, whilst presenting him with a cup of hot elder wine, he inquired, "how feel you now?"

"Much better!" replied the young man, "but for your humanity, I must have perished."

"Say no more on it, I but did my duty," said the cotter, "he who could see fellow-creature perish, and stretch no hand to save him, does not deserve to class with brutes, however he may wear the form of man—it was a dismal sight to see the goodly ship go down, and the poor souls struggling with the waves so near to land.''

" Poor fellows !—think you, that none but me escaped the dreadful wreck ?"

" None, I fear me,'' replied the cotter, " whither are you bound ?"

" My home is many miles from hence,'' said the young man. I intend to set off soon as the morning dawns to-morrow ; order a chaise to be here in waiting at six precisely.''

" Nay, nay, bide here to-morrow, you'll be right welcome,'' replied the cotter's wife, " you are hardly yet recovered, and must be very weak.''

" I thank you,'' replied the young man ; " I am impatient to return, and must away in the morning.''

" Why he's impatient, dame, to see his sweetheart, 'tis very natural,'' said the cotter.

" Believe me,'' replied the young man, " it is my father and my sister that I wish to see.''

" And glad they'll be to see you,'' said the cotter's wife, for what's so pleasing to a parent's heart as a dutiful and loving child ?''

" A dutiful and loving child !'' repeated the young man, soon as the cotter's wife left the room ; " that is a title I do not deserve. I know my going to India grieved my father to the heart; yet I would go—gold was my idol—I thought if I had plenty of that yellow ore, every good must follow—but sadly am I disappointed; will it buy health, happiness, or true friendship?—no,'' he mentally said, " I have proved the reverse.''

Frederick Manby was in the chaise at the appointed hour ; and when he had reached the residence of his father, a most affectionate meeting took place between Frederick, his father, and Celeste. The day of his son's return was one of the most pleasing days ever experienced by Mr. Manby ; he introduced Frederick to Sir James Durant, and to his brother-in-law Osmond, the husband of Celeste.

Frederick heard of the fortune left him by his great uncle Russel, with very little emotion. " I have now plenty of money of my own,'' he said, " and I do not value that metal as I once did ; it will be no unpleasant acquisition.''

Frederick told his father of the narrow escape he had had of being drowned, and of the kindness shown him by the cotter.

" I am now come back, my dear father,'' said Frederick, " and never intend to leave England again ; money I have enough, and the wildness of my youth is over, —you, I know, will forgive me for the grief I have caused you.''

" Forgive you, Frederick ? why I was never angry with you,'' said Mr. Manby, and elated, he sung the following words:—

' Talk no more of old affairs,
They are stale and queerish ;
He who ever growling is,
I think rather bearish.
 Rum ti rum ti rum,
 Rum ti rum ti rido.

' When children wiser grow,
Parents should not flout 'em;
Left your wild oats behind,
And you can do without 'em.
 Rum ti tum ti tum,
 Rum ti rum ti rido.'

" Talk no more of past grievances, my boy,'' said Mr. Manby ; I wished to hear an account of your travels.''

" When I arrived in India, my friend got me a situation, as overlooker in one of his father's plantations,'' said Frederick, " and there I had not been more than a month, when I became acquainted with a Miss Elliot, whose father, a rich lanter, had lately died. This young lady was very partial to me, and with the consent of her mother, who valued her child's happiness above every other consideration, we were married. I then became possessed of what my soul had thirsted after—gold; and to the gratification of my pride, I was flattered by the obsequious homage of my slaves; and with extreme pride, I looked on the plantations, of which I now was lord; 'all these things are mine,' I exultingly said, 'like an eagle I have built my nest on a rock, where the storm cannot harm me.' But at that moment, the angel of death was hovering over my house; trouble and sorrow were about to fall upon me. I had two infant children, the eldest, a boy fifteen months old, and a girl, a babe about six weeks old; the boy was walking with his nurse, when some poisonous reptile stung him just above the ankle bone; the leg swelled to a great size, and in a few hours convulsions ended my boy's little existence."

CHAPTER XL.

Can costly robes, or beds of down,
Or all the gems, that deck the great and fair,
Give health, or ease the brow of care ?   OLD SONG.

" THE uneasiness we felt, concerning our boy, caused us at that time to be unmindful of anything else; but at length my wife thought on her baby, who she had not for several hours seen, and she expressed her surprise that her nurse had not brought the babe for her necessary sustenance. Agnes, a favourite slave, who waited on my wife, was desired to send the nurse with the babe to her mother; but in a fright, Agnes returned, and said—' The nurse and child had left the house for many hours, and had not yet returned.' A search was instantly made in the neighbourhood, when, at length, in a plantation, at about a quarter of a mile from my house, my babe and the nurse were found with both their throats cut; they were both dead and cold. It is impossible for me to describe the grief of my wife; she was a most affectionate mother, and the death of both her children and that in so horrible a manner, completely overcame her: she for a time was quite frantic; but medical skill at length restored her to sanity. But after she recovered her senses, she fell into a nervous fever, of which she died; and in the course of a few days, after the death of her daughter, my wife's mother also died. Who the diabolical perpetrator of the murder of my child and slave was never could be discovered; but there is every reason to believe, it was done by some of the slaves. After the death of my wife, I was taken ill, and my life was long despaired of; I had been very delirious; but at length I became calm and sensible of what was passing, but I was too low, to ask those about me for the nourishment I needed.

" My suffering was great; I had none who had my welfare at heart to attend me, but was surrounded by slaves and hirelings, who though they did not actually put me out of the world, for fear of punishment, yet they tried to hasten my death by the most inhuman neglect.

" The nurse, who attended my wife and her mother, was in the room, with two of my female slaves, who instead of smoothing my pillow, and moistening my parched lips, left me unnoticed to die at my leisure; whilst they regaled themselves with coffee, wine, cakes, and sweetmeats, and amused themselves with surmisin how I should be buried.

" Agnes, who had been treated more like a relation than a slave, came and looked at my ghastly feature as I lay still, and I was more like a corpse than a living being,

" 'Not dead yet !' she said, 'how troublesome—I hate to be stewed up here.'

" I then heard them contrive how they should rob me. ' There is much gold in that chest near his bed,' said Agnes, ' soon as he's dead we'll help ourselves ; he has no relations here—and if he had, death can tell no tales.'

" Too weak to call to my cruel attendants, I laid in extreme suffering. I wanted to be moved in a more easy position, and to have my parched lips moistened, for they clave, as it were, together.

"A quantity of the metal I had so coveted, was locked in a chest that stood beside me; in it there was gold sufficient to satisfy the most avaricious. It was near enough to my bed for me to lay my hand on it, if I had strength to have done so. But of what use was gold then to me? it would not moisten my lips, nor insure me the respect and attention of my slaves, when I could no longer command them.

"Then, then I felt what it was to have plenty of gold, and no affectionate friend; then it was that I thought on my relations, who in sickness had smoothed my pillow. And when I opened my eyes, I saw they were anxiously watching beside me.

"'Accursed gold!' I inwardly said, 'I will no longer place my happiness in thee. Oh! let my death-bed be as the death-bed of the poor cottager,' I inwardly said, 'surrounded by affection, rather than the death-bed of the monarch, left to the care of mercenary hirelings.'

At this juncture, my friend Mr. Mapleton entered the room; when he drew nigh my bed, I made signs to him, for speak I could not.

"What has Mr. Manby taken?" said my friend, "oh, sir, we cannot get him to take anything," said the nurse.

"I will myself try him," said Mr. Mapleton, "you all seem to have everything here in plenty."

"My friend, with his own hand, mixed some wine and water, which he held to my lips. I revived, and as well as I was able, I informed Mr. Mapleton of the conduct of my servants. There was not an hour passed in the day, without my receiving a visit from my kind friend, or some of his family; they took care that I was not neglected. Soon as I got better, I made up my mind to leave India, and come to England; for I longed to see you and my sister. I made up my mind to sell my plantations, and I got a good purchaser for them. After settling all my affairs in India, I entered the first ship that left India, for England; but as I before told you, when near Margate, the ship sprung a leak; but I was not destined to perish, I was picked up by a good cotter, and the bonds I had received for the sale of my estates, were in a small tin box, which I tied by a string round my waist, before I was washed into the sea."

CHAPTER XLI.

Tremble, thou wretch,
That has within thee, undivulged crimes,
Unwhipped of justice, hide thee, thou bloody hand.   SHAKSPERE.

THE news of Frederick Manby's return to England, and that he was now enjoying the society of his father and sister, soon spread in the neighbourhood and many persons with whom Frederick had been acquainted, called to see him, and to welcome his return to Cornwall. Amongst the rest of the visitors, who called, was Miss Devel. Frederick was always a great favourite with that lady, and she was very glad to see him, after his long absence; Miss Devel staid chatting until it was dark, and Frederick escorted the lady home.

Mr. Devel prevailed on Frederick to walk in, and take a glass of wine with him as they were old neighbours, who had not seen each other for so long a time. Miss Jane Devel, who had been from home all day, returned a few moments after Frederick Manby had entered the parlour, understanding from her sister, who was there, Miss Jane was much pleased, and as her dress was rather soiled, in consequence of her being out all day, she wished to change it before she appeared in the parlour. Jane went into the kitchen, to ask one of the servants for a light, but both the maids had been sent out some hours before, on errands for their master, and it being warm weather, the servants had neglected to make up the fire, which had gone out, nor could Jane by any means get a light, without going into the parlour, and that was not to be thought of.

Disappointed of getting a light, Jane thought she would do without one: as she was very careful in placing her things, and knew where to find them in the dark, Jane opened a drawer, and took from thence a white powder, she was in the habit of

using, to blend the lily with the rose, which Miss Jane thought glowed with too lively a red in her cheeks, and gave her more the appearance of a milking girl than a lady.

Having rubbed on some of this powder, Miss Jane put on another dress and a very elegant necklace, she had that day purchased, and having thrown a scarf over her shoulders, she descended to the parlour.

But, oh! unexpected misfortune; Ruth, one of the maids, had been sent up

No, 17.

stairs that morning to polish the stoves, and a supply of black lead was given by Miss Devel. After brushing the stoves, Ruth, who knew Miss Jane was from home, went into her room, in order to make free with some needles, which she knew were in the drawer of Miss Jane; and whilst she was searching for the needles, the paper with the black lead in it, unperceived by Ruth, fell into the drawer; thinking she heard some one coming up stairs, and without thinking of the lead, she hastened out of the apartment, nor did it again enter her mind.

To this accident, Jane owed the mortification that befel her, for she unfortunately, not expecting such a powder was there, rubbed her face with the black lead, instead of the white. Not at all aware of her mistake, she entered the parlour with a smiling countenance, little dreaming of her worse than sooty appearance. The whole party looked at her with amaze, and Miss Devel cried—

"For Heaven's, Jane! what have you been about? have you come with the intention to frighten us all, or do you intend to play the Queen of Ethiopia, in all her glory?"

Jane, at this moment, observed the colour of her hands, and, quite abashed, she ran out of the parlour.

"Why, what's the girl got in her head now? what's the meaning of this freak?" cried Mr. Devel.

Frederick could not help smiling, as he took his leave of Miss Devel and her father, suspecting the true cause, that Miss Jane had mistaken black for white.

Mrs. Immorf very frequently visited Celeste, and Celeste was very often at Ravenswood Castle, with Mrs. Immorf.

Percival and Parrolla Immorf were grown two very fine boys; but the turbulent and morose temper of Parrolla gave his mother much concern.

And what was worse, he seemed to hate his brother, who was a very mild and well-disposed boy. Though so young, this malice towards his brother appeared in the little Parrolla; it seemed as if born with him—a natural antipathy.

Mrs. Immorf thought with pain on the gipsy's prediction; but she hoped that the words spoken by that wild woman, were like most of the gipsies sooth-sayings—false, and built on no other foundation than their own inventive imaginations.

Two years had worn away, and Count Herman was during that time roaming in different parts of the globe, which his preternatural existence enabled him to do.

Again he returned to Naples, and he thought on the Marchese De Gusman, who had returned from Sweden, and was again dwelling in his palace.

Count Herman again watched near the monastery of the Contrite Heart, and again saw the Marchese De Gusman enter that edifice. The countenance of the Marchese bore yet a deeper shade of melancholy.

The marchese, whilst in Sweden, had met one who caused every chord in his heart to vibrate with agony. That person aroused in its full force the worm that never died in his bosom; and caused the marchese to fall for some days into a state of the deepest melancholy.

The person who caused these feelings to arise in the bosom of the marchese, was but a feeble and aged man; but a giant in all his strength and power, could not have struck such terror, nor have caused the tremulous sensation that then passed over the nerves of the marchese. He, who he met creeping along with a stick, which he held in his hand to support himself, was an old man, whose name was Lindo.

The old man seemed to be bent down by age and affliction; but though weak, he appeared still to retain his faculties. And as he passed, his eyes, which were still lustrous, rested on the countenance of the marchese, who they looked on, as the marchese thought, with a reproachful expression, and they reminded him of one who was then no more.

The Marchese De Gusman could not have met a person more repugnant to his feelings than old Lindo. He thought Lindo knew him, and in his glare of scrutiny and hate, seemed to say—

" Where's Rachel ?—where's my daughter ?"

The marchese turned into another street to avoid the old man, who he thought would follow and accost him.

But Lindo had no such intention; he had no knowledge of the person of the marchese, whom, he had never seen but once, and that was when his mind was occupied by anger and terror. On the night of his daughter's elopement, he saw the marchese—then, and then only.

It was the old man's way, to look with scrutiny, dislike, and suspicion on every person; for all he saw, he thought meant to cheat and plunder him.

The old man had left Spain for Sweden, in order to avoid his run-away daughter, who he had made a vow never to see nor forgive. Although he had no child, nor any particular person to whom he wished to leave his wealth, yet he still continued his course of usury, sedulously hoarding up gold.

With a heart untouched by any feelings of benevolence, he still grovelled on to increase that wealth he had not the heart to use.

With feelings excited, and almost worked up to agony by the unexpected sight of the man he had so deeply injured, the marchese pursued his way; but in his mind's eye, the form of Rachel stood before him in all her beauty, as when he first saw her—and he thought on his child; and the exclamation of "Oh. God ? be merciful unto me !" fell from his lips.

Not to keep the reader in suspense, it may now be necessary to give some account of the Marchese De Gusman.

CHAPTER XLII.

See, how she leans her cheek upon her hand.
Oh! that I was a glove upon that hand, that I might touch that cheek.

SHAKSPERE.

JULIAN DE GUSMAN, the second son of the Marchese De Gusman, when about eighteen years of age, left home to reside with an aunt in Spain.

Leonora De Gusman, the sister of the Marchese De Gusman, was married to the Baron De Medina, a Spanish nobleman; and having no children of her own, she sent to Italy for her nephew; and the baron and baroness intended to promote the interest of their nephew all that lay in their power; and as they had no child of their own, they intended to make Julian their heir.

This offer was gladly embraced by Julian De Gusman, who being but a younger brother he needed some further addition to the fortune his father would be able to give him, in order to keep up the dignity of his family.

Julian had resided with his aunt at Madrid about two years, when passing through an obscure street, he saw sitting at a window a very beautiful young woman; although the house was not large nor the appearance of it genteel, yet the lady was richly drest.

The more Julian De Gusman looked at the lady the more he was fascinated by her beauty; and whether she was a respectable person or a lady whose favour was to be bought by a golden introduction, Julian did not know.

The lady, without noticing Julian, left the window.

Julian could get no sleep that night for thinking of the lady; the next day he walked down the obscure street again, but the lady was not visible; but an old man left the house, and after very cautiously shutting the door, he went down the street in a direction to where Julian was standing.

When, to avoid the penetrating glance of the old man, who Julian thought looked at him with some suspicion, he turned down an avenue until the old man was out of sight.

" This will be a good opportunity and such a one as may seldom occur," thought Julian, " I will knock and ask for the lady, now the father, or whoever the old man may be, is gone out. Yet, before I do so," he mentally said, "it were better for me to inquire, and find out the name and condition of the family."

Julian, in order to satisfy himself of this particular, went into a shop in the neighbourhood, where he learnt that the lady did not belong to that class of females he had surmised, on account of the richness of her dress and the meanness of her abode; but that she was a person of character and respectability, living with her father, whose name was Lindo, a merchant dealing in precious stones, a money lender, and was very rich.

And the young lady, Julian found, was his only child.

"I don't think my family would be willing for me to marry a trader's daughter," thought Julian, "they being all of the nobility. But her being a daughter of a trader does not lessen her loveliness, nor can want of birth alter the symmetry of her features, nor dim the lustre of her eyes."

Besides, the words "extremely rich," acted on Julian, whose besetting sin was avarice. He was from a boy of a very interested disposition, and loved money better than most things; yet he was affectionate, and always rather of a melancholy and religious turn of mind.

"Extremely rich!" Julian repeated to himself; "and what thread-bare garments the lank-sided miser had on!"

"When Julian again reached the old man's door, he stood for some time considering whether he should knock or not. "And if he did knock, what should he say to the person who might open the door?"

"Oh, I will ask for the old man himself," thought Julian; "I know he is out and cannot answer me—perhaps the lovely creature herself may open the door."

But in this hope Julian was disappointed; the door was opened by a young man with a pen stuck behind his ear.

Julian inquired of the young man "if his master was at home?"

"He is not," was the reply, "but you can leave your business with me," said the young man.

Julian paid no attention to the words of the scribe; he was listening to hear if he could catch a sound of the lady's voice, and looking down the passage in hopes of seeing her.

The young man repeated, "you can leave your business with me."

"I have occasion to borrow a sum of money," said Julian, hardly knowing what he said.

"Your name, and the security you propose," said the young man.

Rather confused, Julian hesitated, then said, "the sum I need is not large, and my security is undeniable; it is rather a delicate business—I will call to-morrow and see your master."

Julian could not see or hear anything of the lady; but, too much in love to rest, he continually watched the house until he saw the young lady go out. And with little difficulty Julian succeeded in introducing himself to her notice.

When the young lady first left home from the direction she took, Julian thought her intention was to pass through a crowded part of the city; but he was surprised to see that she turned her steps from the crowded streets and walked to a spot some little distance from the city, a place rather lone and unfrequented, situated in a valley, and overshaded by trees.

Here Julian had an opportunity of pleading the violence of his love, to which the young lady listened, and was persuaded to grant Julian another interview.

Meeting after meeting followed, and Julian heard from the young lady, "that many noblemen would be glad if they possessed half the riches her father was master of, besides precious stones to a large amount. And at the death of my father, I shall receive cash to the amount of twenty thousand pounds left me by my uncle," she continued, "but my father must not know of our intimacy."

"And why not?" inquired Julian,

"I will tell you," replied the young lady, "but it is in confidence. My father, though it is not generally known, is a Jew; and never will he, I am sure, suffer me to wed a Christian. Therefore my father must not know of our acquaintance."

Julian had been acquainted with the young lady, whose name was Rachel, about three months, when the nigh approach of winter caused the weather to be unfit for walking, and by that means prevented Rachel from so often seeing her lover.

Nor could she now so frequently leave home; for her father had become suspicious that all was not right with Rachel, on account of her frequent and long absences from home.

This conduct of his daughter gave the old man some uneasiness, as to where she spent her time when abroad.

He had inquired among their friends, and found that his daughter now but very seldom visited them; and when she did, her stay was but of very short duration.

Old Lindo questioned his daughter as to where she spent her time, but could not obtain a satisfactory answer, which made the old man yet more uneasy.

To quiet the suspicion of her father, Rachel now but very seldom left home; but unable to live without seeing her lover, she privately admitted him, when her father, and the clerk, and the female servant were gone to bed.

It happened one night, when the old Jew was rather indisposed, that he was tormented by uneasy dreams of robbers, who he thought were breaking into the house, and carrying off his money. He awoke from his sleep, but the impression of his dream so afflicted his mind, that he really believed he heard the noise the robbers made in forcing his shutters.

Hastily the old man arose, and softly creeping from his bed-room with noiseless steps, he descended the stairs, when he heard persons in coversation, in the lower apartment—he heard the voice of his daughter, and a sound of kisses given and received.

Irritated to madness, the old Jew burst into the room, to see what intruder dare, at that late hour, to enter his dwelling, and the old man was almost choked with passion, when he saw a Christian with his daughter.

He seized Julian by the collar, and as soon as passion would let his words find utterance, he called, "help!—robbers!—mnrder!"

But the strength of the Jew was unequal to that of Julian; he broke from the old man's grasp, and having thrown him down on the floor, he left the house as quickly as possible, not staying to see if her father, who was stunned by the fall, was dead or not. Rachel followed her lover, they took some bye-paths, until they came to an unfrequented spot, where they stopped to take breath.

"This is a most unlucky business," said Julian, "Rachel, I wish at this time you had not left your house.

"And is it already come to this?" said Rachel, bursting into tears. "Do I not forsake friends and religion, and all for you—think you I could again face my father?"

"True—true," replied Julian, kissing away her tears, "all my fear is, that you will be torn from me by your father; and if a noise is made in this affair, it may too prematurely reach the ears of my family; it rather vexes me about your father, who I hope has received no serious injury by his fall; if he has, your being missing might cause unjust suspicion, and cost us some trouble."

"What? then you think his falling with such violence has killed him," said Rachel.

"Perhaps it has."

"But who can blame me? there can be no marks indicative of murder about him, his death would appear to be in consequence of a fall. I shall be very sorry if such is the case; but then I shall receive all my father's property, there is none but myself entitled to it."

This unfeeling speech of Rachel's somewhat opened the eyes of Julian to her real sentiments.

"Rachel is not the tender, disinterested being I thought her," mentally said Julian, "but no matter, perhaps in a wife, it is more to my advantage her being without those fine qualifications; if she is kind and disinterested to me, that's sufficient. Her sentiments respecting the old man perfectly agree with my own, indeed, I feel more than indifference towards him. How often have I wished the old fellow dead, that he might fall down and dislocate his cursed neck, be run over, or in some way be sent to a better world, but not by my hand. If he is indeed dead, his having died in the way he did will give me some uneasiness, yet why should it, on my part, it was quite accidental, he sought his own destruction, the difficulty now was where to place Rachel, and how to provide her with a hat and cloak, for she had on neither."

Since Rachel had admitted Julian into her father's house, he had kept very late hours, which he was unable to do without such fact being known to the servants in his uncle's mansion.

That no tales of the late hours he kept might reach the ears of his uncle and aunt, who were then on a visit at Montpellier; and in order to blind the servants, to prevent their knowing whether he was in or out; Julian privately had a key made, so that he could admit himself whenever he chose.

Availing himself of this circumstance, he again with Rachel entered the city; and having opened the door that led into his aunt's mansion, he left Rachel in a passage, then went up stairs, and made free with the first hat and cloak that hung in his way.

Morn now began to break through the clouds of night, they then left the city, and, after walking a considerable distance, they cam up to a lone cottage overhadowed by trees, at the door of which a venerable old man was standing.

CHAPTER XLIII.

Lady, I can conduct you to a poor,
But loyal cottage.   MILTON.

SEEING two persons stopping near his cottage, the old man approached to meet them.

Julian inquired of the old man if he had a room in his cottage, where his wife (for so he termed Rachel) could rest awhile.

"For she is in a bad state of health," said Julian, "and very faint."

"The lady can rest in my cottage, and welcome," said the old man, "walk in, you will find my dame there."

When Julian reached the cottage, he found the good wife preparing breakfast; Julian informed her that they were sent there by her good man; and desired to know if she could accommodate them with breakfast, for which he would pay her what she required.

"I have nothing but bread, milk, and fresh churned butter, to offer you," said the good woman, "but to that you are heartily welcome."

After they had breakfasted, Rachel complained of being faint, and she went into the garden at the back of the cottage for air; where she was followed by Julian.

And it was agreed between them, that Rachel should remain at the cottage until the next day, meanwhile Julian was to look out an abode for Rachel suitable to the circumstance she was then placed in—a place where she could remain in privacy until they could arrange their affairs; and consult in what maner it would be best to introduce Rachel to his aunt.

Leaving Rachel with the cottager's wife, Julian returned home, and endeavoured to compose his mind, to which the adventure of the preceding night gave but little satisfaction.

Julian had a confidential servant, who knew almost every secret of his master's heart; nor did Julian withhold what had transpired in regard of Rachel; he told

Carlos, for that was the name of his servant, how she had left her father's house, and the unhappiness he felt in not knowing where to place her.

However, Julian at length made up his mind, that Carlos should take a house in his own name, and at length a house was fixed on by Julian, as one that would be suitable.

It was a small detached house, standing in a garden, and entirely hid from the view of any passer-by.

The entrance to the garden was through a gate of a very peculiar make, and the walls of the premises were surrounded by a high wall.

Julian gave his servant money, to purchase furniture as was requisite, and desired that Carlos would not fail to have the house ready for the reception of Rachel, the next evening.

According to desire of Julian, all was ready for the reception of Rachel, with whom he now spent great part of his time.

Julian desired Carlos to learn, if possible, how it fared with old Lindo, and whether any inquiry had been made after Rachel.

That the old man was not dead, was certain, for Carlos saw him leave his house, nor was he broken-hearted on account of the flight of his daughter, for whom he had made no inquiry, and whose absence, for anything, Carlos could learn, was yet a secret in the neighbourhood.

Passing through the street again, Carlos saw that the house was shut up, and on inquiring, he found that Lindo had removed with the greatest privacy, at day-break, that very morning, and no person in the neighbourhood could tell to where he had removed.

"Oh!" cried Rachel, when she heard from Carlos, of her father's removal, "it is on my account that he has removed—he has abandoned me, given me quite up."

"But we may discover to where he is gone," said Julian, "and when he finds you are married, he will not be inexorable; if we find to where he has removed as soon as we are married you shall visit him."

"He has taken no trouble to inquire after me," said Rachel, "and that circumstance convinces me that he never will forgive me; never more must I pollute his dwelling; I know his mind so well, that he would spurn me, were I even to kneel to him, and clinging to him beg for his forgiveness—he would shake me off with abhorrence, and shrink from my unholy touch."

Julian hummed a tune, as was his way when anything vexed or displeased him; he walked to the window;—"immensely rich,—gold and precious stones," he muttered to himself, "and to lose such a windfall, is enough to drive one mad. The old fellow's sudden removal, I hope, is only a start of passion; he never can desert his only child, and leave his wealth to strangers."

Julian now seated himself by the fire, opposite Rachel, who was sitting, leaning on a table, her face resting on her hands; neither of them spoke for some time, they both seemed to be taken up with their own reflections.

At length Julian starting from a deep reverie, said, "for Heaven's sake, Rachel! how are we ever to get the money left you by your uncle. If your father should continue to conceal himself, he may die and go to the lower regions, and we be none the wiser, the executors of course would not pay you the money, until you could prove his death."

"I was thinking of the same thing," said Rachel, "we must make all possible inquiry, and, if we find him, keep an eye on him, without his knowing it."

"That will be our only course," said Julian; "are you sure that your father has no power to prevent you from receiving the money left you by your uncle."

"None in the least, I assure you," said Rachel, "my father receives the interest of my uncle's legacy during his life, but when he dies, the principle must come to me."

CHAPTER XLIV.

A sturdy lad,
With eye so merry, and with foot so light,
That none could chide his gamesomeness.

ION, A TRAGEDY.

THE Baron and Baroness De Medina were now returning from Montpellier, which prevented Julian from spending so much of his time with Rachel; nor had he indeed now the inclination to do so; for though still fond of Rachel, he found her constant complaint, on account of her not being introduced to his aunt, and the delay of their marriage, extremely disagreeable.

For Julian began now to reflect, that to take such steps required some deliberation.

Month after month passed on, but no tidings could be heard of old Lindo, although Julian spared neither expense nor trouble in his endeavour to find him.

Rachel, finding she was soon likely to become a mother, still more importuned her lover, to act by her as he had pledged his word to do.

She had renounced Judaism, was willing to be baptized according to the Christian faith, and to do whatsoever Julian might require; but still the marriage was postponed on one pretence or other.

At length Rachel was delivered of a son, who was called Julian.

The income Julian received from his father was not large, and he found the expense he incurred in the maintenance of Rachel extremely inconvenient.

Julian then wanted nearly twelve months before he became of age; and his fortune would not be large when he was so.

And with vexation he reflected, that it was indeed a great chance if ever he touched one piece of the gold left Rachel by her uncle.

Mortified, he considered that he must, in consequence of supporting Rachel and her child, deprive himself of many enjoyments befitting his age and condition.

Six years had wore away, and yet no tidings were heard of old Lindo.

The little Julian, who was now five years old, could read very well; and knew all the notes of a guitar his father had bought for him.

Julian was very fond of the water, and the only recreation Rachel had, was her accompanying her lover in his aquatic excursions.

Julian would frequently hire a boat, and row several leagues in the course of the day.

Sometimes they would take their wine and provisions with them, and land in some shady spot, where Julian would sit angling by the water-side; whilst Rachel and the child amused themselves as they thought fit.

The elder brother of Julian had been for some time in a very declining state of health, and a letter, Julian received from his father, informed him of the increased indisposition of his brother.

"He is continually talking of death," said the Marchese De Gusman, "and seems fully aware that he will not live long, and sorry am I to say," continued the Marchese, "that his mother and myself are of the same opinion, for we see him daily wasting away, and his disease his physician declares to be consumption.

This letter caused a great change in the mind and manner of Julian: if his brother died, which there was every probability of his doing, he of course would be heir to the family estates, which were large; and Julian found himself not a little elevated, when he contemplated the rent roll, and the income he should receive after his father's death, should his brother not survive.

Julian certainly had loved Rachel, and he still loved her, but not as he had done her disagreeable temper and unamiable disposition very much lessened the regard he had once felt for her, and Julian now much regretted that he had ever known her, he had hoped to finger some of the gold of her father; but as if penetrating into his design, and willing to disappoint him, the old Jew concealed himself so closely, that Julian feared, in case he married Rachel, the treasure of the old Jew would never come into his possession.

To marry Rachel without money, he could never think of; and he knew her temper and disposition were such as would not endear him to his aunt, and at all reconcile her to his marriage with the Jewess.

The lowness of his finances, too, gave Julian great uneasiness, he hardly knew how to procure money for Rachel sufficient to defray the expenses of housekeeping.

Out of temper he came to the cottage; and, as usual, he found Rachel in very

No. 18.

low spirits, on account of Julian being so little at the cottage ; and also on account of the lone and sequestered life she and the child had lived.

"He, poor fellow, is like an idiot," she said, "he knows nothing ; no, not even if he lives in Spain or Greenland ; nor does he know the name or condition of his own father ; you will not suffer him to have a child to play with him ; nor has the poor little hermit been more than six or seven times since its birth beyond the walls that surround him."

"He will see enough of the world in time, and perhaps more than he likes," said Julian, "the urchin is happy enough, and that is sufficient ; would I was as happy as he is ! I know you have but a dull life of it here, Rachel," continued Julian, for he saw that Rachel was in tears ; "what say you to a day upon the water ? and Julian shall go," he said, as he kissed the child, and took him up in his lap.

The proposal of Julian was agreed to by Rachel; and the day after the following was fixed on for their excursion.

CHAPTER XLV.

Vainly thou talkest of loving me alone,
Each man is man, and all the sex are one.					PRIOR.

ON the very day that Julian had promised to accompany Rachel on the water, his uncle proposed that Julian should accompany him and his aunt to a party to which they were invited.

"But from this invitation, Julian excused herself, although it was to his no small mortification, for he would have preferred being of his uncle's party.

But he had promised Rachel, and he knew her temper too well to suppose she would forgive him such a disappointment; he knew it would be the cause of eternal sullenness, and upbraiding.

Much ruffled in mind, Julian reached the cottage, to inform Rachel that the boat was ready.

"She upbraids me with the child's ignorance," thought Julian, "he shall not be like an idiot through my means, nor lose, through taking pleasure, one day's improvement ; he shall take his books in the boat with him, so that he may learn his task, and his guitar he shall also take, that he may practise his notes."

The book and guitar were placed in the boat by Julian, who informed Rachel of his reason for so doing.

Rachel saw Julian was cross and irritable : she thought that spending the day with her and the child was unpleasant to him ; and she too felt ruffled and offended.

"You are too hard upon poor Julian," she said ; "but you are cross and severe to us both."

"He shall be neither a dunce nor an idiot through me !" cried Julian, "I will not be contradicted ;" and his colour rose to crimson.

"You have all your own way," said Rachel ; "you'd crush me like a worm beneath your feet—I that have given up all for you."

"How many times have I heard that before?" said Julian, "it's stale and sickening. If you go on in this way, I'll row back."

Rachel was silent—and more than an hour had passed without either Julian or Rachel having spoken one word; the child was playing over the notes of his guitar, whilst his mother sat reflecting on circumstances of no very pleasing nature; and his father, who now found rowing indeed a toil, was pulling away with all his might to reach land, with his eyes fixed on the altered sky, which was fast overspreading with dark clouds, from whose lowering aspect, Julian saw a dreadful storm was approaching.

Soon loud thunder rolled heavily above them, and the lightning's vivid glare played on the water around.

Rachel had been too absorbed in thought, to observe the changing sky; but now the loud bolt aroused her from her deep reverie, and the lightning's glare mode her tremble with apprehension.

"Had you not better," she said, addressing Julian, "row up to those trees that grow on yonder bank, and let us take shelter there until the storm hath subsided?"

Julian rowed to the spot Rachel had pointed out, and, as he did so, he said—

"I had rather encounter the storms of Heaven than the storm and turbulence of an ill-tempered woman."

The tears stole into Rachel's eyes, when she stepped from the boat; and with a look expressive of resentment, she refused the offered hand of Julian, that was held out to assist her out of the boat.

Without noticing her ire, Julian again stepped into the boat, and took from thence to where Rachel was sitting, not only the wine and eatables they had brought with them, but the child's guitar and books also.

"Come, eat up your dinner!" said Julian to the child, "then run over the notes of your guitar."

The lightning's glare had not yet subsided, and still loud thunder rolled awfully above them.

Awaiting its discontinuance, Julian and Rachel remained beneath the trees where they had sought shelter; and bitter taunts and severe recriminations passed between them.

Rachel reproached Julian with luring her from her father's house, and then ill-treating her; and of his cruel neglect in not marrying her before the birth of her child; "for should you succeed to your family titles and estates," she continued, "in consequence of the death of your brother, my poor boy, my poor Julian!"— and she hugged the child to her bosom, whilst tears flowed fast down her face; "my boy!" she again repeated; "my poor Julian, could not inherit."

"Nor did I mean him to inherit," said Julian, from a spirit of contradiction. "Julian, Julian the illegitimate, shall never inherit the estates of my forefathers."

"Wretch!" cried Rachel, in agony of grief, "Why did you lure me from my home? why seek a daughter of Judah, to make her miserable?"

"A daughter of Judah!" said Julian with a sneer, "rather say a daughter of Moab; did you not give me every encouragement? Did you not turn from the public streets, even at our first interview, into obscure and sequestered walks? your eyes brightened at my approach 'tis true, but it was not the refined passion of love that caused their brilliancy; it was the passion that irradiated the countenance of the dark-eyed Moab, on the night she so plentifully supplied her father with wine. How was it that with your person and fortune none of your own people sought you in marriage?—They knew you too well."

"And what did they know of me?" said Rachel, rage sparkling in her eyes. "Slanderer, what did they know of me?" and she struck Julian on the face, a blow that made the water flow from his eyes, and for some moments almost blinded him.

"Never do that again," cried Julian, much irritated. "Rachel, as you value your own life, never do that again. And you, you little villain," cried Julian, as he struck the child a violent blow; for the passion of Julian was yet more heightened by detecting the little boy making faces at him.

"Do so again," cried Julian, "and I'll trample you beneath my feet."

The violence of the blow given him by his father, caused the blood to flow from the child's nose and mouth.

Seeing that Rachel, with the fury of a tiger, again struck Julian a yet more violent blow in the face.

In a moment of extreme irritation, and almost unconscious what he did, Julian plunged the dagger he wore into the bosom of the unfortunate Rachel.

"Oh! I am murdered," she cried, "I am murdered; but Julian, my child, he shall avenge me," she shrieked, as she fell to the earth.

"Avenge!" was again repeated; not by the dying Rachel, but by a responding echo, that yet more awfully repeated the words of the dying woman.

Pale, ghastly, and saturated in blood, lay the unfortunate Rachel, who in a few minutes ceased to breathe.

Grieved and horror-stricken, Julian beheld the fatal effect of his ungoverned rage; but fear for his own safety superseded every other consideration. He took up the bleeding body of Rachel and threw it into the water—it sunk down like a stone, leaving the water crimsoned with blood.

Julian looked around him for the child; but terrified, the child had fled. Julian called him, but no answer was returned.

The heart's blood of Rachel lay in a crimson stream on the earth. Appalled and trembling he turned from the ghastly sight.

All was now still—no sound was heard by Julian, for the voice of the thunder had ceased, and all but his own bosom seemed serenity and peace.

But a voice seemed to whisper in the ear of the murderer, "blood will have blood—the inquisition awaits thee!"

Footsteps he now thought were approaching, and with extreme dread he jumped into the boat and rowed with all speed from the fatal spot—nor did he again call or look after his child.

With alarm he perceived that there were several spots of blood on his clothes; he wetted his handkerchief in the river, with which he rubbed the spots, and after much trouble caused them to disappear.

It was dark when Julian reached the mansion of his aunt; complaining of illness, he immediately went to bed; but not, as it it may be supposed, to rest.

In imagination, he still beheld the bleeding Rachel lie prostrate on the earth. And if for a moment he closed his eyes in slumber, he thought the officers of the inquisition had arrived, and were loudly demanding the murderer; and once or twice he jumped out of bed, as the words, "Oh, hide me—save me!" issued from his lips. Carlos, who slept in the next chamber to his master, had more than once that night been disturbed by the fearful exclamations of Julian.

To that faithful servant Julian told the fatal story, and spoke of the uneasiness he felt concerning the child. "What to do about him, I don't know," said Julian; "to leave him to his fate, will be barbarous; and to go and look for him would be attended with the greatest danger. He witnessed the whole transaction, and, before this time, has, perhaps, met with some one to whom he has told the whole affair. I might be laid in wait for, and the ground, saturated with blood, would prove the child's evidence."

"Oh, never think of going after the child," said Carlos, "it would be placing yourself in the most imminent danger; he will, I dare say, be taken care of by some goatherd or fisher. And should he not, whose life is of the most consequence, his or yours?"

CHAPTER XLVI.

Not poppy, nor mandragora,
Nor all the drowsy syrups of the world,
Shall ever medicine thee to that sweet sleep
Which thou hast yesterday.   SHAKSPERE.

THE mind of Julian now knew no peace; a dread of his guilt being discovered through the means of the child, embittered every moment of his existence, and he determined to leave Spain and return to the house of his father.

For every footstep he heard behind him made him start and tremble, and every person he conversed with, he thought regarded him with a look of suspicion.

At nights, he was tormented by the horrid visions, that he almost feared to close his eyes in sleep. He dreamed he saw the murdered Rachel lying on the river, and upborne by the water. She had on the same white dress, and her raven locks hung over her shoulders as they used to do. From the wound in her bosom the blood profusely flowed until it had turned the water crimson; the sky, he thought, appeared to be on fire, casting a yellow glare on the river, of blood.

Horrified, Julian awoke from this dream; and he could not close his eyes any more that night.

In the morning he fully made up his mind to tell his uncle and aunt of his intention of returning to Italy, not to stay long he pretended, but merely on a visit to his father and sick brother.

Whilst Julian was planning this excuse, a letter came from his father which imformed him that his brother was worse, his disorder was rapidly increased, and it was deemed impossible, according to all human probability, that he could long survive. The Marchese De Gusman hoped that the Baron and Baroness De Medina would not take it amiss, his wishing the return of Julian, as they must be aware that the unexpected death of his eldest son would make a very great alteration in the circumstances of Julian as he of course would succeed to the family title and estates.

This letter contained news that made the heart of Julian leap for joy, for he was in continual dread.

Julian sought his aunt, and made known to her the contents of his father's letter.

"I am very sorry to part with you, Julian," said his aunt; "but if your father loses your brother, it would be selfish in the baron and myself to wish to detain you."

Preparations were made for the immediate departure of Julian, who in a few days set sail for Italy. Carlos accompanied his master, for he was a great favourite with Julian, and not only that, but now there was a tie between them; Carlos was aware of what passed in the inmost recesses of his master's heart.

Julian was gifted with a fine person and youth, and now every prospect of being possessed of the family title and estates, which his avaricious heart had long coveted, yet notwithstanding all these advantages, he was not happy, nor could he be so.

The worm that never dies gnawed his inmost soul. "Blood will have blood!" seemed to be continually whispering in his ear.

He walked on the deck of the ship to amuse his mind; but the water the more reminded him of the unfortunate Rachel, when she sank down, crimsoning the water with her blood.

When at midnight he heard the turbulent waves beat against the sides of the ship, he thought it was on his account; and in fancy he heard the fretful water say, " Cast forth the murderer ?"

Carlos did all in his power to soothe the troubled mind of his master, and used every argument in his power to dissuade him from thinking on that which never could be recalled.

"It indeed," grieves me to see this continued depression of your spirits," said Carlos. " What is done cannot be undone; you study these things too deeply. Can grief, however poignant, arise the insensate dead, and give decay again its roseate bloom? Will grief re-animate the lifeless body, and in her veins again pour life's warm current? We know it will not; then wherefore waste your health in sorrow? If you go on in this way, a nervous consumption must be the consequence."

"I feel the truth of your words, Carlos," replied Julian; "but you must suppose the impression this dreadful affair has made on me, is not easily to be shaken off! Oh, what a look she gave me! then the echo, 'avenge!' it repeated; ' Julian shall avenge me !' This threatened vengeance dwells upon my mind—Julian, I feel assured, though at some distant period, will cross my path, and bring destruction on me."

"Is it possible that you can be so superstitious, signor," said Carlos; "but these thoughts are occasioned by the weakness of your nerves, which must have suffered a great shock by the dreadful event."

When Julian arrived at his paternal home, he found his brother extremely ill, and reduced to a mere skeleton.

The sight of decaying mortality was no pleasing contemplation for the nervous Julian; but he had not many weeks that melancholy picture before him—his brother was soon borne to the mausoleum of his forefathers.

The Marchese De Gusman was grieved to see the continued depression visible in Julian, and the old gentleman attributed it to the sorrow he felt, and the shock he had sustained, on account of the loss of his brother.

The Marchese De Gusman wished his son to marry, and a match was made up between Julian and the Signora Clementina Di Orriel, a lady of very high birth, and great fortune. The Marchese De Gusman was dead; and the marchese did not live long after his son's marriage.

Julian, now Marchese De Gusman, had no children by his lady, nor did they live very happily together. There was a gloom and heaviness that always hung over him; and any person who observed the marchese, would conclude that all was not right within.

Twenty years and upwards had worn away from the death of the unfortunate Rachel, to the time when Count Herman saw the marchese and his lady step into their carriage to go to the theatre; it was not to please himself that the Marchese De Gusman went there, but to please his lady; for such at that time was the mind of the marchese, that he would have preferred a visit to the monastery of the Contrite Heart, rather than going to any part of pleasure in Naples.

Indeed, the Marchese De Gusman was not now a man fit to mix with the world; for he was remarked by all he happened to be in company with.

. The startled look; the abstracted manner; and deep musings into which the Marchese De Gusman frequently fell, was a subject of conversation amongst persons of his acquaintance.

The haughty marchesa was much displeased and mortified, in consequence of her lord.

"How ridiculous you appear when in company, Julian," she said, "one would really think that some heavy guilt burdened your conscience, and which crime is the cause of your melancholy."

"Crime!" said the marchese, starting, "who says I have been guilty of crime? Cannot a man enjoy his own reflection without being accused? you know, Clementina, I no longer can enjoy the pleasures of the world."

"And wherefore should you not?" replied the marchese; "it is a pity that you married, if you are determined to entirely relinquish the pleasures of the world. I wonder you did not turn monk—indeeed, 'tis not too late now."

"It is not," replied the marchese; and he left the apartment.

CHAPTER XLVII.

What charnel hath been rifled for these bones?
Fie, this is pedantry—they look uncouthly.   Rowe.

SOME few days after this conversation had passed between the marchese and marchesa, the marchese was taken very ill, and his disorder for a long time baffled the skill of his physicians.

Wildly he raved of new-made graves and sepulchres, of rowing in boats on rivers of blood.

"Take away this mummery," he cried, "these bones and skulls, and all those ghastly emblems of death; where did they come from?" he cried, "what tomb have they been raking to find them?" Then in a low voice, almost a whisper, he said, "Tell me, are they Rachel's bones?—Where is Julian?" he raved, "what, would no kind hand offer him a morsel of bread? Must the child of the Marchese De Gusman want bread? Bring out old Lindo's money bags,—his gold, and precious stones; shall his grandchild starve amidst such riches? He must, they will not take them for food. Julian starved; see,—see his skeleton is dancing before me."

All these wild ravings of the marchese were heard by the marchesa, who now felt assured there was a cause for her husband's melancholy.

She, during his intervals of sanity, would have inquired who Rachel and the Julian he rave of were; but the marchese feared to irritate her husband by such questions.

When in pain, and under great depression of spirits, the only consolation of the marchese was the company and spiritual consolation of the good Monk Anselmo; for whom a messenger was frequently sent to the monastery of the Contrite Heart.

The company of the good monk was more efficacious to the troubled mind of the marchese than was the drugs of his physician. Long and protracted was the illness of the marchese, and slow and doubtful was his recovery, but he was at length restored to a state of convalescence.

CHAPTER XLVIII.

But oh! what form of prayer
Can serve my turn? forgive me my foul murder.   SHAKSPERE.

ONE morning, when the marchese was in his library, where he expected to be free from observation or interruption, he betook himself to prayer; and in his prayer, he again solicited pardon on account of the murder of Rachel, and for his having deserted his child.

The marchesa was listening. "Rachel again," she inwardly said, "and the child, now the marchese is perfectly sane; what can he mean by talking of these persons? I will know," and she went into the library.

Giving way to a fiery and jealous temper, although she saw the marchese was in an attitude of prayer, she disturbed him by saying—

"Who is the Rachel I heard you name in your prayers? and whose the child who you also named? you deceived me in saying; your naming them in your delirium, was but the effect of your illness; and the Rachel you raved of, was but the creature of your fevered imagination. You must have known her, or why name her in your prayers, and talk of your name-sake Julian being starved to death—of boats, and rivers of blood."

"Why do you disturb me from my devotion?" said the marchese. "I told you, that what I said about these persons in my delirium was void of any foundation for me to do so. I might have raved of the gipsy queen, or the queen of France, for aught I know."

"No, no, you raved of no such persons," said the marchesa, "Rachel was the person who troubled your mind, and this Julian, when I heard you speak of them, it made me very unhappy. Soon as you got better, I slightly inquired who they were, I saw you start and change countenance, but I would not then press the question, fearing to vex or excite you; but now I will not be put off. I insist in knowing who was the woman, and who was the child?"

At this moment Father Manfride, the confessor of the marchesa, was announced, and he was desired to walk into the library, where the marchese and marchesa were disputing about the marchese's former knowledge of Rachel.

"Good father, hear what I have to say," said the marchese.

"I have been ill, very ill," continued the marchese, and in my wild ravings I chanced to rave, among other things, of some Rachel; and the marchesa insists on knowing who she was."

"You were in your illness thinking of Rachel the daughter of Laban, named rn the scriptures, perhaps," said the father. "Daughter," continued the father Manfride, addressing the marchesa, "you must not be uncharitable, nor surmise evil without a sure foundation to do so. Recollect, if you lack charity, every other virtue is but as a sounding brass and a tinkling cymbal. The marchese has never given you any reason to suspect him of incontinence; then why should he insensate raving of a delirious man fill your bosom with alarm, and cause you o be unhappy?"

The marchesa appeared satisfied; but still a restless curiosity and jealousy consumed her; and she more than ever insisted on the marchese accompanying her to gay parties, where she would watch every action of the marchese with the greatest scrunity, even the very turn of his eye should not escape her notice.

That his lady no longer might suspect that any uneasiness dwelt on his mind, the marchese appeared as cheerful as he possibly could; but when at a party, the theatre, or any resort of the gay, the marchese would frequently fall into a fit of the deepest abstraction.

His conduct towards Rachel and his child seemed every succeeding year to sink deeper into his soul, with yet more accumulated anguish.

When looking from his balcony at moonight, and viewing the fine prospect of the Bay of Naples from the window of his palace, and the serene and cloudless sky, he was ready to exclaim with Calista, in Rowe's Fair Penitent :—

"And you, ye holy, heavenly glittering host of stars,
Hide your fair head in clouds, or I shall blast ye."

But although Rachel had met her inexorable doom, Providence preserved the child from a miserable death.

Julian, as soon as he saw his father stab his mother, ran away much terrified, and hid himself behind some bushes.

But as he saw his father depart in the boat, he came out from behind the trees, where he had hid himself; and he went to the river-side, for from behind the trees, he had seen Julian throw Rachel into the water.

"Mother, mother!" he cried, "Oh! mother, mother!—she's dead! and cannot come to me; she's deep, deep, down in the water! Mother, mother!" he again cried, stamping and tearing his hair.

"Oh! I wish I was a great big man," he said. "If I was, I would kill my father; and when I do grow a man," he cried, "I'll stab him, and throw him into the water. Mother, mother!" he again cried, until sobbing, he fell asleep on the green sward.

Poor child! with no covering to protect thee from the dew of night; no couch, but the cold earth, to receive thy little frame—where now are the arms that so fondly encircled thee, and lulled to sleep, although thou wert nearly six years of age? Where now is the mother who so loved thee?—cold in her watery bed—deaf and unconcious, nor can thy cries awaken her.

When Julian awoke, his eyes were red with weeping, and again he called on his mother; but now the morning sun was shining forth, and the butterfly was pursuing her airy course.

Julian started up, and for a time forgot his sorrow, amused by pursuing and endeavouring to catch the grey insect.

Julian had ever felt a great dislike to the sight of blood, and was at some pains to tear from his dress the marks of blood, with which in places it was saturated, in consequence of the blood flowing from his mouth and nose when struck by his father. He now felt hungered, and recollecting the provision that was brought 3here by his parents, and which was still untouched, he ate of it a hearty breakfast.

But the provision did not last him many days; and poor Julian was without food, his clothes were all in tatters, through his having torn away the stains of blood; his hands and face were covered with dirt, and his long black locks hanged ngledand matted together.

Fever raged in his little frame, and the want of food was no longer felt by Julian; he laid in a torpid state upon the bare earth, and his mother and all his sorrows were forgotten.

In this state he was found by a goatherd, who in search of a stray goat had wandered that way. With surprise the man viewed the sleeping child, whom he believed to be the deserted offspring of some wandering vagrant.

The man tried to awaken Julian; but the torpid child only opened his eyes for a moment, then closed them again.

The good man pitied the child; and without staying longer to look for his stray goat, he took Julian in his arms, and carried him to his cottage.

The goatherd's wife washed Julian and put him to bed, and poured down his throat from time to time such remedies as she knew to be good in fevers.

No. 19.

CHAPTER XLIX.

Here, to the houseless child of want, my door is open still.

GOLDSMITH.

FOR six weeks the child struggled, as it were, between life and death; but at length he recovered, so that he could take a little nourishment.

The good woman perceived that he had entirely lost his hearing, in consequence of the cold he caught whilst lying on the ground. He could not understand any questions she or her husband put to him; but in the course of a few weeks, when he had recovered his strength, so that he could walk about, he could hear, if spoken to very loud.

That Julian was the child of respectable parents, from his appearance when found neither the goatherd nor his wife could believe.

And the account the child gave of his mother being stabbed and thrown into the water, they could not think was true: they believed it to be but a mere delusion of the child's fevered imagination.

But when Julian so often repeated the same statement, and gave so clear an account of the transaction, the goatherd began to believe there was some truth in the child's story.

And when Julian had gained sufficient strength, the goatherd took him to the very spot where he (the goatherd) had picked him up when labouring under a raging fever. The child pointed out the spot where the murder had taken place.

Julian's books and the guitar were still there, and near the river edge the goatherd picked up a dagger; the handle was of silver, and of curious workmanship; the blade was corroded and eaten in places with rust, and on the handle were to be traced spots of blood.

These evidences were strong proofs of the child's assertion; but in what part of Spain he had lived he could not tell, nor the name of his parents, except that his mother was called Rachel by his father, and by Carlos, madam.

He did not know that his father had any other name than Julian, which name he was called by his mother.

"This is indeed very strange," said the goatherd's wife; "the child's statement seems to be correct. Murder may have been done, and Heaven directed you, Peres, to the spot to save the life of this innocent child."

When the goatherd went to the market with his kids, he thought he would make inquiry in the town about Julian, Rachel, and Carlos, and endeavour to bring to light the horrid affair. "But instead of doing right, I may only do wrong," thought the goatherd, "and by some means get myself into trouble; it is best for me not to intermeddle. I will not say anything about it, but take care of the poor child, and leave the rest to Heaven."

The goatherd sent Julian to school with some other peasant children, to a village where a school was kept, at about half a mile distant from his cottage, to learn to read and write; read he already could, almost as well as his schoolmaser.

Julian's guitar was almost spoilt, by lying on the ground exposed to damp and heat; but his foster-father went to the expense of having it new strung and repaired. Julian greatly delighted in this instrument, and improved himself very much in playing on his guitar.

As he grew older, the dreadful scene of his mother's death, instead of wearing off, was the more strongly impressed on his mind. He would frequently stroll along the river's brink, where his mother was thrown in; and he would sit there for hours, crying and bewailing her loss, and execrating with bitterness the hand that shed her blood.

In one of these rambles, Julian picked up, attached to a piece of broken ribbon a miniature, which he knew to be the exact resemblance of his father. He viewed the portrait then with scorn and abhorrence, and threw it from him; he thought the eyes glared with anger, as did the original's on the day he stabbed his mother.

Julian told the goatherd this circumstance, and the goatherd blamed him for throwing away the portrait. "That picture may enable us to find out to whom you belong;" and he immediately took Julian with him to point out the spot where he had thrown the portrait. Julian with little trouble again found the portrait, and he gave it to the goatherd.

With surprise the man viewed it. "If this be thy father," he said, "he was indeed a fine don; and it is a pity that thou art not sought after by him. Not that I wish to part with thee, boy; but thou wouldst then be better provided for than I c n provide for thee. I would inquire into the mystery that hangs over thee, but I fear I should be but fishing in troubled water."

"I don't wish to see him until I grow a man," cried the boy, "and then let him look to himself."

CHAPTER L.

From childish sports he'd turn aside to weep.

By the Authoress of Eva.

The goatherd carefully wrapped up the portrait, and placed it in a box with the dagger, thinking that at some future time it might be useful in proving the identity of the child.

There were some traits in the character of Julian that gave the goatherd much concern, for the goatherd loved Julian as if he had been his own son, and he was sorry to see that he was of a very unforgiving temper when offended; and he was apt to pilfer any little articles from his schoolfellows and playmates, if he unobserved could take anything from them.

It was spring, and Julian went with his foster-father to visit a neighbour, who took them into his garden to see how finely the seeds he had sown were coming up.

Julian walked behind the man: he thought himself unobserved, but the goatherd, who happened to turn his head, caught him in the act of slily treading down the young crop.

For this malicious conduct, when Julian got home, he was severely reprimanded by his foster-father, who inquired the cause of his so doing.

"I had no particular cause," said the boy; "but I remember my mother told me I ought to spoil every one's things if I could; and then, if their things were spoilt, they would get poor and come to me to borrow money. And she said, that if I lent them one piece of gold, they must give me two for it. And then she said I should get rich and care for no one, and that every one must care for me. My mother said, I should have plenty of money when I was a man; for one of my grandfathers had bags full of gold and diamonds, and my other grandfather she said was a nobleman, and lived in Italy."

"Dear, dear, how could your mother fill your little head with such pride, and your heart with such bitterness?" said the goatherd's wife; "how very wicked!"

"If you call my mother wicked, I'll strike you!" said Julian, "I'll always strike any one who says my mother was wicked." And he began to cry, "Oh! my poor mother, my poor mother!"

Year after year rolled on, until Julian was able to assist his foster-father in looking after the goats, cultivating the vines, digging up the earth, and doing cheerfully whatever his strength would permit him to do.

But, when Julian was about seventeen years old, he went with his fostermother to pay a visit to her sister, who lived servant in a nobleman's family at Madrid.

It was then that Julian first became discontented with his situation in life.

He was struck when he saw the gay dons ride about in their carriages and on horseback.

The finery of their dress he contrasted with his own coarse clothing, and the elegance of their persons with his own rustic and awkward appearance. And when he returned with the goatherd's wife to their humble dwelling, he was gloomy, morose, and discontented; and now, with tears in his eyes, assisted his fosterfather in his daily labour.

He would now more frequently wander by the river-side, and bewail his mother, and with increased invectives vow a deadly vengeance on his father, should he ever cross his path.

_____

CHAPTER LI.

Thou shalt lull my sorrow,
And thy plaintive harmony speak of the grief that oppresses me.

BY THE AUTHORESS OF EVA.

JULIAN was very fond of his guitar, and he played that instrument with the most touching pathos: the sound of his guitar, more than anything, seemed to soothe his melancholy, and drove away for a time the remembrance of the troubles of his youth.

He, too, was very fond of reading, and he would now do little else.

The spring was again approaching, and he was desired by his foster-father to follow him with a spade, to help dig up a piece of ground at the back of the cottage.

Without speaking one word, he assisted the goatherd in digging up the ground; but when he followed his foster-father home to dinner, tears were in his eyes, and a gloomy moroseness sat on his countenance; he ate no dinner, from which he excused himself by complaining of being sick.

" Poor boy! he has worked too hard, and fatigued himself," said the goatherd's wife. " Art thou not tired, child?"

" I hate digging," replied Julian; " my hands are hard and blistered with the spade; and when summer comes, my face will be browned and scorched by the sun."

" Thou wert never fair, boy," said the goatherd, " and must work as I do to get thy living."

Julian sullenly leant his head on the table, and the goatherd went to work without his companion.

When Julian got over his sullen mood, he left the cottage, and having caught the goatherd's ass that was grazing in a field hard by, he mounted it, and rode up and down the road before his foster-father's cottage. There was much haughtiness in the countenance and manner of Julian as he sat on his beast, with great stateliness, in imitation of the dons he had seen at Madrid.

The alteration in the manner of Julian was noticed by his companions; for of late he had been more reserved and distant towards them, and assumed a consequence that caused him to be disliked and ridiculed.

And when they saw him ride with such stateliness on his ass, with his legs reaching to the ground, they laughed and derided him. "Good senor," they cried, " thy legs are too long for thine ass—he cannot raise thee from the ground;" which was actually the case; for Julian, though but seventeen years of age, was very tall, and of a lank appearance. His face was long and narrow, and his eyes were of the most jetty blackness, and when Julian was angry, they expressed the greatest malignancy; but the angry glare of Julian was disregarded by the peasant boys, who followed him with shouts and mockery.

Irritated to madness, Julian sprung from his ass, and pursued the flying youngsters. "Vagabonds!—scum!" he cried, "if I catch ye, I'll strike ye dead to the earth."

Grieved and offended at the affronts he had received, Julian was gloomy and reserved, and his frequent sighs did not escape the notice of his foster-mother.

"Why art thou so sad? what has vexed thee, my child?" said the old woman; "it grieves me to hear thee sigh so."

"Can I be happy," said Julian, "when I think on my poor mother? How can I be happy, when I behold the splendour and magnificent of the great? I was contented before I went with you to Madrid, but now I am miserable. I know my father is equal to any of the great dons I saw there, and that I am heir to riches and grandeur. How can I be happy, when deprived of what I ought to enjoy, and live here in meanness and comparative poverty? I was not borne to drive forth and milk the goats, nor to have my hands spread, embrowned, and blistered with turning up the stubborn earth. Some evil star must have ruled the hour of my birth; Heaven hath abandoned me, and made me the mark of its ire."

"Oh, hush! stop thy sinful tongue, Julian," said his foster-mother. "Heaven hath protected thee, and directed my poor husband to the spot where thou in thy helplessness had laid thee, and Heaven in its own good time will restore thee to thy birth-right; and if not, we have no child, and what we possess at our death will be thine."

"And think you that the life of a goatherd will content me?" said Julian. "No; sooner would I turn bandit," he would have said, had not the goatherd's wife prevented him by saying—

"Say no more, Julian, I prithee say no more, for this is grievous talk. Get thee to bed, child and pray Heaven will give thee peace and a contented heart; it is most sinful to be of a murmuring and repining spirit. Pray to the Almighty that thou mayest be restored to thy relations, if it is not His good pleasure to give thee a contented mind."

From this time Julian endeavoured to hide his discontent, and to appear before the goatherd and his wife with a cheerful countenance.

It happened that the manager of a company of strolling players, who were going to Madrid, was taken suddenly ill, and obliged to stop for some days at a little inn, which stood near the goatherd's dwelling.

The sound of Julian's guitar attracted the notice of the player, and he listened with much pleasure to its plaintive sound.

When the player recovered from his illness, and before he left the inn, he sought Julian, who was sitting beneath a shady tree, with his foster-father's goats browsing around him.

The manager got into conversation with Julian, who he found was very discontented with his station in life. The offer of joining the company of strollers was given to Julian, and by him very readily accepted.

When he informed his foster-father and mother of the resolution he had taken they were much grieved, and would have dissuaded him from entering on such a wandering and irregular life, but Julian would not be persuaded.

Before he left the cottage, the goatherd gave him some money to take with him; and he said, "My door shall be ever open to receive you, and when you are tired of a rambling life, return here, Julian, to peace and comfort."

For twelve months he remained with the players; and he improved so much, that in a little time he was able to undertake principal business, and strut on the stage, decorated with crown, robe, and sceptre. Julian not only played, but he wrote the pieces which were to be performed, and several songs which he sang, accompanied by his guitar. Amongst the rest he wrote the following song, which was sung on their stage by the performers, dressed as a lady, a woodman, and boy.

WOODMAN.

"In this lone wild and pathless way,
Wither, lady, dost thou stray ?
A place to thee with ills beset ;
Here robbers lurk——the grass is wet."

LADY.

"My life I dedicate to God,
O'er hill and dale my feet have trod ;
Oh say, wilt thou my lone steps guide
To convent near yon mountain side ?"

WOODMAN.

"Its distant spire in gloom is lost,
This wild to-night thou ne'er must cross ;
The winds are raising their fierce power,
And clouds foretell a heavy shower.

"Twilight her mantle soon will spread,
The birds have sought their leafy bed ;
'Tis here that fell assasins wait:
Then come away, nor brave thy fate.

"Oh, come and leave this dreary spot,
And thou shalt rest thee in my cot—
My cot, where dwells my wife, my Rose—
My cot, where peace and love repose."

WOODMAN AND BOY.

"Then in the morn with the rising lark,
Cheerily, cheerily shalt thou depart."

Julian did not long remain with the players, in consequence of the breaking-up of the company, through the sudden death of the manager, and whose whole wardrobe, scenes, &c. were distrained on for rent.

Julian now became quite distressed, and he thought of returning to the goatherd's cottage.

"I have not a single coin left ; and it will not do to stay here and starve," thought Julian. "I will leave Madrid to-morrow ; the old people, I know, will be glad to see me again."

His mind occupied with this thought, and whilst rambling about the skirts of the city, he saw standing, in a sequestered spot, a house he recollected he had seen before. The house seemed familiar to him ; and the more he looked at it, the fresher it came to his memory.

The peculiar fashioned gate in the fore-court ; and the tree that hung over it, were objects he particularly called to mind ; and he felt convinced that this was the very house his father and mother had lived in. And he determined to ascertain, if possible, who twenty years back had lived there.

After some trouble, Julian at length found to whom the house belonged. He called on the landlord, and found that, twenty years before that time, the house was let to a family who conducted themselves in a very strange and mysterious manner.

"As near as I can recollect," said the man, "it being so long back ; nor could I have told you at all, senor, nor have remembered anything about it, if there, as I said before, had not been something very mysterious in their conduct, which at the time struck me. The gentleman was a gay don ; then there was another man, but he seemed to be of inferior note ; then there was a lady and a child, but they never went out. The man of inferior appearance called and paid the rent, and he gave me the key of the house: ' the family are gone on their travels,' he said ; ' it is quite a sudden affair.' I went into the house to see in what condition they had left it, and was surprised to find they had left all their moveables behind them, and a lady's and child's clothes; their departure was very sudden, or they certainly would not have left their clothes behind them. Ah! there was something," said the man, shrugging up his shoulders, "more than you or I can guess ; it altogether was a strange piece of business, that their journey was so sudden."

"Sudden, indeed !" groaned Julian ; "alas ! my poor mother—sudden, indeed, was thy journey to eternity !"

"Your mother !" cried the man, "was the lady your mother—and are you the child that was then ?"

"I am," replied Julian, "and the gay don you spoke of was my father. Have you not seen him since ?—and is there none you can think of, of whom I might inquire ?"

"Oh, no, Senor, that I do not," said the man; "they were so close, and acquainted with no person in the neighbourhood, nor anyone else, that I am aware of."

"In what name did they take the house ?" inquired Julian; "to know that is of the greatest consequence to me."

"I never heard the name of the parties," said the landlord, "nor was it necessary for me to make the inquiry. They paid me a quarter's rent beforehand, and continued to do so all the time they were there; nor did they ever require a receipt for the same."

"Oh, miserable that I am !" said Julian, mentally, "I fear that poverty will ever be my lot. That the house in which I spent the days of my childhood I have now seen, I am certain ; but never, I fear, shall I obtain more information ; a strange mystery seems to hang over my parents. The house is but small, though respectable, but not equal in appearance to those who inhabited it."

Julian again went and surveyed the outside of the house; he saw a child walking in the fore-court. "Tell your father or mother I would speak with one of them," he said. A female followed the child to the gate which led to the house.

<hr/>

CHAPTER LII.

Dear, lovely bower of innocence and ease,
Scene of my youth, when every sport would please.　　GOLDSMITH.

WHEN the female approached near to where Julian was standing, he apologized for the trouble he had given her in leaving her house to come and speak to him. "But I could not resist the longing desire I feel to view these premises," he said ; "it was the seat of my childhood, where I dwelt with a fond mother, who is now no more. And I request, as a peculiar favour, that you will allow me once more to retrace my steps in those apartments, and to view the garden ; it will afford me a melancholy satisfaction, and do me a favour greater than I have words to express."

"Walk in, Senor," said the female, "you are welcome to go over the house and garden, if it pleases you to do so."

Julian went into the house. "Ah! there's the room where my poor mother used to sit," he said; "and there's the kitchen ; and there's the room where we slept." He stood some time viewing these objects, then went into the garden.

There still was the arbour; the pond ; and the flowering shrubs that grew near its surface, with their branches drooping down, and wooing the refreshing water.

Julian was affected: "this is the place of my childhood, and most likely of my birth," he mentally said. "Dear objects of a long remembrance ! When I lived here, I had a mother and a father; but now I stand alone on the earth, for there is none with whom I can claim kindred."

It was nearly twilight when Julian left the abode of his infancy; and he bent his steps to the village where he had slept the night before. It was some miles distant, but he could sleep there without paying ready money, which to him was an object; for, as it has before been said, he had not a single coin left.

Without money to get any refreshment, Julian, faint and fatigued, went on. "I will go to bed soon as I reach my lodging," he thought, "and rise before daybreak, and set out for the cottage of my foster-father."

With a heavy heart, Julian pursued his lonely way; for he yet was more than a mile from the little inn at which he lodged. The night birds chaunted their dismal lay as he passed along the green lane; and dark and lurid clouds, as if concordant with his feelings, overspread the sky. Soon the lightning's vivid flash played awfully around him, and thunder rolled in one lengthened reverberation.

"Beneath a sky so dark, and such sounds as these, did the bleeding body of my mother lay stretched on the green sward," thought Julian; "from behind the trees I saw, by the lightning's glare, the gory wound—then the water encrimsoned with her blood received her. Oh! why was I spared," he cried—" left friendless, and in poverty? it was not mercy, it was cruelty. Why did not the lightning's vivid fire strike me dead, and the convulsed earth heave me into the watery grave of my mother?"

Again a yet more vivid flash played around him, and a louder burst of thunder shook the ground beneath him.

This scene was more than Julian could bear, with any degree of calmness. The sight of the house in which he had spent his childish years; the garden, and each distinct room, so forcibly called his loved mother and her unhappy fate to his recollection, that his mind before the storm was in a state of the greatest excitement, and the storm still added to his frenzy; for it seemed to him that then, and but then, the bloody deed was committed.

With eyes wildly glaring, he threw his hat on the green sward, then bared his bosom to the fire of heaven, which yet more awfully played around him.

"Strike! strike!" he cried; "I brave the vengeance of that Heaven, which unmoved could look on, and behold my mother's murder!"

During the stillness that succeeded a burst of thunder, a deep groan sounded on the ear of Julian—then a kind of rustling amongst the bushes behind him. He turned his head, and beheld a shadowy figure; it was the form of a female, and she resembled the cherished idea Julian always bore in mind of his lamented mother.

A kind of halo shone around her form; but when she disappeared, the light disappeared with her, leaving each object again obscured by the darkness of the night. Julian was overcome for the moment, and he stood without the power of utterance; but when somewhat recovered from his surprise, he said, "It was—it was my mother—no illusion raised up by my distempered brain. I saw her, as my fancy as ever pictured her. But wherefore was that groan? Too surely my impiety in accusing Heaven, and daring it in its wrath to strike me with its forked fire, hath called up the disquieted spirit of my mother. "Oh, forgive me! merciful Heaven, forgive me!" he cried, "the words I in the anguish of my soul uttered."

The thunder had died away, and the lightning's glare no longer shone with terrific brightness, when Julian reached his humble pallet. Without undressing, he threw himself on his bed; and although he felt much fatigued, it was long before he could compose himself to sleep. When he did so, he dreamed that his mother stood before him: "My son, you will find your father," she said, "and he will do justice unto you. Reproach not Heaven with impious tongue," he thought she continued, "but bow with humbled heart to its all-wise dispensations."

Julian awoke refreshed and comforted in mind, by what he believed to be a communication from the dead, and before daybreak he set out for the cottage of his foster-father.

CHAPTER LIII.

Where'er he trod, the verdure wither'd,
Where'er he look'd, a blight seem'd by,
Each evil passion round him hover'd,
A scathful glance was in his eye.

By the Authoress of Eva.

JULIAN was with joy received by the goatherd and his wife, to whom Julian gave an account of what had befallen him.

The goatherd, with surprise, heard that Julian had recognised the abode of his childhood, after an absence of so many years.

"I do not think it at all strange that Julian should recollect his home," said the goathred's wife. "I can remember many things that happened before I was five years of age."

No. 20.

"I had no money to support myself," said Julian, "it was but on that account that I returned so soon. If I had wherewithal to support myself, I should have staid longer about Madrid and its environs, and made every possible inquiry."

"Money thou shalt have," replied the goatherd, "nor be prevented from inquiring after thy father on that account; I have great hope that thy endeavours to find him will be ultimately crowned with success, on account of the dream or vision which passed before thee."

"I think differently from you, Peres," said the goatherd's wife, "Spain is a large place, and to what part of it his father has removed, Julian is not aware, nor does he know for certain that he is in Spain at all. How canst thou find thy father, child? when even his name is not known to thee, no further than that it is Julian; there are many Julians,—and much, I fear me, thou'lt never find him; and for thy dream, I think nothing of that; when the mind is troubled, it causes strange fancies in sleep to rise before us. Be ruled by me, Julian, and go no more roving about, but content thee at home with us, child; and when thou art inclined to take thee a wife, Peres will buy thee household goods; and he has often told me he would share his goats with thee."

Julian thanked his foster-mother for her kind intention, but he assured her that he could not think of living a goatherd's life, when he believed himself born to fill a very different station.

"Well, boy, since thou hast made up thy mind to go in search of thy father, I will, as I promised, assist thee all that lay in my power; when dost thou intend to commence thy journey?"

"I will enjoy this day in the company of you and my mother," said Julian, "and commence my journey to-morrow morning."

"Well, God speed thee!" said the goatherd; "I will now give thee what money I have by me."

And he opened a box, and took out what money it contained, and he handed it to Julian.

"I fear that sum will not be sufficient for thy purpose," said the goatherd, "but it is all I now have in my possession. And thou must take this portrait with thee," continued the goatherd, as he took the likeness of Julian's father from the box.

The eyes of Julian glared with a vengeful lustre, as he viewed the portrait. "Villain, murderer!" he cried; then he sat for some moments with his eyes fixed on vacancy.

"Come, arouse thee, arouse thee, Julian!" said the goatherd, "or thou wilt have thy fits again come upon thee."

"What need I of that daub to enable me to find the original," cried Julian, pointing to the portrait, "when every feature is engraven on my soul in characters of fire?"

"But this may be of use to me," cried Julian, and he snatched the dagger that had belonged to his father from the box, and put it into his bosom.

"Give over this vengeful mood, Julian," said the goatherd, "it will but make thee miserable; it is now many years since this sad circumstance happened, and it is best for thee, if thou shouldst find thy father, to harbour in thy heart no evil against him; he may greatly have repented of his crime, and he may be willing to receive, and to do thee justice."

"If he does that, it may cause my vengeance to sleep," replied Julian, "but if he will not do me justice, we'll sink in one common ruin."

After some persuasion, Julian agreed to take the portrait of his father with him, and he put it in his pocket for that purpose.

The evening of this day was serenely beautiful; and the goatherd's wife had prepared a little treat, on account of the presence of Julian. And the party sat enjoying themselves beneath the shelter of a clustering vine, that formed a bower over the rustic seats in front of the goatherd's cottage.

Walking close beside the hedge that separated the vineyard from the public way, was seen the tall figure of Count Herman, walking with his usual slow and stately step towards the goatherd's cottage.

When he drew nigh, he greeted the party, by saying, "Much good may it do you, my friends; may no moment of your lives be worse than the present!"

The goatherd, with his usual good nature, went into his cottage and brought out a stool, and begged that the count would be seated and partake of what they had, telling the count that he should be right welcome.

Count Herman accepted the goatherd's invitation; and, after they had supped, the intended journey of Julian in search of his father was spoken of.

" And where does he intend to go in search of him?" said Count Herman.

" He cannot, with any hope of success, search any other place than Spain," said e goatherd; " for he is not aware that his father lived in any other place."

" I think I could direct Julian where to find his father," said Count Herman; but not in Spain."

" Oh! where can I find him?" cried Julian; " how did you discover him?— was it in consequence of the portrait?"

" Partly through that, and partly through other circumstances," said the count; "but before I inform you of the name and abode of your father, you must tell me, and that without disguise, the reason of his deserting you. I must know all particulars;—where is your mother?"

Before Julian had time to answer, the goatherd replied,

"Senor, there are secrets in all families : and I entreat you will spare this youth from relating circumstances that can be by no means pleasant to you to hear, nor prudent in him to speak of.

" Then I will never divulge that which I know," cried Count Herman; "but on the condition I have named, will I inform him."

" Why should I withhold the truth?" said Julian; " I will inform the senor of the particulars."

The goatherd made no reply.

And Julian began his story, and he told Count Herman every particular that he could recollect from his earliest infancy.

" And shall the murderer escape?" cried Count Herman. " The officers of the inquisition should be made acquainted with this foul deed. Does not your mother's blood cry for vengeance on her murderer? Fear not, for he who is now feasting in his palace, surrounded by every luxury, must give up to thee, when he is seized by the officers of the inquisition, all that pertaineth unto thee, and which in right of birth thou art heir to; thy father is the Marchese de Gusman, living in his palace near the bay of Naples. I am going to Naples, and thou, Julian, shall accompany me. I will bear thy expenses, and to-morrow I will call for thee."

After the departure of Count Herman, the goatherd said to Julian, " I like not that man, there is something more than mortal in the overpowering lustre of his eyes, and glad was I when I saw him depart; hearken not to him, boy, when he persuadeth thee to impeach thy father, for whatever may be thy father's crimes, it is not thy place to cause the bolt of justice to fall on his guilty head—no, thou must not do it. And in point of thy being heir to the Marchese de Gusman, how know you that you legally are so—who can prove the marriage of your father and mother? and until such proof, you cannot inherit without the consent of your father. Listen to me, Julian —I who you know have your welfare at heart. Go to Italy and see the Marchese de Gusman; make thyself known to him, and he will do thee justice; but stay with us until next week, and I will raise thee a greater supply of money to enable thee to journey to Italy."

Julian agreed to take his foster-father's advice. And when Count Herman came again he was told by the goatherd that Julian declined going with him to Italy. But the count would not so easily take his denial : " this is the old fellow's doings," he inwardly said; " I will watch for the youth, and work upon him.'

Peres set off the next morning for Madrid, to the relation who was in the service of a nobleman there; and of her he borrowed the sum he wanted.

During the absence of Peres Count Herman watched about the goatherd's cottage in hopes of seeing Julian; but in that he was disappointed, for Julian had set out at an early hour to accompany his foster-father part of his way to Madrid, and he did not return until late in the evening.

"How unfortunate," mentally said the count; "I must watch until I see the boy. That the Marchese de Gusman, if accused of the murder of the boy's mother, would fall into the hands of the inquisition, I am certain; and when hopeless and despairing in his dark cell, I would visit him, propose my terms, and obtain a victim: he must and shall accuse his father."

As the shades of evening overspread the earth, again Count Herman lingered near the goatherd's cottage, and he then saw Julian sitting on the bench before the cottage-door, beneath the shade of the vines.

"I will not go up to the cottage to speak to the youth," thought the count; "the old man or woman may come out and foil my design," and he beckoned Julian to where he was standing. Julian arose from the bench, and with a slow and hesitating step joined the count, whose token he was somewhat undecided whether he should obey or not. As he advanced, Count Herman motioned Julian to follow him into a grove of palm trees, that grew near the spot. Julian followed the count into the palm grove, when the count said:—

"I would not come into the cottage of that ungrateful old man who denied you to me, notwithstanding all I have done for you; through my means you will be raised from poverty to opulence, and that one circumstance alone demands some gratitude. After having seen the portrait of your father, I determined to take every pains to find him, and what was my motive—a desire to serve you, you an entire stranger to me; but I felt for you, and have fortunately succeeded in my undertaking. I am a rich man, you are but poor, and in consideration of your taking a journey to Naples, which you could not of course do, without a very considerable expense, and which expense you I am confident would find it very inconvenient to defray; this expense I generously offer to defray for you. But certainly there are conditions—I love justice, and detest the crime of murder; your mother's blood, you must not let go unavenged."

"Senor," said Julian, "I will not be tied down to any conditions. For the kind offer of your bearing my expenses to Naples, I thank you; and for all the trouble you have taken on my account, and especially for the service you have done me, in making known to me the name and condition of my father; for which kindness I hope at a future time to be able in some way to repay you,—but to promise you that I will be evidence against my father, I will not. I shall act according as circumstances may direct me."

"Then you decline my offer," said Count Herman.

"I do," replied Julian.

"Will you accompany me to Naples?" said the count.

"I cannot," replied Julian, "it would displease my protectors."

"We shall meet again," said Count Herman, "I will see thee in Naples."

Saying this, Count Herman turned into the palm-grove, and Julian returned to the goatherd's cottage.

CHAPTER LIV.

'Tis Slander,
Whose edge is sharper than the sword, whose tongue
Outvenoms all the worms of Nile, whose breath
Rides on the posting winds.   AUTHOR UNKNOWN.

ALTHOUGH Julian was of a revengeful temper, pride in him was a stronger principle than revenge; and he attentively considered the words used by the goatherd in their last conference, namely, whether he could or not claim as rightful heir the honours of his father's house.

When he considered the mystery in which the affairs of his parent was concealed, and the meanness and obscurity of the house they lived in, compared to that which a man of the Marchese De Gusman's consequence might be reasonably expected to live in. In short, a fear now broke on the mind of Julian, that he was the child of privacy and disgrace; and of no pretension to claim the honours of his forefathers.

Words that he had not before thought on, came fresh to his memory; namely, the words used by his father, when the fatal quarrel between himself and Rachel took place: the words were these—" He shall not inherit! Julian the illegitimate shall never inherit."

" These were the very words before the fatal blow was struck," thought Julian. " 'Tis evident I am no lawful heir."

" Would that I had died, when I lay fever-parched on the earth, for the longer I live, the more my sorrow increases. When raised to the highest pinnacle of hope, by a sad retrospection, I am suddenly again plunged into the very depth of despair."

" But I will hide these thoughts in my own bosom," thought Julian, " and see my father self-possessed, and nothing wanting in my lofty bearing of that consequence suitable to the heir of De Gusman."

The very evening after Count Herman left Julian in the palm grove, he (Count Herman) was in England, roving from place to place, restless, and unable to stay long anywhere.

He again visited Cornwall, again viewed the tomb of his old friend, Sir Parrolla Immorf, and again viewed the mansion where his friend when in life had resided.

At that mansion again was the sigh of sorrow heard; for in one little week Mr. and Mrs. Phillimore (the sister and brother-in-law of Mrs. Immorf) were no more; they were on a visit at the castle with their two children, when, seized with a fever, they both expired within an hour of each other, leaving Mr. Immorf executor to their immense property, and guardian to their children.

Olando and Lisbia Phillimore now lived in Ravenswood Castle, with their aunt and uncle, who were as fond of them as they were of their own children.

Percival Immorf was all that could be desired in a child; but Parrolla Immorf, as his person grew, so his evil quality grew with it.

Cruel, revengeful, obstinate, and disobedient to his parents, were but some of the evil traits evinced in the conduct of Parrolla.

He was very jealous of his brother Percival, who he thought his parents regarded with more affection than they did himself; on that account, he was very spiteful to Percival.

He would privately throw away his toys; make holes in the kites of his brother; tear leaves out of his books, and do all he could to annoy him.

A circumstance happened, which gave both Mr. and Mrs. Immorf, and likewise Lady Immorf his grandmother, much uneasiness.

Mrs. Immorf's maid by some means offended Parrolla, and he stole a diamond ring from out of his mother's casket of jewels, and threw it into a ditch at some little distance from the castle.

For, though but young, he had cunning enough to know that the ring was very valuable, and he thought it would be a pity to throw it into the sea.

And after the servant was punished for the theft, Parrolla thought that he could pretend that he had just found it where the servant artfully must have placed it.

The ring was missed, and not only Mrs. Immorf's maid, but the other servants also were called to a strict account concerning the ring.

But Mrs. Immorf did not entirely believe that any of the servants had stolen it; she had always found them honest, and she hoped that the ring was but mislaid, and would yet be found.

Vexed that the servant had escaped the snare he had laid for her, the wicked boy did not know what other plan to devise to get her into disgrace and trouble.

There was a boy, a helper in the stable, to whom Parrolla was rather partial.

To this boy, Parrolla told, as a good joke, how he had thrown the ring away, and named the particular spot where he had flung it; and he expressed his sorrow that his mother's maid had escaped being punished for the theft.

The poor stable-boy, though ignorant, was learned enough to know that the action Master Parrolla had been guilty of was a very bad one to thieve his mother's ring, and for no other reason than to make an innocent person suffer for what he had done.

Shocked at what he heard, the boy told his mother, who thought it but right that Mrs. Immorf should be made acquainted with her son's delinquency.

" For, if things are suffered to go on in this way, there is no knowing what may be lost, or who may be blamed; you, boy," said the stable-boy's mother, speaking to her son, " may be accused of theft and sent to prison for a thing you are entirely innocent of, should Master Parrolla take a dislike to you. I will make bold to call on Mrs. Immorf and tell her the whole truth of the affair."

The woman was as good as her word: she went to the castle and begged to see Mrs. Immorf, to whom she related the whole affair.

Shocked and grieved at the wickedness of her son, Mrs. Immorf sent a servant, who she could rely on, with the stable-boy to look for the ring in the precise spot where Parrolla said he had flung it. After a long search, imbedded in mud, the glistening stone was discovered.

Parrolla was taxed with his crime—he could not deny it.

" I hate Ann," he cried, " and, if she offends me, I'll serve her so again."

For this base conduct Parrolla was in great disgrace, nor permitted to see his parents for a fortnight.

But, during that time, he contrived to get into the stable, and he lamed one of his father's horses that the stable-boy might get blamed for neglecting the animal.

This was done by Parrolla to punish him for telling about the ring.

Every day Mrs. Immorf grew more uneasy about Parrolla, and she more than ever thought on the gipsy's prophecy. His grandmother, Lady Immorf, too, was very uneasy about Parrolla, for she feared he would take after his grandfather, and she inwardly lamented the oath by which she was bound not to destroy the magic book.

Whilst Count Herman was passing through the high street in Cornwall, he heard two men discoursing, and he listened to their conversation, as it was his custom to do. " There he goes," said one of the men, " and I dare swear he has hardly tasted bread to-day. As I was telling you, I am his own sister's son, he is as rich as Crœsus, and has neither wife nor child nor any relation to leave his pelf to excepting myself; I am his only relation, and yesterday, when I called on him and only requested the loan of a shilling, he refused it me."

" ' No, no, Mark,' he said, ' I cannot lend thee a shilling, I have not got it for myself; hear how bad my asthma is,' he continued, whilst he was attacked with a violent fit of coughing, ' cough, cough, cough, and I cannot afford one penny to get anything to ease it. I know I shall die for want.' "

" What ? with all your hoarded bags of money," I said, " and talk of dying for want, I only wish I had the handling of them, I warrant I would not die for want."

" I have no money I tell you," roared the old man. " What ? I suppose you will come some time and murder me, in expectation of finding money. Get out of my house, you graceless dog, and never darken my door again." Saying this, the old man held up his stick, and I verily believe he would have knocked me down, if I had not left the house."

" He looks almost bent double with age," said the other man. " How old is he ?"

" How old ? Why, upwards of eighty," replied the other, " and he has as great an objection to leave the world as if he was but twenty."

This was enough for Count Herman. " He will answer my purpose," thought the count; " and he followed the old man, who was just seized with a violent fit of coughing as the count got up to him.

CHAPTER LVI.

The lanksided miser, the worst of felons,
Who robs his back and belly of their proper cheer.   BLAIR.

"DEAR me, what a dreadful cough you have!" said the count : "I have a most excellent remedy at home which has cured many persons, and a very expensive medicine it is."

"Expensive," said the old man, turning up his eyes as soon as he could recover breath, ' an expensive medicine, did you say ? What! and I suppose you are the maker of it ; but you need not puff off your expensive medicines to me—me a poor man, who has not wherewithal to buy bread."

"The medicine I speak of," said Count Herman, "you shall be welcome to. free of all expense ; it has cured hundreds; many even at the advanced age of ninety years. And I'll answer for it that, if you take it, in less than one month you will be upright, nimble, and free from cough as I am : it is, indeed, a golden elixir."

"A golden elixir ?" said the old man, well as he could speak for coughing, " a golden elixir? then I 'am sure it must be a good elixir. No elixir can be so good as a golden elixir. And you say I am to have it gratis."

"Gratis, and as much gold as you can carry into the bargain," said the count, " if we can agree upon terms."

"As much gold as I can carry ?" cried the old man; "you are mad, sir, you're mad,—tell me where there is so much gold to be got ? ."

"Where?—why, in the mines to be sure," replied Count Herman.

"In the mines!—I could have told you that," said the old man ; " but what are we the better for that ?"

"A great deal," said Count Herman. " I will call on you in a short time with the elixir I spoke of, if agreeable to you, and then I will let you see what I am the better for the gold that lies in the bowels of the earth ; I will produce as much of the ore as will fill the crown of your hat."

"I'll not believe it," cried, the old man ; " you banter me."

"No! on my honour I am serious," said Count Herman ; "the gold of Peru is at my service ; but for such favour there must be a return."

"A return !" cried the old man, " and what return could you make, adequate to such a good ?"

"And that is not the only good," said Count Herman, " long, long life, and a second youth."

"Why, I should not care what I gave for such benefits," said the old man, "I'd do anything."

"Well, I shall see you again, and we'll talk this matter over," said Count Herman,—"where do you reside ? "

The old man gave the count his direction, which he had written in his pocket, and as he did so, he said,—" I shall now be on thorns until I see you ; but tell me, sir,' he continued, " are you a philosopher, an alchemist, or a cabalist ? "

"No matter at the present," replied Count Herman : " when we again meet, all shall be explained."

Saying this, Count Herman turned off in another direction, leaving the old man in wonder and amaze, at the conversation of the mysterious stranger, whose promised visit he now looked for with the greatest impatience.

Count Herman bore in mind the Marchese De Gusman, whom he hoped yet to get in his power ; he went to Naples—but there he could see nothing of Julian.

"He may not yet have left his foster-father's cottage," thought the count ; and he was in Spain by the dawn of the following day. He inquired of a goatherd who lived near the cottage of old Peres, and he found that Julian had departed.

He bent his steps to Seville, and there he was observing and prying into every incident that fell under his notice, in hopes of meeting with such as would serve his purpose.

One morning, whilst walking down the chief street in the city, he was most disagreeably surprised, by meeting Dollabella, the old sexton's daughter. Count Herman would have avoided her, but she saw him, and flew at him like a tigress.

"Where's my poor father's head?" she bawled out. "Villain! where's my father's head?"

"Oh, my dear Dollabella, how glad I am to see you !" cried Count Herman; "nothing but the most unfortunate circumstance could ever have induced me to quit you. I was now coming to seek you."

"To seek me?" said Dollabella, squinting most horribly; "to seek me? that won't do, senor."

A crowd had gathered round them. Count Herman attempted to pass, but the persons there congregated prevented him, or, at least, tried to do so.

"Let him not pass, I command you," cried Dollabella; "some of ye secure him, and give him into the hands of justice. I accuse him of having sacrilegiously entered the vault beneath the church, where the corse of my father was interred, and stealing from the body the head of my father."

"Wretch! for what purpose did you steal it ?" demanded one in the crowd.

"To eat it, no doubt," said another; "he is one of those who prowl about graves and charnel-houses, to feast on the bodies of the dead."

And they proceeded to lay hands on Count Herman, in order to deliver him over to the magistrate. But Count Herman in one moment shook them off; and those who had endeavoured to seize him, stood looking at him paralysed and motionless.

"Touch me not !" cried Count Herman : " ye cannot detain me; for know I hold a charmed life, which ye cannot destroy !"

Terrified, the crowd of persons there collected made way for him to pass; and he with all speed left the city. It was very unpleasant to Count Herman to act as he did; for he knew, if ever he met with any of the persons who had joined with Dollabella to detain him, they would point him out as a magician, and he would then become a mark of general observation, which was what he greatly abhorred, as it might be the means of leading him into much trouble; and, in consequence of his being recognised as one holding a charmed life, he would be shunned by all who knew it, and, in that case, he would be unable to find victims.

"I will not trouble myself to go to Naples, after this Marchese de Gusman," thought Count Herman; "through that business I met that scarecrow Dollabella. No; I will again go to England, I thing my victim there pretty sure. Gold will lure the old miser, and he will be sure to fall into the snare. Snare!" mentally continued Count Herman; " I did not once think it a snare, or I should not have taken such pains to have made myself miserable; for what I read before my fall, now forcibly strikes me; when a boy, I read a book I dare not touch now. In that book it says, 'The wicked are like a troubled sea, casting up mire and dirt,' and such do I. I hate myself; I hate the good; I hate the bad, and all created things in the world : I have no joy. I, too, have read in that book I now dare not open, 'What shall it profit a man, though he gain the whole world, and after all lose his own soul ?' that I have lost, nor dare I ask for mercy; I am excluded— and for what ?—for that which I vainly thought the good of this life. But with the power to gratify my every wish, the inclination is gone; the fiend hath cheated me. And if I fail to get a victim, torture unspeakable must be my doom. I had all—all that man could reasonably desire, and yet I coveted more. Happy is the man who reclines at night on his bed of straw, with hope springing in his heart. But hope is lost to me—despair and dreadful anticipation must ever be my portion !"

CHAPTER LVII.

With that, methought, a legion of foul fiends
Environ'd me, and howled in mine ears
Such hideous cries, that with the very noise
I trembling waked; and for a season after,
  Could not believe but that I was in hell. —SHAKSPERE.

THE place Count Herman had walked to was a sequestered valley, overshade by trees.

Tired in body, and harassed in mind, he threw himself on the green sward and, after some time spent in fearful apprehension of the future, he fell asleep. He dreamed that the crisis of his fate was come, and that he could not procure a victim.

The Demon Zinegratta, in all his native ugliness, he thought, stood before him

No. 21.

and in a voice, to which the united sound of a thousand roaring seas, and th
howling of as many blustering winds, would have been melody, he said,—

"My victim! I am come for my victim!"

Count Herman thought he fell on his knees before the demon, and besought hi
to grant him longer time to procure a victim, in which he now had failed.

But the inexorable demon answered in the same appalling voice,—

"Your time is come!"

Then stretching out his claws, to which the talons of an eagle were harmles
he stuck them into the shoulders of Count Herman, and bore him to the lof
Vesuvius; and the demon, he thought, descended with him into the bowels of th
mount.

Oh! what a dreadful scene, he thought was there, a suffocating smoke,
smell of bitumen, sulphur, and putridity that overcame the fainting senses, an
made being insupportable.

Yet, however agonising the suffocating smoke, and the scorching flame th
flared up with it, it could not destroy the immortal essence.

Count Herman thought he was borne by the claws of the Demon Zinegrat
deeper down into the fearful cavern, whose length nor breadth the e e could measur

There, numberless fountains spouted forth liquid fire; and in the midst of th
dire region, was a lake, in which the souls of the wicked were lying; whos
shrieks and agonising groans awakened, in the greatest terror, Count Herman.

Secluded by trees, and near to the spot where Count Herman was lyin
stood a monastry. At the moment Count Herman awoke, the monks were singin
a requiem over a newly departed brother; the solemn and holy strain vibrate
through his whole frame, and in an agony of mind he stamped and tore his hair.

"Oh! mad and foolish man, that I am!" he cried; "never for me shall sound
like these be uttered; no ineffectual voice will be raised for me, to sue for tha
mercy that never would be granted. Those sounds seem to proceed from th
Heaven I have lost; and in a vision I have seen the torments of the damned—
torments of which I must be a partaker."

Stamping and tearing his hair, he gnashed his teeth in agony.

Then rising from the ground, with a slow step and a melancholy and dejecte
countenance, he pursued his way.

CHAPTER LVIII.

With wild convulsive start,
And all the father kindled in his heart.—DARWIN.

WHEN Julian reached Naples, his first care was to find out the palace of th
Marchese de Gusman.

There the angel of death hovered, for the marchese lay at the point of death.

Julian watched about, but he could not see the marchese go out; and he coul
not summon resolution to inquire for him at his palace.

But after waiting three days, walking about in suspense, he determined to knoch
and inquire for the marchese.

But when he did so, the servant who opened the gate, inquired his business; on
being told by Julian, that he wished to speak to the marchese, the man eyed him
from head to foot, and with a sneer, said—

"What is your business?"

"It is of great importance," said Julian.

"It may be of great importance to you, and but of little to the marchese," said
the man; "and I must tell you, friend, that the marchese will see no persons, but
his very particular friends, for the marchesa is now lying at the point of death,
and is not expected to survive many hours."

Disappointed, Julian left the palace of his father, and remained at the inn where he had taken up his abode ; but he spent great part of his time in inquiring whether the marchesa was yet alive, and watching about to see the marchese leave his palace. At length he was informed, by inquiry, that the marchesa was dead.

Seven days more passed away, and Julian was yet wandering near the palace of the Marchese De Gusman. On that day he saw the grand funeral procession of the Marchesa De Gusman issue from the palace ; Julian followed the pompous cavalcade to the cathedral, where it was interred.

And amongst the mourners, he saw a face that caused a strange sensation to run through every fibre ; for in that countenance, he felt, he knew he saw his father.

But no longer the gay don, the portrait represented, though the features were the same. But how different the expression of countenance ; no longer of a lively gay, but haughty character ; now bowed down, melancholy and subdued.

Julian no longer felt a vindictive sentiment towards the marchese, who seemed so melancholy and heart-stricken, and, as Julian thought, repentant.

After his return to the inn, he called to mind every circumstance, that he could recollect having occurred from his earliest childhood.

And having done so, the Marchese De Gusman, in some measure, stood acquitted by Julian.

For now no longer prejudiced, nor his feelings biassed by the grief he felt for his tender mother, in consequence of his seeing his father; who now, though but in the prime of life, was but the ruin of what he had been.

" Where is now the lively and laughing eye, the haughty and commanding mein ? —gone ! " thought Julian, " no doubt through that deed which has made us both miserable. Surely I have been wrong in harbouring such hostile thoughts against him, for doing an act which he, in all probability, has lamented as much as myself. I now call to mind, that my mother, in her anger, struck him twice, and in his rage he pierced her bosom."

Julian now felt for his father ; and again shed tears for the death of his unfortunate mother.

The next day he left his inn, with the intention of demanding an interview with the Marchese De Gusman.

He arrived at the gate of the palace, and after Julian had knocked thereat, the same servant opened the door, and inquired the business of Julian.

" I must see the Marchese De Gusman," said Julian.

" Send up your name, signor," said the man.

Julian hesitated; he could not think of doing that.

" What is your name?" again inquired the man; " unless you send up that, I will not trouble my master."

" Tell him," said Julian, " one would see him on an affair of great importance."

" I shall do no such thing," said the man ; " I suppose you are come on some errand to crave charity. We have too many of such visitors ; I beg you'll come here no more, friend, troubling me," and he slammed the gate in Julian's face.

Grieved and disconcerted, Julian returned to his inn ; perplexed in mind, and studying what means would be the most advisable for him to adopt, in order to obtain an interview with his father.

He walked about, and watched near the palace of the marchese, hoping he should see him come out ; but in that hope he was disappointed.

On the second day of his watch, Julian was more fortunate. He saw the Marchese De Gusman leave his palace; it was the time when the evening bell was chiming to vespers.

" I will not speak to him near his palace," thought Julian, " we shall be observed, and that I do not wish ; for a time may come, when I should be mortified at being recognised as one who ever wore such clothes as these."

The Marchese De Gusman proceeded on his way with a slow and stately step, with eyes bent on the ground, neither looking one way nor the other, nor regarding any passing object.

He bent his steps towards the monastery of the Contrite Heart, for there he was gong to vespers.

Julian followed close behind the marchese; and he made several efforts to speak, but his courage failed him, besides, he was behind the Marchese De Gusman, and in an awkward position to address him.

Julian with hasty steps took a circuitous way behind the trees, and stood before the Marchese De Gusman, just as he had reached the monastery door.

"Signor, I would speak with you," said Julian.

The marchese started. "What would you?" he said.

"What I have to communicate is of a private nature," said Julian; "I do not wish to be overheard in that I have to say. Let us step to some little distance, between those trees."

The Marchese De Gusman did not object; he followed Julian to some little distance amongst the trees.

They stopped; and the marchese said,—"This place is private, if your business with me is of a secret nature, here you may speak without danger of being overheard."

For some moments, Julian stood before the Marchese De Gusman, without being able to utter one word. But at length he said, in a tremulous voice, "I would tell you, that I, Julian, your first born, am come to claim my birthright."

The Marchese De Gusman appeared to be overcome with surprise and emotion, confused, and hardly knowing what he said.

"Julian," he faltered out; "Julian, I do not recollect."

The colour rose in Julian's face; he will not acknowledge me, thought Julian.

"If the name of Julian is forgotten by you, signor," said Julian, as he pulled the fatal dagger from his bosom, and displayed it to the marchese, "this will assist your memory. Remember this dagger, and the day you used it."

The marchese, for a moment, gazed upon the dagger; then, faint and overcome by his feelings, he leaned against a tree for support.

"Surely you do not mean to deny that I am your first-born and rightful heir?" cried Julian, in a threatening tone; "too long have I been neglected, but now I expect to have justice done me! You will find I am one not easily to be shaken off; if righted, all is well; but if injured, like Samson of old, I'll put my hands to the pillars of the tower, and crushed in one common ruin, I'd die with my oppressors rather than live a life of privation and beggary."

The Marchese De Gusman was now somewhat recovered from his surprise, and the emotion that had rendered him, when Julian first discovered himself, almost speechless; he took the hand of Julian, and tears were in his eyes. "Poor youth," he said, "thou shalt be righted; but where hast thou been living, and who has protected thee?"

"I have been living in Spain, where you left me," said Julian, "and was found by an honest goatherd who had no children of his own; he pitied my helplessness, and acted a father's part to me. If you have yet any doubts," continued Julian, "of the truth of my statement, in order to rid you of these doubts, behold this portrait—it is your own likeness—it dropped from my poor mother's neck—I found it in the grass that grew beside the river."

"Put it up—put it up!" cried the marchese, "nor cause my wounded heart to bleed anew. I loved your mother, and the act I in my rage committed, I have never ceased to regret since that fatal hour. I have now no happiness; my life has been one continual scene of repentance and penance; poor boy, I have no doubt of thy identity," continued the marchese, "thou hast thy mother's eyes and complexion, and the haughty bearing that once distinguished me. Here is money; provide thyself with clothes fit for the son of the Marchese De Gusman to wear; but thou must provide thyself with them at a distance from hence, for I would not have thee known and again recognised. Meet me again in seven days in this place, and at this hour, and I then will arrange when thou shalt come to my palace, and be acknowledged for my son; I hope it is unnecessary for me to warn thee not to say anything respecting the death of thy mother; thy own good sense and feeling for a father, made wretched through an evil destiny, will cause thee to be silent on that subject; I feel assured that thou wilt hold sacred, nor expose to prying curiosity that mysterious grief that preys on thy parent's heart. Fail not to meet me here, my son, at the time I have appointed," continued the marchese "for I have much to say to thee."

Julian assured the marchese that he would be punctual, and they then separated.

The marchese returned to his palace, without visiting the monastery of the Contrite Heart; and Julian to procure such raiment as was suitable for the son of the Marchese de Gusman to appear in.

CHAPTER LIX.

In Padua, far beyond the sea,
Men said he changed his mortal frame
By feat of magic mystery ;
For when in studious mood he paced
St. Andrew's cloistered hall,
His form no darkening shadow traced
Upon the sunny wall. WALTER SCOTT.

IT was evening, when Count Herman knocked at the door of the mean house occupied by the asthmatic old man.

Twice he knocked before any one answered; at length the old man came to the door himself.

"Ah, is it you?" he said, with a pleased countenance, "I fear it was that villain, Mark; well, come in, come in—but have you brought the golden elixir with you?"

"I have," replied Count Herman, "I would not on any account have come without it; when I promise, I hold my word sacred."

"But remember you said I was to have it gratis," said the old man; "ay, gratis—don't think that I'll pay anything for it—you remember you said I should have it gratis."

"And gratis you shall have it," said Count Herman.

Count Herman was lighted up stairs, into a small and mean apartment, by the penurious old man, who desired him to be seated. The old man placed the glimmering light on the table; there was hardly a spark of fire in the grate, and the feeble rays of the small candle but little illumined the gloomy chamber.

"You see, sir, how poor I am," said the old man, "and yet that graceless dog, Mark, is always hunting me for money—but where is the elixir?"

Count Herman gave the old man a bottle, in which was a mixture he had from a physician; it was a good medicine for the cure of asthma. As he gave it to the old man, he said,—

"Here is the golden elixir I promised you; and here," said he, "are the bars of gold, I promised to bring to show you;" and he took from his pocket two bars of gold, about eight inches in length, and two inches in thickness.

"That is not gold," said the the old man, "you are deceiving me; it cannot be gold—only consider the worth of two such pieces. No, no, you are having a joke at my expense—something you have covered with a shining metal, to deceive me."

"I am surprised that you should entertain such an opinion of me," said Count Herman; "I am not a person either apt to joke, or deceive. Are you a judge of gold?" inquired Count Herman.

"I am," replied the old man.

"Then examine that bar, and tell me, is there a piece of metal of that size, that would weigh as heavy as that bar does, if it was not gold."

The old man put on his spectacles, and he held out his hand for the bar.

"It is gold, sure enough!" he cried; "Let me look at the other bar—gold too, as I live! Oh, precious—precious metal; and you have brought these as a present to me as well as the elixir."

"Oh, no," cried Count Herman; "I must indeed be a liberal man to do that; gold must be earned."

"Alas! I am old and weak," said the old man; "'tis too late for me to earn gold—I wish I was a young man like you."

"I have before told you, you may be young if you please," said Count Herman, "and have the wealth of Peru, and all the jewels the East can boast, at your disposal. But if you are a scrupulous, religious man, I will not explain—what is your mode of worship?"

"I worship that, which all the world worship, revere, and love," said the old man, "that which all the world labour to obtain."

"How mean you?" inquired Count Herman.

"I mean gold," cried the old man—"all-powerful gold! what is loved like gold?—what is coveted like gold?—what does the soldier fight for, but gold?—what does the parson preach for, but gold?—what does the counsel plead for, but gold?—what does the physician visit the sick for, but gold?—what does the poor man work for, but gold?—in short, the love of gold is the mainspring of every action."

"But gold has not the power of adding years to the aged, nor of turning infirmity into youthful freshness. With your asthma, and the infirmities of age, gold to you would be but of little service, because you could not live long to enjoy it."

"Not enjoy it!" cried the old man; "I should see it, and know I had got it—would not that be enjoyment?"

"Ay, but not such enjoyment as you might procure with gold, if you were a young man," said Count Herman. "I know a secret, and have a friend, who, if you will apply to him, and do his bidding, will not only lay the treasures of the earth at your feet, but he will give you a renewed being—youth, and years, that will endure as long as this sure and firm-set earth will last—on but one condition."

"But on one condition!" cried the enraptured old man, who now began to place implicit faith in the words of Count Herman; "and what is that condition?"

"Is it not written," said Count Herman. "All things will I give thee, if thou will fall down and worship me."

"And are you the giver of such good?—is the condition on which it is granted, adoration?—do you require that I shall fall down and worship you?—if so, for the gifts you promise, I will worship you with pleasure."

"It is not I who demand such homage," said Count Herman, "nor can I bestow such favours—it is the master who I serve; if you are desirous to accept his terms, I will introduce you to him."

"When will he come?" said the impatient old man; "bring him to-night."

"No;" said Count Herman, "I will bring him to-morrow evening at this hour—be alone."

CHAPTER LX.

Somewhat was he chilled with dread,
And his hair did bristle upon his head.—WALTER SCOTT.

THE old asthmatic man was a stranger to those mysteries, of which Count Herman had made himself master; he had never opened books that treated upon magic, nor had he ever thought that dealings between earthly and unearthly beings was possible.

And when Count Herman called the next evening, with his tall, dark companion, the miser felt a shuddering sensation run through his frame, when he looked on the strange form, whose eye of tawny glare shot midnight lightning's lurid ray; however, with the thought of gain, he conquered his feelings of terror, and begged that both the gentlemen would be seated.

The Demon Zinegratta, for him it was who accompanied Count Herman in his visit to the miser, then appeared in mortal guise, lest he should terrify his expected victim; to whom riches, long life, on certain conditions, and all that could tempt the avaricious and worldly-minded, was offered to the miser, by Count Herman, who accepted the proposal, and the assent of the dreaded stranger was given to the agreement.

The mysterious contract was entered into, and the form of the miser was transformed from age to youth; then was heard voices unlike the voice of man, and strange sounds of howling and laughter, as if the fiends kept holiday. The sounds were such as described by Sir Walter Scott.

> Is it the wind that swings the oak?
> Is it the echo from the rocks?
> What may it be?—the heavy sound!
>
> The unearthly voices ceast,
> And the heavy sound was still;
> It died on the river's breast,
> It died on the side of the hill.

At length all was accomplished, and Count Herman was sure of another seven years liberty to range this terrestrial globe. Still he lingered about Cornwall,—and three years more passed away.

He knew that the grandson, and namesake of Sir Parrolla Immorf, was likely to become his victim; and he often strolled near Ravenswood Castle.

Percival was now near eighteen years of age, and Parrolla nearly sixteen, Olando Phillimore was fifteen, and his sister Lisbia, was thirteen.

Often when at play, they had lifted the curtain of black cloth that covered the portrait of Count Herman, then run away, crying,—
" The tall gentleman in black is coming."

The portrait of Count Herman had been, and was still a bugbear to the young people, and particularly to Lisbia, who, though with a feeling of terror, would frequently contemplate the dark countenance, and fearful eye of that singular being.

Three years more had rolled away, and Lisbia was now nearly sixteen, and reckoned the most beautiful girl in Cornwall, but she was of a melancholy turn of mind, and fond of wandering in the meadows and green lanes, with no other companion than her little dog; and frequently she strolled near the house of Mildmay, who was now become a miller in a flourishing way of business, and he had a family of two sons and one daughter.

Edwin, the eldest son, was seventeen years of age, and generally went by the name of the handsome miller.

Rose Mildmay was a most lovely girl, and nearly two years younger than her brother Edwin; she was as handsome, and very much resembled her unfortunate aunt, whose name she bore.

Lisbia, during one of her rambles, had walked a considerable distance along the sea-shore; tired, she seated herself on a cliff that overhung the sea, and she opened a book she had with her, and read some pages of a story, which greatly affected her; the tale was of an orphan, and the death-bed scene of that orphan's parents.

Lisbia was the most sensitive creature on earth. The tale greatly affected her—it brought to her mind the loss she had sustained in the death of her own parents; for, though her aunt and uncle were exceedingly kind to her, yet Lisbia felt her loss, and deeply deplored it.

Whilst sitting absorbed in grief, by the tender recollection, she heard a footstep behind her, and turning her head to see who it might be, and she saw it was Edwin Mildmay.

In consequence of her so suddenly turning her head, she slipped from her seat and would have fell from he cliff into the sea beneath, if Edwin had not, with the greatest presence of mind, rushed forward and caught hold of her arm, and stayed her from falling into the bosom of the deep.

Lisbia, blushing, faultered out her thanks, whilst the modest youth stood bowing and hardly dared lift his eyes to that form he so often, unseen, had watched and admired.

Lisbia, though so young, was not insensible of the manly beauty of Edwin Mildmay ; she had often rejoiced in her own mind, for Lisbia had no sister or friend to whom she could disclose the feelings of her heart ; and as before has been said, she often rejoiced in her own mind, when she on a Sunday heard the bell sound, announcing the hour for public worship, for then she knew she should see young Mildmay, whose form was but seldom absent from her thoughts.

Edwin walked by the side of Lisbia along the sea-shore, and across the meadow that led to Ravenswood Castle ; he assisted Lisbia to get over a stile that lay in her way to the castle, and as he did so, he involuntarily pressed her hand ; as if ashamed of his presumption, his eyes were instantly cast on the ground, and his cheeks were flushed with a yet deeper crimson.

Lisbia saw that Edwin Mildmay loved her—rapture was in the thought ; but when cool reflection came, what would her uncle and aunt say to her forming such a connexion so far beneath what she reasonably might expect ; for however handsome and well educated he might be, still he was but the miller's son, and that man's son, who would not have been what he then was, had it not been, Lisbia had heard, for the liberality of her uncle.

CHAPTER LXI.

Love rules the court, the camp, the grove,
And men below, and saints above,
For love is Heaven, and Heaven is love.

WALTER SCOTT.

FEW days were happy days now to Lisbia, excepting Sunday, for then she saw Edwin Mildmay, whose eyes were continually fixed on the pew in which Lisbia was sitting ; but if he thought himself noticed, he would instantly withdraw them.

Lisbia felt that she loved Edwin, and that she could never love another. She lost her spirits, and more than ever loved to roam in the most solitary places she could pick out ; lone and unfrequented situations were those that Lisbia best loved, for there she could, unobserved, indulge in the grief that preyed upon her. The churchyard, too, was a favourite walk of Lisbia's ; there she would often visit the graves of her deceased parents.

Coming down the yew-tree walk from such a visit, she saw, gliding down the avenue before the church, the very being whose painted likeness had so often terrified her ; and now, as on the painting that hung in her aunt's chamber, though terrified, she could not withdraw her eyes from the object of her terror.

She saw she must come almost in contact with this dreaded being if she proceeded, and she could not well turn back, as they were now near each other.

She proceeded, and Count Herman passed Lisbia, who hurried on ; but never did Lisbia forget the glaring lustre of those terrible eyes, that viewed her as she passed. Terrified, she reached Ravenswood Castle, and sought her aunt, whom she informed of her having met the original of the picture covered with the black cloth, who she supposed had been dead long since. " And," said Lisbia, " whether it was a man or a spectre that I met, I am not aware, but he certainly appeared more like a spectre, than a being of this earth."

Mrs. Immorf communicated to her mother-in-law, Lady Immorf, what was told to her by Lisbia. How she had seen the original of the very singular portrait that ung in the chamber covered with a black cloth.

"Good Heaven! and is that man, or demon, I know not which to call him, still lurking near the castle?" said Lady Immorf. " It grieves me to hear that he is in the neighbourhood, for I believe his presence is an omen of evil. I should be sorry if Lisbia knew of the connexion between that person and Sir Parrolla, nor would I have my grandsons know it on any account."

"Never from me shall they hear it," said Mrs. Immorf; "nor would I have Lisbia acquainted with a circumstance which ought to be buried in oblivion."

"Would I had met this person, this Count Herman, instead of Lisbia!" said Lady Immorf; " I would have spoken to him, and desired that he would take away his portrait and the magic book; those things being here is truly burdensome to me; they seem to me, as if they cast an evil spell on me and mine. Was I left to my own choice, I would this very night order a great fire to be made, and they should be consumed therein, but both I and my son are bound down by an oath never to destroy them. No doubt Sir Parrolla, when he so enjoined his on and myself, expected Count Herman would fetch them away, and I earnestly hope and trust, that now he is in the neighbourhood he will do so. However horrific an interview would be with him, I would not shrink from it, could I but get rid of the book and portrait."

Lisbia could not drive the thought of Count Herman from her mind, and she hoped no more to behold that dreaded personage.

The thought of Lisbia having seen Count Herman, gave Mrs. Immorf, as well as her mother-in-law much uneasiness, fearing that Count Herman might by some sorcery, delude and injure in some way the unsuspecting girl.

Poor Mrs. Immorf had quite uneasiness enough on her mind, without any additional sorrow. Parrolla was indeed a heavy affliction to both his father and mother; his insolent and overbearing temper, and the malice and hatred it was evident he harboured towards his amiable brother, though hid under the mask of seeming love, greatly distressed his parents.

The affectionate heart of Mrs. Immorf was much pained, on account of her nephew, Olando, whose weak understanding did not improve with his years. Olando was mischievous, and troublesome as a monkey, and almost as ugly; there was frequent complaints made by the maid servants to Mrs. Immorf, on account of the rudeness of Olando, who took a great delight in being in the kitchen amongst the female servants. For Olando though very silly, was a great admirer of female beauty, and whether gentle or simple it was all one to Olando, who had no pride and was very good natured, when he had all his own way; but when crossed or disappointed in any thing he wished, he was fierce as a firebrand, and not only passionate, but malicious.

Poor Lisbia was now no longer the gay, lively girl she used to be, and her altered manner was noticed by her aunt, who feared that the change in Lisbia's manner was owing to her not being in so good health as she had been.

Lisbia smiled at her aunt's fears, and she declared that nothing was the matter with her. And she now endeavoured to force her spirits in the presence of her aunt; but extreme uneasiness dwelt on the mind of Lisbia—the love she bore Edwin she knew would not be approved of by her natural protectors, her aunt and uncle; they, it could not be supposed, would suffer with their consent to marry one so much her inferior both in point of birth and fortune; but Lisbia could not forget Edwin, his tender glance dwelt on her recollection, and the heart of Lisbia felt the tender and never to be forgotten feeling of first love. And her thoughts dwelt on Edwin with all the devotion of youthful affection.

The woods and wilds, and all the romantic and gloomy scenery by which Ravenswood Castle was surrounded, but increased and nursed the passion that Lisbia had conceived for Edwin.

Lisbia felt by anticipation all the grief of disappointed love; and there were other circumstances also that gave Lisbia much uneasiness, she feared that both her cousins, Percival and Parrolla, regarded her with more than fraternal affection.

Lisbia plainly saw that her cousin Percival did all in his power to please her, and gain her good opinion; and, though he had never spoken to her on the subject of love, Lisbia much feared that he meaned to do so, for she read in the look and every action of Percival's the love he bore her.

And that love she thought was observed and disproved of by Parrolla, whose dark and threatening glance spoke the but ill concealed anger of his envenomed mind.

" Should my aunt inform me of Percival's love, and propose that I should become his wife," thought Lisbia, " what could I say? How could I refuse my amiable cousin, who is almost without fault either in person or disposition? I could not refuse Percival without assigning a reason for so doing; for if I could assign no reason for refusing my cousin, my uncle and aunt would suppose it was from personal dislike to that amiable youth, and that they should think that would make me most unhappy. And, if my aunt should make me such a proposal, I must take my choice of three things, either to make myself miserable for life by marrying Percival; suffer my uncle and aunt to think that I have a personal dislike to their son, and by that means lose their regard; or confess my love for Edwin, which I can never do."

CHAPTER LXII.

A sudden storm did from the south arise,
And horrid black began to hang the skies,
By slow advances loaded clouds ascend,
And cross the air their lowering front extend;
Heaven's loud artillery began to play,
And wrath divine in dreadful peals convey;
Darkness and raging winds, their terrors join,
And storms of rain, with storms of fire combine.

DRYDEN'S VIRGIL.

IN the afternoon of a day which had been unusually close, Lisbia sat at the window of her chamber. It commanded a fine view of the sea, and also of the cliffs that extend in wild succession along the coast. As she sat at the window, many a melancholy thought entered the mind of Lisbia; and, to banish such thoughts from her mind, she prepared to take a walk, and join her brother Olando who she knew was gone out to walk along the sea-shore.

The fiery rays of the sun had now subsided; it was setting in glory beyon l the cliffs, tinging the sea with the most vivid hues. Lisbia walked to a considerable distance, in the hope of seeing Olando or her cousins, for she knew they were out; but Lisbia was unsuccessful in meeting either her brother or her cousins. Disappointed, she turned back, and it was fortunate she did so; for dark gathering clouds overspread the sky, and frequent bursts of thunder, and flashes of very vivid lightning, caused Lisbia to quicken her pace, and she regretted having taken so long a walk.

Heavy rain drops came pattering down, and Lisbia feared she should be wet through before she could reach the castle.

The miller's house was nigh, and gladly would Lisbia have requested shelter from the storm there, but an undefinable feeling prevented her. It was the dwelling of Edwin, who, in all but words, had told her how he loved her; if she sought shelter there, and should Edwin be at home, he might think she made the storm an excuse to visit his dwelling. "No," thought Lisbia, "sooner would I brave the fury of the elements than go uninvited to Mildmay's."

It would not be an easy task to define the motive Lisbia had for avoiding the miller's house, when every inmate there would have been proud to have served her. The conduct of Lisbia, in this respect, might have proceeded from sensibility, delicacy, or pride, or, perhaps, all put together.

For Lisbia feared that Edwin knew the secret of her heart, and, perhaps, might think that she came there on his account.

As Lisbia was hastening on, she heard a footstep behind her, and in a few moments Patty, the miller's wife, stood by her side.

"Good Heaven! Miss Phillimore," said Mrs. Mildmay, "surely you are not proceeding to the castle in this storm, and when our house is so nigh, too; pray walk in and wait till the storm is over."

So invited, Lisbia could not, or did she refuse; she went into the house with Mrs. Mildmay.

The smiling Rose ran and placed a chair for Lisbia to sit down, and in a few minutes afterwards, Edwin came into the parlour. The youth appeared to be struck with surprise and pleasure, when he saw who was the visitant. And such feelings were plainly to be perceived in the intelligent dark hazel eyes of Edwin, whilst the blue eyes of Lisbia were cast on the ground, and her cheeks were suffused with a yet more rosy red.

At that moment, a loud knocking was heard at the street-door, and Rose ran to open it, when Lisbia heard a loud, boisterous voice say,—

"Come, make haste, open the door. Don't you see we are almost drowned?"

The voice Lisbia knew to be that of her cousin Parrolla. Percival was with him, and came into the parlour, whilst Parrolla staid in the passage, trying to snatch a kiss from Rose, who was indignant at the rudeness of Parrolla, and she called on her mother to come and take her part; but Edwin went into the passage, he heard the story of his unfortunate aunt, and high words would have passed between the parties, if Parrolla had continued to detain Rose.

As it was, Parrolla and Edwin eyed each other in no friendly way, and Parrolla started back with surprise when he saw his cousin Lisbia, sitting in the parlour.

"Lisbia!" said Parrolla, with much scorn in his manner. "I was not aware that you were in the habit of visiting here," and his eyes shot fire as he glanced at Edwin.

Lisbia felt the full force of her cousin's insinuation, and her face became the colour of crimson.

"Neither am I, sir," she replied; "but Mrs. Mildmay kindly invited me in, to take shelter from the storm."

The room in which they were sitting was very handsomely furnished, at least for the parlour of a miller. There were several pictures hanging there in gilt frames, and amongst them were the portraits of the miller, his wife, Edwin, and Rose.

Parrolla hardly knew how to conceal his spleen. He thought he saw a tender glance pass between Lisbia and Edwin, but he was not certain; and if he had been certain, what could he have said? He felt himself provoked and irritated, and very much displeased with Edwin.

Impatiently Parrolla paced the room; he wanted to begone, but still the rain came down heavily.

"You have some very expensive paintings here, old miller," said Parrolla, to old Mildmay, who had just come into the room. "Yours is a good trade—a little out of one sack, and a little out of another, those perquisites will pay for the painting of a family portrait or two."

"I don't know what you mean, sir," said old Mildmay, "no person can impeach the honesty of either me or my son."

"Oh, very likely—very likely," said Parrolla, "you take care of that, I dare say; but you have throve wonderfully, Mildmay; you are very differently situated now, from when you and your son lived in the cottage at the end of the green lane—at least, so I have been told; I mean the cottage where you lived at the time your daughter committed suicide, and thew herself into the sea, just where the willows hangs over the cliff. Was it a disappointment in love?—or what could induce the girl to take such a desperate leap—are you aware, old man?"

The insolence and unfeeling manner of young Immorf, greatly hurt the feelings of old Mildmay; and he answered, whilst a tear ran down his aged cheeks, as he thought on his injured daughter.

"If you inquire, sir, you may perhaps, hear the particulars of that sad story you will then find on whom the disgrace falls."

Percival looked as if ashamed of his brother's behaviour.

The rain had now ceased, and Lisbia, after thanking the miller for the shelter he had given her, she, with Percival and Parrolla, made their way to Ravenswood Castle.

CHAPTER LXIII.

Let youth beware of love :
Of the smooth glance beware ; for 'tis too late,
When on the soul the torrent softness pours,
Then wisdom prostrate lies : while the fond soul
Wrapt in gay visions of unreal bliss,
Still paints the illusive form.—THOMPSON.

ORLANDO had reached home before the commencement of the storm, and Mr and Mrs. Immorf were glad to see their children and Lisbia come in without getti n' wet, and uninjured by the storm, which had raged with extreme violence while it lasted.

"Mrs. Mildmay, belonging to the mill, invited me into her house to take shelter, or I must have been wet through," said Lisbia, " and I gladly accepted her offer."

"No doubt you did," replied Parrolla, sneeringly ; " what a pert, conceited jackanapes that son of theirs is—the fellow don't seem to think a little of himself."

"He has some reason to be a little vain of his person," said Mr. Immorf, " for he really is a handsome youth, and so well behaved too. I believe his father has given him a good education, which his prosperity has enabled him to do. I am very glad to see industry crowned with success."

"But the poor old man has been very unfortunate in his time," said Lisbia ; "Parrolla asked him the reason why his daughter committed suicide. She threw herself from the cliff where the willow droops over the sea it seems ; surely such a dreadful circumstance must have made him very unhappy. Do you remember the affair, uncle ?"

"I do," replied Mr. Immorf, and a tear forced itself into his eye ; " it was a melancholy affair, and I request, Lisbia, that you never more will touch on that subject. And is it possible, Parrolla," continued Mr. Immorf, " that you, having heard of that sad affair, could so unfeelingly inquire of the poor old man, the reason of his daughter's committing the fatal deed. Why did you remind him of his grief ? it was a cruel and heartless inquiry."

"Oh, I did it to vex him, and mortify his pride," said Parrolla, " to see his parlour decorated out, and hung round with family portraits ; I don't like to see such serfs ape their betters. I did not know that asking the old man, what could induce his daughter to take the lover's leap, was any harm ; my father seems to feel it, perhaps it was on his account."

"Leave the room, sir !" said Mr. Immorf, " and presume no more to come into my presence, until you think proper to act to me, as it becomes you to act to a parent !"

"Everything I do is a fault," muttered Parrolla, as he left the room, " if my brother, the favourite, had said so, it would have been all right."

Parrolla now, on account of the angry words he had had with his father, bore the Mildmay's a great animosity, and he determined to annoy them all that lay in his power.

Mildmay was now not only a miller, but a farmer also, and a very fine harvest he was likely to have ; it was a most luxuriant season, and the full ears of corn were nearly ready for the labourer's sickle.

"I'll have some fine sport in the old man's fields," thought Parrolla ; " through him I have had words with my father, and in some way I am determined to be revenged on him."

CHAPTER LXIV.

Since love from silent looks can language draw,
That scorn the same impertinence of wit.—MILTON.

WHEN Lisbia was in the retirement of her chamber, she thought on every tender glance the miller's son had directed towards her.

"Poor Edwin, had he been born the child of wealth," mentally, said Lisbia, "with what pleasure and pride should I have received his addresses, because then my friends would not have objected. But I, though born in affluence, if I had none to consult but my own heart, gladly would I share with him some lowly cot, and find myself much happier in being the miller's wife, than I am now in all the splendour that surrounds me."

Lisbia read in the dark and malignant eye of her cousin, Parrolla, that he had discovered the guarded secret of her heart, she observed, when she was at the house of Mildmay waiting for the discontinuance of the storm, with what suspicion Parrolla had watched her every look, and the looks of Edwin also. And she felt assured, that Parrolla had discovered something in the speaking glance of Edwin which had given him much offence, and had caused his rude behaviour to old Mildmay. Lisbia feared that Parrolla would acquaint her aunt and uncle of his suspicions, and that they, perhaps, might send her to reside with some relation who lived at a distance, in order to break off the connexion. For Lisbia felt well assured, that her uncle and aunt would never consent to such a union the low birth, and want of fortune of Edwin, she felt would be an inseparable barrier betwixt her and the miller's son; at least, while she was under age.

"And then I would rather almost break my heart," thought Lisbia, "than displease my uncle and aunt, who are so very kind to me, and perhaps, Edwin, hopeless of obtaining me for a wife, may turn his thoughts elsewhere," that thought was agony, and Lisbia was ready to exclaim with Ossian—

"Why did I not pass away in secret, like the flower of
The rock that lifts its fair head unseen, and strews its
Withered leaves on the blast."

The following day was Sunday, and Lisbia again saw at church, him on whom all her happiness was fixed.

Edwin looked more pale than usual, but what he lost in the beauty of his appearance, he gained in the interesting languishment that sat on his beautiful countenance, and the pensive and melancholy softness which appeared through the long lashes of his dark hazel eyes, rendered him yet more interesting.

The change in Edwin's countenance was perceived by Lisbia, as she looked from her pew, on the object of her fondest affection.

Looking from the seat on which Edwin sat, towards her cousin Parrolla, she saw his eyes were fixed upon her, and she thought a malicious smile sat on his countenance.

"Is this the conduct we ought to pursue in the House of God," thought Lisbia, "my thoughts wander from my duty to earthly objects, and my cousin is watching me with a yet worse feeling; he wishes to oppress and make me unhappy."

When Lisbia had left the church with her kindred, and had nearly reached Ravenswood Castle, she turned her head, and saw Edwin standing at an angle of the road; he was looking after her, as far as his eyes could trace her receding figure.

CHAPTER LXV.

Insolent serf, I'll him provoke,
Leap o'er his fence of hawthorn bound,
And trample down his yellow corn,
With the fleet step of horse and hound.

BY THE AUTHORESS OF EVA.

ON the following day, Lisba strolled to the cliff, where grew the willow, whose branches drooped into the sea, and where she had heard a young person, the miller's daughter, had ended her existence.

"Poor girl, I pity her," sighed Lisbia, "love no doubt was the cause of her taking the fatal resolution. How I should like to hear all the particulars of her sad story, but my uncle has enjoined me not to mention the subject."

It was a lovely morning, and still Lisbia strolled on, but as she had been out a long time, she thought her aunt might be surprised at her long absence from home, and she turned back. In her way home, she passed the corn-fields that belonged to old Mildmay, and she stood for some moments looking over the hedge, and viewing the abundant crop of wheat in the old man's ground.

Presently, Lisbia saw a horseman followed by his dogs, leap over the hedge of the farmer, and another horseman followed the example of the preceding one, they galloped all over the standing corn, trampling it beneath their feet as they went; and by the noise they made, they encouraged their dogs to tread down the wheat in all directions, smelling for such game as they might find.

Lisbia saw on nearer inspection, that one of these destructive horsemen, was her cousin Parrolla, and the other was his groom.

She saw old Mildmay with passion, he appeared to be reproving the unwelcome visitors; but Lisbia was too far off to distinguish their words, but she saw by their gestures, that both parties were in a great passion. Parrolla cut Mildmay with his horse-whip, then rode close by him with such force, that the old man was thrown down by the horse, and whether he was alive or dead, Lisbia did not know, neither did the horsemen care, for they turned their horses' heads in another direction, and again leaped the hedge, followed by their dogs.

With tears in her eyes, Lisbia witnessed this cruel act, her heart was good to have gone into the field and assisted the poor old man up, if indeed he was not dead, or too much injured to rise; but Lisbia dared not do that, she saw that her cousin Parrolla hated the family of the Mildmay's, and a blush rose in her cheeks, when she recollected the insinuations Parrolla had thrown out respecting Edwin. Alarmed by these thoughts, Lisbia thought it would be best for her to hasten home, and take no notice of what she had seen. For Lisbia was aware, that if her cousin Parrolla knew that she had been near either the dwelling or the grounds of Mildmay, it would call forth from him some ungenerous surmise, and not only that, if it were known to her uncle or aunt that she had witnessed the affair, she might be called on to speak of what she had seen; and as she could not with truth speak in favour of her cousin, she wished to decline speaking on the subject at all.

It was towards evening when William Mildmay, the miller's son, came to Ravenswood Castle, and inquired if Mr. Immorf was at home, for he wished to speak to him.

Mr. Immorf, kindly asked Mildmay in, and desired him to be seated.

CHAPTER LXVI.

Sure some malignant plant,
Which long has spared me, now of late begins
To shed on me its baneful influence.—TRAP.

"WHAT is the matter, my good young man?" said Mr. Immorf to William Mildmay; "you look grieved and unhappy; I hope nothing is amiss."

"Would I could say so, worthy sir," replied William Mildmay, "but my poor father, I fear, has received his death blow; he is, indeed, very, very bad."

"Is there anything I can do to serve you?" inquired Mr. Immorf, "if there is, don't be afraid to speak, for if it is anything that lies in my power, I will do it with pleasure."

Mildmay shook his head.

"Your kindness, sir," he said, "first raised my father in the world; he has been very successful, and for the field of wheat that is trodden down, that, comparatively speaking, is of no consequence; but to knock my poor father down, and then to ride over him, was a most cruel act."

"And who has dared to do such a thing?" cried Mr. Immorf; "what barbarian could have the heart to hurt one white hair on his aged head?"

"It was—it was your son Parrolla!" replied Mildmay, in a voice tremulous, and almost choked with grief, "unprovoked, and with no othor view than to injure. Your son and his servant leaped the hedge that separates the wheat-field from the meadows; they were followed by their dogs; and for some time they were trampling down the field of wheat with impunity; but at length they were observed by my father, who desired Mr. Parrolla would instantly quit his field, and no longer with his horses and dogs try to ruin a poor man's crop. Mr. Parrolla refused to leave the field; angry words ensued, and my father was knocked down, either by the horse or the handle of the horse-whip; and when he was down your son rode over him."

Mr. Immorf rang his bell, and when the servant answered the summons, he said,—

"Tell Parrolla I wish to speak with him directly."

When Parrolla came into the room, and saw William Mildmay there, the colour forsook his cheeks, and he would have left the room.

But his father detained him by saying in an authoritative tone, "stay sir, whither are you going?"

"I was going to retire, I thought you were engaged," said Parrolla.

"No sir, I am not engaged," said Mr. Immorf, "I sent for you here to make answer to a most heinous charge, that of leaping the hedge of Mr. Mildmay, treading down his corn, and purposely riding over his aged father."

"I certainly plead guilty to leaping the hedge," said Parrolla. "A hare started, I had my dogs with me, and I could not resist the temptation of following it. Old Mildmay came up to me, and he behaved in a very insolent manner; and when he saw how his corn was trodden down, he said,—

"'I would to Heaven that there was not a Parrolla on the face of the earth; that name has been my bane, my curse.'"

"So insulted, I would have knocked any one down."

"So then, you are to spoil a poor man's crop; and because he remonstrates with you on the impropriety of your conduct, you think yourself justified in riding over him, and taking his life away."

"I am sure I have not hurt him, at least I did not mean to do so," said Parrolla, "nor do I believe I have done much harm to the wheat."

"The injury you have done, I am bound in justice to pay for; and tell Richard to come up to me; and—do you hear, sir? await my coming in the library.'

Parrolla left the room, and as hid so, he cast on Mildmay a threatening and revengeful look.

"Of what does your father mostly complain?" inquired Mr. Immorf; "in what part of his body is he most hurt?"

"He complains greatly of his head, and he is much bruised in his body," replied William Mildmay. "When I came to acquaint you with what has happened, which I thought it but right you should know, I left him groaning with pain—I staid till I could bear it no longer."

"You did very right to let me know of my son's misconduct," said Mr. Immorf.

"I did so, to prevent him from acting again in so cruel a manner," said Mildmay, "I am sure Mr. Percival would not have done so."

Richard now came into the room, and Mr. Immorf ordered him to saddle a horse, and go with all speed for Doctor Milbourn, who Mr. Immorf ordered Richard to take to Mildmay's. "And," said Mr. Immorf, "if a surgeon is wanting beg Doctor Milbourn to send for one, or more, if a consultation is necessary."

When Mr. Immorf went into the library, it was to be seen in his countenance how much he was grieved and irritated at the conduct of Parrolla, who was sitting gloomily leaning on a table, looking haughty and displeased, and more like one who had been injured, than an inflicter of injuries.

"I am surprised, Parrolla," said Mr. Immorf, "at the extreme wickedness and cruelty of your conduct; your brother Percival, I am sure, could not have acted so."

"Whatever I do is a grievous fault, and whatever he does is right; but, it always is, when we are hated."

"Hated! God forbid, I should hate my own child!" said Mr. Immorf; "it is your faults that I hate, Parrolla, not you; I would have you consider how you have acted on more occasions than one; and when you have taken such a retrospect, I am sure you will own yourself to blame, and set about amending your conduct."

"I suppose I must neither look nor speak," said Parrolla, "but sit with my hands before me, like some boarding-school miss; but that will never do for me; I hate to be so curbed. I am now nineteen, and I'd sooner that you would give me the patrimony I am to have, and then I will entirely leave Ravenswood, where I am such a nuisance;—yes," said Parrolla, with bitterness, "I would leave Ravenswood to my cherished, fondled, elder brother, who I dare say, in time, you will find out."

"Speak not against Percival!" said Mr. Immorf; "he is a good youth, and happy am I that he is my eldest son."

"But he may not be always so," said Parrolla, with a bitter smile.

"He may not," replied Mr. Immorf, "but I hope I shall never live to see that day."

Here their conversation ended; and, much displeased, they both left the library.

CHAPTER LXVII.

> Wherefore look'st thou sad,
> When everything doth make a gleeful boast?
> The birds chaunt melody in every bush;
> The snake lies rolled in the cheerful sun;
> The green leaves quiver with the cooling wind,
> And make a chequer'd shadow on the ground,
> Under their sweet shade.—SHAKSPERE.

THE fears entertained by the affectionate William Mildway, on account of his aged father, greatly distressed his mind. But when Doctor Milbourn had seen the old man, and had examined him, he found that there was no fracture of the skull, his apprehensive son had feared, nor had he any broken bones, but several very severe and painful bruises; and he likewise was ill, in consequence of the shock his nervous system had received, and which he could hardly bear up against.

For as it is beautifully said in the scriptures—"A grasshopper is a burden to the aged."

In the course of a few days, it was ascertained that Mildmay was in no danger of death, from the injury he had received from the horse.

And the old man, considering his advanced years, was very rapidly amending.

The younger Mildmay perceived a very great change in his son Edwin; from being one of the most lively youths in the neighbourhood, he was become dull, thoughtful, and so absent, that when he was spoken to, he was often not aware of it.

His flute and violin instruments that he had taken such delight in, were now thrown aside, or only used when he with his voice accompanied the latter-named instrument, and sung words he had written descriptive of his feelings; the words were these :—

> "Oh! why did I gaze on that lovely maiden,
> So high her estate—but lowly my station?
> How fair is her face, where ringlets stray over;
> How thrilling her glance, when cast on her lover!

> "How could I aspire to such peerless perfection?
> Oh no, I must only meet scorn and rejection;
> But in my faithful bosom, her image I'll cherish,
> And in the battles loud clangour, gains laurels, or perish"

Company was disagreeable to Edwin, and nothing suited him so well as roaming in lone and solitary places, where he could, undisturbed, brood over his ill-placed affection—an affection he could not hope would meet with a return.

This thought disturbed his peace, and precluded hope. The object of his love being so differently situated from himself, caused Edwin to despair of ever obtaining her hand; and that despair drove from his cheek the rich hue of health.

Edwin felt that he could not stay in Cornwall, and see Lisbia Phillimore the bride of another.

Not far from Ravenswood Castle, there was a long, winding path, edged with high trees and brushwood; this path wound up the cliff, and here ruminating on her ill-placed love, Lisbia was walking. She had walked a good way up the path, when, to her surprise, she saw Edwin Mildmay sitting on the root of a tree, with his head resting on his hand, his countenance bore the stamp of melancholy; and in so deep a reverie was the love-lorn youth, that he neither heard the tread, nor saw the form of Lisbia, until she was close to him; but when he saw Lisbia, he arose from his recumbent posture, and bowed to her as she passed him.

Lisbia stopped, and inquired after old Mildmay, "who," she said, "she had heard had met with an accident."

Edwin said, "his grandfather was much better, and he was very thankful that he was so. For I should be very sorry," said Edwin, "to leave home, whilst the recovery of my grandfather was dubious."

"Then you are going to leave home," said Lisbia.

"Yes," replied Edwin, "home loses its charm when the heart is no longer at ease;" and he sighed deeply. "I intend to solicit my father to obtain a situation for me in the army."

"And is it possible that you can choose the life of a soldier?" said Lisbia.

"I do not like it," said Edwin, "but I think the change and bustle of military life is the best of all things calculated to drive from the heart a settled grief; there being in that profession but little time for reflection."

Lisbia turned pale as death, when she heard Edwin's determination; and fearing lest he might observe the change in her countenance, she went no further along the walk up the cliff, but turned her steps homewards.

Edwin still walked by her side; he cleared away the intruding brushwood, and snatched away the obtrusive thistles that impeded her in her way down the shelving path.

When Lisbia had reached nearly the end of the walk, she stopped, and her cheeks were suffused with blushes; she appeared as if she wished to say something, but could not give utterance to that which she wished to say; but, feeling the necessity of the injunction she was about to give, in order to preserve her own happiness, as well as the safety of Edwin, she at length said,—

"I must request you will turn back, for I should feel distressed and unhappy, were I now to meet my cousin Parrolla."

Truly might Edwin have answered, in the words of Romeo, "Alack! there lies more peril in thine eyes than twenty of their swords; look thou but sweet, and I am proof against their enmity."

"I will do as you request," said Edwin, "however repugnant to my own feelings, could I but hope to see you in this walk again; what pleasure would a repetition of such delightful moments give me!"

Then suddenly checking himself, he said, "I am too presumptuous: can it be supposed, that Miss Phillimore, lovely, rich, and happy, will bestow one thought on me; on me the miller's son?"

"Grandeur does not always bring happiness," said Lisbia, "would I were but a miller's daughter."

And a blush rose to the cheek of Lisbia, as she said so.

Edwin was enraptured, he caught the idea Lisbia's words conveyed. "She wished that she was but a miller's daughter, their fortunes then would be equal, nor worldly pride prevent their union."

Again he said, " could I but hope to see you here again, when far away, what pleasure, what extacy would the dear remembrance give me; if I thought you would again walk here, I would watch for that dear moment from the dawn of day, until the earth was enshrouded in darkness.   Do not destroy my hope—say Miss Phillimore, shall you again walk this way?"

" I may," said the blushing Lisbia.

" To-morrow ?" inquired Edwin.

" Not to-morrow," said Lisbia, " my cousin Percival is of age, the day after to-morrow; and we then shall have much company at the castle, my aunt will give a ball, and to-morrow she will think it unkind if I go out ; she wishes me to assist her fancy, in arranging the flowers and ornaments to be used on that occasion."

" Then on the third day from this," said Edwin, " I will watch your coming."

CHAPTER LXVIII.

White was her wimple and her veil,
And her loose locks a chaplet pale,
Of whitest roses bound.—WALTER SCOTT.

IN the solitude of her chamber, Lisbia thought on her lover ; she repeated every word he had spoken to her, and his affectionate, but respectful admiration, sank deep into her heart.   His image was still before her, and in fancy she yet saw the glance of admiration and respectful love beam from the dark languishing eyes of her lover.

Oh what pleasure was in the idea of being so beloved, that happiness in the pleasing thought !   Yet what would her aunt and uncle say to the attachment she had formed, and some time or other they must know it ; then, the violence of her cousin Parrolla's temper, she reflected on with dismay, and she feared from the behaviour of the gentle Perceval that her marriage with another would give him pain.

These thoughts caused Lisbia to be very unhappy, but when she thought on Edwin, she thought on happiness, and every unpleasant thought for the moment vanished from her mind, as do the dews of morn from the refulgent beams of the mid-day sun.

The rooms in the castle were arranged for the reception of company, and the ball-room hung with wreaths of flowers.

But no flower looked more lovely than the blooming Lisbia, the simplicity of whose dress but added to her charms, and of whom it might be said in the word of the poet,—

" Beauty like yours needs not the aid
    Of foreign ornament, and is, when unadorned,
    Adorned the most."

Lisbia wore but a white robe, and the locks of her beautiful hair was bound in a chaplet of roses of the same snowy hue.

Lovely and graceful in every movement she looked like some sylph, as she lightl trod the mazy dance, admired by all.

Some part of the evening she danced with Parrolla, and then with Percival, and as it was customary to change partners, the latter part of the night, she danced with a gentleman named Dashwood.

Lisbia happened to turn her head, and she saw her cousin Percival watching her whilst she was speaking to Mr. Dashwood, and in his look Lisbia thought she saw love and admiration strongly blended.

Far from being vain, or wishing to gain love where she knew she could not return it, Lisbia was grieved at a further conviction of what she before suspected; she loved Percival with a brotherly love, but nothing more.

When the dance was over, and the company left the ball-room for the supper-rooms, Percival handed his cousin to the table, and procured for her the greatest dainties there, and his behaviour that night was both tender and impassioned.

The conduct of Percival did not escape the scrutinising glance of his brother Parrolla; and fierce, gloomy, and revengeful was his look, and with sorrow it was observed by Lisbia, who dreaded the vengeful Parrolla; she had heard of the story about the diamond ring, how he threw it into a ditch merely from a malicious motive to criminate his mother's servant, who had offended him, and she herself had witnessed his wicked and malicious conduct to old Mildmay.

"If I offend him," thought Lisbia, "I, by some means, may become the victim of his malice."

It was long past midnight before the company—departed it was near two in the morning; but although Lisbia had danced a good deal and was fatigued, she felt not the least inclination to sleep.

She seated herself at her chamber-window, full of uneasy thoughts.

The darkness of night still hung upon the distant hills, and a solemn silence reigned around.

"All nature seems concordant with my feelings," thought Lisbia, "all dark and gloomy. I have been dancing, and spent a brilliant evening with a seeming light and joyous spirit, gay in the possession of youth and prosperity; but I have a secret grief lies here," mentally said Lisbia, as she placed her hand on her bosom, "a dread and foreboding of evil, that I cannot overcome."

The heavy-toned church-clock broke on the silence; it sounded the hour of two, as if awakened by the heavy sound the death-owl loudly shrieked from an adjacent tree, and long did she continue her ill-omened screech.

The spirits of Lisbia were low, and the death-owl's note filled her mind with terror.

"Too surely death hangs over this house," thought Lisbia; she closed her window and went to bed, but not to rest, for it was long before Lisbia could close her eyes to sleep.

CHAPTER LXIX.

Ere to black Hecate's summons,
The shard-borne beetle, with his drowsy hums,
Hath rung night's yawning peal,—
There shall be done a deed of dreadful note.—SHAKSPERE.

AFTER long wakefulness, Lisbia at length fell asleep, but when she did so, fearful and horrific visions passed before her.

She dreamed she was in the ruin of an old chapel, of a gloomy and dilapidated appearance.

The ivy that ran up the front of the building had crept through the time-worn apertures, covering some part of the inside wall with its verdure. The pavement, of black marble, was strewed with human bones, and near the broken altar was an open grave; suddenly Lisbia thought she heard the most heavenly sounds, and the form of a youth, clothed in white garments, arose from the grave.

He was encircled by a halo, that by far outshone the sun, when in its meridian splendour. Awe-struck, Lisbia awoke; disturbed in her mind, she could not remain in bed; she got up and looked through her window; the beams of morn had not yet illumined the earth, and Lisbia felt a strange sensation pass over her mind; she felt as if she had left her earthly existence, and was awakened into another state of being. But this idea was but of short duration, and caused by the impression the dream had made on her spirits.

Lisbia feared, indeed she felt assured, that death would claim some member of her family, or some one very dear to her. Who the youth was that Lisbia in her dream saw rise from the grave, she could not tell, so transient was the glance she had of his person, for when encircled by the halo, he was too resplendent for mortal eyes to look on. "All I intimately know are in good health, and in no danger of death," thought Lisbia ; "what could the appearance of the youth I saw in my dream, indicate ? Surely the revengeful Parrolla does not meditate evil against the beloved of my heart, Edwin !" the thought was agony. "Parrolla could not conceal the dislike he has to Edwin when he sought shelter from the storm at Mildmays," thought Lisbia ; "he even now may be planning his destruction—I will not walk up the cliff—Parrolla may surprise me in conversation with Edwin, and fatal might be the result—I will not go. But then how cruel will think me—he, indeed, will be in despair."

Irresolute, Lisbia joined her aunt, uncle, and cousins at the breakfast-table. Percival was more particular than ever in his attentions to Lisbia, to the evident displeasure of the scowling Parrolla. The pallid look of Lisbia was noticed by her aunt, who thought that she was not so well in consequence of over-exerting herself in dancing

After breakfast the family separated, each to pursue their own avocations; Lisbia knew not what to do, whether to go out and meet Edwin, or stay at home. Undecided how to act, after dressing, she went down stairs again, where she was relieved from her embarrassment, by hearing Parrolla ask his brother if he would go out in a sailing-boat.

"I should like it of all things," said Percival. And Lisbia had the pleasure of seeing them depart. She watched them from the castle, and thought she should now have an hour to herself, free from the presence of Parrolla. But a new trouble presented itself ; the poor idiot, Olando, seeing his sister was preparing for a walk, said,—"What, are you going out, Lisbia ? I'll go with you."

Lisbia was again embarrassed ; she never before had refused to take her poor idiot brother with her—what could she say ? It would not do to let him see Edwin, for, though an idiot, he was fully capable of every passion that actuates the heart, and of knowing and reporting that Lisbia and Edwin had met, should such fact fall under his observation, and that their conversation was of love.

What to do, Lisbia did not know ; what would her aunt think if she heard that she, Lisbia, would not take her brother with her, but wished to go out privily and alone. But Lisbia was relieved from this perplexity ; for Olando ran out in a hurry, crying, "Oh, I have forgot to feed my peacocks—I have forgot to feed my peacocks !"

Taking the advantage of her brother's absence, Lisbia left the castle, and walked up the cliff, where she saw the expecting Edwin. Their meeting was extremely tender ; Edwin now gave up all thoughts of going into the army ; for Lisbia promised to be his as soon as she became of age.

Fearing to be seen, Lisbia did not long remain with her lover, who watched her receding steps, till distance hid her from his view. When Lisbia returned, her brother Olando was quite offended with her.

"It was very unkind of you, to run away whilst I was feeding my peacocks," he said ; "but I'll be revenged of you, I'll go out after dinner, and take a walk by myself."

On this day there was a party at the castle, and amongst the company was Mr. and Mrs. Durant, late Celeste Manby, who still looked as lovely as ever. Parrolla and Percival had returned from their aquatic excursion, and were sitting in the drawing-room with the rest of the company, taking their fruit and wine. Whilst they were so engaged, Olando, who had been as good as his word, and had been out to take a walk, came running in. He was quite out of breath ; and the first words he could utter were addressed to Mr. Immorf.

"Oh, uncle, I have got a wife !" he cried ; "and such a one—so pretty—oh so pretty !"

Though Olando was never ridiculed, but pitied, on account of his having a weak understanding, no one present could help laughing at the simplicity with which these words were uttered.

"Pooh! pooh!" said Mr. Immorf, laughing; "you must not think of a wife yet, Olando."

"Not think of a wife! but I must think of a wife, and I will have one too. And who do think she is?"

"I cannot guess," replied Mr. Immorf.

"Then I'll tell you," said Olando, "Rose Mildmay."

"Rose Mildmay!" cried Parrolla. "I am sick of the very name of these beggars. Mr. Edwin has a very, pretty romantic name, and he is a very pretty fellow altogether; and no doubt the vanity of the puppy will cause him to aspire to the hand of some lady of fortune. And pretty harmless Rose, so she wishes to inveigle you—ah, Olando, this pretty Rose."

"And she is pretty Rose, and a very pretty Rose too," said Olando; "if you had seen her, as I did, bending so kindly over the little lambkins, but so sorrowful, for one of them had its leg broke."

"And where did you see this?" inquired Mr. Immorf.

"Oh, in the field before her father's house; she knelt down on her knees, and looked at them so kindly, I thought she was agoing to take them into her arms, and if she had, I should not have liked it," said Orlando.

"And why not?" inquired Mr. Immorf.

"Indeed, I think she had better have made much of me than the lambs," said Olando; "and if she had taken them up in her arms, I should have offended her. I mean to marry her, and then you know, uncle, she must not notice anything, or anybody but me."

"This is idle talk," said Mr. Immorf, "you must look higher, Olando; you must marry a lady, and not a miller's daughter."

"No, I will have Rose, and nobody else."

"I beg, sir, I may hear no more of this nonsense," cried Mr. Immorf. "Hold your tongue, sir, and let me hear no more of the miller's daughter; if you persevere in this conduct, I shall confine you to the castle."

"Well, I know I must mind you now, because you are my guardian," said the poor idiot, half crying; "but when I am of age, and come to my fortune, I'll do as I like."

Lisbia went up to her brother, and taking him by the hand, she said, "Come, Olando, let you and I take a walk, you will only make uncle angry;" and they went out of the room together.

Percival and Parrolla Immorf were now frequently out in the sailing boat together, and Percival often wished Lisbia to accompany them, but she always declined.

Indeed, she was as little in Percival's company as she could help, for his attention to her became every day more marked, and he was all but her declared lover.

The attention shown to Lisbia by Percival was pleasing to Mr. and Mrs. Immorf, but very much the contrary to Parrolla, who thought his brother superseded him in all things, for which he bore him, though under the guise of fraternal love, a deadly animosity.

Percival and Parolla, being so much out in their sailing boat, gave Lisbia a much greater opportunity of seeing Edwin than she otherwise would have had, for when her cousins were walking, there was no knowing where they might ramble; but when they were out on a sailing excursion, Lisbia considered herself safe.

And often in their absence did she wander with Edwin, in the lone retired walks, with which that part of the country abounded.

But the long and narrow walk up the cliff, where through the trees she could view the sea, was the favourite walk of Lisbia.

Often would Edwin lament, that his station in life was not equal to Lisbia's, for Edwin had all a lover's fears; he feared to lose the object of his fondest love, in consequence of his want of birth and wealth. Some lover suitatble to Lisbia's own rank might intervene, and that lover favoured by her uncle and aunt, might cause a change in the sentiments of Lisbia.

Such fears filled the breast of poor Edwin, and when Lisbia saw the melancholy that oppressed him, she insisted on knowing the cause.

But when Edward explained to her the cause of his uneasiness, Lisbia was much hurt and grieved, that Edward should think her regard for him so light and wavering.

" You have gained my regard too easily," said Lisbia, almost in tears ; " what opinion can you form of me ? who to meet you have left my uncle's house, in fear and secrecy, and that only to meet the object of a light love, a love ready to be bestowed on the next lover who may ask it. No ! was not my mind fixed, and my heart incapable of change, I would not privily leave my home, risking my good name, and the displeasure of my relations."

" Forgive me, dearest Miss Phillimore," said Edwin, " I know that you are not of a light, or changeable disposition, but when I think of your station and my own, it causes fears to arise in my mind."

Lisbia assured Edwin, that she should never change her mind, unless he gave her cause to do so, and that she felt certain he would not.

The lovers parted ; and Lisbia promised Edwin that she would meet him again the first time she thought herself safe from the intrusion of her cousin Parrolla.

When Lisbia retired to her chamber, she called to mind the words of Edwin respecting his fear of her changing her mind.

She took up her guitar, and sang in concert with its soft tones, the following words :—

" Unkind Mildmay, to doubt the truth,
  Of her who loves thee so sincere ;
  Who feels no joy when thou art away,
  Who sees none else when thou art near.

" Thy image fills my nightly dream,
  Oh ! could I ever near thee be ;
  If absent at my dying hour,
  My last sad sigh would be for thee !"

The frequent use made of the sailing boat by Percival and Parrolla gave Lisbia many opportunities of seeing her lover ; and on an evening when they were absent, Lisbia walked up the cliff to meet her Edwin.

It was past six o'clock when she set out to go, for Lisbia had been detained by her uncle, who had requested her to play over some new music.

Lisbia then would not have gone out, but she feared Edwin would be much disappointed if she did not and his mind would be distracted by a—hundred fears, fears that she was wavering respecting him, and careless whether she came or not.

In consequence of these thoughts, Lisbia went to the appointed spot, and there found Edwin awaiting her coming.

Time passes unheeded by lovers ; and the evening sun was fast sinking behind the western hills, as they still lingered on the cliff.

And as they stood hid behind the embowering trees, they looked at the sea, which at that time was rather rough, and seemed to indicate that a storm was nigh.

As Lisbia stood watching the curling waves, she saw, sa far off as she could distinguish objects, a sailing boat advancing, and as it nearer approached, Lisbia saw two persons in it, and she recognised in those persons, her cousins, Percival and Parrolla.

" I will leave you now," said Lisbia ; " I will hasten home. Beware, Edwin, of being seen by Parrolla."

" Oh, do not go yet," said Edwin, " we stand here screened by the trees, they cannot see us ; besides, they are still at a distance, and they will not land near this place."

Before these words had died on the lips of Edwin, Lisbia gave a loud shriek.

"Oh!" she cried, " one of my cousins has fallen into the water, and I think it is Percival ! "

Edwin turned his eyes to the spot, and saw but one person in the boat, and he was engaged in splashing about the water with his oar.

Edwin turned his head, and saw that Lisbia was fainting ; her face and lips were colourless, and she would have fallen to the earth, if Edwin had not caught her in his arms.

Too much engaged with Lisbia to think of anything else, Edwin no longer observed the boat.

But as soon as Lisbia revived and regained her consciousness, she said,—

"Is Percival safe ? Has he again got into the boat ?"

Edwin looked through the trees, and he still saw the boat, but there was only one person in it.

'Oh ! let me fly to the castle, and relate what I have seen," cried Lisbia, " and do you, Edwin, get a boat, and see if you can render any assistance."

No. 24.

Saying this, Lisbia was hastening down the cliff, when she stumbled over the intersected roots of some trees, and was again nearly fainting, when Edwin raised her in his arms.

"Oh, go!" said Lisbia; "fly to the assistance of my cousins—cruel to thus linger here."

"I cannot leave you, dear Lisbia, in this state," said Edwin; "you must not go to the castle by yourself."

"Oh, think not of me!" cried Lisbia; "run, and if possible assist my cousin."

Edwin would have remained with Lisbia, but she hastened past him; her feet were winged with terror; but as she did so, she cried, "Go, and if possible, save my cousin!"

She hastened to the castle, and into the room where her uncle and aunt usually sat.

"Oh! go and save him!" she cried, catching hold of her uncle's arm; "go and save him!" Overcome, Lisbia could utter no more, but with an hysterical laugh, she sank on her aunt's shoulder.

At that moment, Parrolla came running in.

"Oh, that I had died before I had witnessed my poor brother's death" cried Parrolla; "oh, that I had fallen into the sea, instead of him!"

"Percival fallen into the sea!" cried Mrs. Immorf, and she sank senseless on the floor.

"Whereabouts did he fall in?" cried Mr. Immorf, as he snatched up his hat; "come and show me where."

Sobbing, Parrolla ran on before his father, and he pointed to the spot where the accident had happened.

"Oh, God!—oh, God!" cried Parrolla, still in tears, "I wish it had been my fate, instead of my brother's. He overreached himself in trying to get his hat, that had fallen off into the sea, and the boat was nearly upset; I held out an oar, and endeavoured to save him all I could, but he sank down, and rose no more."

Ravenswood Castle was now the house of mourning; and whether the loss of Percival was mourned most by his mother, or Lady Immorf, his grandmother, it would be difficult to determine, for Lady Immorf loved her grandson, the amiable Percival, as well as she ever loved her own son.

Mr. Immorf bore this calamity with manly fortitude, and Christian resignation to the will of Heaven. But it was a fatal blow to his happiness; and he was heard to say, "No more whilst on this earth shall I find comfort."

It is a strange circumstance; but this melancholy affair happened near to that cliff from which the willow droops into the sea, and where the unfortunate Rose had perished.

Several days after the fatal accident had happened, Edwin Mildmay was walking along the sea-shore in very low spirits, and thinking on Lisbia, whom he had not seen since the death of her cousin.

He saw something floating on the water; it was washed by the waves nearer and nearer to where Edwin stood; he saw it was the body of a man, and it at length was washed so near to where he stood, that he succeeded in pulling the person on shore—it was the body of Percival!

Edwin procured help; and the body was removed to Mildmay's house, which was now nearer to that fatal cliff than was Ravenswood Castle; besides, Edwin thought it was proper to inform the parents of the deceased of what had happened, in respect of the body of Percival being found, before it too rashly was taken into their presence.

Mr. Mildmay thought his son had acted with great caution and prudence. "For," said Mr. Mildmay, "if the corse of their son had unexpectedly been presented to the view of his parents, the sight of him would have shocked them more than if they were prepared to expect him. I will go on the mournful errand," said Mildmay, "and ask Mr. Immorf when he will choose to have his son brought home."

Without delay, Mildmay went to the castle, and the parents of Percival hardly knew how to be thankful enough, for the sea having given up her dead; they had the satisfactory hope of having the body of their loved son placed in the tomb of his forefathers, instead of being devoured by the monsters of the deep.

Oh! what a scene was there, when the corse of Percival was brought to the castle!

He looked almost as he did in life; the bloom had not fled from his cheek, nor were his features distorted by the hand of death; the same placid and heavenly composure sat on his countenance.

When Lady Immorf saw the procession that attended her grandson to the place of his interment wind its funeral way along the angle in the road from the castle to the church, it reminded her of the funeral of her late husband; but Percival was not buried in the tomb of Sir Parrolla—he was buried with the Morningtons.

Gloom and heaviness now reigned in Ravenswood Castle, and Lisbia grieved for Percival as much as if he had been her own brother.

CHAPTER LXX.

The lonely mountain o'er,
And the resounding shore;
A voice of weeping heard and loud lament,
From haunted spring and dale,
Edged with the poplar pale.—MILTON.

THE grief of Mrs. Immorf for the loss of her favourite son seemed rather to increase than diminish by time. She called to mind the meekness and pliability of his temper, and the affection and tenderness of his upright heart.

The words Parrolla had used to his father—"Percival may not always be your eldest son,"—struck forcibly on her mind; and she thought on the sibyl's dreadful prediction—"a homicide! a parricide! and a tamperer in the black art!"

"And that self-same woman said, the murderer's hand would fall on my husband," thought Mrs. Immorf. "False and unfounded, I hope, will be her prediction. I have but one child left; and he to be such a demon—avert it Heaven, or let me die before such misery falls on me. My poor son! surely his brother—Oh, no!" she mentally said, clasping her forehead with her hands, "I will not give it a thought."

At this moment, Peter came into the room.

"There are those pests of gipsies in the neighbourhood again," said Peter; "their coming, I think, bodes nothing but ill-luck; I shan't very easily forget the scrape I got into, concerning Margaret's babbling. I wish master would make the vagabonds troop out of the neighbourhood."

"The gipsies here!" exclaimed Mrs. Immorf; "they have not been here before, since the old gipsy predicted evil to Parrolla; and they were here too, when I was married, and now to come at a time like this. I would know for certain whether they have yet amongst them the old woman who predicted to me and mine such evil."

"What, old Cassandra, as they called her?" said Peter. "Shall I go down into the dell, the place of their encampment, and inquire if she is yet amongst them?"

"I would not wish you to inquire," said Mrs. Immorf, "you can look amongst them, and perhaps you may see the old woman, that is to say, if you personally know her—if you can recollect her."

"Oh, yes, madam, I well recollect the hag; she caused me too much vexation for me easily to forget her.'

Peter went down into the dell, and there he saw a large assemblage of gipsies, for the gipsies' families had greatly increased since their last visit to Cornwall.

Sitting amongst their tribe, by a fire they had kindled under a hedge, Peter saw old Cassandra; she was sitting on a three-legged stool, smoking a short pipe.

He did not speak to the old woman, but returned to the castle, and told Mrs. Immorf that the prophetess of evil was yet living, and with her people remained in the dell.

"I have been much annoyed by that woman," said Mrs. Immorf, "yet I have a great desire to se her, in order to ask her some questions. It almost appears to me that there is a fate hangs over the Immorf family that can be neither avoided or overcome ; and however dreadful the contemplation is, yet I fear that the words uttered by that fearful woman will yet come to pass. I speak freely to you, Peter," cntinued Mrs. Immorf; "I know your attachment to my husband's family; it is almost natural to you, having lived in it nearly all your life."

"I have, madam," replied Peter, "and I love my master and his family as much as if they were my nearest relations, and allied to me by the ties of blood."

"I believe you, Peter," said Mrs. Immorf, "and there is no person in existence in whom I can place more confidence, than I can in you. Go to the dell where the gipsies are encampted, and tell that old woman to come to me."

Peter again went to the dell, and found Cassandra still smoking before the fire; when she heard that Mrs. Immorf desired she would come to the castle, a scornful smile sat on her countenance.

"Your mistress does not now despise my forebodings," said the sibyl, "has part of my soothsaying come to pass."

"I know not," replied Peter, "I do not pry into the affairs of my superiors."

"But you have done so," said the sibyl, holding up her withered finger, "remember!"

"I ask you no questions," said Peter, "I merely came to tell you that my mistress desires to see you."

"Well, l will come," said the old woman, "but not to be called fiend and demon."

"And when shall I tell my mistress you will come?" inquired Peter.

"I will come to her about the hour of eight this evening," said the gipsey, "when clouds and darkness enshroud the fair face of night's brilliant orb, even as black and heavy clouds as hang over yon castle;" and she pointed her lean finger towards Ravenswood Castle, "tell your mistress then to expect me."

Agitated, Mrs. Immorf walked on the lawn before the castle ; she watched the receding day: the splendid moon rose in triumphant glory, illumening every tower and tree ; but soon dark clouds enveloped her brightness, and shadows could no longer be traced o the earth.

At this moment, the old gipsy Cassandra appeared on the lawn, at nearly the same hour, and on the same spot where she had visited Mrs. Immorf on her wedding night. But how altered were both parties ! Mrs. Immorf then was very young—no care had ever dulled her spirits—she hailed the rosy hours as they advanced—and then did not give a thought to those ills that ever attend on human life.

Now Mrs. Immorf was much altered ; she had lost the elastic figure of youth, was much stouter, and a care-worn countenance superseded the smiling dimples of her youthful days.

The gipsy was some sixty years of age, when she first stood before Mrs. Immorf on her wedding-day, which was twenty-two years back, so that the gipsy Cassandra was now upwards of eighty years of age.

Her shrivelled and yellow skin bore the appearance of parchment; and in consequence of her being very thin her large black eyes appeared as if protruding from their sockets. No longer was her figure erect and commanding ; but, bent almost double with age and weakness, she approached to meet Mrs. Immorf.

"From circumstances that have lately transpired," said Mrs. Immorf, "I begin to fear that you have a preternatural knowledge of that which will come to pass ; I say, I fear you have, for evil hath been the destiny you have foretold to the house of Ravenswood. I have sent for you, to hear if you are still the predicter of bad tidings—there is money for you," said Mrs. Immorf, as she gave the gipsy gold. "Tell me, but tell me truly, if you really have the gift of prying into futurity, what is the fate that awaits me and mine ?"

"Call me not demon and fiend !" said the old woman, "for telling thee that which is written in the volume of fate. For thyself, short will be thy earthly pilgrimage; and of others I have already spoken."

"And do you still persist in the horrid augury?" said Mrs. Immorf; "will my husband fall by the assassin's hand, and my son be guilty of the dreadful deeds that are predicted?"

"I spoke no lies," said the sibyl; "the spirit of prophecy was on me, and what I then said shall come to pass."

Faint, and overcome by grief, Mrs. Immorf leaned against a tree for support, or she must have fallen on the earth; and the gipsy, supported by her stick, left the lawn, and took her way to the dell, to join her tribe.

CHAPTER LXXI.

Thou hast heard the lie,
The common lie, that every peasant tells
Of me his master—that I slew the boy.
   *   *   *   *
My very mother—Jove, I canno t bear
To speak it!—now looks freezingly upon me.—TALFOURD,

THE words of the gipsy were severely felt by Mrs. Immorf, whose existence was now almost burdensome to her. She every day expected to see her husband a bleeding corse. Grief and horror she had felt, and yet more she feared, was about to fall upon her.

Her heart was still bleeding for the loss of her beloved son, whose death she feared Parrolla was not entirely guiltless of, for so the gipsy strongly intimated. "He is to be a homicide, a parricide, and a tamperer in the black art. Dreadful foreboding! Oh, that he had died in infancy, unsuffering and unsinning! But God's will must be done. I will hope for the best, nor put too implicit a faith in the gipsy's prediction. I must not think too hardly of my son, who may be innocent; nor shall he know I in the least suspect him of crime."

So reasoned Mrs. Immorf with herself; but all her sophistry could not persuade her to be happy, nor calm the fears under which she laboured.

While suffering this tumult of feeling, which rent her heart with grief and apprehension, she did not wish to go into the castle, for her eyes flowed with unbidden tears, nor could she suppress them.

The threatened crimes of her youngest son, and the unabated grief she felt for the loss of her first-born, together, were trials more than the tender Mrs. Immorf could bear.

She thought on that dear son, who had passed away like the gust of wind on the mountain; he, whose brief existence had been almost without blot or failing.

"Ah, little did I think when I saw thee leave the castle, that thou wouldst no more return," sighed Mrs. Immorf, and her tears redoubled.

The shock of Percival's death greatly affected his grandmother, and Lady Immorf, in less than a month, was laid in the tomb.

Lisbia but seldom could venture to meet Edwin, for she dreaded being seen by Parrolla, who now was more arrogant than ever.

The once happy inhabitants of Ravenswood Castle, where the tale, the song, and instruments of music had resounded, were silent and gloomy, and a prey to sorrow.

The approach of winter, too, made dulness yet more dull; and as Lisbia walked pensively down the green lanes, the wind blew by her cold and cheerless, strewing in her path the yellow leaves that the autumnal blast had withered.

Gloomy and dejected, she returned to the castle, for a great heaviness sat on her spirits; for she was thinking on her dream, and the death-owl's note.

When Lisbia went into the room where her uncle was sitting, her brother was there.

"It is of no use talking to me, uncle," said Olando; "I must and will have Rose Mildmay for a wife. Oh, was you but to see her feed the poultry, you'd be quite in love with her; I know she would like my peacocks, and when she's my wife, I'll make her feed them too."

"Olando, do not let me hear you talk in this way," said Mr. Immorf; "Rose is not a fit wife for you—you must marry a lady."

"But I don't like ladies," said Olando; "I shall have money enough, and I think I ought to have who I like."

"No, not to degrade yourself," said Mr. Immorf. "I enjoin you, Olando, to think no more about Rose."

"But I must think of her, and I will think of her," said the idiot. "What is it to you, uncle?" said Olando, almost crying. "You want me to break my heart, I know you do."

"Brother, you must be ruled by your uncle," said Lisbia.

"I shan't be ruled by anybody," said Olando, "for have Rose I will."

CHAPTER LXXII.

Like some baneful herb,
His poisonous qualities, extended with his growth.

BY THE AUTHORESS OF EVA.

PARROLLA now was but little in the company of his parents, he was frequently out all day and great part of the night, and his conduct became in the course of a few months riotous, and very unbecoming the conduct of a gentleman.

There were several formers' sons with whom he kept company, Parrolla not being very particular in that respect, and these young men, who thought themselves honoured by the notice of one so much their superior, followed the degrading conduct of the heir of Ravenswood.

Trampling down the crops, tearing up young trees, and breaking windows when they were out shooting, was fine sport to Parrolla and his companions, and when the flaunting wassailers had left their bowl, not a female could pass them without being insulted.

This conduct of Parrolla was most grievous to his father and mother, and they mildly remonstrated with him.

But Parrolla would not hearken to them; he declared he was tired of the dullness of Ravenswood, and meant to visit foreign climes, where he could act as he pleased without being reprimanded.

"It will not do to be always in leading-strings," said Parrolla; "in fact, I am tired of being controlled; I shall visit Italy, for they say it is a beautiful place, and every gentleman ought to visit it; if a person has not seen Italy they have seen but little."

"I really am surprised at your thinking of leaving us," said Mr. Immorf; "indeed it is very unkind, your brother so lately dead, too."

"If I stay in Cornwall you will only find fault with me, and so I have made up my mind to go. But I don't much like to leave Lisbia," he continued, "for she's to be my wife. When I come back I'll marry her; you must not think of any one else, Lisbia," he continued, "if you do, some one must fall."

"I cannot bear to hear you speak in this assassin-like manner," replied Mr. Immorf; "Lisbia will be her own mistress when she is of age, and no one will have any right to control her, for she will then be her own mistress."

"You are always trying to thwart me," cried Parrolla, "that's not a father's part. If Lisbia refuses me, I'll know who's the cause of it, and let him take what follows. What say you, Lisbia," said Parrolla, boisterously taking her hand, "when I come back will you have me or not? I know you liked my brother Percival best, but now he's dead, and you can't have him!"

Lisbia looked terrified at the violent Parrolla—she seemed almost ready to faint.

"Parrolla, I will not suffer you to behave in this way to Lisbia," said Mr. Immorf. "Retire, my dear," he said to Lisbia, "your aunt is in her dressing-room."

"I suppose I am too rough for Lisbia," said Parrolla, "she wants more compliments and flattery than I know how to give her. I am sincere, flattery and folly is nonsense—I can't bear it;—however, I shall expect Lisbia will have me when I return from Italy, or she and I shan't be friends."

"I am sure as you go on, it is not the way to get her; your behaviour is rude and ungentleman-like, and such as would disgrace the lowest peasant. Parrolla, I have given you education, but you are ignorant by nature."

"Ah, I am everything that's bad, but one good thing is, that I soon shall be out of your way;" saying this Parrolla went off in a huff.

Finding that Parrolla was fully bent on going abroad, his father no longer objected, neither did his mother; indeed she was not sorry that he had formed such a resolution; for Mrs. Immorf thought that if Parrolla went abroad, it would delay, if not prevent, that which always dwelt on her mind, though she feared even to herself to acknowledge that it did so—namely, the gipsy's prophecy.

All things were arranged for the departure of Parrolla, who in a few weeks was to leave the castle, and be on his passage to Italy.

Mr. Immorf wished Peter to accompany Parrolla, as Peter was now between thirty and forty years of age, a sober and discreet man, and one much attached to his master, and the interest of his family. But Parrolla was dissatisfied with Peter for an attendant; he wished to have a younger man, one more of his own age, neither did Peter wish to go; his young master was too hair-brained for him; besides, from boyhood Peter had never left Ravenswood Castle, and he had no wish to do so now.

But Parrolla was not long before he found a travelling attendant, one Anthony Halman, the son of a decayed tradesman, who wanted a situation, and he was hired by Parrolla.

Mrs. Immorf saw her son depart; he went from the home of his childhood with a light and merry heart—he left his paternal home with as much joy as a bird would have done when escaped from his wiry cage, or as a captive would have done when emancipated from captivity.

But the heart of Mr. Immorf was heavy when he saw his son depart.

And tears filled the eyes of his weeping mother. "Oh! what feelings are mine!" mentally said Mrs. Immorf, "to weep for the departure of my son, and yet I am glad that he is going;—glad that he is going! My only son!—his brother so lately drowned too! Could I once have parted with him?—Oh, no! but then it is in the hope that his absence will avert a dreadful destiny. I will pray; Heaven will hear a mother's prayer when it is addressed to the throne of grace for a child. But if it is the ordination of Heaven that he is to fulfil the dark destiny predicted, oh that my eyes may be closed in eternal night before the dreadful fulfilment of his fate!

CHAPTER LXXIII.

A wight he was, who had but little wit,
But full of spleen and hate in angry fit.

BY THE AUTHORESS OF EVA.

OLANDO every day became more enamoured of Rose Mildmay, and he oft
came to the farm when Rose was sitting at work.

"What are you making, Rose," he would say, "shirts for Edwin? Oh, wh
you are my wife, you must make shirts for me."

"You are jocular, sir," Mr. Mildmay would reply; "Rose is to be a farmer
wife, she must not marry a gentleman."

"A farmer!" said Olando; "I'd shoot the first man who offered to marry h
Don't you have nobody but me, Rose; I'll keep a carriage for you to ride
and you shall have horses, and dogs, and peacocks, and servants."

Rose smiled, and showed her pretty white teeth when Olando made her th
tempting offers.

But it vexed Mr. Mildmay, when he heard Olando express himself as he d
for he feared that Olando really meant what he spoke, and that he was in no jest

He determined to put a stop to the visits of Olando: "If I do not, Mr. Imm
may think that I wish to take advantage of the weak understanding of his nephe
and entrap him into a marriage with my daughter," thought Mildmay.

Soon as Olando was gone, Mildmay desired Rose to give Olando no encoura
ment. "You know, Rose, that unfortunately for Mr. Phillimore, he is v
deficient in understanding, and his friends may think that I have some sinis
views in encouraging him here, with an eye to his property. You must lo
cross at him, Rose, and give him no reason to think his visits are agreeable
neither should I think they are. Mr. Phillimore is not a man calculated fo
young woman to fall in love with."

"In love with him?" cried Rose, "he is the ugliest man I ever saw.]
father, I would not have Mr. Phillimore, if he could give me a golden coac
instead of a wooden one."

"I am glad to hear you say that, Rose," said her father; "when he om
again, you must look cross, and hardly answer him."

"Oh, I hate to look cross," said Rose, "it makes one look so disagreeable, and
can't but answer Mr. Phillimore."

"You must like him, for I see you don't like to lose his good opinion," sa
Mr. Mildmay; "but don't flatter yourself, Rose, he never must be your husband

"My husband! la, father, what odd notions you have. I tell you, I would n
have Mr. Phillimore; no, not if it was to save his life; for I am sure, if I sav
his life, I must lose my own. No, sooner than I would marry Mr. Phillimore, I
die where Aunt Rose did. Who would have such an ugly, foolish creature as
is? Don't think, father, I think of him; for if I was compelled to have him for
husband, I would throw myself from that very cliff where the willow droops in
the sea."

"Who could compel you to marry Mr. Phillimore?" said her father; "and
they could, and did, that would be no reason why you should commit so great
crime. You have been very strange and romantic in your way and manner !
some time, Rose," continued Mr. Mildmay; "your temper, that used to be so mil
has become extremely altered; there is a restlessness and petulance in your mann
I do not like; what has occasioned this alteraton?"

"La, father, you are always fancying something," said Rose; "I am sure, if
am restless and petulant, I don't know it; and if I do anything to offend you an
mother, I am sorry for it. I hope you are not angry with me?"

"Angry with you! no, my good girl," said Mr. Mildmay, "and hope I sha
never have any cause to be so. But I wish to get rid he visits of your

Phillimore; I don't like his skulking about the meadows, and coming to the farm. I know it is on your account ;—when he comes again, you must seem distant and look sour."

"Look sour! oh no! I can't do that," said Rose, "I have been praised for always looking smiling; young Squire Manby told me, that when I smiled, I had dimples like Venus."

"Pooh! pooh!" said Mr. Mildmay, "you must not believe his flattery. But I again desire, Rose, that you would look sour at Mr. Phillimore."

"Oh, I can't look sour at him, if I do, I shan't look pretty."

"You need not care what he thinks, said Mr. Mildmay, "as you say you had rather die than have him for a husband."

"So I would," said Rose; "but then I can't bear to be thought not pretty by any body; and if Mr. Phillimore loves me, I can't help that."

"And you wish to smile and look attractive, and to fascinate him yet more?"

No. 25.

"If he will like me, how can I help it?" said Rose; "I wish everybody to like me."

"It is very proper that you should wish your friends to like you," said her father, "but not young men; what is a greater grief to the heart than unrequited affection? I tell you, Rose, you must look sour at Mr. Phillimore."

"I cannot look sour and ugly for anybody," said Rose.

"Rose, I begin to fear that you are a thorough coquette."

Rose told her father true; she did not like Olando,—that is to say, she would not have liked him for a hushand, as such he would have been to her most hateful.

But though young and innocent, Rose had woman enough in her to know that the reign of youth was but for a season, and that the attentions of so wealthy a young man as Mr. Phillimore was, would alarm the jealousy of him she wished to interest; besides, the beauty of Rose had been praised, and she thought that love and homage was but her due.

Parrolla found Italy quite suitable to his taste; and at the Opera, or in a midnight carousal or brawl, there you might find Parrolla. He more than once had like to have been poniarded; and his servant, Anthony Halman, was severely wounded in the arm through being in an affray with his master.

———

CHAPTER LXXIV.

Was I to curse the man I hate,
Hope and disappointments be his fate.—AUTHOR UNKNOWN.

JULIAN was punctual in meeting the Marchese de Gusman; but the marchese from prudent motives, had altered his mind respecting Julian; he intended to have given him a larger sum of money—a sum sufficient to have procured horses and dresses for servants, that Julian might have come to the palace of De Gusman, with an equipage befitting the heir of the marchese.

But, on due consideration, he thought that by such display he should only awaken the enmity of his nephew Don Roderiquis de Gusman.

The nervous marchese thought, that before it was publicly known that he had a son, it would be better to break the matter to Roderiquis, who now considered himself heir to his uncle, in right of his father, who was dead, and was the only brother of the marchese.

The income of Don Roderiquis, and his widowed mother, was hardly sufficient to support their rank, and the Marchese de Gusman was well aware that the introduction of Julian would be as a thunderbolt falling at the feet of Roderiquis.

And the marchese feared that the defeat of his nephew's ambitious prospects would cause much strife and bitterness in the family.

The marchese, therefore, intended to break the matter to his sister-in-law, and her son, before they heard of Julian. He (the marchese) intended to soften the unpleasing intelligence to them, with all the skill he was master of. He felt for them, on account of their disappointment; but his own child, the marchese thought, ought to inherit, if not all, the greater part of his property.

"Poor fellow! he has met with privations enough," thought the marchese; "it is my duty now to make him what amends I can. He is my child and heir in the law of nature, and if he is not my heir according to law, I will make him so, at least as far as I can.

Though without equipage, Julian's apparel was fit for the first noble in Spain, and he walked to the palace De Gusman with his father.

When seated, and served with a luxurious collation that the marchese had ordered to be provided in honour of his son, the marchese said,—

"I assure you, Julian, this is the proudest day, I for many long years have felt;

and I think that the hand of Providence hath directed you to your paternal home, and that Heaven hath been pleased in its mercy to take the marchesa out of a world of turmoil to another and a better world.

"If she had been living, I am sure she never would have been reconciled to your appearance; and what to say, or how to break the matter out to your aunt and cousin, I am quite at a loss."

"They are not your directors," said Julian with much haughtiness. "Are you not master of your own property, and by no means accountable to them?"

"Certainly!" said the marchese, with much mildness; "but you are not aware, Julian, it is dangerous to provoke anger."

"I have provoked no anger," said Julian.

"But you are the innocent cause of a great disappointment to your cousin Roderiquis De Gusman, and sometimes, who is more vengeful than a disappointed man to the object who caused that disappointment?"

"You don't think he'll poniard me, for stepping in between him and your property?" said Julian.

"God forbid!" exclaimed the marchese, "no; Roderiquis, however disappointed, would not do that."

The conversation here dropped, and the Marchese De Gusman showed Julian over his palace, with which he was much delighted, for never before had Julian seen such grandeur.

The marchese showed Julian the portrait of the late marchesa, a very handsome woman, but there was much haughtiness expressed in her countenance.

"I thought on you, Julian," said the marchese, "and in the restless slumber of sickness, I frequently called on your name. Often hath that bosom," and he pointed to the portrait, "heaved with jealous anger at my doing so; and she suspected that others shared with her my affection. I could not, dare not, make known to her the grief that destroyed my peace; had there been one person in the world to whom I could have confided my secret sorrow, it would have been a relief to me; but had the marchesa known the deed, that in a moment of passion I committed, she would have looked on me with abhorrence. Nor would she ever have looked on you, on account of the circumstances under which you were born."

"What were these circumstances?" cried Julian, his face reddening with anger, for a strong conviction of what he had before suspected, passed over his mind. And he again repeated, "what were these circumstances?"

The marchese was silent.

Julian continued. "Am I then not your lawful issue—nought but the child of dishonour, an illegitimate? Then my bright dream of pride, alas! is ended. I awake, and find myself a wretched, nameless being—a child of shame!"

"Do not reproach me!" said the marchese, much affected. "All that is in my power to give, you shall receive from me. I had an immense fortune with the late marchesa in money, and large possessions, she had no heirs excepting myself; and all that I have at my disposal shall be yours."

"But the title of Marchese De Gusman, must I give up that?" inquired Julian.

"Not without Roderiquis makes your birth a matter of cavil."

"And will you expose that circumstance, and bring ignominy on me, for a fault not mine? It behoves you to say that I am a legal heir to the title and estates of De Gusman."

"If I say so, I cannot prove it," replied the marchese.

"Then let them disprove it," exclaimed Julian. "I dare them to that."

"Let us hope for the best," said the marchese. "I am not sure that Roderiquis will dispute your title, nor feel himself injured by your possessing it; but I am well acquainted with his proud, ambitious, and revengeful spirit; and such knowledge causes my fears to arise. To-morrow, I will see my sister-in-law and her son, and break the matter out to them; it certainly is no pleasant thing for a man, who has considered a large property his own, as much as if he was in possession thereof, to see see such property in a moment wrested from his grasp

is enough at the first impulse of disappointment to cause angry thoughts to aris
in his bosom; but when he gets cool and reasonable, and finds another ha
a prior claim, he becomes satisfied, and relinquishes the hope of havin
that to which he had no just claim.   Julian, I have committed sin, and but to
well are you of aware that; I have severely repented of the heinous deed I com
mitted in the days of my youth; and many heavy penances have I undergone,-
and many more shall I have to undergo.   If I by falsehood support your claim t
the title and estates of De Gusman, shall I not be plunging myself deepe
in crime?"

"No," replied Julian, "if by falsehood you support my claim, you will but b
doing me an act of justice; am I not your first-born and heir, by the right of birt
and nature, though not according to the ordinance of man; that ordinance yo
neglected, and who doth the penalty fall on, but on me?——

"By this omission, I may be bereft of my title, estate, and honour; I am no
the legal heir, and who but you have brought this privation upon me?   And t
prevent your having the crime of injustice, and the want of paternal affection t
answer for, it were better for me, and less sin would lie at your door, if by tellin
a few untruths, you can establish my claim; let not any silly qualms of con
science cause you to admit that I am not a lawful heir to the title and estates
De Gusman; if you do, you will commit the double sin of injustice, and a war
of paternal affection, whilst lying can be but one sin, and it were better to comm
one sin than two."

"You are an excellent casuist, Julian," said the marchese; "I suppose I mu
take your advice, and commit the lesser sin, to avoid the greater.   As I befor
said, I will to-morrow see my nephew; he is the only person who would objec
or in any way interfere with your claim.

"There is one thing I will show you, Julian," said the marchese.   "I hav
kept it many, many years, in secresy and safety.   Safely has it happened, an
from the eyes of prying curiosity; for, had it been discovered, greater than eve
would have been my domestic jars."

The marchese opened a cabinet that stood in his library, and having touched
secret spring, he opened a small drawer which before appeared but as a part of th
back of the cabinet.

The marchese took from hence a portrait.   "This, Julian," he said, "is you
mother."

Julian looked at the portrait with a feeling of affection and admiration of he
superior beauty; yet there was an apathy in his look, which but ill-accorded wit
that unbounded love and veneration that he had once expressed for his mother.

He now knew that she was not what he, in the enthusiasm of youth, had sup
posed her to be—an exalted and immaculate being, an angelic and suffering martyr

Julian found that his mother was but as other women,—fallible, and that she
had fallen into error.

CHAPTER LXXV.

There were old rumours of an infant born,
And strangely vanishing—a tale of guilt.—ION, A TRAGEDY.

ON the following day, the Marchese de Gusman ordered his carriage to drive
to the house of the Signora de Gusman's; that lady and her son Roderiquis, were
both at home.   After the first compliments had passed—

"I am come," said the Marchese de Gusman, "to inform you, sister, and my
nephew, of a circumstance, that I dare say will not a little surprise you.   I have
found one, who I thought was lost to me; and who in this world I no more expected
to behold."

"What!" cried the signora, with great surprise, "has the marchesa risen from the dead? Has she burst the confines of the tomb, and again come to visit you?"

"Sister, you totally misunderstand me," said the marchese; "I allude to the living not to the dead."

"Whom do you allude to?" inquired the signora.

"Give me your patience, and you shall hear," said the marchese.

"During the time I was residing in Spain with my aunt—it was before the death of my elder brother—I became acquainted with a young lady who made a great impression on my heart; her father was immensely rich, but unfortunately she was of a different faith from myself. We were privately married by a priest."

"Then, you were married!" said the signora, colouring; "but you had no family," she continued, apparently much agitated.

"I had one son," replied the marchese.

"And is he living?" inquired the signora.

"He is."

The colour of the signora became a yet deeper crimson, and the eyes of Roderiquis were cast on the ground.

At length the signora, somewhat recovered from the surprise this disagreeable intelligence had occasioned her, inquired, but as if almost afraid of what the answer might be,—

"And do you intend to publicly acknowledge him as your son?"

"Certainly," said the marchese.

"And have you not led everybody to suppose that Roderiquis would be heir to your title and estates?" said the signora; "what a deception!"

"My son has paid his addresses to the Signora Olivia de Almeira, as heir-presumptive to the title and estates of De Gusman."

"You, marchese, by your false representations, will cause Roderiquis to appear more like an impostor than an honourable grandee of Spain; but the disgrace and deception lay with you. My son is guiltless, and injured by his father's brother, the Marchese de Gusman."

"But where has this son been concealed," continued the signora, "in what hovel hath the heir of De Gusman been hidden for twenty years, not even credulity would believe so absurd a story; and, granting it true, why have you deceived Roderiquis into a belief that he was your heir? To me the whole affair appears strange, mysterious, and unaccountable. If you really have a son, and a legitimate son, why keep him in secrecy?"

"You talk to me, signora, in a very haughty and unceremonious manner," said the marchese; "however, I shall condescend to account for this seeming mystery. I before told you, signora," continued the Marchese de Gusman, "that on account of the difference in our faith, neither my friends, nor the friends of the lady, would have been agreeeble to our union. My income then was not sufficient to maintain a wife, according to the rank I held in society, without the assistance of my family, and that I did not choose to solicit, nor could my wife, under circumstances, apply to her father for pecuniary assistance, although he was as rich as Crœsus."

"What! then she eloped, I suppose," said the signora, "and trusted to the honour of her lover."

"I have already told you, signora, that we were married," said the marchese; "but on account of the difference in our faith, we knew that neither of our families would be reconciled to us, and that prevented the application."

"Oh," said the signora, with a very significant look.

"But to proceed," said the marchese, "in consequence of my limited income, we took a cottage, secluded but rspectable; it was a place very suitable for the circumstances we were then in: we kept no company, nor did I reside there, but with my aunt, visiting the cottage occasionally."

"Very romantic indeed," said the signora; "and what faith did the lady profess,—an heretic no doubt?"

"You are deceived," said the marchese, "she was not an heretic, but what her manner of worship was, is now of no consequence. In the cottage I was speaking of, my son was born; when he was about five years old, he strayed away from his home, and I heard nothing of him until within these few weeks; the loss of our child was the death of his mother,—she never held up her head afterwards. My aunt, uncle, nor any of my friends did not know anything of the affair, neither did I ever name it to the late marchesa. The loss of the child was a grief to me, and a subject I never wished to speak on; neither did I ever name my first wife to the marchesa : it was useless raking up the ashes of the dead. Besides, you know the peculiarity of the late marchesa ; she would have been jealous even of the dead ; if I by chance had sighed, she would have thought I had been sighing on account of the death of my first wife, and that she held but a small place in my affection."

"My sister-in-law was certainly rather odd in her way," said the signora, "but of this youth, whom you suppose to be your son—who brought him up, and of what age is he ?"

"He is not yet twenty," replied the marchese; "he is a fine manly youth, and looks older than he is."

"And where has he been living all these years ?" inquired the signora.

"He was found by a goatherd, who brought the child up as his own."

"And did you not make inquiry after him—did you take no pains to regain your lost child."

"1 made every inquiry, but without effect."

"And how was it that you found him now ?" said the signora.

"Most providentially," replied the marchese, "by the means of a portrait."

"What portrait was that ?" inquired the signora.

The marchese was rather nonplused; he had said too much, and had got himself in a difficulty, from which he knew not how to extricate himself. Hardly knowing what reply to make, he said,—

"By the means of my portrait he took with him, as a toy to play with, when he strolled away."

"And is that portrait all the evidence you have, to prove the youth your son, after this lapse of years? The child could not have walked miles—and if you had properly inquired for him, as you say you did, and have offered a reward for the recovery of the child, he, if living, would have been brought back to you. Your child must have fell into some pit or river, where he never was found. Depend upon it, the vile goatherd has palmed his son, or grandson, upon you, with a view of the youth enjoying the estates and titles of De Gusman, to the exclusion of the lawful heir ; can you, marchese, suffer yourself to be so imposed upon ?"

"Quite a rustic, I suppose," cried Roderiquis, who had not before spoken; "a very fit representative, indeed, for the house of De Gusman."

"He has by no means the manner of a rustic," replied the marchese; "he is well informed, and his bearing is as lofty as your own. But we will not disagree on this matter; I hope to see you to dine with me to-morrow, and you shall judge for yourselves." So saying, the marchese departed.

CHAPTER LXXVI.

Proud Spaniard, thou shalt feel me.—YOUNG.

"So it appears, Roderiquis, that you are after all to be robbed of your inheritance," said the signora ; "however, please Heaven, we will go to-morrow; and see this youth who hath dropped from the clouds."

"It is to me a very strange and mysterious piece of business," continued the signora, " but be prudent, Roderiquis, and seem to be in friendship. with your new-found cousin, whatever may be the feelings of your heart."

The marchese sent cards of invitation to a number of his most particular friends, requesting their company to dine with him the next day.

The Signora de Gusman and her son were the first who arrived; and Julian was introduced to them by his father.

With but ill-concealed spite and envy the signora viewed the youthful Julian, and contrasted him, whom she had termed a rustic, with her own high-bred son, who was not by any means a handsome youth.

Whilst the appearance of Julian was most striking, he had been but a tall, lank, and awkward boy, but his figure had amplified, and he was now a graceful and handsome youth, of a tall and commanding figure. His face was oval, and the hue of the damask rose enlivened his clear brown cheek, for the complexion of Julian was dark, as were his eyes, that, now inspired with pleasure, shone with more than common lustre through his long black eye-lashes. His dress was of green velvet after the Italian fashion, and the appearance of Julian was handsome, graceful, and commanding.

The Marchese de Gusman introduced Julian to all his guests as his long lost son.

The Signora de Gusman, and her son Roderiquis, were quite vexed and con-founded at the appearance of Julian, and at the congratulations received by both Julian and the Marchese de Gusman on that occasion.

Julian now was as grand as the highest don in Naples; he devoted some hours of the day to study and the improvement of his mind, and the rest of his time he, like other gentlemen, devoted to pleasure.

But the Marchese de Gusman at times was more melancholy and conscience-stricken than ever, and he still very frequently visited the monastery of the Con-trite Heart.

The effort he had made to place Julian in a position to succeed him in his title and estates was an exertion most unpleasant to a man in the state of mind the Marchese de Gusman was in, and the untruths he was obliged to tell in support of that claim did not sit easy on his conscience.

The Marchese de Gusman, having found his son was soon publicly known at Naples, and finding that Roderiquis was likely to lose the title and estates of De Gusman, the family of the Lady Olivia de Almeria, Roderiquis thought, looked rather cool at him, as did the lady herself.

On a night Julian was at the Opera he happened to sit near the box of the Lady Olivia, whose eyes were frequently directed towards Julian.

This was enough to arouse the passion of jealousy in the breast of Roderiquis, who sat, as it were on thorns, all the evening, whilst Julian looked pleased and triumphant in his new-found honours.

To his mother, the Signora de Gusman, Roderiquis told his heart-burnings, and that lady participated in the feelings of her son.

" Would I could administer a dose of poison to this new-found heir," she said, " or put a stop to his pride by the point of a poniard!"

" Your thoughts and mine exactly correspond," replied Roderiquis. " I'll watch him to some secret place, and lay low the enemy of my peace and fortunes."

" Hush, rash boy!" cried the signora, " walls have ears. You must be more guarded; lay aside this rashness, and well consider and mature your plan, before you put it into action. Recollect the penalty of what you spoke of: you must be secret and silent."

" But Italian vengeance will not sleep," replied Roderiquis.

" Of that I am well aware," replied the signora; " mine will not sleep, nor must yours."

CHAPTER LXXVII.

' I told thee I'd meet thee at Philippi.'—SHAKSPERE.

JULIAN wrote to his foster-father and mother, and informed them of all that had happened to him ; and he sent them a large sum of money, and invited them to come and remain for some time at the palace of De Gusman.

"Be not afraid of coming here amongst the great and gay," said Julian ; "every one knows that I was lost by my father, and found by a good goatherd, who protected me. Come and remain with us for a time," continued Julian, "and you will be caressed, loved, and respected for your humanity."

Julian, though proud and ambitious, was not so lifted up by his prosperity, as to cause him to forget or despise the humble persons who had protected his infancy.

The old goatherd accepted the invitation of their foster-son, and they were kindly received by the Marchese de Gusman, who knew not how to make enough of the old people, who were shown to the friends of the marchese, as the humane persons who had fostered and treated, as their own, the heir of De Gusman, without any prospect of the least remuneration.

" They at first supposed the child to be some vagrant's offspring, and when they had reason to think that he was differently connected, they had no hope that he would find his father."

As Julian was walking one fine evening on the bay, accompanied by the young Marchese de Alvera, who was expatiating on the charms of an opera dancer, the time glided insensibly away until it was near midnight. The fishermen had long since retired to their lowly pallets, and the busy minds and industrious fingers of these men, whom Julian and his friend had observed as they passed them, now lay entranced in sleep.

All was silent and serene, and the friends stood for some time viewing the lofty Vesuvius.

" Here is a scene of sublimity and grandeur !" cried Julian ; " one would think that when it overflows, it would consume this terrestrial globe with vivid fire. But no; like unto the raging sea, it hath its bounds—an Almighty power hath restrained it, and said, ' So far shalt thou go, and no farther.' "

The friends now turned to go home ; and when they came to an angle, where a number of olive-trees were growing, the Marchese de Alvera pointed to Julian.

" Look," said he, " observe, there is some one skulking behind those trees."

" I see nothing," said Julian.

" There, in the obscurity behind those trees," said the Marchese de Alvera, pointing with his fingers to a dark spot covered with olive-trees. " There, as the moon partially illumined that spot, I saw the outline of a tall dark figure."

" Mere fancy, you may depend on it," said Julian ; " don't alarm yourself, it was but a shadow caused by the moonlight falling on your or my figure."

" Let us be cautious, my friend," said De Alvera, " we are watched—there are assassins abroad. I suspect I have a rival, one who envys me the favour of the Signora Seraphina ; but I know him, he is of short stature ; but the person whom I saw skulking behind those trees is a tall dark figure."

" Some person like ourselves, no doubt," said Julian, " walking here to enjoy the beauty of the night, and to inhale the perfume shed by the fragrant flowers that so profusely grow in this neighbourhood."

" If such was his intention, why skulk behind the trees, fearful of being seen? That we are watched, I am certain," said De Alvera ; " let us make the best of our way."

Again they caught a glimpse of the person, and Julian saw enough of his figure, to lead him to suppose it was the same mysterious being, who had so haunted him whilst he dwelt with his foster-father in Spain.

"Why should he watch me?" thought Julian, "for me, I have doubt, it is whom he is watching. He told we should meet in Naples. and he is as good as his word; but why does he watch my steps like some hired bravo?"

Again he was seen beneath the dusky umbrage, and De Alvera again caught a sight of his figure; but in a moment, he glided away behind the green foliage that crossed the perspective.

"He is now yonder, hid behind those trees," said the Marchese De Alvera; "I suppose I shall be poniarded before I reach home—depend on it, my life is in danger on account of Seraphina."

"Do not alarm yourself," replied Julian; "it is I who that person is watching. I plainly discriminated his figure, and know him to be a person I several times have seen before."

"Is he any enemy?" inquired De Alvera.

No. 26.

" I should think not,'" said Julian ; " I never gave him any reason to be so."

" Then, why does he skulk about in darkness and secrecy ?" said De Alvera ; " what motive can he have for doing so, unless he meant to waylay, and thrust his poniard into your heart ?   I would always avoid so suspicious a character, nor give him an opportunity to harm me."

" That is my intention," said Julian.

They had now reached the palace of De Gusman, and the friends separated.

CHAPTER LXXVIII.

Hast read his eye of silent agony ?—MATURIN.

THE strange conduct of Count Herman gave Julian some uneasiness ; and he was very sorry that he had opened his mind to that mysterious man, concerning how he had been left by his father, and the death of his mother.

" My father has behaved like a father to me," thought Julian, " and he is the only person I now have in the world to love and venerate, excepting the good old people who brought me up. I heretofore looked on my father as a murderer," thought Julian, " as the murderer of my mother, and for which crime I vowed a deadly vengeance upon him ; but now my mind is altered—I see the anguish under which he labours, for an act done unpremeditated, and in a moment of provocation and rage. I now feel the affinity there is between us ; my heart acknowledges the duty I owe him, and that which will dishonour him will dishonour me.

" There must be some particular motive in that mysterious man, who forced himself into my confidence when in Spain ; he must know, and hate the marchese, and wish to bring destruction on him, or why urge me to turn evidence against my father, and make known to the Inquisition what has occurred ? It was he no doubt who watched me, and that for the purpose of persuading me to impeach my father."

Julian had wished a heavy retribution to fall on his father on account of his mother ; but now he felt he had a parent, and that parent he meant to shield from harm all that lay in his power.

The old goatherd and his wife, who now had been in Naples a month, returned to their cottage, laden with presents.

Nor did the vindictive Signora De Gusman and her son withhold their presents to the old people, for the service they had done the marchese in restoring to him his son, although they were planning in their hearts how they could destroy that son.

It happened on a night when Julian was sitting in a box at the Opera, he saw sitting in a box near him the very man of all others he wished to avoid ; for he feared lest Count Herman might speak of circumstances he now wished to be concealed.

Julian kept his eye on the count to see if he was observed by that strange personage, and to his great mortification he saw he was.

There were two persons in the box with the count, one of them the very last person in the world he wished to have seen there in company with Count Herman; it was his cousin Roderiquis.

The other person was a stranger to Julian, and that person was Parrolla Immorf, who now was the gayest of the gay, and the depravest of the depraved.

Both Roderiquis and Parrolla were strangers to Count Herman, but Julian observed the count was in deep discourse with them, and he suspected they were talking of him, for their eyes frequently wandered in a direction to where he was sitting; neither the fine strains of music nor the warbling of some of the finest singers in the world, could entirely arrest their attention.

They all three seemed engaged in some very interesting conversation, which prevented their much noticing the performance, and they annoyed those who sat near them with so much talk.

Vexed at what he had observed, Julian soon left the theatre, but he did not mention that which had disturbed his mind to his father, who he saw was low-spirited and nervous enough without any additional uneasiness.

Whilst Count Herman was sitting in the box at the Opera, awaiting the drawing up of the curtain, Roderiquis came into the same box, and soon after Parrolla Immorf,—they were all strangers to each other.

Count Herman—who for some time had been looking at Julian, said to Roderiquis, who sat near him. "Look at yonder fine don, the upstart, I have no patience with him!"

"Who do you mean?" inquired Roderiquis.

"Why, that handsome signor there in green, with the white feather in his hat, the new-found heir of the Marchese de Gusman."

"You mean him, do you?" replied Roderiquis.

"Yes," replied Count Herman, "it raises my choler to see that peasant boy ape the gentleman. It was a good thing for him that the Marchese de Gusman lost his son; that circumstance was known to the subtle old goatherd, and he, with an artful story, palmed his own tawny son on the nervous marchese."

Roderiquis was much agitated; though glad to hear this intelligence, which he would not appear much to notice, he coolly replied, "He is rather a handsome young fellow, though dark."

"Dark!" replied Count Herman; "one would almost swear from his appearance, that he was the son of some vagrant Jew, or gipsy. If he is not the old man's son, and the old man found him as he pretends, it is more likely that yonder fine don is the illegitimate offspring of some such parents, than the true issue of the Marchese de Gusman."

"He may be the son of the marchese, though not the legitimate son," replied Roderiquis. "I have heard he was in Spain when young, and there is no answering for any one. The marchese might have been captivated with some vagrant woman, belonging to one of the tribes you speak of."

Count Herman had not yet spoken to Parrolla, who all along had been eyeing the count with deep scrutiny; and though listening to the discourse, he had not yet spoken, although Count Herman by his glance appeared to address his discourse to Parrolla as well as to Roderiquis.

It was evident that the discourse of Count Herman annoyed those who sat near them; therefore, the discourse was dropped.

But when the opera was over, Roderiquis gave Count Herman his card, and said, "He should be glad of an hour of his company when convenient."

After Roderiquis had departed, Count Herman looked round for Parrolla, but he was no longer to be seen; the fact was, that Parrolla was thunderstruck, as it were, when he saw the countenance of Count Herman, which he did not immediately do when he first came into the box at the Opera.

If Parrolla had seen the count, he certainly would not have gone into that box; but when there, he felt a kind of fascination, that, as it were, rooted him to the spot; he well knew the face and figure of Count Herman, having so often contemplated the very singular person of that mysterious being.

Parrolla remembered the portrait as long as he could remember anything; he recollected how himself, his brother, and cousins had often lifted up the black curtain that hung before the portrait of the count, then ran away frightened, crying "The gentleman in black is coming!"

Parrolla had always thought that the portrait of Count Herman looked as if it had a great deal of the infernal in it; and now that he saw the original, he thought the same of that.

And what surprised Parrolla was, that the original looked much younger than the portrait, which Parrolla had heard was brought to the castle when his father was but a baby. " Yet there is no change in his countenance," thought Parrolla, " all these years have made no change—he cannot be mortal. When I return home, I will inquire the history of that portrait."

————

CHAPTER LXXIX.

Ha ! it dawns—
It rises to me like a new-found world,
To mariners long distressed at sea—
Sore from a storm, and all their viands spent.—YOUNG.

WHEN Roderiquis returned home, he told his mother, the Signora de Gusman, of the conversation he had had at the Opera, concerning Julian de Gusman being the son of the Marchese de Gusman, and how much that circumstance was doubted by a gentleman, who happened to be in the same box with him (Roderiquis), and who knew Julian, and those who brought him up when in Spain; " and that person says," continued Roderiquis, " that this new-found heir is more likely to be the child of some vagabond Jew, or vagrant gipsy, than the child of the Marchese de Gusman."

" I should like to see that person," said the marchesa.

" He has promised to call," replied Roderiquis.

" I cannot tell what to make of it," said the signora; " it is altogether a most strange affair."

" So strange, that I shall be cheated out of my title and possessions if I don't do something to prevent it," said Roderiquis; " mother, I cannot rest, something must be done."

" Something must be done," said the marchesa, " but you must not run any risk."

At this moment, the Count Herman was announced; and at the same moment Parrolla Immorf, who had become intimate with Roderiquis. But the moment Parrolla saw Count Herman, he made his adieus, and departed.

And a long conversation was now entered into, between the Signora De Gusman and Count Herman, when the latter informed the signora and her son, that the Marchese De Gusman in his youth had certainly been a very great sinner, he having committed a murder, and that on the body of Julian's mother; " this the youth, Julian, told me himself, when he was in Spain," said Count Herman.

" And I have not the least doubt but it is true," continued the count. " For I heard the marchese himself acknowledge the fact."

" Then, you are acquainted with him," said the signora.

" Not at all," replied the count. " But as the marchese came from the monastery of the Contrite Heart, he betook himself to prayer. He begged to be forgiven for the foul crime of murder; and begged no more to be tormented by the shade of the murdered Rachel!"

" Then this Rachel, you think, was the boy's mother," said the signora.

" Certainly," replied Count Herman.

" Rachel!" cried Roderiquis. " Why, you said, signor, that the new-found heir looked like the offspring of a Jew or gipsy; and, from the circumstance of his mother's name being Rachel, I think he must have sprung from the former tribe."

" I wished the youth, Julian, to acquaint the Inquisition with the crime of the marchese," said Count Herman; " but we would not do that."

" That, indeed, would be madness," replied the signora; " for should the murder be proved upon him, his estates might be forfeited to the State."

The signora now rang her bell, and ordered the servant who answered the summons, to tell the housekeeper to bring up refreshments. The refreshments were brought up by a short limping woman. And Count Herman was wondering in his mind how the signora could have such an object about her. But the income of the signora may be straightened," thought the count · ' she may work for low wages, not being every one's money; and her abilities may be good, though her person is against her. Surely, I never saw a more ungainly servant."

These thoughts were passing in the mind of Count Herman when the female, who was in the act of placing the tray she had in her hands on the table, happened to turn eyes on Count Herman, when, in the squinting glance, he saw the dreaded Dollabella, who at the same moment recognised Count Herman.

She let fall the tray and all thereon, breaking the glass and china, and strewing the carpet with the viands.

"Ho! signora!" cried Dollabella; "harbour not that monster—he is a vampire, one who feasts upon the dead!—He stole my poor father's head from the tomb, where we saw him quietly interred."

"Wretch!" she cried. "Where's my father's head?—Give me my father's head!" Then she burst into a violent hysterical fit of laughing and crying, alternately.

"Your servant has certainly become insane," cried the count. "I would advise you, signora, to have her confined in a straight waistcoat—she may be mischievous —to see any one in this state is quite distressing. The poor wretch is certainly in a most rabid state."

Somewhat recovered from the hysterical affection occasioned by passion, Dollabella started up.

"Where is my poor father's head?" she again cried. "For what purpose did you steal it from the tomb? Was it to feast your unnatural appetite, or to forward some accurst scheme of magic? Did you not promise to marry me? and then ran away, villain? I'll tear your eyes out!" and Dollabella was about to lay violent hands on Count Herman, but she was prevented, and held by Roderiquis. Again she relapsed into an hysterical fit, and lay struggling on the carpet.

"This is not to be borne," cried the signora; "come, signora," she said, speaking to Count Herman, "let us go into another apartment."

"No," replied the count, "I'll not trust myself longer in the house with that mad woman;" saying this, he left the house of the signora, and Naples also, fearing again to encounter the fury of Dollabella, whose physical strength he had but little fear of; it was exposure that he dreaded—a fear of its being known that he was what he really was, as he, in that case, would be shunned and avoided by everybody, and then no victim could be obtained.

Full of these thoughts, he left Naples, and again visited England.

CHAPTER LXXX.

Ye subtle demons which reside
In courts, and do your work with bows and smiles;
That little engenry more mischievous
Than fleets, and armies, and the cannons murder;
Teach me to look a lie—give me your maze
Of gloomy thoughts and intricate designs,
To catch the man I hate, and then devour.—YOUNG.

THE Signora de Gusman weighed in her mind the information given her by Count Herman respecting the Marchese de Gusman.

"From the habits of the marchese, I could not have thought he was a man likely to commit a murder," thought the signora; "yet I have marked his abstraction and his melancholy ; his sudden starts and the apprehensive look, as if fearing something yet untold would come out. But it would degrade the family of De Gusman if this were known ;—no, it must not be known ; I will conceal my thoughts, and dissemble with the marchese and the vagrant boy. But shall he inherit the estates of De Gusman, to the hindrance of Roderiquis ? Oh, no ; that must not be ; he must be confined where none can hear his wail, or else a poniard must drink his blood."

Unconscious of what was passing in the minds of his enemies, Julian was happy in his new-found honours.

But as there is seldom any happiness without an alloy, so it was with Julian ; who feared that through the means of Count Herman, his mother's death would be talked of, and that his father might be called on to answer for that deed.

But Julian determined, if such an accusasion should take place, in consequence of what he had told Count Herman, that he would deny it altogether. And severely did he repent telling Count Herman of the fatal affair.

With every succeeding day the mortification of Roderiquis increased. He was no longer looked upon as the heir of De Gusman. The preference of the Lady Olivia de Almeria was no longer shown to Roderiquis ; and the beauty of Julian de Gusman was generally spoken of, as was his affability and gentlemanly deportment.

Although much company came to the house of the Marchese De Gusman, it was on account of Julian ; for the marchese, as usual, took but little pleasure in worldly matters—his time was mostly spent with his confessor.

At a party given by the Marchesa de Almeira, the mother of the Lady Olivia, both Julian and Roderiquis were invited. The smiles that Olivia directed to Julian were as daggers to the heart of the jealous Roderiquis ; but he put on as good a face as he could on the matter, and behaved with a greater appearance of friendship to Julian than ever, although his heart was full of bitterness towards him.

Whilst Julian was paying some very high-flown compliments to the Lady Olivia, the heart of Roderiquis was bursting with rage, and he, by an involuntary movement of his hand, drew his sword almost from its scabbard.

This action was not noticed either by Julian or Olivia ; if it had, they certainly would have thought it very odd.

When Olivia spoke to Roderiquis, rage caused his face to glow, and complaining of heat, he withdrew to walk in the garden, for he could no longer hide his angry feelings.

He strolled down a walk where the laburnum fell with its golden flowers, streaming down the path before him, and the white syringe, and flowering lilacs shed their sweetness on the breeze. The moon was at her height, in a clear and cloudless sky, and there seemed a freshness and sacred solemnity, as if the work of creation was but just completed ; and the glorious firmament, and every plant and flower looked bright as in its pristine freshness and beauty; but no local circumstances could interest the mind of Roderiquis.

Disappointed and revengeful, and full of malignant thoughts towards Julian deGusman, he paced the walks, vowing a deadly vengeance on the heir of De Gusman.

" This earth will not contain us both," he mentally said ; "no, one of us must fall ere yon moon shall again illumine the earth with renewed lustre."

" Insolent usurper !" he cried, stamping on the earth, " you have robbed me of my title, my lands, my wealth, and my love also. I have suffered by thee, and thy blood shall pay for it."

He seated himself in a retired arbour, and there he wept in the agony of grief ; but fearing his absence would be thought strange, he composed himself as well as he could, and entered the balcony where Julian, the Lady de Almeria were sitting, to view the beauty of the evening.

" 'Tis evident she loves him," mentally said Roderiquis ; " he is triumphant, and I am miserable."

He found he could not for long conceal the conflicting passions with which his mind was torn; namely, the passions of grief, anger, and revenge. Roderiquis, therefore, without showing any displeasure, took his leave, before any of the party thought of breaking up, pretending that he was indisposed.

When he reached home, he immediately retired to his chamber, and he threw himself on his bed without undressing, and bewailed his miserable fate.

"Crossed and disappointed in all I set my heart on," mentally said Roderiquis; "I thought myself happy, but the despoiler has banished hope, and has left me nought but despair."

CHAPTER LXXXI.

Go dance around their bower, and close them in,
And tell them that I sent thee to salute them;
Profane the ground; and for the ambrosial rose
And breath of jassamine, let hemlock blacken
And deadly nightshade poison all the air.
For the sweet nightingale, may ravens croak,
Toads pant, and adders rustle through the leaves;
May serpents winding up the trees, let fall
Their hissing necks upon them from above,
And mingle kisses—such as I would give them.—YOUNG.

THAT Olivia intended to be the Marchese de Gusman, Roderiquis did not doubt, and agony was in the thought.

"Either he or I must die," inwardly said Roderiquis; "is it not enough that he has intervened between me and fortune?—no, even that will not content him."

"He shall not only have Olivia for his bride, but a winding sheet also; he shall lie in state in the cold tomb, and wreathing worms shall be his wedding guests."

Wrath and bitterness now filled the mind of Roderiquis; and he determined to be the murderer of Julian, and such determination he made known to his mother.

"Lay aside such a thought, Roderiquis," said the signora; "should you fail, and be discovered;—think not of doing the deed yourself, there are men who live by their traffic in blood—for gold they will do your bidding."

"I know none such," replied Roderiquis; "this arm must rid me of my enemy; I'll watch him, and when a fit opportunity occurs, my poniard shall reach his heart."

"Give up the thought," replied the signora, "there's great danger in it; inquire diligently, and you will find enough to serve you."

"I cannot depend on a villain," said Roderiquis; "he might take my money and not do the deed; but tell Julian of my intention."

"No," said the signora, "those bravos, who get a living by ridding a man of an enemy, have honour in their trade of blood; if they had not, the great would not employ them. I will tell you, Roderiquis," continued the signora, "your father had an enemy, he caused him to be slain, and by one of these persons I have mentioned."

"But where does he live?" inquired Roderiquis.

"That I do not exactly remember," said the signora, "but I took such notice of the man, that I know him personally; for often hath your father pointed him out to me, for not one circumstance did he withhold from my knowledge."

"It may be some time before this man is to be met with," replied Roderiquis; "and my revenge is impatient—I thirst for the minion's blood."

"Be not so rash," said the signora, "all in good time."

"There is no time to lose," said Roderiquis. "I tell you, mother, Olivia loves this new-found heir ; I saw it in her looks and every action. I fear their marriage will take place before my vengeance is accomplished. What is the bravo's name ?" inquired Roderiquis.

"His name is Paulo Zimperetti," said the signor ; " he lives in an obscure street at the eastern end of the city ; but we will go to the public walks, and there we shall see him—you must have your card ready, and slip it into his hand as you pass him : he will understand you, and you will see him here."

Roderiquis approved of his mother's council, and they towards evening walked to a spot where, when the sun was down, much company assembled ; here was generally to be seen the fell Paulo Zimperetti, but on this evening he was not there. With the utmost scrutiny the Signora de Gusman observed every passer-by, but Zimperetti's countenence the signora could nowbere discover.

Disappointed, the signora and Roderiquis returned home ; but they determined on the next evening to again visit the same spot.

On the following morning, Parrolla Inimorf, with whom Roderiquis had made an acquaintance, called to see his friend, and they, to pass an hour, strolled along the bay.

The sudden starts, and agitated manner of Roderiquis was noticed by Parrolla, and he inquired what had happened to disturb him.

"To you, I don't mind unburdening my heart," said Roderiquis ; " I hate that upstart, Julian de Gusman—a name, between you and I, to which he has no title. How hard to have this spurious heir come forward and claim a title and estates, mine by lawful succession."

"You must poniard him." said Parrolla.

"I fear the crime would be known—and then the punishment," replied Roderiquis.

"For the crime," said Parrolla, " I think it no crime at all. If a wasp comes to sting us, do we not kill it ?—if we meet a serpent in our path, do we not slay it ?—it is but an act of self-defence. If a man comes to rob you of your property, and supersedes you in your right, you have as much right to slay that man, as you have to take the life of a wasp, or an adder. Neither father nor brother should stand between me and my interest ; I would push them into the sea, or give them the point of a poniard."

"Inimorf, you are a friend," said Roderiquis ; " you speak the sentiments of my own heart—will you assist me ?—If so, you may command me in any way you please. I will serve you, even if it is at the hazard of my life."

"The thing you can best serve me in, is money," replied Parrolla ; " my father is a niggard, and he keeps me very short of money. But to come to the point at once," he continued, " for money I'll do anything to serve you."

"You speak like a friend," said Roderiquis, " and when the being I detest is no more, you shall use my purse as if it was your own. We must watch and waylay him," said Roderiquis ; "his bleeding corse shall lay on the green sward ; he often walks on the bay, and there it will be best to do the deed."

"I agree with you, my friend," said Parrolla ; " but I must leave you, for I have an appointment—to-morrow we will meet again."

CHAPTER LXXXII.

"Thou Zanga, thou my solemn friends invite,
From the dark realms of everlasting night :
Call vengeance, call furies, call despair,
And death, our chief-invited guest be there.—YOUNG.

RODERIQUIS told his mother, the Signora de Gusman, of the conversation he had with his English friend, Mr. Immorf, who, with the sympathy of a friend, felt the njuries that he (Roderiquis) laboured under, through the means of the person who called himself Julian De Gusman.

"My friend," continued Roderiquis, " speaks the very sentiments of my heart. He advises me to lay this Julian on the spot from which he never more shall rise."

"What!" said the signora, "and have you confided the secret of your soul to a friend, and that the friend of a day, and a foreigner likewise ?—foolish young man!"

"But he will help me to do the deed," cried Roderiquis, " for money he himself will strike the fatal blow."

"What, then, is he an assassin, one who lives by shedding the blood of others ?' said the Signora de Gusman—" and are you then sunk so low, to take as your bosom-friend, your boon companion, an hired assassin? Is such conduct befitting a branch of the house of De Gusman? These men of blood are useful when they

No. 27.

are wanted, but shunned and despised when not needed. I beg that you'll have no further intimacy with such a character."

" Mr. Parrolla Immorf is a gentleman, and no hired assassin," replied Roderiquis. " If he assists me to dispatch the upstart Julian, it would be done to avenge my injuries."

" But you said he would do the deed for money," said the signora.

" I did say he was in want of money," said Roderiquis, "for the father of Mr. Immorf, though extremely rich, does not allow his son money sufficient to defray the travelling expenses of a gentleman; of course if he obliges me in helping me to dispatch my enemy, it is but my duty to assist him in pecuniary affairs."

" Roderiquis, I think you act extremely imprudent!" said the signora, " and I insist that you will have nothing to do with that young man in this affair. Paulo Zimpretti must be the man.'"

" But I have engaged with Mr. Immorf," said Roderiquis.

" What folly!" said the signora. " I tremble for the consequence of your imprudence to trust a stranger with a secret of such deep importance. If this Julian is to die, Paulo Zimpretti must be the hand to slay him."

" You must tell Mr. Immorf, that what you said was uttered in a moment of passion, because Julian had offended you; and that you had no such real intentions ; tell him that you love Julian as if he were your own brother, and that if any one was to injure him you would be the first to take his part."

After the heat of the day had subsided, the Signora de Gusman and her son again walked in the much frequented walk; but although there were a great number of persons there, the signora could not distinguish the features of the bravo Zimpretti.

The signora was disappointed, but she still continued walking in the frequented lounge.

The day was fast departing, and the shades of twilight were gathering fast around when the stern and under look of the bravo, Paulo Zimpretti, met her view.

A speaking look passed between the signora and Zimpretti, who went on, but soon returned, and passed close to the signora.

As he did so, the signora with caution, and favoured by the dim twilight, slipped her card into the hand of Zimpretti as he passed her.

CHAPTER LXXXIII.

Away, you study these things too deeply.—SHAKSPERE.

ON the following evening, as the shades of twilight were veiling the earth with her darkening shadows, the bravo Paulo Zimpretti, went to the residence of the Signora de Gusman, and was there long closeted with the signora in close conference.

The sum was named for the business required to be done, and the terms were agreed to by the signora. All was settled, and Roderiquis was to be hard by when the assassination took place. A thousand doubts and fears pervaded the mind of the signora ; she was of a very cautious and wary temper, and feared, lest Zimpretti should betray her to Julian, and get a yet larger sum than she had given him, from Julian, for his information ; but she consoled herself with the thought " that Zimpretti was known to be a man honourable in his profession, and the last man in the trade of blood who would inform against his employer. But then, should any wandering step intrude, see the blow given, or hear the death-cry. If Zimpretti should be taken in the act, and confess who was his instigator, I shall have no peace until the deed is done," thought the signora.

' And then Roderiquis to make a confidant of that English boy, he must see him, and laugh the matter off as a mere jest; to be sure, this Immorf's young, and may not think deeply—nor should I conclude he does, from the thoughtless and dissipated life I hear he leads. But when a man is told of a murder in contemplation—it is no every-day affair; and the impression he has received at the hearing thereof may not be easily obliterated from his mind. Besides, he offered himself to do the deed for money—he will be disappointed; and, when he hears of Julian's death, the truth will flash upon him. I am maddened!" cried the signora, holding her head with her hands; "I am maddened!"

That very night Roderiquis sought Parrolla Immorf, for he knew his resort, amougst courtezans and men wild and profligate as himself.

After some conversation, Parrolla and Roderiquis were talking of titles and grandeur, when Roderiquis said,—

"I like titles and grandeur as well as any man, if fairly obtained; but I would not burden my conscience, or soil my honour, to be an emperor."

"This is a very different doctrine to that which you held forth yesterday," said Parrolla.

"Yesterday! Oh, yesterday is an eternity," said Roderiquis, laughing; "I am sure I don't know what I said yesterday—some of my rodomontade, I suppose?"

"You were talking of poniarding Julian," said Parrolla.

"Is it possible that you could believe me serious?" said Roderiquis.

"Serious! why not?" said Parrolla; "I would poniard any one that stood between me and my interest. I have not poniarded, but I have done the same thing," said Parrolla, "and would do it again."

"Come, come, let us change this subject," cried Roderiquis, "for by the mass 'tis an unpleasant one. Was you at the opera last night?"

"No," replied Parrolla, "I was otherwise engaged."

After some further discourse, Roderiquis and Parrolla separated, Roderiquis thinking that he had completely blinded Parrolla as to his intention respecting Julian.

But Parrolla saw through the art of Roderiquis. "He wishes to deceive me," said Parrolla, mentally, "but he shall not do that; I'll keep a watch upon him—perhaps he fears to trust me, or has hired a hand more ready and expert—a bravo, used to the trade of blood. But I will not be deceived; be he where he will, he shall find me at his elbow."

Roderiquis told his mother, the Signora de Gusman what had passed between himself and Parolla.

"The Englishman is suspicious," said the signora. "I cannot express the vexation I feel, when I think of your folly, in exposing to a stranger the secrets of your heart. We must now wait some little time, until the circumstance is forgotten by this Mr. Immorf, or at least is not so fresh in his recollection."

"I will not wait long," said Roderiquis, "before many hours, there shall be an end of him or me; besides, you have agreed with Paulo Zimpretti, don't think that he'll be played with."

"Played with!" said the signora, "then do you suppose that I don't intend the murder of Julian to take place?—All I mean is, but to be cautious. You, Roderiquis, are too rash and open-minded; it will be best to see Paulo Zimpretti, and inform him of the reason why the business is delayed."

"I tell you, mother, once for all," said Roderiquis, "that if Zimpretti does not murder Julian between this and eight-and-forty hours, I'll murder him myself!"

"He may not have an opportunity," said the signora, alarmed at the violence of her son.

"Well, do not you interfere," said Roderiquis; "leave the matter to me and Zimpretti. I know Julian usually wanders on the bay by moonlight—the moon rises late, it will be the very time for our enterprise."

"I tremble," said the signora; "be cautious; I pray you, Roderiquis, be cautious."

"No one can be more so," replied Roderiquis.

"There I differ from you," said the signora.   "Was that a mark of caution, to name your intention respecting Julian to that Englishman ?"

"Telling me of that again," said Roderiquis; "I own it was foolish, but no matter, Immorf will think no more about it—you are too fearful, and study these things too deeply ;—he will lie in his gory bed, and none suspect the hand that has done the deed."

———

CHAPTER LXXXIV.

In bleeding state I saw him on the earth,
From whence with life he never more sprang up.—SHAKSPERE.

THE assassin Zimpretti was now generally at the heels of Julian, but no opportunity had yet occurred.

Roderiquis was impatient; for ten days had passed since Zimpretti had received his wages of blood.

He sought the assassin, and reproached him with his tardiness.

"Since I have received my hire, I have often seen him you wish laid low," said the bravo in a gruff voice ; and as he said this, the evil glance of his scowling eyes, in which might be read a propensity to commit crimes of the darkest hue, almost terrified Roderiquis, who however summoned up courage to inquire,—

"Where shall you be this evening ?"

"On the bay," was the reply of Zimpretti ; "I then hope to finish the business," he continued, "there is risk and trouble enough ; and by Saint Peter, 'tis little enough we get for our labour."

"You was paid what you required, I believe," said Roderiquis.

"I was," replied Zimpretti ; "but I am too moderate in my demands ; I expect another sum of the same amount."

"That shall be paid you, and without the least hesitation," said Roderiquis, "only perform, and the money is yours."

"What money have you about you ?" inquired the ruffian.

"I have but five pieces of gold," replied Roderiquis.

"Then give them to me in part of my further recompence," said the bravo.

And the gold was given by Roderiquis.

"I shall be near the palace of De Gusman at nine o'clock," said Zimpretti.

"Then I will be near the spot where I see you lurking," said Roderiquis.

And he left the dwelling of the bravo.

Although Julian was happy in the accomplishment of his wishes respecting finding his father, and placed in that splendour he thirsted after.

Yet at times he was troubled with lowness of spirits ; for the events of the childhood of Julian had greatly affected his nervous system; and as the twilight of evening advanced, his spirits drooped with the day.

Early habits are but rarely forgotten or overcome ; and so it was with Julian.

From a child he had always loved the orb of night; and when grown to be a young man, and had learned to play the flute, he would sit beneath the shade of some spreading tree, by the moon's silvery light, playing on the instrument he loved tunes so soft, and full of melancholy pathos, that no person unmoved could have listened to him.

This conduct of Julian's had annoyed the good old people who brought him up, for they wished their foster-son to retire to rest when they did.

Even now would Julian have been gratified in playing his flute beneath the bright rays of a beaming moon.

But as the son of the Marchese de Gusman, Julian knew that it would not be proper for him to leave his father's hall, and play on the instrument he loved, beneath the moon's silvery ray, like some wandering minstrel; such conduct would have subjected him to too much notice; and would have been improper for the heir of De Gusman.

But as a consolation to himself, and concordant with his late habits, he would now frequently, even to a late hour of the night, stroll along the bay.

That Julian was happy in having found his father was certain; but his mind was not altogether easy on account of his illegitimacy, for he feared that the tenure he held in his new-found possessions, was but on an insecure and uncertain foundation.

And should his father, the Marchese de Gusman, die, Julian feared that he should be involved in some unpleasant litigation with his cousin Roderiquis.

For though Roderiquis appeared to be on friendly terms with Julian, and expressed pleasure in Julian having found his father, yet there was something in the manner of Roderiquis, that showed when he made those professions, that his heart and tongue did not go together.

It was a lovely night, and the beauteous moon was shining in the clear Italian sky, when Julian left the palace of de Guzman, and was walking slowly along the bay, meditating on the subject of his birth, and some other circumstances, not to him of a pleasant nature.

In a deep reverie, he was passing the very angle where he had noticed the dark outline of Count Herman's figure partially hidden behind the trees.

As Julian passed them, he heard a rustling amongst the leaves, but thinking that it was only some night-bird alarmed by his approach, he proceeded on without taking further notice.

But in a moment he heard a footstep behind him, and before he could turn his head to look who it might be, he felt that he was wounded in the side, and he sunk down covered with blood.

The blow was not repeated; and the poniard with which the blow was given, was left still sticking in the flesh, for the bravo or bravos had run away, they hearing coming footsteps.

The person who had so opportunely approached, was Parrolla Immorf. He had kept his eye on the movements of Roderiquis, and had privily followed him and Paulo Zimpretti to the bay.

"Stop!" cried Parrolla, "and take your poniard with you. Stop, Roderiquis de Gusman! 'Tis but I, your friend and confidant, Parrolla Immorf."

Parrolla then went up to Julian de Gusman, who he found was not yet dead.

Leaving the body of Julian on the ground, Parrolla hastened to the palace of De Gusman, which was not more than a quarter of a mile distant, and informed the household of the marchese of that which had happened.

Julian was conveyed to the house of his father, and every attention paid him that surgical skill could devise.

But though the wound was not considered to be mortal, Julian was so weak from the loss of blood, that his recovery was a matter of the greatest doubt.

The Marchese de Gusman was at the house of a friend on a visit, when the assassination took place; but an express was immediately sent off to inform the marchese of what had happened.

CHAPTER LXXXV.

I see the approaching torches of the guard,
Flash their red light athwart the forest's shade.—MATURIN.

SOON as Julian was taken into the palace of De Gusman, a number of the servants set off in all directions in search of the assassins, and not a place escaped their search for at least half a mile round the palace of the marchese : they searched amongst the shrubs and brushwood, and in the woody dell near the monaste y of the Contrite Heart, but no person was to be seen.

As the servants were returning to the palace of De Gusman, they picked up a very handsome silver-handled dagger.

"This," said one of the servants, "the assassin must have dropped; 'tis fortunate we have found it; it may lead to a discovery of the assassin."

Breathless and pale, Roderiquis reached his home.

"Julian is wounded, but I fear not slain," he said to the signora. "All seems to go unlucky, I have dropped my dagger, which if found will create suspicion. Immorf sprang out upon me—he, I fear, will make all known."

"Fool! idiot!" cried the signora, "to trust a boy; but say, Roderiquis, are you sure Julian is not dead, and for what purpose did the Englishman spring out upon you?"

"Julian may be dead," said Roderiquis, "but I, fear he is not, for it was but one wound he received from the hand of Zimpretti; before Zimpretti had time to strike again, Immorf, who must have watched us, sprang from his concealment behind the trees."

"All will come out now," said the signora, "a dungeon's depth will be your doom."

At this moment a loud knock was heard at the door, and another quick knock immediately succeeded it.

"Fly, fly, Roderiquis," said the signora, "they are come in pursuit of you."

Roderiquis snatched up a poniard that was in the room.

"Easily I will not be taken," he said, as he left the apartment. "This shall reach the heart's blood of some of them if they offer to take me."

The door was opened, and the bravo Zimpretti without ceremony walked into the room where the signora was sitting.

Fierce and savage was his look, as he said, "When friends come, your servants should not keep them waiting; 'tis well that I was not seen and recognised."

The signora did not reply; for in consequence of the quick and successive knocking of Zimpretti, and the unpleasant intelligence of Roderiquis, her nervous system underwent a terrible shock.

"This a fine business," said Zimpretti; "we were watched, but let the spy look to himself. I must keep out of the way, and you must let me have money to enable me to do so."

"Money!" cried the signora, "I gave you a large sum, and you do not know that the deed is performed. How is it possible that you can ask for more?"

"How is it possible I can ask for more?" said Zimpretti, and his countenance expressed the malignity of a demon, "but I do ask for more, and more I'll have. You shall give me as much now, as you gave me before."

"Insolent! I have fulfilled my agreement," said the signora.

"And so have I," said Zimpretti. "My reward was given to stab Julian de Gusman, and I have done so; if the wound proves not to be mortal, that's no fault of mine—I stabbed him. The fee I now ask, is for hush-money, and I'll have it, or swear that your son did the deed. Refuse me, and the authorities shall know it. When Roderiquis ran, I saw a dagger fall from his hand, nor did he stay to pick it up; that dagger will be found, and conspire with my evidence to criminate your son."

"Oh, God! what a strait have I brought myself into," cried the signora; "thus it is when we have to do with the unprincipled."

"Unprincipled!" exclaimed the bravo, "don't be insulting. You are a very principled lady, are you not, to hire an assassin to murder your own nephew;—what are you better than I am? I only tell you, unless you instantly come down with the gold, I'll acquaint the authorities—be quick in your decision, for I stay here in danger."

The signora for a moment hesitated.

"Be quick in your decision," cried Zimpretti with impatience.

With a trembling hand the signora unlocked a cabinet that stood in the room, and she took from there a number of pieces of gold, and with a trembling hand she counted them.

"I have not the money you require in the house," she said.

"I will accept no less," said Zimpretti.

The signora burst into tears.

"Unfeeling man!" she said, "have you no compunction!"

"Compunction!" cried Zimpretti, "who but a fool could expect to find compunction in one who trades in blood. I'll have the money, or this moment I'll——"

"Stay!" said the signora; and with a tearful eye and trembling hand, she caught hold of the arm of the bravo Zimpretti. "Oh, stay!" she cried, "will nothing but gold content ye?—here is a diamond cross, worth ten times the money you require; take it as a pledge, and to-morrow, if you come, I will redeem it."

The bravo held out his hand for the cross, and his eyes brightened with pleasure as he looked on it.

"You will return it, on being paid the sum deficient," said the signora.

"I may," replied Zimpretti.

"I believe it will be but little matter to me, whether you do or not," said the signora. "I fear I now shall have but little occasion for ornaments, for my sun is fast setting in clouds and darkness."

Then clasping her hands in mental agony, she cried "a heavy foreboding sits on my heart, I feel ruin and death hover over me."

Without noticing the agony of feeling that overpowered the signora, or speaking to her one word of comfort, the bravo put up the diamond cross, and a sneer sat on this malicious countenance, as he said—

"As you have given me what I demanded, I am dumb on this business; but l'd have you beware of a young Englishman, named Immorf. He witnessed the whole transaction, and he shouted, as we ran away, after the stabbing of Julian de Gusman, "'Stop! 'stop' cried the Englishman, 'Roderiquis de Gusman, and take your poniard with you.—'Tis but I, your friend and confident Parrolla Immorf.'

"I tell you this. signora, to clear myself from any imputation that may be cast on me." Saying this, Zimpretti left the house.

"Oh Heaven have mercy on me!" cried the signora, falling on her knees in an attitude of despair.—"Have mercy! Oh have mercy on me, miserable sinner that I am!

"If I once get over this trouble, never more will I barter my integrity for ambition. Oh my poor Roderiquis! on a scaffold, amidst scorn and mockery, I fear thy young days will be ended!"

The signora sat down quite exhausted with her grief, and gave way to a flood of bitter tears.

Roderiquis had concealed himself, so that he could see who the person was that came in, and he saw that it was Zimpretti; but Roderiquis did not again go into the apartment in which his mother was, until he saw the bravo depart, when Roderiquis went into the room where his mother was sitting.

Seeing her in such deep affliction, Roderiquis inquired if any fresh disagreeable had occurred, that occasioned her to be in such distress of mind.

The signora related to her son the conversation that had passed between herself and the bravo Zimpretti, and she spoke in strong terms of the uneasiness under which she laboured on account of Roderiquis having trusted Parrolla Immorf.

"All is now over," continued the signora. "That you will be accused of poniarding Julian de Guzman, I am certain—all I could do to prevent such accusation, I have done. The ruffian Zimpretti demanded as large a sum as I at first gave him to keep the matter secret; and not having so much in the house, I let him take as a pledge, until I did pay him, the diamond cross given me by your father."

"And think you I shall be suspected by my uncle?" said Roderiquis. "Julian I am sure did not see me—and he may be dead. Immorf, who offered to assist me in the murder, he I think, would not be base enough to betray me, even if he had seen me do the deed."

Before these words had died on the lips of Roderiquis, the signora Mazzinghi, the sister of the Signora de Gusman, entered the room.

"For Heaven's sake, Zelinda, what is the matter?" said the Signora Mazzinghi, "I am terrified to death—strange news is abroad ; it was now told that Roderiquis had stabbed the new-found son of the Marchese de Gusman, and that the whole affair was witnessed by a young Englishman, who has called at the palace of De Gusman, and he has acquainted the marchese, who is inconsolable, with all particulars. And more than that, it is said that the dagger of Roderiquis was picked up near the spot where the assassination took place. So the report goes," said the Signora Mazzinghi ; "but I hope and trust, Zelinda, that there is no truth in the report."

With clasped hands, and her teeth chattering in her head, as if suffering from the effect of ague, the Signora de Gusman's head sunk on the shoulder of her sister. She had fainted, and was then lost to a sense of her anguish, whilst Roderiquis seemed to be labouring under the greatest mental agony ; for he tore his hair and stamped on the floor, and looked as wild as if in a state of the greatest frenzy ; but before the Signora de Gusman's senses were recalled to a consciousness of the trouble by which she was surrounded, Roderiquis had left the apartment.

A copious flood of tears, in some measure, relieved the signora, and she was able to answer the anxious questions of her sister, who from what she could see and hear, concluded that there was but too much truth in the report she had heard.

"Oh! that I had died but one month back !" cried the Signora de Gusman, "then would my soul have been less clogged with sin, and my heart less broken by suffering. Oriel, my dear sister, no more in this world is there peace for me."

"What am I to think—oh what am I to conjecture?" said the Signora Mazzinghi.

"Ask me not !—name not the dreadful circumstance," cried the Signora de Gusman ; "but where is Roderiquis—where is my son?"

"I don't know where he is gone ; but he left the room in a state of great agitation and excitement," said the Signora Mazzinghi.

"Do, pray do inquire of the servants if he is gone, my dear sister," said the Signora de Gusman ; "I cannot inquire, for the agitation under which I labour would be noticed, and that I should not wish."

The Signora Mazzinghi rang the bell, and inquired of the servant who answered it, if the Signor Roderiquis had gone from home ?

"He has not, signora," said the man ; "the signor, some short time back, went into the garden ; I saw him pass through the glass doors that lead to the green-house."

"Let us seek him," said the Signora de Gusman to her sister, and they went into the garden.

It was now past the hour of midnight, and the moon was yet riding in the firmament, so that every object was plainly to be distinguished. The Signora de Gusman and her sister searched every walk and avenue in the garden, but Roderiquis was not there.

The Signora de Gusman called on her son, but no answer was returned.

At length they went into a kind of temple, that stood on a mount in an elevated part of the garden, where the signora and her son had often sat for hours to enjoy the cool shade of this temple, it being surrounded by trees, and screened from the mid-day sun.

There a shocking sight presented itself,—Roderiquis lay a bleeding corse, deluged in blood ! The screams of the signora and her sister soon brought the servants to the spot, and the lifeless corse of Roderiquis was borne into the house and laid on a bed ; medical aid was procured, but it was all in vain, the vital spark had fled from the body of the unfortunate Roderiquis, who had stabbed himself in the temple, immediately after leaving the apartment of his fainting mother.

"My son, my son !" cried the grief and horror-stricken mother. "Why did I encourage thee in thy ambition? Rather ought I to have taught thee humility and submission to the will of fate."

Julian was not dead; but Parrolla Immorf, without the advice or concurrence of the Marchese de Gusman, went the next morning and acquainted the chief

magistrate with what had happened. Then an officer was sent to the house of the Signora de Gusman to speak to her son, and inquire into the affair; but when the officer requested to see the Signor Roderiquis, the answer returned was,—

" He is dead!"

No. 28.

CHAPTER LXXXVI.

In Hasson's hall,
The lonely spider's thin grey pall,
Waves slowly widening o'er the wall,
And in the fortress of his power,
The owl usurps the second tower.—LORD BYRON.

GRIEF threw the Signora de Gusman on a bed of sickness, from which she was doomed to rise no more.

Nor after she had beheld her son's bleeding corse, did she evermore see that form on which her eyes had looked on with such delight.

Roderiquis was interred in the tomb of his forefathers, leaving his mother to lament the death of her only son.

And when she reflected that he might have still been alive, had she checked rather than encouraged his ambition and pride, which pride had caused his down-fall,—the thought cut her to the heart.

But one month the Signora de Gusman lived after her son ; and the greater part of her property she bequeathed to the Marchese de Gusman, and the remainder to her sister the Signora Mazzinghi.

The Signora de Gusman left the Marchese de Gusman her property in order, if possible, to preserve the good name of herself and son. For although the signora feared to send to the palace of De Gusman to inquire after Julian, lest an answer might be sent back, unpleasant to her feelings.

She wished to seem ignorant of what had occurred.

Whilst the marchese, who heard of the untimely death of his nephew, felt sorry for the mother of the ill-fated youth.

For he did not in the least suppose that the signora was at all accessary to the assassination of his son.

Julian yet lived, and his wound was healed, but the blood he had lost so weak-ened his frame that he went into a rapid decline.

CHAPTER LXXXVII.

I know my fault, and feel my punishment
Not less, because I suffer it unbent.
That thou wert beautiful, and I not blind,
Hath been the sin that shuts me from mankind.—LAMENT OF TASSO.

THE decay of Julian was rapid ; and when he knew that no medicine nor human aid could afford him relief, he wished to see, before his departure from this life, his foster-father and mother ; for Julian had always felt great love for the good old people.

They, when they arrived at the palace of the marchese, were surprised and grieved at the alteration they saw in Julian, whom they loved with as much af-fection as if he had been their own son.

And when they heard how Julian had been assassinated, and left weltering in his blood through which such weakness was caused, that it precluded all hope of recovery, they bothwept in an agony of grief.

" It seemed the will of Heaven, that the heir of De Gusman should be a goat-herd," said his foster-mother, " but poor Julian was not satisfied with such a life ; he wished to be a don, and see the consequence. He was ruddy, and beau-tiful as a rose," said the weeping old woman, " but now the poor child looks wan as a tenant of the tomb. Much I feared, that in Naples some harm would befal him."

"We did all in our power to restrain him," said the old man, "but it was not to be. Julian was fated to die by the hand of the assassin, and no human power could have prevented, or altered his destiny."

"All, every circumstance hath conspired to bring about that which hath now happened, and all we can do is patiently to submit to the will of Heaven."

"We ought to do so," cried the weeping old woman, "but how can I submit to the stern decree, without feeling and deeply feeling too? Think you, Peres," continued the old woman, "that I can look on that dear youth, and see his wasted form and hollow eye unmoved; 'tis not in nature, is he not blest with youth, and raised from a goatherd's humble cot, to a princely domain, surrounded, with wealth and honours, then in a moment, as if to fulfil a sad destiny, he is death-stricken, and lost to us for ever!"

"Whilst there is life there is hope," said the tremulous voice of the old man, "Heaven can yet raise him."

"He will never more rise!" said the sorrowing old woman, "he goes like a flower that is cut down in the bud, whilst its parent stem is left shrunk and withered by the hand of adversity and grief."·

"But yet a brighter bloom shall he wear, when in the bower of paradise," said the old man, "he will shine a seraph in celestial beauty. We are loth to lose him, think then, what must be the feelings of his father, who is called on to resign his only hope; his all, even as Jacob was called on to resign Isaac his son."

The old man and woman watched by Julian until a late hour, when worn out by grief, and the fatigue of their journey, they were shown to their chamber, but ten days were the good old people at the palace of De Gusman, before Julian yielded his last breath to Him who gave it.

All now was grief at the palace of De Gusman, for Julian was beloved by all.

In a rich coffin of crimson velvet, adorned with golden ornaments, lay Julian; pomp and grandeur he had coveted, and now he lay in that state, that royalty could hardly have exceeded; for the walls of the chamber of death were hung with black velvet, and large and massive silver branches were fixed in different parts of the room, in each of which burned a wax taper.

The goatherd and his wife were suffered to attend their foster-son to the grave; and as the gorgeous procession moved slowly on, bearing the youthful corse to its everlasting home, busy were the tongues of the spectators, in talking of the mysterious birth of Julian, and the assassination of the unfortunate youth.

In consequence of the death of Julian, the Marchese De Gusman was now entirely disgusted with a world, which he had long since been indifferent to; and soon as he had arranged his affairs, he intended to enter the monastry of the Contrite Heart, and to become a monk of that order.

The Marchese De Gusman sent for the sister of the late Signora De Gusman, and he gave that lady an order to receive the legacy left him by her sister.

On the goatherd and his wife he settled a very handsome income, whom the marchese offered a very pleasant house on the bay as a gift, for it belonged to the marchese, but the goatherd and his wife declined the proffered gift.

They were grateful to the marchese for his liberal offer, but they preferred returning to their peaceful cottage.

"To stay in Naples would but remind us of the dear departed Julian," said the old man; "a peaceful and retired life best befits us; and if we were young, we are not well educated, nor fit to mix in company with the great, as your bounty, signor, would enable us to do. We have no ambition, our rustic neighbours are the best society for us; and what we can spare from our income shall be given to the needy."

The marchese approved of the plan of old Peres.

"Happy are they," said the marchese, "who are contented with an humble life. Through ambition, Lucifer, he was of the first order of angels, fell. Ambition it was that caused misery to fall upon me; and what but ambition has brought my sister-in-law and her son to the grave? The mother of Julian I thought did not rank sufficiently high in life for me to introduce her to my relations. I loved her, but when I found my elder brother could not survive, I felt reluctant to fulfil my engagement to the mother of Julian; so that pride, the first of all deadly sins, hath wrought this ruin on the house of De Gusman."

CHAPTER LXXXVIII.

For sin committed in life's early noon,
I pray ere matin hour in cloisters gloom.

BY THE AUTHORESS OF EVA.

THE Marchese de Gusman had a very grand and expensive monument erected in memory of his son.

The monument was of white marble, ornamented with the figures of angels, bearing the spirit of Julian from the tomb to the bright atmosphere, which in glorious brilliancy appeared to be shining above them.

Whilst angels with their harps seemed with holy joy to welcome the beatified spirit.

On the monument was inscribed

" TO THE MEMORY OF

JULIAN DE GUSMAN,

Who died September the 3rd, 1702,

IN CONSEQUENCE OF WOUNDS

HE RECEIVED FROM THE HAND OF AN ASSASSIN."

Soon after the interment of Julian, the Marchese De Gusman entirely gave up the world, and he entered the monastery of the Contrite Heart.

And of which holy community he became a member.

The goatherd and his wife returned to their peaceful cottage, thankful that providence had not placed them amongst the great, where crimes, even amounting to murder, were committed through ambition. They fully coincided with the wise and pious request of,—

" Give me neither poverty nor riches, lest if I am rich I be lifted up and forget God ; and if poor, I steal."

These wise, though unlearned persons, valued a contented mind, and a clear conscience, above all the wealth the world could give them.

Parrolla Immorf witnessed the interment of Julian, and he was sorry that he had not, before the assassination of Julian took place, acquainted him with the foul intentions of his cousin Roderiquis.

" As by that means," thought Parrolla, " I should have ingratiated myself into the favour of the marchese ; and knowing that I was a foreigner, and disappointed in my remittances, I might have borrowed a large sum of him until I received them, particularly as he would have been under an obligation to me, for saving the life of his son, through making known to him the intention of Roderiquis."

The means of Parrolla were now but low, for he had squandered his money with the greatest profusion : and after he had borrowed money of every one he could, and ran in debt with whom he could, he left Naples, and was on his way to England.

When Parrolla reached Ravenswood Castle, he found his mother in a very ill-state of health. Mr. Immorf was but in very low spirits ; and Lisbia became pale as a corse, when she saw Parolla open the door of the apartment in which she was sitting with her uncle and aunt.

The foolish young man, Orlando, ran jumping up to Parrolla, kissing his hand, and patting his cheek, and in a variety of antics, evinced the love he bore Parrolla.

Lisbia now feared to go out to meet Edwin, for she plainly saw that the eye of Parrolla was upon her every action.

In consequence of the ill-health of Mrs. Immorf, but little company came to the castle, excepting friends, who came to visit the invalid. Nor did many friends come to visit Mr. Immorf; for what had already transpired in his family, and what it was foretold was still to come, completely preyed on the nervous system of that gentleman.

He thought on the death of his mother, cut off, when hardly past the meridian of her days. He thought on his son—his darling son, whose death had been so sudden, and under circumstances of a very suspicious nature.

"But to whom does the suspicion attach?" said Mr. Immorf, mentally; "to his brother—my own son!—Oh, dreadful suspicion! But if Parrolla is guiltless, how would such an accusation break his heart,—that heart which none but the Most High knows the secrets of. I hope he is innocent of the foul deed; and never shall Parrolla know from me that such a suspicion has crossed my mind."

But the more Mr. Immorf tried to persuade himself of the innocence of Parrolla, concerning the death of his brother, the stronger it was impressed upon his mind.

And such thoughts caused great unhappiness to Mr. Immorf, as did the declining health of his wife, who he knew entertained the same suspicions concerning the fate of the loved Percival; but such conversation never passed between Mr. Immorf and his wife, the subject was too distress ng, and the bare idea of such being the case was a dagger to both their hearts.

The dulness that prevailed at Ravenswood Castle made Parrolla hate his home; and he now spent great part of his time in the town, in company with the same set of dissipated young men, whom he kept company with, before he went to Naples.

Returning home one night on foot, and without any attendant, a heavy shower came on, and Parrolla, whose nearest way was through the church-yard, stood up to take shelter from the rain beneath the yew-trees that formed a grove in front of the church.

Whilst standing there, he saw pass him, the same person he had seen at the opera when he was at Naples. This person was the original of the portrait that hung in his mother's bed-room. He was stalking through the church-yard with a slow and stately step, nor did he in the least seem to heed the storm.

"That man seems to be everywhere," thought Parrolla, "he seems to be a young man, yet he must be very old. When I get home, I will ask my father if he knows the history of that singular being, and if he is related to the family, and the reason of his portrait being hung in the bed-room of my mother, with a black curtain before it."

When Parrolla reached home, both Mr. and Mrs. Immorf were in bed, therefore he could not ask any questions about Count Herman; but the next morning when the family were seated at breakfast, Parrolla said,—

"Pray, father, who is that dark, demon-looking man, who hangs in your bed-room, screened from observation by means of the black curtain which hangs before him? I have often wondered who that person could be, when a child, and wherefore he was hidden behind the black curtain. I remember having heard yn or my mother say, that the portrait of that peculiar-looking being, hung there ever since my father was but a baby, and yet I saw him at the opera when I was at Naples; and again I saw him last night, whilst I stood beneath the yew-trees in the church-yard, to screen me from the storm. So tall, so dark, so stately, methought he looked like the prince of darkness, roaming to and fro the earth, in search of whom he might devour. I would know," said Parrolla, "what connexion there is between the house of Ravenswood and that man."

Mr. Immorf looked amazed at this very unexpected question of his son's, and he did not directly reply.

Then Parrolla said—" Is the portrait of that man, who appears to preserve perpetual youth, any relation to our family ?"

" He a relation !" cried Mr. Immorf, " God forbid !"

" God forbid !" said Parrolla, " and why God forbid ? You seem to scorn him and you cry God forbid that he should be a relation of mine, when, at the same time, you suffer his portrait to hang in your chamber covered with a curtain either to preserve the loved countenance from dust and injury ; or otherwise, it is covered up as a face not fit to be looked upon. But if so, why keep it there ?"

" Make no further inquiries," said Mr. Immorf, " it is a subject I do not wish to touch on."

" You certainly like the picture to hang there ; if not, you would take it down And if it is hateful to you, why not burn it out of the way ?"

Mr. Immorf looked affected, as he said,—

" I dare not."

" Dare not ! and who could prevent you ?" inquired Parrolla.

" I am prevented by an oath I made not to destroy it," said Mr. Immorf.

" And why did you take that oath ?" said Parrolla.

" It was a fatal necessity," said Mr. Immorf, " I was sworn never to destroy that portrait."

" And why did you of your own free will be so bound down ?"

" I could not avoid it," replied Mr. Immorf, " I hold a promise sacred, especially when given to the dead."

" And who was the person that made such a request ?"

" Ask me no more, for no further will I speak on the subject," said Mr. Immorf.

" This is all very mysterious," said Parrolla ; " if I again should meet that man I will of him myself make the inquiry."

" Speak not to him !" cried Mr. Immorf, " his breath is pestilential, and ac curst is the ground on which he treads. The birds stop their blithe notes at his approach, and seathed and blighted appears the green verdure when he is present Know, Parrolla, that man is the enemy of thy Creator !—shun him as you would pestilence !"

" What ! then he is the devil himself, and that is the long and short of it," said Parrolla ; " but I would not keep his portrait in my house."

" I have told you I dare not remove it," said Mr. Immorf.

" Who hung it there ?" inquired Parrolla.

" I will not tell you," replied his father ; " the knowledge of who pa ced that picture against the wall where it now is can be of no benefit to you, therefore we will no longer speak on the subject."

Saying this, Mr. Immorf left the apartment.

CHAPTER LXXXIX.

Ever charming, ever new,
When will the landscape tire the view?
The fountains fall, the rivers flow
The woody vallies warm and low;
The windy summit wild and high,
Roughly rushing to the sky;
The pleasant seat, the ruin'd tower,
The naked rock, the shady bower.—YER.

THE winter had worn away, and the Spring again, in her verdant robe, had re- visited and enlivened every object with her cheering presence.

And now Lisbia again could wander in her favourite walks ; she could again ascend the hill, and view the wide extent of country, until every tower and tree was lost in the distance.

Again was the white thorn and the dog-rose in bloom, and the blue-bell, and the violet, and the anemone. All around looked cheerful as it was wont to do, when Nature shone forth resplendent in renewed beauty.

But Lisbia could not view these objects with the delight she formerly had done. Fear preyed on her mind, a dread and a terror of her ruffianly cousin Parrolla, whom she feared on account of his persecuting her with his odious addresses.

She saw how much her uncle was incensed at the thought of Olando wishing to marry Rose Mildmay. "What then would he say," thought Lisbia, "if I refuse my cousin Parrolla for Edwin?"

These thoughts caused Lisbia to be very unhappy. She was now, and had some time been, the betrothed of Edwin; but during the wintry months she could but seldom see her affianced bridegroom; the weather being unfit for walking, Lisbia could on no pretence leave the castle; and very rarely excepting at church on Sundays, did Lisbia see that countenance which was the whole week the subject of her contemplation.

Very rarely, as it before hath been said, could Lisbia speak to Edwin, on account of the season of the year. For what young lady by choice, unless they had some motive for so doing, would roam abroad, amidst fields and lanes, clothed in the genial season with verdure and fragrance, but then robbed by the wintry winds of their green attire? where leaves had clustered, there icicles hung, and instead of the king-cup and daisy, there had the drifted snow settled.

But though the desolate season had now given place to young-eyed spring, yet the walks of Lisbia were still restrained, though not by stern winter, yet by one, fierce, headstrong, and unrelenting as the ungovernable tempest, when it comes howling across the wood, tearing up, scattering, and causing desolation to all around.

Fearing lest she might meet her cousin Parrolla in her walks, and that in company with Edwin, Lisbia seldom stirred from home.

But on an evening, when she knew that Parrolla was deeply engaged with a party of his friends who had dined at the castle, Lisbia went out in the hopes of meeting Edwin, for she knew that Parrolla was not in the least likely at that time to annoy her, he being deeply engaged in playing at dice with his companions.

Lisbia passed the house of Mildmay, and she saw standing at the door the mother of Edwin.

Lisbia spoke to Mrs. Mildmay, for now that she had received the vows of Edwin, and had promised to become his wife, Lisbia was not so scrupulous as she had been in talking to the relations of Edwin; for heretofore she had feared that he had discovered the love she bore him, and would think, if she came near his dwelling, that it was to throw herself in his way. But that fear now no longer troubled the mind of Lisbia, since a mutual explanation had taken place, and Lisbia looked upon Edwin as her affianced husband. She therefore had not those scruples, and considered that Edwin would not think her wishing to see him a want of delicacy, but a proof of esteem to him, who Lisbia had confessed held the first place in her heart.

"This lovely evening has tempted me to walk out," said Lisbia, to Mrs. Mildmay, whom she saw standing at her door.

"Yes, it is a very pleasant evening, indeed," said Mrs. Mildmay, but I had rather it were otherwise, for Edwin has gone out in a sailing-boat, and since the melancholy death of young Mr. Immorf, I have ever feared the sea. How is your aunt, Miss Phillimore?" inquired Mrs. Mildmay.

"She is very ill," said Lisbia, "and with concern I look on my dear aunt, thinking every day that she becomes weaker and weaker. She has never been so well, since the shock she received, when my cousin was drowned," said Lisbia; "I should almost break my heart, if my aunt dies, for I love her as if she were my mother."

Lisbia was going, when Mrs. Mildmay said, "I wish to speak to you, Miss Phillimore, concerning your brother, Mr. Phillimore. He will come to the farm to see Rose, and all my husband can say won't keep him away. I fear Mr. and Mrs Immorf should think that I encourage their nephew, but it is no such thing; and I am sure that Rose don't encourage him, for I believe she has other views.

"Olando is continually talking of Rose," said Lisbia, "and I really believe he loves her, but unfortunately the understanding of my poor brother is rather weak and he is very obstinate, and spiteful when offended. But if Olando wished to marry Rose, and his friends were even agreeable to their union, Olando, I fear would not be preferred by Rose."

"Oh, no," replied Mrs. Mildmay, "Rose would not prefer Mr. Phillmore, she think, has bestowed her heart elsewhere; but he haunts her like a shadow."

"I will speak to my uncle to talk to Olando," said Lisbia, "and he will poin out to my brother the impropriety of his conduct."

With her thoughts on Edwin, Lisbia walked up the long winding path, when she had so often passed moments of delight in the company of her lover—where he by every look and action had made known the idolitry with which he regarde her; she recalled to mind how they had met in this very path—how Edwin had attended her down the shelving path, snatching aside the brushwood, and ever obstrusive thistle that impeded her in her way down the declivity.

Lisbia seated herself on a bank, screened behind the trees, but through an opening between them, she watched the motion of the swelling waves : she saw at a distance several sailing-boats, but Lisbia could not recognise the form o her lover.

Filled with uneasy apprehensions, Lisbia sat on the bank. Whilst waiting there, she had long since seen the splendid sun sinking in glory behind the wester hills, and the night was fast coming on.

"He cannot be long," thought Lisbia, "and near this place he certainly wil land. Surely he will not stay until it is dark ; there must be then danger in being in an open boat on the water.

In terror, Lisbia still watched the sea; and she thought on the melancholy fate o her cousin Percival.

Twilight advanced, cloathing the earth in her mantle of grey, and the bat, and beetle with his drowsy hums, flitted across her path.

The sea appeared a perfect calm, and a sacred solemnity seemed to reign through nature. Amidst this silence, Lisbia heard an advancing footstep ; she feared that her cousin Parrolla had discovered her route, and was come in pursuit of her; but the footsteps were not coming in a direction from the castle.

In breathless suspense, Lisbia listened to the approaching footsteps, and in a moment the tall figure of Count Herman stood before her.

He at this time wore a dress similar to that he wore when his likeness was taken,—a large round hat, long black feather, and black wrapping cloak.

Lisbia had always from a child been terrified at the portrait, and an extreme dread and terror pervaded her frame, now that she beheld the original of that dreaded portrait.

With the fleetness of a fawn she would have fled on before him, but his gaunt limbs could soon have overtaken her.

Lisbia thought on that, and she thought it were best to continue lo ing at the sea without noticing that any one was passing, and she hoped that the dreaded gentleman in the black wrapping cloak would pass on without heeding her. But Lisbia was mistaken, he placed himself by her side, and stood viewing the slumber-ng water.

Faintly could Lisbia now discern through the gloom an approaching boat; in it were two persons, and one of them Lisbia believed to be Edwin.

Eased of her fears, she was hastening to the castle, when Count Herman followed her, and said,—

"Permit me, gentle lady, to be your guard. The road is lone, and the shades of night are darkening all around."

"I need no guard," replied Lisbia, and she was hastening on when Count Herman said,—

"Lady, you are wrong in saying you need no guard; beauty like yours might tempt an anchoret! the lover of beauty might steal you from your friends, and beneath the veil of night, place you in that seclusion, where you no more might be heard of. Then, gentle lady, permit me to see you to your home."

"There is no danger," said Lisbia. "I beg, sir, that you will leave me."

"That I cannot do," said Count Herman; "the happiness of my life depends on you; your image I have cherished in my heart; for, though unknown to yourself, I have often seen you."

"And I have often seen you," said Lisbia. "Your person is not unknown to me."

"Often seen me," said the count, "when and where? angelic being, tell me! and that you entertained a hope that we should meet again?" As Count Herman said this, his gaze met the view of Lisbia, who shrank from again

No. 29.

beholding the preternatural glare which shot from the eyes of that mysterious being. "And did you hope that we should again meet?" said the count, in a softened tone,

"Hope that we should again meet!" cried Lisbia. "Oh, no! I hoped that I should never see the original of the person I have often seen the portrait of!—and which portrait I have viewed with fear and dislike." Saying this, Lisbia quickened her pace, nor stopped until she reached Ravensworth Castle. When to her infinite satisfaction, Count Herman was no longer there.

CHAPTER XC.

Methought I heard a seraph say,
Come, leave thy suffering sister, come away;
The harps prepared to sing thy Maker's praise,
In songs of glory's never-ending lays.
Let not one lingering thought on him behind,
Retard thy passage on thy heavenly road ;
God in his own good time can him subdue,
And he may join thee in thy bright abode.—BY THE AUTHORESS OF EVA.

GLAD was Lisbia when she got into the castle, and got rid of her fearful visitor. Her uncle was engaged in the library, and her aunt, who was extremely indisposed, had lain down on the sofa, where she had fallen into an unquiet slumber.

Lisbia stood by her sleeping aunt, and surveyed with anguish her altered countenance ; with grief she listened to the low moan, and saw the fevered start; and heard her aunt in broken accents beseeching the Almighty to turn the heart of her son.

Affected, Lisbia left the parlour, and went into her aunt's room, where the portrait of Count Herman was hanging.

Lisbia put aside the black curtain, and once more she viewed the demoniac features of the count.

" 'Twas him," said Lisbia, mentally. " Who can he be ? I will inquire of my aunt. 'Tis strange that the ugly resemblance of that fearful man should remain here, and that with his features concealed with a black curtain."

The noisy mirth of Parrolla and his guests resounded in the halls of the castle; nor was the illness of his mother at all heeded by her unnatural son, who was either from home, or causing the castle to be in a continual uproar with his riotous companions.

Lisbia was now suffered to remain at peace by Parrolla, for he had taken a liking to a young female, who had been seduced by a gentleman who had become tired of her, and he had turned her over to one of his acquaintance.

The awkward country girl disdained to pine for her lover. She sang with the female in Milton's *Comus*,—

" The wanton God who pierces hearts,
Dips in gall his pointed darts ;
But the nymph disdains to pine,
Who bathes the wound in rosy wine.

" Farewell lovers when they are cloy'd,
If I am scorned because enjoyed ;
Sure the squeamish fops are free
To rid me of dull company."

This Molly Moxley was once one of the shyest girls in the village, where her parents had dwelt for many years, getting their living by working for the farmers.

Her father's work was reaping, mowing, or following the plough, as his employers thought fit ; whilst Molly and her mother were employed on the farmers' grounds, making hay in the summer, and picking stones in the winter, or working at what the farmers chose to employ them in.

Old Moxley lived in his thatched cottage in peace and content, notwithstanding the lowness of his wages. And, what with one thing and the other, he lived as well as most of the poor men in the neighbourhood.

He had a pig in the sty at the back of his cottage, and what with the corn his wife and daughter gleaned in the summer and the turnips, apples, and poultry he abstracted from the fields, gardens, and yards of the farmers ; and the practice of snaring hares and rabbits occupied the hours of Moxley, after he had done the business of his master, so that no one could say that Moxley was an idle man.

His daughter Molly was reckoned the prettiest girl in the village, and she had been the cause of many broken heads and bloody noses, for, when the village swains, at a wake or fair, got more ale in their heads than they were used to take, they would become quarrelsome, all being candidates for the hand of fair Molly in the dance, each of them declaring that he had the most right to that honour.

The fact was, that Molly was very liberal in her favours to all. And when young Squire Haden went on a visit into Somersetshire, he saw Molly gracefully tossing the hay with her fork.

Mr. Haden thought Molly a very pretty girl—he chucked her under the chin, and pinched her arm, whilst Molly cried, " Don t 'ce, sir!" but smiled, and simpered at the notice taken of her.

Mr. Haden told Molly a tale of love, and she promised to meet him at the five-barred gate, near her father's cottage, that night. But Molly returned no more ; a post-chaise was hired by Mr. Haden, and Molly went to London with her lover.

There for a time she was decked in all the splendour of the East ; but soon she became stale and valueless to her keeper—he left her.

But Molly was yet in the full bloom of her beauty, and she found a yet more generous keeper.

No jewel, however costly, was thought too expensive for the fair Molly ; and, in a very short time, she caused, by her extravagance, such embarrasments to fall on her generous keeper, that he became the inmate of a prison. To him another lover and another succeeded, and at length she became acquainted with Parrolla Immorf, who kept her and her servant in lodgings, at a farm-house at about two miles' distant from Ravenswood Castle, pretending that she was a heiress of great fortune.

Most of the young men, at least those of fortune, with whom Parrolla was acquainted with, had their ladies.

Parrolla gave an invitation to all his friends, for so he called his profligate companions, to come to a banquet at the castle. The musicians were seated, and the tapers were lit ; all looked splendour and gaiety, excepting in the chamber of sickness, for there lay Mrs. Immorf, who was considerably worse.

But, notwithstanding the illness of that mother, who had so loved him, who had watched him in sickness, nor would have suffered even the closing of a door to disturb his repose—she, that mother—lay, as it were, at the point of death, and the son she had so loved now made her abode ring with the sound of revelry.

Neither Mr. Immorf nor Lisbia were of the party. Mr. Immorf felt hurt at the conduct of his unfeeling son, who showed so little regard for his sick mother ; neither could Lisbia think of joining the party when her aunt was so very ill.

She saw the company come, from the window of her chamber, and was disgusted with the bold faces and tawdry appearance of the ladies.

But Lisbia could not help admiring the beauty of person of one of the females, notwithstanding her assured manner. This female was Molly Moxley, now called Miss Delamere.

Olando was of the party, and the poor idiot was in his glory. He danced to the sound of the harp, fondled and talked to the ladies, and drank wine until he was intoxicated.

" These ladies are pretty, Cousin Parrolla," cried Olando, " but not so pretty as

Rose, that they aint; I will marry Rose, and we'll have all these pretty ladies to live with us."

Parrolla laughed at the idea of Olando, respecting the ladies. " Then you like pretty ladies, Olando," he said ; " come, let us go and join them ; but you can't walk straight, Olando."

" Not walk straight !" cried Olando, " I can walk and dance too;" and he went capering into the room amongst the company, and joined in a song that a lady was singing, which put her completely out, she not being of the mildest temper in the world—and, moreover, she was in a very ill-humour, as some persons are when they take rather more strong drink than does them good.

She was very angry with Olando, and could not again be prevailed on to sing.

" No," said the lady, " I will not again be interrupted by the mockery of that monkey."

" Mockery !" cried Olando, " I am sure I never mocked you ; I was helping you to sing ; and I won't be called a monkey by you: Rose never called me monkey, and I am sure she's prettier than you are." Saying this, Olando staggered into a corner, where he seated himself and fell asleep, overcome by the wine he had taken. Nor were any of the company very sober ; not even the ladies.

Miss Delamere looked but coolly on Parrolla ; all her kindness was directed to a Mr. Mason, a young gentleman, one of Parrolla's guests.

She snatched a rose which he had in his bosom, and placed it beside the white feather she wore in her hair; she then reclined on the shoulder of Mr. Mason, and threw the dregs of the wine she had been drinking in the face of Parrolla.

Enraged, Parrolla started up inflamed with jealousy, and he flew at both Miss Delamere and Mr. Mason, like an enraged lion; the blows were returned, and general hostilities commenced amongst the inebriated party, some taking the part of Parrolla, and some that of Mason.

During this fray, so disgraceful in the house of a gentleman, Miss Delamere was knocked down, and her face coming in contact with a glass decanter, the bridge of her nose was quite shattered and broken, and the tip of it entirely cut off ; so that poor Miss Delamere, according to her new name, or Molly Moxley, according to her old, was maimed and disfigured ; and she now looked a fright instead of a beauty.

The screams of the women and the voices of the gentlemen concerned in this disgraceful affray, reached the ears of Mrs. Immorf ; terrified, she could hardly be persuaded to remain in bed. Violent spasms came on, and before morning dawned, Mrs. Immorf was a corpse.

" These are fine doings," said Peter, mentally, as he helped the footman pick up the broken glass, " but it is all through the curse that rested on old Sir Parrolla." For three days Mr. Immorf confined himself to his chamber ; he held no converse with Parrolla, nor did he name to him his most disgraceful and outrageous conduct; for Mr. Immorf saw that all remonstrance was in vain to one so hardened as Parrolla was. He was gay as usual all the time his mother lay in the house ; and at her funeral he was not seen to shed a tear.

And but one month after his mother was interred, the same riotous party was again invited to the castle, with the exception of Mr. Mason and Miss Delamere, who could not have accepted the invitation, even had she been so invited, on account of the injury she had received from the decanter.

Mr. Immorf was provoked beyond measure when he heard the song and loud laugh of his son's gay companions, and he could no longer restrain his anger at the unnatural and indecorous behaviour of his son. He went into the room where Parrolla and his guests were sitting, and said,—

" Parrolla, if you have neither natural feeling, nor even decency, 'tis fit that I should ; I therefore command these persons to depart from the castle. And, Peter, 'tis my orders that you immediately remove these viands, bottles, and glasses, nor bring here another bottle of wine, ale, or spirits, at your peril."

" Are you not ashamed," said Parrolla to his father, " to treat a son of my age in this way? I am not going to be treated like a babe in leading strings. My friends shall neither go, nor be insulted."

"Peter, lock up the cellars, and bring me the keys," said Mr. Immorf, "I am determined to put a stop to these proceedings."

CHAPTER XCI.

Have you a ruffian that will swear, drink, dance,
Revel the night, rob, murder, and commit
The oldest sins, the newest kind of ways ?"—SHAKSPEAR.

THE party broke up, and Parrolla was left alone in the banquet-room, with none but the foolish Olando.

Gloomy and morose, he sat leaning on a table, and he vowed a deadly revenge on his father.

"What a shame it is, Cousin Parrolla," said Olando, "that uncle has sent all the company away, and the pretty ladies too. I would not care—I'd have them here for all him; but it is just like him—he won't let me marry Rose; and I think, by-and-by, that he'll wring the necks of my peacocks, for, when the poor things sang before it rained yesterday, he said,—

"'What a yell! how I hate these hideous screams—the sound of their discordant voices to me is hateful.'"

"Oh, everything is hateful to him," cried Parrolla, "when he, above all, is the most hateful himself. But you don't mean that he shall prevent your marrying the pretty Rose?"

"I don't know, he's always a browbeating me so," said Olando. "I can't do as I like for him; he says I am foolish—now I think myself as wise as anybody."

"At least you know how to please yourself," said Parrolla. "But we'll talk on this matter again; you had better go to bed."

Mr. Immorf was now very cool with Parrolla, and Parrolla was gloomy and reserved in the presence of his father.

Poor Lisbia could now but seldom see Edwin; for notwithstanding Parrolla was so much taken up with Miss Delamare, as she styled herself, he had continued to watch Lisbia, and he did so still, though he did not so much pester her with his addresses.

She rarely saw Edwin, except on a Sunday at church, and then she thought her every look was watched by her cousin Parrolla, if he happened to be there, which he sometimes was for appearance' sake.

It was a melancholy sight to see the Immorf family seated in their seats at church, all in deep mourning for the lamented lady of the castle, when there had so recently been such continual mourning in that family for Lady Immorf, Percival, and now Mrs. Immorf; indeed, it was generally thought that an evil fate hung over that house, on account of the misdeeds of old Sir Parrolla; for of what he had been guilty by some means got whispered abroad, and it was thought that his sins were falling on the third and fourth generation.

Parrolla now was in want of money, and in consequence of the coolness that subsisted between him and his father, he hardly liked to speak to him on that subject, especially as he, during the time he was at Naples, and likewise since he came back, had expended a great deal of money.

Having no cash, he was compelled to speak to his father, and to request a further supply. For that purpose he put as good a face as he could on the matter, and knocked at the door of the library, in which his father was sitting. It was but seldom that Parrolla felt the blush of shame crimson his cheek; but he felt awed, and repugnant to appear in the presence of his father, with the request he was going to make; however, he summoned all his courage to his aid, and again he knocked, for Mr. Immorf, who was deeply engaged in study, did not hear any one knock until the knock was repeated. Mr. Immorf desired the person who knocked to come in, and Parrolla stood in the library before his father.

"On what account am I to attribute this visit?" said Mr. Immorf, looking sternly at Parrolla. "Speak, what has brought you here?"

"I want money," stammered out Parrolla.

"Then money you will not have of me," said Mr. Immorf; "your extravagance would ruin a dukedom."

"Then I must get it where I can," said Parrolla; "money I must and will have."

Parrolla, knowing the money he had run through, and the displeasure under which he laboured with his father, when first he appeared in the presence of him, felt some shame; but now the ice was broken, as it were, Parrolla cared not what his father thought of him, and he bravadoed in that of which he ought to have been ashamed.

"Then you will not let me have money?" said Parrolla.

"I will not," said Mr. Immorf; "consider the sums you have lately squandered. If I uphold you in spending money with your profligate companions, and in supporting harlots, I should be equally culpable as yourself—I will not do it."

"Then take the consequence," said Parrolla, and he flung out of the apartment.

At the moment Parrolla left the presence of his father, Olando came running in.

"Where's my uncle?" he cried; "I must see my uncle," and he ran into the library, crying, "Oh, uncle! I shall lose Rose, if I don't marry her to-morrow. I saw her with Mr. Manby, and he kissed her hand; I'd have knocked him down, but I was afraid that he would have turned again. Let Peter saddle a horse directly, and go for a licence."

"Why, Olando, are you gone mad?" said Mr. Immorf, who was in no pleasant temper of mind, having been a good deal put out of the way by Parrolla. "I have told you before, that I entirely set my face against your having anything to do with that girl, who could not love you—she would marry you merely for a home."

"Not love me!" cried Olando; "but I know she does love me; she always laughs every time she sees me—and I will have her."

"You must wait till you are of age, then," said Mr. Immorf; "whilst you are under my guardianship, I'll never consent to any such thing. To your study, sir, that will better become you, than thinking of marriage."

Olando left the presence of his uncle, bellowing like a great calf. He was quite sullen all day, and would not eat anything; in the evening he again saw Mr. Immorf, when he again spoke of marrying Rose; but Mr. Immorf would not hear the subject mentioned.

On the following day, Olando told Parrolla how ill his uncle had used him, in preventing his marriage with Rose.

"Oh, can't you see through his drift?" cried Parrolla; "he don't mean you to marry at all; he means to keep all your money himself. Whilst you are a bachelor, you will remain with him, and won't want your fortune out of his hands; but if you were married, of course you would want your fortune."

"Ah!" said Olando, "that is it, sure enough; I know he's very stingy, for he wishes the peacocks were dead. I dare say 'tis only because they eat victuals. I am sure I wish he was dead, that I do. I'd marry Rose the very next day."

"He is not immortal," said Parrolla, "death is as likely to overtake him as any one else. He is more like a tyrant than a father to me," continued Parrolla; "he will not let me have any money. You wish him dead, and so do I."

"Suppose," said Olando, and he whispered in the ear of Parrolla.

"Oh, fie!" said Parrolla, laughing, "and you would do that to get Rose."

"I would do anything to get Rose. And if I were my own master, and not under the control of my uncle, I'd have such a fine house, and horses, and dogs and peacocks, and Rose should be mistress of them all."

" What signifies talking of what you would do," said Parrolla, " when you know you can't do it. Are you not kept like a babe in leading-strings by my father ? What young fellow of spirit would put up with it ? If he was not my father, and he served me as he does you, I know what I'd do."

" And what would you do ?" cried Olando.

" That which would put you in possession of your fortune, and cause Rose to become your wife."

" What is it ?—what is it ?" cried the poor idiot ; " tell me, and I'll do any-thing to get Rose. Tell me, Cousin Parrolla, what I must do."

" Hush !" whispered Parrolla, " I hear footsteps—some one's coming ;" and he listened. " No, I was mistaken," he said, " all's quiet; it was but the wind forcing its way through the long galleries. You are so rash, Olando—you must be more guarded ; we will converse further, but not here : walls have ears. Meet me to-morrow at sunset in the obscured path that winds up the cliff near the sea—be punctual, and tell no one."

CHAPTER XCII.

Baron of Muckelmide, may the foul fiend drive thee,
And all to pieces rive thee, for building such a town,
Where there's neither man's meat, nor horses' meat,
Nor a chair to sit down.—SCOTT.

LADY Mackenzie, late Lady Nettleby, set out for Scotland with her husband ; her ladyship was in very high spirits, and she was quite pleased with the thought of the castle in Scotland, to which they were hastening.

But the nearer Mr. Mackenzie got to his native land, the more he appeared to be out of spirits ; and that his mind was employed in some deep cogitations was observed by her ladyship.

" What is the matter, 'Kenzie, love ?" said her ladyship ; " of what are you thinking ?"

" Oh, nothing particular," replied Mr. Mackenzie.

" Nay, don't say so," said her ladyship.

" Well, if I must tell you," replied Mr. Mackenzie, " I was thinking on what I ought to have thought on before."

" And what is that ?" inquired her ladyship ; " you don't repent our union, I hope."

Lady Mackenzie looked rather confused as she said so ; for a suspicion crossed her mind, that Mr. Mackenzie had heard how much she, through her extravagances had overrun her income, and how deeply she was in debt, which debts he, in con-sequence of his marriage, was bound to pay.

Lady Mackenzie thought herself the biter, nor did she in the least suspect that she was bitten, and that Mr. Mackenzie was too far north for her.

" Repent of our union ! Oh, no," replied Mr. Mackenzie ; " I was thinking, love, that I ought to have left you in London, and have gone into Scotland my-self, and seen that my castle was in proper repair to have received your ladyship ; but the violence of my love was such, that I on no account could leave you be-hind ; and now I have a thousand fears, thinking that the bleak north winds may have blown the roof away, or that these cursed highland thieves have stolen every article of furniture."

" And have you left no one in care of your castle ?" inquired Lady Mackenzie.

" Oh, yes, there is the old housekeeper, but it is five years since I left Scotland and three years ago the auld laird, my father, died ; of that circumstance I was apprised by old Madge, the housekeeper, who got a letter written and sent to me with the information—and that my uncle, my father's brother, was coming to live there ; and since that time I have heard no further."

" What ! and did you not attend the funeral of your father ?" cried Lady Mackenzie.

" No, I was too much engaged at that time ; I could not then leave London."

" Good Heaven ! what a wild-goose chase we are upon," cried Lady Mackenzie, " going to a ruinous old castle, with no other domestic than an old woman, lame, and purblind more likely than not, and the old man your uncle ; perhaps, when we get to this fine domain, the old people may be dead, and there may not be a brick left standing."

" Not so bad as that, neither, I hope," said Mr. Mackenzie, " but you must not be angry ; but attribute this disappointment, dearest, to the violence of my love, which would not permit me to think of anything else."

Lady Mackenzie and her husband reached Scotland ; and on a wide barren heath, stood the mansion of the Mackenzies, wearing an aspect of the greatest desolation.

The court-yard that surrounded the house was equally ruinous ; the old and broken flag-stones were displaced, and grass, dock, and thistles sprung up between them.

Mr. Mackenzie went through the court-yard, and knocked at the door of the mansion, but no answer was returned ; he pushed the rotten door—it gave way.

And the appearance of what they called the hall was by no means pleasing to Lady Mackenzie—an old oak table, and two what are called tub chairs, which chairs had formerly been covered with leather, but now only partially so, for the hay, with which they were stuffed, was largely projecting in more places than one ; and a pair of stags' horns and a rusted gun hung over the mantel-piece.

" Is this your castle ?" cried Lady Mackenzie ; " I would to Heaven that I had never left London !"

" The old housekeeper, I dare say, is dead," said Mr. Mackenzie, " and there being no one here to take care of the place, all the valuables, I fear, are abstracted—such a quantity of valuable old family plate as there ; was here 'tis enough to make one mad to think of it ! Unfortunate man that I am !" he cried, as he stamped about the beggarly-looking hall, as if he were frantic. " Oh, what a fool I was, to fall in love !" continued Mr. Mackenzie. " You, Gertrude, have been my ruin ! through my passion for you, I could think of nothing else ;— instead of courting you, if I had come down to my castle before the old woman died, all would have been well ; but when those cursed highlanders found there was no one to take care of my property, they have come and taken away everything worth having."

" But they have not robbed you of your hall chairs," said Lady Mackenzie, with a sneer. " 'Tis a wonder they did not take them with the rest of your valuables. What, sir, could be your reason for bringing me here ?"

" Do you doubt my honour, madam ?" replied Mr. Mackenzie. " I told you that I had a mansian in Scotland, and you find that I have not deceived you."

" A mansion !—a castle you told me," said Lady Mackenzie, " which I was led to believe was inhabited by the servants that you had retained since the death of your father. Did you not tell me that you studied the law for a mere amusement—that you needed no addition to your income, having large possessions ?— Where are these possessoins ?" inquired Lady Mackenzie.

" Those possessions I have," replied Mr. Mackenzie ; " dare you doubt my honour ?" and he gave Lady Mackenzie a look that made her tremble.

CHAPTER XCIII.

Oh, lover of the desert hail !
Say in what deep and pathless vale,
Or on what hoary mountain side,
'Midst falls of water you reside ;
'Midst broken rocks a rugged scene,
With green and grassy dales between ;
'Midst forests dark of aged oak,
Ne'er echoing with the woodman's stroke.—AUTHOR UNKNOWN.

FINDING the mansion of her husband was in no fit condition for her reception, Lady Mackenzie desired to go back to the inn, and hoped that as things had

No. 30.

turned out so differently from what Mr. Mackenzie had expected, they might return to London without delay.

Not a sentence more did Lady Mackenzie breathe on account of her disappointment, in finding the boasted castle of her husband but a house, and that not an over large one ; 'tis true that the top of the house resembled two turrets, and it certainly was fortified with the rusted gun that hung over the mantel-shelf; however, Lady Mackenzie, whatever she thought, said nothing. She now feared that which she never before had feared, and that was to provoke her lord ; she remembered the look he had given her—it almost petrified her. She would have gone into hysterics, whilst viewing her husband's castle, but it was an inconvenient place ; there was none by to assist her.

Full of disagreeable ruminations, Lady Mackenzie, when she reached the inn, sat at the window, seeming to be noticing what was passing in the street ; but her thoughts were not on the passing objects.

Silently Mr. Mackenzie sat at a table in the room ; he did not interrupt the cogitation of his lady, his thoughts were full of the business that brought him to Scotland.

The father of the present Mr. Mackenzie had been a very wild and extravagant man, and he had mortgaged his grounds and house, called a castle, on account of the turrets at the top, for a very considerable sum of money.

At the death of his brother, the younger Mackenzie took possession of the house and lands, for he it was who had lent the money on the house and lands, for which his brother had given him a bond and judgment payable six months after his decease; the money not being paid, the uncle of the present Mr. Mackenzie had entered up judgment ; and Mr. Mackenzie, having married Lady Nettleby, thought to make terms with his uncle, and pay the mortgage out of the money he expected to become master of, in consequence of his marrying that lady, when, to his surprise when he reached Scotland, he found that his uncle was dead, and that the house was without an inhabitant.

What he had told his lady about the high winds, and the thievish highlanders, was but a subterfuge, to prepare her for not finding his castle, as he called it, what he had represented it to be, but an old shattered building, needing repair. And as to the plate that he pretended the highland thieves had stolen, he to prevent such of an occurrence, had wisely sent for it up to London, assoon as he heard of the death his father.

But though this same house, or castle, was a good deal out of repair, and it stood in a very lone and unfrequented spot, yet Mr. Mackenzie, although he had for some years been in London, and had partaken of the dissipation of that gay city, still retained a love for the land of his forefathers, and intended to have the old place of his birth repaired and newly furnished ; that is to say, if he could get the consent of his lady to remain there. And what with the income arising from his lands and the jointure of his wife, he thought to cut a very good figure amongst his own countrymen.

But Lady Mackenzie on no account would be persuaded to stay in Scotland, and that caused many words between her ladyship and Mr. Mackenzie.

"Do you think I'll stay to be buried alive here ?" said her ladyship. "No, sir, I have always had an elegant house, splendidly furnished ; and can you for a moment suppose that I will live here in a dog-kennel ?"

Mr. Mackenzie was quite indignant with his lady for expressing herself as she had done. But at length it was agreed that Mr. Mackenzie should give orders for the repairing of his paternal home ; that they should then go to London, and return to Scotland the following summer ; and if Lady Mackenzie found the place such as she could dwell in, they were to remain there entirely ; if not, they were to stay there but during the summer, and to return to town in the winter.

Things being thus arranged to the satisfaction of both parties, they set off to London in good spirits.

But, unfortunately, Lady Mackenzie had but just stepped out of the chariot, and was going into the hotel, when Lady Mackenzie saw a Mr. Pearson passing by, and he saw her ladyship.

However, he took no notice, nor did she. But the sight of Mr. Pearson caused an unpleasant sensation to run through the frame of her ladyship; for she feared that Mr. Pearson would broach an unpleasant subject. And glad was her ladyship when she saw him pass by without taking any notice.

But Mr. Pearson stood where Lady Mackenzie could not observe him; and as soon as he had seen her luggage taken into the hotel, he went to his attorney, and a writ was issued against Mr. Mackenzie for a debt of two hundred and fifty pounds, the sum Lady Mackenzie owed her upholsterer.

That very evening, whilst Mr. Mackenzie was seated reading to his lady the news of the day, these rude and disagreeable persons, agents to John Doe and Richard Roe, made their appearance, they having abruptly entered the room without the least ceremony, and arrested Mr. Mackenzie for the sum of two hundred and fifty pounds, due to the said Pearson, for goods had by her ladyship.

"Good God!" cried Mr. Mackenzie, "how is it possible you could have been so neglectful as to leave this sum unpaid—you certainly ought to have paid it before you went to Scotland. The man, I suppose, thought you intended cheating him out of his money, and has put you to the expense of this writ; you had better instantly discharge it, that is to say, if it is a just debt."

Lady Mackenzie was all of a tremble, and her face was of an ashy paleness.

"Pay it!" she said.

"Yes, pay it," cried Mr. Mackenzie. "But for what is it owing?"

"For the white-figured satin chairs, and sofa with the gold mouldings that I had in my drawing-room; a table-clock, and looking-glass."

"D—d extravagant, madam! Do not let me be disgraced—instantly pay it."

"Pay it!" again said Lady Mackenzie.

"Pay it, certainly!" cried her enraged husband.

"I have not the money," said her ladyship.

"Not the money!" cried Mr. Mackenzie. "So, then, I am to be dragged to prison for a debt not mine—caged up through marrying a mere adventuress. By Gad, madam, you are nothing better in my estimation than a female sharper—a scheming, plotting, manœuvring widow; but one comfort is, that I am as wide awake as yourself. And since I must go to prison with this fellow, with his writ of mandamus, for your debts, you may pawn your jointure to get me out again. Lead the way," continued Mr. Mackenzie, speaking to the men, for he was now more cool; and not surmising that his wife owed yet other debts, he thought that he had the best of the match, as his lands would not produce at most more than seventy pounds per year, and her ladyship's jointure was five hundred.

Lady Mackenzie had now no other means to get her husband out of durance vile than to raise money on her jointure; this she did for two years, and for the thousand pounds that she would have received during that period she could not get more than six hundred.

The money was paid, and Mr. Mackenzie was liberated; but before Lady Mackenzie paid such sum, she inquired of Mr. Pearson, if he had informed her other creditors of what had happened: he assured her that he had not, neither would he if her ladyship paid him; on that condition the money was paid.

This affair made many words between Mr. Mackenzie and his lady; and he in a severe, authoritative tone, demanded if he was still in danger of losing his liberty on account of her debts; Lady Mackenzie assured her husband that he was not.

Humbled and terrified, and fearing that the truth would come out, (for she was still three hundred pounds in debt,) Lady Mackenzie would willingly have left London, and gone anywhere, to prevent such knowledge coming to the ears of her husband, of whom she stood in much greater fear than she had ever done of her poor dear dead Sir Nicholas.

CHAPTER XCIV.

This is no flattery, these are counsellors
That feelingly persuade me what I am;
Sweet are the uses of adversity!'—SHAKSPERE.

SOON as Mr. Mackenzie was liberated from his confinement, he took ready furnished lodgings at Paddington, and he told his lady they must now begin to economise.

"That chariot of yours is quite a superfluous thing," said Mr. Mackenzie; "when persons are of a hale and robust constitution, like you, they have no need of a carriage; besides, you are so very obese, much walking would be of great service to you."

Tears were ready to start into the eyes of Lady Mackenzie.

"Robust!" she said, "you mistake, sir, I am not robust; I was always reckoned very delicate—a carriage I have always been used to, nor can I, nor will I, do without one."

"But I say you must, and shall do without one!" thundered out Mr. Mackenzie; "consider, through your extravagance, your jointure will bring you nothing for two years, then how are we to keep a carriage?"

"We have yet some hundreds by us," said Lady Mackenzie, "and your income."

"My income," said Mr. Mackenzie, "at present is worse than no income at all. My uncle died, and no person in Scotland knew where to write to me, so that my lands have become, as it were, a mere wilderness, covered with stones, thorns, and thistles, and labour and expense will be necessary to put them in proper order."

"And who is to bear that expense?" inquired Lady Mackenzie, haughtily, "for it appears you have no money; my purse-strings I am obliged to undraw for all that's wanted; therefore, I should be glad to know who is to find money for the labourers, and other expenses."

"Who? why you, to be sure," said Mr. Mackenzie, "my wife; certainly whilst she has one farthing at her command she must produce it for the benefit of her husband. You have now several hundred pounds which you received in advance on your jointure, that will do well to lay out in ploughing, manuring, and sowing my lands; and you will see oats and rye grow, where there is now nought but dock, furze, and thistles; and you, love, will have the pleasure of saying, 'I am Lady Mackenzie, and these are my lands.'"

"I cannot think of parting with my chariot," said Lady Mackenzie, "'tis cruel of you to request it, my poor dear dead Sir Nicholas would rather have broke his neck in a fox-chase, than have made such a request."

"What he did was one thing, and what I do is another," said Mr. Mackenzie; "you said that he was obliged to mortgage some of his estates, now I mean to keep mine clear, and free from incumbrance."

"And starve, and break your wife's heart, to preserve them," said Lady Mackenzie. "I never will put down my chariot, I assure you; what would the world say?—I should be ashamed to show my face. I suppose you would have me walk on foot through the miry streets, like some poor and draggled-tailed drab of the lowest grade of society," and Lady Mackenzie sobbed with vexation.

"Come, come, Gertrude," said Mr. Mackenzie, "you know the proverb that says, 'that which cannot be cured must be endured.' To deal plainly with you, 'tis my intention to leave London in the course of a month, and by that time my castle, or house, whichever you choose to call it, I hope will be ready."

This was heart-breaking news to Lady Mackenzie; but she bore such intelligence with more calmness than she would have done before the arrest of her husband, for she was now in continual fear of meeting some one to whom she owed money, and such debts coming to the ears of her husband, whose ire she dreaded to provoke; and though she was quite miserable and melancholy at the thought of going to live on that rude spot, where her husband's house or castle stood, yet she had even a greater dread of Mr. Mackenzie finding out that she had deceived him.

CHAPTER XCV.

Instead of ball, and masquerade, and play,
'Midst cows and poultry, pine my hours away.—BY THE AUTHORESS OF EVA.

THE chariot and horses of Lady Mackenzie were sold, and she went into Scotland with her lord.

The repairs of the house or castle were not finished; but there were one or two rooms of which her ladyship could make use. She took her waiting maid, Elizabeth, with her, and this girl was all the society Lady Mackenzie had.

Elizabeth despised Mr. Mackenzie's domain as much as her lady, and declared that if she had known what sort of a place she was coming to, nothing would have tempted her to have left London; for Elizabeth declared that it was the horridest, strangest, outlandish place she ever saw in her life, and she was sure her lady would not live three months there.

"Oh, no, madam," said Elizabeth, addressing her lady, "it is impossible that you can live here—not a soul to be seen—nothing but tall trees, hedges, and ditches; and if you do by chance see a human face, 'tis only one of those nasty Scotchmen without unmentionables, a sight enough to put any modest body to the blush. I am sure I would not go out after dark for the world; and I am very sorry, but I give your ladyship warning."

"For Heaven's sake, Elizabeth, don't leave me!" said Lady Mackenzie. "It would indeed be cruel of you to do so; you know I have no other servant than that rude, uncouth, gaping Scotch wench that serves for both cook and housemaid. I'll raise your wages, but pray don't leave me."

"I would willingly oblige your ladyship, madam," said Elizabeth, "but I am sure I could not live a month here—there is no one here that I can 'sociate with; and your ladyship knows I have always been used to the highest of company. I have even kept company with the servants of his Grace, my Lord the Duke of Beaufort, and the servants of my Lord Harcourt; and does your ladyship think that I can condescend to keep company with these here ignorant creatures, who knows nothing of what's going on in the fashionable world? No, madam, I cannot think of staying here," continued Elizabeth; "until my warning is out, I will stay, but no longer."

The winter came on, and all was gloom around the domains of Mr. Mackenzie; the icicled trees and the snow-covered hills were but a dismal prospect for Lady Mackenzie. She was not one of those persons who could hail the varying seasons, and view each object around her with delight.

The beauties of Nature had no charms for her, and her mind sank into despondency in her dreary solitude.

All her schemes had failed, and it might be said, "that the pit she had dug for another she had fallen into herself."

Mr. Mackenzie did not behave with much kindness to his lady, and she had none now to comfort her, or show the least regard or fondness for her; no, she had not even a little dog to welcome his mistress home, nor a bird to come chirping with pleasure when he saw his protectress return. Lady Mackenzie was not fond of animals, and the grateful though speechless eloquence of the brute creation were never noticed by her; nor would it have been remarked with pleasure by her ladyship, had she done so. Disappointed in all her schemes, and the dupe of her artifice, Lady Mackenzie entirely lost her spirits, and at times her mind seemed labouring under error. Her senses were wandering and unsettled. She awoke Mr. Mackenzie one night, saying,—

"Maria is here, with her carriage and two footmen ! Oh ! how ashamed I am of my mean appearance ! Get up, Mackenzie, and say I am at our town-house."

"Nonsense !" said Mr. Mackenzie. "There is no Maria here."

"There is, I tell you !" said Lady Mackenzie. "I saw the splendid liveries of her servants, white, turned up with lemon-colour, and silver shoulder-knots—I am so ashamed," and she hid her face in the bed-clothes.

Mr. Mackenzie found that his lady was labouring under some delusion of mind, which every day appeared to increase. And when Lady Mackenzie was walking out, or standing at her window, the children would say,—

"Run, run, here comes the mad woman !"

It was not only disappointed pride that unsettled the mind of Lady Mackenzie, there were other matters that weighed heavily on her spirits ; she was brow-beat, and bullied by her unpolished Scotch husband, and much neglected by him. She spent a great part of her time in entire solitude ; for Lady Mackenzie had now no other attendant than an awkward, red-haired Scotch wench, who stared and grinned at everything her mistress said to her. There was another source of vexation, too, for Lady Mackenzie ; there was a Mrs. Butler, a widow lady, possessed of much property ; she was a sprightly woman, without any incumbrance, and seemed nothing loth to enter the marriage state again. This lady had invited Mr. and Lady Mackenzie to her house, after she had first visited them, on their arrival in Scotland ; and they had often been to see the widow Butler, until Lady Mackenzie dropped going, having taken offence with the widow, who she found had been an old sweetheart of Mr. Mackenzie's, before he left Scotland. And Lady Mackenzie felt a jealousy arise in her mind concerning this widow, who, she believed, Mr. Mackenzie would have preferred to herself.

One day, after a severe quarrel between Lady Mackenzie and her husband, Mr. Mackenzie said,—

"You shall no longer annoy me—I'll not be plagued with the freaks of a mad woman."

That same day the widow Butler called, and Lady Mackenzie, who listened, heard Mr. Mackenzie say to Mrs. Butler,—

"Oh, she's quite insane. I'll place her in some lunatic asylum, and that before the week's out."

"It certainly is the best place for her," replied Mrs. Butler; "any one can see she is quite deranged."

Lady Mackenzie was certainly far from being in a sound state of mind, and, acting with the cunning peculiar to mad people, she, to frustrate the intention of her husband, to whom she took no notice of what she heard, got up the following morning, and made herself mistress of what money there was in the house, which was no large sum, and a bundle of clothes ; she left her home, with the intention of seeking her niece Celeste, from whom she expected to find more kindness than she did from her own children.

It was a long journey from Scotland to Cornwall, particularly to one in the state of mind Lady Mackenzie was then in. Her oddities rather alarmed the persons in the stage-coach ; however, she got to her journey's end, and that without being pursued by her husband, who hoped he might never hear of her any mor , making himself quite happy in the company of the widow Butler. Mr. Mack nzie was now in easy circumstances, the money of Lady Mackenzie having put his heretofore wilderness of an estate into good order.

———

CHAPTER XCVI.

It was a wild and strange retreat,
As e'er was trod by outlaw's feet.
The dell upon the mountain's crest,
Yawn'd like a gash in a warrior's breast.
The oak and birch, with mingled shade,
At noon-day there a twilight made;
From such a den the wolf had sprung—
In such the wild cat leaves her young.—SCOTT.

LADY MACKENZIE reached the house which Mr. Manby had occupied, when she last visited them, for notwithstanding her malady, she still remembered that place, and finding it shut up (for it was then without an inhabitant) her disordered brain concluded that all the family of her brother were dead.

Disappointed in the protection that she expected to receive from Celeste, Lady Mackenzie now knew not what to do; every step she took she thought her husband was behind her; and when that fancy strongly possessed her mind, she would run on until she was quite exhausted, and ready to drop; for she feared that Mr. Mackenzie was following her, in order to place her in a madhouse.

Full of this idea, she hid herself in some lonely spot all day, and at night, as soon as darkness enshrouded the earth, she went forth to purchase food

Wandering about one moonlight night, near the sea-beach, she saw a mud-built hut standing, though almost obscured from view by the veteran oaks, and hardy elms, with which that spot abounded.

"This shall be my castle," said Lady Mackenzie, as she entered the hut. There was a door which opened into a wide chasm; in it there was a path, which appeared to be of a gradual descent.

Although Lady Mackenzie's senses were now completely deranged, yet she had understanding enough to think that this place contained some secret, in consequence of the obscureness of the situation.

"All will be found out now," she cried; "they have gone out, and left the door open."

This was exactly the case; for the persons who used this place as a depot to put the proceeds of their illicit trade in, had drank too freely of the spirits they had there concealed, and in the jovial hilarity of the moment, they had forgotten to close the well-constructed door, which was so fitted, that no person would have suspected that any illicit trade was carried on there, or that there was any passage beyond the hovel with which it was at all connected.

Lady Mackenzie proceeded down the passage, which was not entirely dark, there being some small iron bars, about seven inches in length, placed across the surface of the earth, so that a small portion of light issued between these bars into the subterraneous passage.

Lady Mackenzie pursued her way until she came into a spacious cavern, which was partially illumined by the rays of the moon, by the same means as the subterraneous passage.

Here Lady Mackenzie found a quantity of hay, and the branches and leaves of trees, and a quantity of furze and other rubbish.

"This shall be my dwelling," said Lady Mackenzie; "here in my castle will I repose myself, and sleep in safety on my bed of down; but where are my servants? All gone to some merry-making, I suppose—well, I must make my bed myself." And she shook up the hay and leaves, and then extended herself upon them.

CHAPTER XCVII.

The drowsy night grows on the world, and now
The busy craftsmen, and the o'erlabour'd hind,
Forget the travail of the day in sleep ;
Care only wakes, and moping pensiveness :
With meagre, discontented looks, they sit,
And watch the wasting of the midnight taper ;
Such vigils I must keep. So wakes my soul,
Restless and self-tormented. Oh, false Hastings,
Thou hast destroyed my peace.—Rowe.

At a little distance from Ravenswood Castle, there stood a rude hut : it had been built by some wandering gipsies, who had taken up their residence some months in Cornwall ; but had long since abdicated their clay-built dwelling.

In this hovel there now dwelt a family consisting of a man, woman, and a child about three months old. The poor woman looked like one who had seen better days ; there was something superior in her carriage, though she was clothed but in very poor attire, and a heavy grief sat on her meagre countenance.

A pot was on the fire, which was supported by bricks and pieces of iron, and a very small rush candle stuck in a lump of clay, but feebly illumined the miserable dwelling.

On a bed of straw lay a child—it was ill, and its envious mother was watching its heavy breathing. With a tearful eye she raised the babe from its wretched couch, and put its little lips to her breast, in which, from want of necessary support, there was scarcely one drop of milk to moisten the fever-parched lips of her infant.

"Come, my babe, we must go," she said, speaking to the child. "We must go and endeavour to get some turnips from the field, and cook them against thy father's return."

She wrapped her babe in its mantle, and went forth to purloin some turnips from a field hard by the hovel in which she dwelt.

Whilst she was drawing the turnips from the ground, she was much startled by seeing the figure of a woman stand before her, with a face pale and wan as the inhabitant of the tomb ; believing the female to be such, the poor woman fled, leaving the turnips in the field.

When she reached her hovel, her husband was come home.

"Are the turnips ready ?" he said, "I yet have eaten nothing to-day, luck has been against me ;—all I have been able to get is this loaf, and for that I had a narrow escape of being taken into custody. Come, put the child down, and bring the turnips."

"I have not got any," said his wife ; "I could not go to get them until it was dark, and just as I had got them in my lap—"

"You were caught, I suppose— you should be more careful ; you are a rare help-mate for a man, fit for nothing but to dress, and sit with your hands before you."

"Dress !" cried the woman, raising her tearful eyes to heaven. "Good Heaven! how can you talk of dress, when you know these rags are all I have to stand upright in !"

"And good enough too !" replied the man, "you are now suffering for your former vanity. I shall think of you not getting the turnips ready; if I don't, curse me ! Put that child down, and see if you can get me an onion or two to relish my bread."

"I cannot go, Robert," said the woman wildly, "indeed, I cannot. To-night, whilst I was pulling the turnips, I saw an apparition, and I was so terrified, that let the turnips I had in my apron fall. I dare not go to get you any onions, for the universe: I should expire with terror."

" Tell me none of your nonsense," cried the man, "'tis all your cursed laziness. There you sit squatting all day with that child in your arms, and will do nothing else."

" I never was used to do anything," cried the weeping woman, "I had alway Persons to wait on me. If you had the least feeling, you could not talk in thi way. I am almost starved, and this poor sick child is perishing for want of medicine which I cannot procure."

" How can I help it?" replied the man sullenly. "I have had no chance of getting anything for these three days ; but I'll not go on so, something I' have, or

No. 31

I'll swing for it. There is much money and plate, I understand, in the house of Squire Durant; the family, I hear, in a short time are going to leave home on a visit for a few days; it will then be a good opportunity. I mean to force a shutter, and carry off what valuables I can. Sooner would I swing on a gibbet than remain in this wretched plight."

The woman was still weeping. "Is there no trade you can turn your hand to?" she said; "can you do nothng else to get a living?"

"Trade!" replied the man, contemptuously, "it is so long since I have worked at a trade, that I have forgotten all about it; and if I had not, think you that I'd starve on the wages of a mechanic? No, no, I have tasted of luxury too much to do that."

"Oh! consider the risk," cried the woman, "should you be taken."

"I can but die," said the man, "and 'tis better to die by the halter than by starvation. Why don't you apply to your mother? If you could get a hundred or two from her, with that sum, I'd go on such a game, that instead of those wretched rags, you should stand alone in silks."

The woman wiped her weeping eyes, and with a faint smile, said, "Oh! Robert! never I fear, will that day come again; broken down and dejected as I am, I have not the face to apply to my mother, who I certainly used very ill; and if I could summon resolution to see her, I could not in this plight. You know my mother is a worldly-minded woman; I know her disposition so well, that was I to appear before her in these rags, though her own child, she, instead of commiserating my misery, would look on me with contempt and loathing. When I have better clothing, the silks you spoke of, I will try what I can do, but not before."

"And silks you shall have in a short time," said the man, "and lace and ornaments too, or I'll die for it."

All the following day the man was out, and the poor woman had no other subsistence to support herself, and enable her to suckle her baby on, than a portion of the bread that was left on the preceding night; but towards evening, the man came into the hovel. "Maria," he said, "you must lay aside your silly fears, and get a good quantity of turnips to-night, for I am inclined to steal a lamb."

The lamb was brought home and dressed, and the famished woman once more enjoyed a good meal, but she dreaded the consequences of her husband's lawless life; and trembled for what might occur from the intended burglary in the house of Mr. Durant.

Olando met Parrolla, according to appointment, in the obscure and unfrequented walk up the cliff, where he upheld Olando in all the complaints he had to make against his uncle, respec ing Mr. Immorf being against Olando marrying Rose.

"Through my father's means, you'll lose her," said Parrolla. "Manby will marry her if something speedy is not done to prevent it: it were well if he were dead—I mean my father."

"I don't mind telling you," said Olando, "because I know you are my friend, Cousin Parrolla, and won't tell him; but I'd do it if I could."

"Do what?" inquired Parrolla.

"Why kill him."

"Kill him!" said Parrolla; "why, you'd never have courage to do that?"

"Should I not," said Olando, "I only wish I had a good opportunity when he is asleep, and there was no fear of his turning again."

"Why of course if he was dead, you would be your own master," said Parrolla, "and have none to control you. He generally goes to sleep in his library after dinner."

Olando was going to answer, when Parrolla put his finger to his mouth.

"Hush!" he said, "I thought I heard footsteps," and he listened. "No there is none by," he said, "it was the wind rustling amongst the leaves; but speakl ow —be more cautious."

". If he is asleep to-morrow in the library," said Olando, in a whisper, "Ill take the poker, and knock him on the head."

"You will not have that courage," said Parrolla, "no, not even to get Rose."

"You shall see," said Olando; and here the conversation ended.

CHAPTER XCVIII.

And all the courses of my life do show,
I am not in the roll of common men.
SHAKSPEARE.

THE wretched inhabitant of the hovel, no longer able to bear the privation brought on by his own dissipation, determined at all risk to break into the house of Mr. Durant, nor wait for that gentleman's absence from home.

And he began his operations that very night, about the hour of twelve; he had skulked around the premises for some time, and when he saw the family had retired to rest, he with the tools he had, with as little noise as possible, succeeded in getting into the house. He got into the butler's pantry. and packed up a large quantity of plate; and having tied it up in a bundle, he was going to make off with his booty, and was rejoicing within himself, thinking how well he had succeeded, when the gardener, who had been watching him all the time, fired a gun he held in his hand,—the robber dropped his bundle, and fell a corse on the earth.

All was now confusion in the house of Mr. Durant; the corse of the robber was laid in an outhouse, and a crowd of persons congregated to see the body, but he was a stranger, and known to no one.

After the crowd of persons who had come to view the corse of the man were departed, they having fully satisfied their curiosity, and found that the deceased was one they had never seen before, Mrs. Durant wished to see the felon's corse.

When she went into the outhouse for that purpose, she saw a woman standing near the corse, her eyes were bathed in tears, and her appearance was wretched in the extreme.

Mrs. Durant was affected, and she felt for the wretched object before her.

"Was that man your husband?" inquired Mrs. Durant; when the woman, in the greatest surprise, cried, "Great God!—my cousin Celeste!"

And Mrs. Durant was equally surprised to find in the wretched woman her cousin Maria, and in the deceased robber, she recollected the features of Mr. Synegall, the friend of the pretended Count le Mar.

Mrs. Durant requested Mrs. Synegall would walk in and tell her what way she could be most serviceable to her.

But Mrs. Synegall said, in a voice rendered inarticulate by grief,—

"I cannot stay now, I have an infant at home in a dying state. I must hasten home, and when I have seen after my child, I will come back, and accept you kindness."

"I will walk with you," said Mrs. Durant, and she accompanied Mrs. Synegall to her miserable abode; and as she did so, she thought on the time when Maria, like a divinity, only seen to be worshipped, sat carelessly reclining on the white satin sofa, with her lace scarf, and white feather sweeping her left shoulder, strewing around her the fragrant leaves of a white rose; and a deep sigh issued from her bosom, as she thought on the change.

The unhappy mother flew to her child; but its little spirit had fled—it had breathed its last sigh during the absence of its mother; whilst she, whose husband had died by the hand of violence, was lamenting over her babe.

A noise was heard in one corner of the hut, and in a moment, a woman of a wild and strange appearance stood before them. [She burst into a wild and frantic laugh.

"I am glad the brat's gone !" she cried. "It would only have lived to have picked your eyes out ; but I have run away, and left them all. I am a queen now—and the birds of the air and the beasts of the field are my subjects."

Saying this, she with affected dignity walked up to where Mrs. Durant and the poor inhabitant of the hovel were standing.

And in the maniac Mrs. Durant discovered her aunt, and Mrs. Synegall her mother.

But the senses of Lady Mackenzie were too much disordered for her to know either her daughter or her niece.

"Oh, mother ! don't you know me ?" cried Mrs. Synegall; "don't you know your poor unfortunate Maria ?"

"Maria ! Maria !" said Lady Mackenzie, and she held her hand to her head, as if endeavouring to recollect. "Oh, Maria, I remember ; she was turned into a butterfly, and she flew away one fine sunshiny day, and we have never seen her since. Oh, no, she never came back again. But have you seen Mackenzie ?— hush, speak low, some of his emissaries may be about; he wants to put me in the madhouse, but he shan't—I'll kill him !"

Maria wept. "Oh, my poor mother !" she {cried, "little did I expect this meeting—and now to see thee but the ruin of thy former self. A butterfly, my poor mother said I was ; alas ! I am but a caterpillar now—a poor, miserable, grovelling insect ;" and Mrs. Synegall's tears redoubled.

"Dear Maria, let me not see you thus depressed," said Mrs. Durant; "better days await you ; and your mother I hope will recover her reason, when she is placed under proper care, and that she shall be ; I will get the first physician in cases of lunacy to attend her."

Mrs. Synegall could hardly find words to express her thanks to the generous Celeste, who immediately provided a house for the poor maniac, and furniture from her own residence, to make the place comfortable ; and whilst the house was being got ready, she took Mrs. Synegall and Lady Mackenzie to her own home.

She sent one of her servants to do the drudgery of the house, and wait on Mrs. Synegall; and a woman who had formerly been cook to Mrs. Durant, was for the present appointed to take charge of Lady Mackenzie.

Far from ever speaking of what had transpired, or owing any ill-will to her aunt, on account of her vile conduct concerning the pretended Count le Mar, Mrs. Durant, now that her aunt was in affliction, sincerely forgave her the injuries she had received at her hands, and rejoiced in having the ability to serve her unhappy relative.

The corse of Mr. Synegall was taken in a coffin by an undertaker to the house of his wife, as was the corse of the child.

And Mrs. Durant gave the unhappy widow money to purchase mourning, and to settle the funerals, and pay every expense.

The health and spirits of Mrs. Synegall were greatly broken, and the malady of Lady Mackenzie was by no means amended ; at times she was tolerably calm, then she would become very violent, fancying that she saw Mr. Mackenzie, who she declared should die by her hand.

CHAPTER XCIX.

Come ye furies,
Daughters of hate and hell, arise; inflame
My murderous purpose; pour into my veins
Your gall, your scorpion fillness.—EURYDICE.

OLANDO now narrowly watched his uncle, to find an opportunity to execute his murderous purpose; and when Mr. Immorf retired to his library, Olando frequently went into that room; for which he made some excuse to his uncle, who was surprised at the intrusion of Olando; but Olando had no opportunity that day, for Mr. Immorf was much engaged in reading, and did not, according to his usual custom, fall asleep. Disappointed, Olando became irritated and out of patience; he sought Parrolla, and cried as soon as he saw him—"He won't go to sleep Cousin Parrolla! What's to be done?"

Parrolla held his finger to his lip, and frowned at Olando; but still the idiot would go on. "Do you think he'd turn again?" he cried, "if I thought he would not, I'd go and knock him down now he is awake."

"Hush!" cried Parrolla. "Come, let us go and take a walk down by the seaside." There they wandered, talking and devising schemes for the destruction of Mr. Immorf; but nothing appeared to them so safe a way, and the least likely to prevent suspicion, as to knock him on the head whilst he slept, and then his death, when found lying on the floor, would seem as if it happened through a fall.

"If there is an opportunity, you must make use of it," said Parrolla; "if not, we will meet here the evening after to-morrow, and concert new plans."

Parrolla having spent all the money he had in his own possession, and not being able to obtain a fresh supply from his father, he could not now go on in the riotous manner he had done; and greatly mortified on that account, he kept at home, went out in a sailing-boat, or strolled along the seashore, not on account of his being the least amended in his conduct, or repenting of that which he had been guilty of, but to wile away an hour that he could not employ more to his own satisfaction.

Lisbia knew that Parrolla was much on the water; and when she knew he was there, she considered herself safe from his discovering that she was in company with Edwin, which she now sometimes was; but their meetings were conducted with the greatest secrecy, for Parrolla had now broke off his acquaintance with Miss Delamere, and again more than ever pestered Lisbia with his addresses. Love, Parrolla could never feel for any one; but he had two very strong inducements to court Lisbia: those inducements were her lovely person, and immense fortune.

On the evening after Parrolla and Olando had met to plan the murder of Mr. Immorf, Lisbia, thinking Parrolla safe, had ventured to walk with Edwin in the retired walk up the cliff; they were conversing on their mutual passion, and Lisbia was speaking in what manner she should, when she became of age, make known to her uncle her intention of becoming Edwin's wife; before the words had died on the lips of Lisbia, she heard footsteps approaching, and Lisbia saw with terror that it was her cousin Parrolla. She knew the violence of Parrolla's temper, and she dreaded lest he should insult Edwin, who, she knew, would not tamely brook an insult.

But, to the surprise of Lisbia, Parrolla passed on without speaking, but he gave her a side look, which fully conveyed to her the meaning of his rancorous heart. Lisbia was ready to expire with fright and vexation at being seen with Edwin by Parrolla, of whom she had the greatest dread.

Edwin said all in his power to comfort Lisbia, but he could not pacify her fears. "I know the malignant temper of my cousin Parrolla," she said, "he will never be at rest until he has done you some serious injury. Remember how suspicious he was, and how malicious he seemed to be, when I was invited in by your mother to take shelter from the storm. You must recollect how insolent he behaved when he and poor Percival came to your house to request shelter."

"Very few persons will give your cousin Parrolla a good word," said Edwin; "but, dearest Lisbia, let us not feel trouble by anticipation. I am not sure that your cousin observed us; and if he did, you are not under his control, nor accountable to him for your conduct; indeed, I do not think he noticed us; he walked on in deep thought; if he had seen you, he certainly would have spoken."

"Ah! no, he would not," said Lisbia, "I know my cousin's temper better than you do—you would not think that Parrolla did not observe us, had you seen the evil look he gave me; I dread, lest he should have overheard our conversation. I had rather it had remained a secret until I am of age; and that on no other account, than I do not wish to act in contradiction to the will of my uncle, who I know will not be agreeable to our union; and when informed that I walk with you, he will, no doubt, forbid our acquaintance, on account of your want of birth and fortune. My uncle has always behaved as a father to me, and as such I respect him; he I know acts by me as he would by his own daughter. Thinking my union with you would not be to my advantage, and through a mistaken notion of worldly interest, he would sacrifice the happiness of his niece."

"Ah! Lisbia, I shall at last lose you," said Edwin; "if your cousin acquaints his father, that he saw us taking an evening walk up this retired path, and you confess your regard for me, I fear it will be the ruin of my happiness; your uncle will take you to London, or perhaps France, or Italy, in order to break off our connexion; and when you are surrounded by the rich and great, you will forget the poor humble Edwin."

Dejected, he seated himself on the intersected roots of an oak, and with gentle violence he pulled Lisbia down, and seated her beside him. His voice was tremulous, and Lisbia saw he was much affected, as he said,—

"Do not go yet, and leave me so miserable and apprehensive; I fear, Lisbia, that we shall meet no more."

"Do not distress yourself, by thinking on that which will never happen," said Lisbia, "unless it is through death. That my uncle will be displeased with our acquaintance, I am certain, but he cannot prevent our marriage. During my minority, he may take me to London, or where he pleases; but no change of scene will ever drive you from my heart; take this ring," said Lisbia, and she drew a ring from her finger, and gave it to Edwin; "it was my mother's," she said, "wear it for my sake—think of me when you look on it, and be assured that my love, like the gold of that ring, will remain unchanged, nor suffer decay—as soon may you expect to see the pure metal melt, and drop from your finger."

With the anticipation of a severe lecture from her uncle, Lisbia returned to the castle; and Edwin, after watching her until she was out of sight, returned home with his thoughts full of love and Lisbia.

CHAPTER C.

"Yet doth he live!" exclaims the impatient heir,
And sighs for sables, which he must not wear.
A hundred scutcheons deck with gloomy grace,
The Laras last and longest dwelling-place.
But one is absent from the mouldering file,
That now were welcome in that Gothic pile.—LORD BYRON.

GREAT was the rage and malice that agitated the breast of Parrolla, when he saw Lisbia in company with Edwin; but he suppressed his angry feelings.

"She loves him, the low-bred serf," he inwardly said; "yes, she prefers him to Parrolla Immorf—but he shall suffer for his insolent presumption; and she shall be mine, both her person and fortune. I'll smother my ire, nor let them know that I noticed them."

"Full of uneasy thoughts, he strolled along the seashore, meditating in what way he could best dispose of Edwin,

No opportunity had yet occurred for Olando to fulfil his murderous purpose and on that subject, too, the thoughts of Parrolla were deeply engaged.

"My father must die, and that soon," thought Parrolla; "I cannot put up with such privation, as to be kept without money, I'd sooner die. This very night I'll drug his wine with opium, go into his room, and cut his throat myself, when he's sleeping; nor at all trust the idiot with my purpose; the bloody weapon being found near him, will cause the world to think that he did the deed himself."

Thinking on and planning his diabolical purpose, he walked along, ruminating, until it became dark; when a sudden agitation of the sea made Parrolla think that some bark was drawing towards the shore, and he stood watching to see who the persons might be.

Soon as they drew near the shore, which was situate near that spot where Lady Mackenzie had found shelter in the cavern, amongst the straw, dried leaves, and brambles, the men alighted from their bark, and began to haul some casks on shore, which they rolled into the cavern.

Parrolla came from the place of his concealment."

"Hilloa, my jolly boys," cried Parrolla, "what are you about there? Placing good liquor on my domain without paying rent. Pray, what remuneration am I to receive for suffering this?"

"Whatever you please to require," said a bluff-looking fellow, who seemed to be the head of the party; he looked a weather-beaten man, about forty years of age, dressed like a sailor, with a black beard and large whiskers.

"Whatever your honour requires you shall have," said the man, "but don't betray us."

"Betray you! no, no, my hearty fellow, I'll not betray you. But what have you got in those casks?"

"What! but some of the right stuff, to be sure. We'll tap a cask for your honour to taste, if you will come into the cavern; there we have deposited our goods for these twenty years, and never before has the least shadow of suspicion rested on us—but you have discovered our hoard."

"Well, well," said Parrolla, "what if I have? You shall receive no injury from me; and I will taste your liquor, and drink success to your trade."

Parrolla followed the men into the cavern, after one of them had kindled a light with some materials they kept in the cavern for that purpose.

Parrolla saw that these smugglers, for such they were, kept their stores in a recess Nature had formed in this cavern, in the front of which they piled up a quantity of straw, dried leaves, and brambles, in order to conceal their hoard.

They made a seat for Parrolla on one of the barrels, and having pulled out from beneath the rubbish, a flagon and horn cup, they abstracted from one of the barrels a flagon of brandy.

Having stuck their torch in the ground, they formed a group round Parrolla, who looked as if he was the sovereign of a lawless band. The cup went round, and Parrolla seemed quite at home with the smugglers, who all declared that they would serve the Lord of Ravenswood with the last drop of their blood.

"These professions sound well," said Parrolla, "if, when called on, the performance equals the promise; perhaps if I tell you in what way you can materially serve me, you may hesitate."

"Try us!" cried the smugglers, with one voice; "try us! Lord of Ravenswood."

"If an obnoxious reptile crawled before you," cried Parrolla, "one who would destroy your peace, your hope for ever, would you not crush him?"

"Ay," cried the band with one voice, and at the same time each man clapped his hand on a pistol which he wore in his belt; "his blood should no longer

remain in his body, nor his brains in his head," cried the man who appeared to b[ ]
the captain.

"I find you are men of spirit, and such as would not submit to injury," cried
Parrolla. "I have no doubt of your generous sentiments, and feel assured tha[t]
you feel as much interest in avenging the wrongs of a friend, as if the ill was don[e]
to yourselves. I am your friend—this secret retreat at the base of this castle, whic[h]
now is my father's; but in consequence of the age and infirmity of my parent, i[t]
will not be his long, it must soon be mine ; and here I swear never to disturb no[r]
molest you, but to give you free egress to this cavern to secrete your goods in, a[s]
much so as if it were your own freehold ; but I shall expect a service in return."

"What service do you require ?" cried the smugglers, with one voice. "Speak
Lord of Ravenswood—there is nothing we will hesitate at to serve you."

"There is one whose existence is hateful to me," said Parrolla; "I would no[t]
breathe the same vital air with him, living, this same globe must not contain u[s]
both—one of us must cease to be."

"Then you wish him dead ?"

"I do," cried Parrolla.

"His death warrant's signed," cried the band, with one voice, "his destructio[n]
is certain—point him out and he dies—who is the person ? Is it man or woman?

"It is but a youth," said Parrolla, "scarcely attained the age of manhood
but he stands between me and my happiness ; I'd have him removed—you un[der]
derstand me ?"

"Yes, yes, we understand you," cried the men—"he dies !"

"And where shall we find our victim ?" inquired the captain.

"At but a short distance from hence," said Parrolla, "'tis Edwin Mildmay, th[e]
miller's son."

"Edwin Mildmay, the miller's son !" exclaimed the captain. "I would it wer[e]
any other."

"That is the way," cried Parrolla, "men who are so very liberal in thei[r]
promises of service, are generally very slow in their performance ; but tell the[m]
what they can do, and they will find an objection."

"No objection should be on my part," said the captain, "but that youth I hav[e]
often nursed on my knee ; I love the boy—he is my sister's son."

"No matter," cried a sturdy-looking fellow, who now rose from his seat, and ap[-]
peared to be spokesman for the rest. "No matter," he said, whilst he pulled up hi[s]
unmentionables with one hand, and tucked a quid of tobacco into his mouth wit[h]
the other. "No matter," he again said, "if he is your sister's son. I'll tell yo[u]
what it is, captain, private feelings must give place to public interest ; if the Lor[d]
of Ravenswood requires it, the youth must be sacrificed."

"By G—d ! his life shall not be taken," cried the captain, "I'd sooner los[e]
my own."

"Cannot you compromise the matter ?" cried one of the crew. "Suppose w[e]
take him, and leave him amongst the savages, or somewhere thereabouts ?"

"Well, that will do," said Parrolla, "keep him but out of my way for a fe[w]
months, and I don't care."

"That I will do," said the captain, "he must first be enticed here ; we will the[n]
haul him into the ship."

All things were arranged between Parrolla and the smugglers, whilst poo[r]
Edwin slept, dreaming of his adored Lisbia, little thinking of the ev[il] that wa[s]
brewing against him.

CHAPTER CI.

I go, and it is done, the bell invites me.
Hear it not Duncan, for it is a knell,
That summons thee to heaven or hell.—SHAKSPEARE.

AFTER Parrolla had left the smugglers' cavern, he walked slowly on, ruminating on the strange adventure of the evening, and congratulating himself on his

address in bending the smugglers to his mind, respecting young Mildmay, whom
he now made sure of getting rid of.

It was a serene, but starless and dark night, and all things seemed buried in profound repose.

No. 32.

As Parrolla walked on, he heard the cathedral clock heavily sound the hour of midnight.

"My father is in bed long before this time," he mentally said. "I wish that he would sleep the sleep of death; and in that unwaking slumber he soon shall lay. Ay, this very night, or rather morning, if opportunity serves."

At that moment, Parrolla was startled by hearing a deep groan—it was thrice repeated. The affrighted night birds came fluttering round him; what had startled them he knew not, unless it was those awful groans that made even his firm nerves tremble. The night was no longer serenely still. The death owl's shriek sounded long, loud, and awfully; and as he passed along the elm-skirted path, every leaf, as if agitated by a tempest, shook and trembled.

Notwithstanding Parrolla felt somewhat shocked at the groans he had heard, which sounds had disturbed even the night birds, and made every leaf tremble, yet he remained resolutely bent on his purpose, and determined when he reached home, to fulfil his murderous intention, should opportunity offer.

Instead of going to bed, he sat in his chamber, until the bell sounded the hour of two.

Then shading his lamp, and with a stealthy step, he went into his father's chamber, whom he found lying prostrate on the floor. Thinking him asleep, Parrolla stooped to listen to his breathing, when he found that no breath issued from the lifeless corse.

"Mr. Immorf was dead; he had that night retired to rest about the hour of ten, and as soon as he entered his chamber, he was seized with a fit of apoplexy, and having no help by, he expired.

"Death has here superseded me," said Parrolla; "I am glad he has. I shall now sleep easy; to-morrow I shall be Lord of Ravenswood."

He left the corse of his father, and retired to his chamber, where he sat forming plans how he should best enjoy himself, now that he had become master of the property which had belonged to his father.

In the morning Parrolla did not rise at his usual hour, but rang the bell in his chamber, and when the servant answered it, he complained of illness, and ordered the man to bring his breakfast up to bed.

Mr. Immorf was a man of very regular habits, and always rose by seven in the morning; but seven o'clock came, nine and ten o'clock, when the servants became alarmed, particularly Peter, who proposed that the servant who usually waited on Mr. Immorf, should go up and knock at his master's door. The servant did so; but no answer was returned. Peter then went up and opened the door of his master's room; and, grieved and horror-struck, he beheld him lying a blackened corse on the floor.

All was now confusion in the castle—the servants loudly lamenting their beloved master. And Parrolla, when informed of his father's demise, appeared to be in the deepest sorrow.

A physician was sent for, who declared that all the art of a physician was unavailing, for the deceased had been dead many hours.

Here had the prediction of the gipsy failed; in all other matters her prophecy had been correct.

But Heaven, in its mercy, intervened; and had hearkened to the prayer of Parrolla's dying mother, who had prayed, and that incessantly, that her husband might not fall beneath the assassin's hand, nor her son become the murderer of his father. Yet of the intention Parrolla was guilty, though not of the actual deed; that foul sin was not added to the catalogue of his crimes, in consequence of the beatified spirit being called from the misery he experienced in this sublunary world, to partake of those joys no tongue can utter.

Poor Lisbia was in great grief concerning the death of her uncle, whom she loved as if he had been her own father. Nor did the selfish consideration of having none now to oppose her marriage with Edwin at all console the affectionate Lisbia, who knew that when she lost her uncle, she lost the best friend she had in the world. Besides, she was uneasy at being an inmate in the house of her cousin Parrolla, of whom she had a very bad opinion; and she intended, as soon as her lamented uncle was interred, to go into Devonshire to visit some relations she had there.

Never was any man more beloved and lamented by all in the neighbourhood than was Mr. Immorf, excepting by his own son, and the idiot, Olando, who, soon as he heard his uncle was dead, ran up to Mr. Mildmay's,—

"Where's Rose?" he cried; "uncle's dead, and I'll marry her to-morrow!"

"Your uncle dead!" cried Mr. Mildmay; "you surprise me. Is it a fact?—Is he really dead?"

"Dead!" cried Olando, "to be sure, he is; and I'll marry Rose to-morr o !"

"I am surprised to hear you express yourself in this unfeeling way," replied Mr. Mildmay; "and for Rose, 'tis useless for you to think of her, she is going to be married to Mr. Manby."

Olando was much chagrined at this intelligence; and he went back to Ravenswood, sighing and weeping, in consequence of his disappointment.

The light and indecent way in which Parrolla conducted himself at his father's funeral was much talked of by all in the neighbourhood who witnessed Mr. Immorf's interment; and the amiable qualities of that gentleman, and the unworthy conduct of his reprobate son, was a general topic of conversation.

CHAPTER CII.

His bristling locks of sable, brow of gloom,
And the wide waving of his shaken plume,
Glanced like a spectre's attributes; and gave
His aspect all that terror gives the grave.—LORD BYRON.

It was evening, and Peter was now somewhat recovered from the shock he felt on account of the sudden demise of his beloved master, and he went into the room in which Parrolla was sitting, and begged to be indulged with a little conversation on a matter of the greatest importance.

"Why really," said Parrolla, "I have not much time to spare, to listen to old men's tales. I suppose this important matter is some quarrel between you and the other servants, or some little mistake in your accounts which you wish adjusted."

"No, sir," cried Peter, "I would speak to you on a subject of the greatest importance. I would not intrude on you, now you are in such grief for the loss of your lamented father, with such trivial matters as you speak of; what I have to say deeply concerns you, and all who dwell in the castle."

"Well, Peter," said Parrolla, "do not be tedious in your talk, but tell me, in as few words as possible, what you have to say."

"I will, sir," said Peter, as he wiped the perspiration from his forehead; "I will tell you. You know, sir, there's a portrait covered with a black cloth hanging in the chamber of your late father, that portrait must be taken down and burnt."

"Indeed, Peter," replied Parrolla, "and who has made you a lawgiver? You presume very much on having lived so long in the family."

"Oh, sir, forgive me, if I have said anything to offend you," said Peter; "but, indeed, I but speak the words your honoured father would have spoken had he been living."

"My father wished the portrait to be burnt!" said Parrolla, "then why did he not do so?"

"He could not—dared not," replied Peter; "he wished it away—he wished it destroyed—but he was bound down by a fearful oath to let it remain uninjured."

"'Tis very strange," said Parrolla, "I saw the original of that portrait when I was at Naples, and I inquired of my father concerning that singular man, but he declined giving me any information. I suppose he must be some relation, as his portrait is hanging here."

"A relation! God forbid!" cried Peter; "he is one who studies magic, and holds a charmed existence."

"Studies magic, does he?" cried Parrolla. "I thought there was something very strange and unearthly in his appearance. His dark complexion, and eyes of fire—then his dress gives him more the appearance of a spectre than a living man. But how came my father to agree to be bound down by such an oath?" inquired Parrolla.

"He could not help it," said Peter; "his father, old Sir Parrolla, on his death-bed, required him to take it; he made my late honoured master and his mother, swear they would never destroy, directly or indirectly, neither the portrait nor the magic book. The magic book was given old Sir Parrolla by the original of the portrait, Count Herman."

"What, then, there is a magic book!" cried Parrolla: "where is it?—is it in the castle?"

"It is in the disused eastern turret," said Peter, "and I hope, sir, that you will permit me to make a bonfire of both the book and the portrait."

"By no means," cried Parrolla; "my grandfather's edict shall be punctually attended to by me."

"Oh, say not so!" cried Peter; "follow not the ways of old Sir Parrolla; he killed his own child, and caused the death of Rose Mildmay."

"What! then he was a murderer!" cried Parrolla.

"He was," said Peter, "and an awful scene was the hour of his death. He called for the magic book, and would have bargained with fiends to have prolonged his life, but death was upon him; he opened the magic book, but his power of vision was gone; he wished Lady Immorf to read the book at the leaf he had turned down, but her ladyship would not touch it, neither would your honoured father.

"They would have had the magic book, and the portrait of the magician, burnt the moment the breath was out of the body of old Sir Parrolla, for they felt the greatest dread at keeping those things in the castle; but they could not break the solemn oath they had so unwillingly entered into; for they were not aware that the portrait was the likeness of a magician, nor that the book was a treatise on magic.

"I was ordered to place the magic book again in the crimson velvet bag, from whence I had taken it; I did as I was desired, and placed the bag in the iron box that stood in the eastern turret; when I had done so, I locked the box, and took the key down to my mistress, but she would not touch it.

"'Hang it up,' said Lady Immorf, 'over the portrait, and if the original of the portrait comes for his likeness, and the magic book, he shall have them; for, though I am bound not to destroy them, I must not refuse them to their owner.'

"'And if he does not fetch them away,' said your honoured father, 'may mildew rot and consume every page of that accursed book, for perdition must bafal him who reads it.'"

"How foolish of you, Peter, to think of destoying this book," said Parrolla; "that the owner of it is in existence I am well aware, as not long since I myself beheld him. It would be but bad policy to enrage a magician; he, in his power, might raise a storm, and cause the castle to fall about our ears. No, no, Peter, the magic book must not be destroyed, I will myself take care of it.

"Fetch me the key," he continued, "we will go and take the book from the iron box in the eastern turret. Fetch it directly." Seeing Peter hesitated, Parrolla said, "I'll have the key—dare not dispute my commands."

"I beg, I intreat, sir," said Peter, much affected, "that you will have nothing to do with that accursed book; nothing shall induce me to lay one finger upon it—not for worlds would I read one page of that diabolical book."

"Nonsense!" cried Parrolla; "take one of those tapers, and light me up to the eastern turret."

"Oh! do not go up there, nor touch that fatal book, unless it is with the intention of burning it," said Peter; " it has brought trouble and death on the house of Ravenswood."

"Dastard!" cried Parrolla; and snatching up the taper, he went to the chamber where hung the portrait of Count Herman, and having taken the key from the nail on which the portrait hung, he hastened up to the eastern turret.

CHAPTER CIII.

The waving banner and the clapping door,
The rustling tapestry and the echoing floor ;
The long dim shadow of surrounding trees,
The flapping bat—the night song of the breeze.—LORD BYRON.

In the hall of Ravenswood Castle, there were two niches, and in each niche stood a tall carved figure, representing a man in armour, bearing in his hand a silk banner.

Parrolla was a man of strong nerves; but as he passed these figures, which he did in his way to the eastern turret, he was rather startled, by seeing the banners borne by these figures much agitated ; and he thought that the figure of the warrior he was passing, looked frowningly upon him.

"'Tis strange," thought Parrolla, " that the banners held by these figures should be so agitated, when there is not even a breath of air stirring."

But he went on, and he entered the eastern turret, which had not been entered for so many years—no, not since the birth of Parrolla.

He opened the iron box, and took from thence the crimson velvet bag ; and so great was the impatience of Parrolla to read the magic book, that he seated himself on the iron box, and he began to turn over the leaves.

The letters were in many places quite pale and colourless, in consequence of the damps, so that the words could not be distinguished; whilst other parts of the book were in a good state of preservation.

Parrolla's eyes had just rested on that page, where it explained how to call on supernatural agency to procure a lengthened existence ; but Parrolla could not read one single line in peace ; for the branches of the high elm trees rattled against the windows of the turret, and a dismal sound of wailing, and heartrending groans met his ear; then yells and laughter, as if the fiends of darkness were keeping holiday.

These sounds were by no means agreeable to Parrolla ; and with the magic book in one hand, and the taper in the other, he hastened down stairs.

And as he again passed through the hall, the banners held by the carved figures were yet more violently agitated ; and a moan, as if proceeding from some one in mental or bodily anguish, sounded on his ear.

But so intent was Parrolla on reading the magic book, that events so uncommon were but little heeded by him. And when again seated in his parlour, he hastily ran over the characters therein written.

"This book is more valuable to me than all my father's estates," inwardly said Parrolla; " life, long as this terrestrial globe shall last, if a victim can be procured, and how easy that will be. Riches, and all the world can give, will be at my command. And for the murderer's skull, that's necessary to complete the charm. Thanks to Peter; he, in his zeal to prevent my having recourse to magic, has given me every facility to do so."

In high spirits Parrolla closed the book, and determined at all events to possess himself of his grandfather's, old Sir Parrolla's, skull, and then at once to put the charm into operation.

On the following morning, Peter ventured to say, " I hope and trust, sir, you have altered your mind concerning that accursed book which, if used by you, mus certainly tend to your eternal perdition.

"I hope, sir," continued Peter, in a tremulous voice, that you have not removed it from the eastern turret."

"Ask me no questions," cried Parolla, haughtily. "Recollect, to question and direct your master is no part of your duty."

"Forgive me, sir!" said Peter; "forgive me for being solicitous for your welfare; for you must be well aware that that is my only motive. I have nursed you in my arms, when you were but an infant, and now feel as much affection for you, as if you were my own son; and on my knees I beg that you will not touch that magic book;" and Peter knelt down, with his face bathed in tears, as he clung to the knees of Parrolla.

"What would my late honoured master say?" cried Peter; "could he speak from the grave, would he not beg you to desist from your fearful purpose, nor touch a book so impious and opposite to the will of your Creator?"

"I am my own master," cried Parrolla. "And I shall use my own will; I will not be dictated to by a servant. If you cannot conduct yourself otherwise, you must leave my service."

Although the death of his father was a source of great satisfaction to Parrolla, there was one thing which much vexed and mortified him.

And that thing was, the smugglers had failed in taking Edwin Mildmay with them, as they had promised to do.

The fact was, they had waited until they were tired, in hopes of getting him into their power, but as no opportunity offered, they determined to try a scheme which they thought would not fail.

Towards evening, one of the men lurked about the cottage of Mildmay, until they saw Edwin. When the man, who had had his lesson from Parrolla, said,—

"There is a young lady, sir, that wishes to speak with you."

"Where is she?" cried Edwin, eagerly, not in the least doubting but that it was Lisbia whom the man alluded to. "Where is she?" cried Edwin.

"Follow me, and I will take you to her," said the man.

"What go at your tardy pace," cried Edwin. "Tell me, and tell me quickly where she is, that I may fly to her; is she in the walk leading up the cliff?"

"No, no," said the man, gruffly; "she is not there, she fears to be seen by the Lord of Ravenswood; and she awaits your coming by the seaside, in the cavern near where the huge willow droops into the sea."

"Quicken your pace," cried Edwin.

"Be not in such a hurry, you will be there in good time, I warrant me," said the man.

"What mean you?" inquired Edwin.

"Oh, nothing," said the man. "All I mean is, I don't like to be hurried."

"Lisbia has pitched upon a dismal spot for our meeting," said Edwin mentally, as he listened to the fretful waves, as they came foaming up towards the sea-beaten shore.

"She fears to be seen by her cousin Parrolla," thought Edwin. "Dearest Lisbia, and hast thou overcome the extreme timidity of thy nature, and assumed a courage foreign to thy soul, for a few moments converse with thy lover?"

"I fear there will be a storm," said Edwin, speaking to his guide. "The birds are making to their nests, and low, louring clouds hasten on the coming twilight."

The man made no reply.

"I fear there will be a storm," repeated Edwin.

"No matter," said his gruff companion, "you will be safely housed."

"Housed!" said Edwin, "what mean you?"

"Mean, oh, nothing!" said the man. "All I mean is, that you can take shelter in the cavern should a storm come on."

They were now at the mouth of the cavern.

"Where is the young lady?" demanded Edwin.

"I dare say she is gone into the cavern to prevent her being observed," said the man.

Edwin went a few paces into the cavern, and he called on the name of Lisbia, but no answer was returned.

The man put a whistle to his mouth, and in a moment several men were at the mouth of the cavern.

They seized Edwin, and, notwithstanding the resistance he made, he was overpowered by the men, and carried into the cavern.

"It is useless to make any resistance, young fellow," said the men; "you must go with us; we shall only take you a short voyage to sea, it will be for the benefit of your health, resistance is vain, therefore you may as well go peaceably. '

"Why have you lured me to this place under a false pretence?" said Edwin. "But I guess who is your employer. Ye shall not find it so easy a matter to compel me to go with you, sooner shall you take my life. '

Edwin was seized by four of the men, who were dragging him to their vessel, when breathless and in haste, came into the cavern the father of Edwin.

Mildmay had seen Edwin follow the man, whose appearance Mildmay did not like, and he had followed at a distance; and now that he had come into the cavern, and seen with what violence they were treating his son, his fears were realised.

"Villains! instantly let go that young man, for what purpose do you detain him?"

The men were for a moment stunned at so unexpectedly seeing a stranger amongst them.

Mildmay recognised Robert Alterton in the captain of these men—and Robert Alterton was his wife's brother.

"What Robert!" can you stand by and see your own nephew murdered?" cried Mildmay. Desist!" he cried, "and let go your hold on my son."

The bludgeon of one of the smugglers was up in a moment, and Mildmay would have been felled to the earth, had not the captain interfered.

"I will not suffer this," he cried; "let us come to a parley, matters must be differently arranged.

"Differently arranged!" cried the men, with one voice; "what mean you, captain? Have you not given your word? we never yet found you to be a weathercock, but staunch to your purpose. If you do not act according to your promise, the ruin of our company will follow."

"And what is this promise that you have entered into, Robert?" tremblingly inquired Mr. Mildmay; "surely you could not be wicked enough to engage to murder Edwin."

"No, no; bad as I am, I am not so bad as that, neither," cried Robert Alterton. "Let go the boy," he cried; "I'll do as I ever have done—be true to the interest of my company, but never will I be a hired assassin, to slay my own flesh and blood."

"It is now eighteen years since we last met, Robert," said Mildmay; "we all thought you were dead, little did I expect to find that you had turned bandit."

"Bandit?" cried Alterton; "I scorn the name. No, we are not banditti."

"Then what course are you pursuing?" tremulously inquired Mildmay.

"No matter for my course of life," replied Alterton, "that's to myself; and for my nephew, notwithstanding my engagement, I will let him go."

"What! and bring imprisonment and ruin on us all?" cried the men; "we will not be sacrificed."

"Nor shall you," said Alterton; "my brother-in-law must promise that his son shall keep house for one month, nor stir from thence, to which promise my nephew must agree; and they must likewise both swear never to name this transaction, nor to say they have seen me—they must banish this meeting from their recollection, and let all thoughts of it die away as if it never had been. Surely that will satisfy you," said Alterton, addressing the rest of the men who sullenly stood by.

"Who is there amongst you who would wish me to imbrue my hands in the blood of my nearest relation? If ye would, I am mistaken in your characters; if there is here a man so sanguinary, let him speak."

"No, no, we wish for no murder to be done," grumbled the men; "all we wish, is our own safety, and to be unmolested in our way of life."

"Your safety shall be uninjured by us," said Mildmay; "we will take any oath you require—that we will be secret, nor never name the transaction."

The terms were accepted by the company, the oath administered, and Mildmay and his son were suffered to depart.

CHAPTER CIV.

By Heaven I'll tear thee joint from joint,
And strew the hungry churchyard with thy limbs.
The time and my intent is fierce and wild."—SHAKSPEARE.

"How fortunate that I am possessed of the magic book," thought Parrolla; "not even Count Herman, though he should come for it himself, shall get it from me. How can I be sure that it belongs to him? My father never named it to me, and what signifies the evidence of stupid old Peter? No, no, I will never part with it.

"But lest any cross accident should happen, it will be prudent in me to secure the skull of my grandfather, old Sir Parrolla—delays are dangerous; if his being a murderer is publicly known, some one else for the same purpose may steal it, if they have not already done so. He has been so long dead, that his skull may have crumbled to dust, and if it is not, it may be so putrid that to touch it might be dangerous. But that will not deter me, have it I will. This night I will take a walk and survey the church, and find out if there is a possibility of my gaining an entrance into it without my employing a second person."

With this intent, Parrolla stole privily out of the castle after midnight. He provided himself with the implements he thought he should want, and likewise a dark lantern; and he took with him the velvet bag which had contained the magic book, to put old Sir Parrolla's skull in.

"There is now no fear of my being discovered in forcing an entrance into the church," thought Parrolla; "the drowsy world little dream of the errand on which I am going."

He had now reached the yew-tree walk in front of the church, and as he walked on, he was startled by hearing a deep groan sound near him. He turned his head, and saw a receding figure pass between the trees.

It was the form of his father! Parrolla for a moment was somewhat daunted, but he soon recovered himself.

"What childishness is this," he mentally said, "to be frightened at a spectre, which perhaps was but an imaginary form of my own disordered fancy? Nothing shall turn me from my purpose—at least no ideal form."

He proceeded on until he reached the church; he put his lantern down, and tried several of the windows of the church, to discover if any of them had been left unfastened, but to his disappointment they were all fast. He then endeavoured to force one of the windows, that seemed to be looser than the rest.

Whilst so employed, he heard a voice cry—"Forbear! oh, forbear!"

Parrolla desisted from his sacrilegious attempt; he jumped down from the window, and for a moment he appeared to be quite stunned at being detected in his guilt.

But whether it was mortal or immortal—from whence the voice proceeded,—he was at a loss to conjecture. He looked around him, but he could not see any one,

However, he was too much put out to make any further attempt to gain possession of the skull that night, or rather morning, for it now wanted but little of one o'clock.

As he pursued his way, he thought he saw Peter, who, by his movements, seemed as if he was endeavouring to hide himself from the notice of his master.

Parrolla went on without taking any notice of his faithful servant Peter; but he was extremely angry with him.

"He must have heard me go out, and perhaps guessing on what errand I was going, he has watched me. I hope he did not see me try to get into the church.

No. 33.

I will take no notice, but pick some quarrel with him, and turn away the officious fool."

Parrola was much vexed at being disappointed of getting the skull. However, he determined to go again, and leave no scheme untried, until he became its possessor.

The following morning, Peter came into the room where Parrolla was sitting, on some business he had with his master, when Peter said,—

"I hope, sir, you will pardon the liberty I take, in again speaking to you concerning that accursed magic book; do not attribute to idle curiosity what only proceeds from the regard I have for you. I found that the bag that contained that fatal book is taken from the iron box standing in the eastern turret, and when I found that you had left the castle at the hour of midnight last night, I felt miserable—I could not refrain from following your steps—a dreadful presentiment came over me. You bent your steps to the churchyard—I saw you walk up the yew-tree walk, and then you tried to open a window in the church. Oh, sir, for what reason did you do that? Tell me; for with dreadful apprehensions my heart is sinking within me."

"Follow me!—to be a spy!—and an observer of my actions!" cried Parrolla, "Presumptuous wretch! 'tis well that I did not fell thee to the earth. Never, as you value your life, watch me; and for this insolence, I here give you warning to quit my service."

Peter would have excused himself, would have pleaded the affection he had for his master, as an excuse for his temerity; he would have humbled himself to the dust before his incensed master; but Parrolla would not hear one word. He took Peter by the shoulder, and pushed him out of the room; and again Parrolla desired Peter would quit Ravenswood Castle.

Lisbia had made up her mind to quit Ravenswood; but she thought it not prudent to acquaint Parrolla with her intention of not again returning.

Lisbia therefore told Parrolla that she should go for a few weeks on a visit into Devonshire, as she was extremely dull and low spirited since the death of her uncle, and she thought that a change of scene would enliven her, and raise her spirits.

"Indeed," said Lisbia, "if it was not for Mrs. White, the housekeeper, who has been very kind to me, I don't know what I should do."

"And you would leave me here alone in solitude," said Parrolla, knitting his brow. "No, you must first be my bride, and then I will accompany you."

"And is it possible that you can think of marriage so soon after the death of your lamented father," said Lisbia; "do not, I entreat, at this time mention such a subject."

"Well, you shall reign my sovereign, and I will obey you," said Parrolla. "When do you think of leaving Ravenswood?"

Lisbia informed Parolla that she thought of setting off for Devonshire the following week.

"Your will shall be as a law to me," said Parrolla; "but I must request, that before your departure, you will take leave of those friends with whom you have been intimate; for," added Parrolla, laughing, "if you do not say that you are going, and where you are going, they will not be satisfied, and may think that I have, as some great ogre would have done, eat you up by way of a delicious morsel."

Lisbia smiled at this strange conceit of Parrolla's.

"No," she said, "they would hardly think that;" and pleased at the seeming ready acquiescence of Parrolla for her to go into Devonshire, Lisbia was in good spirits, for she had feared that Parrolla would not so readily consent to her going.

But though Parrolla seemed willing for Lisbia to go into Devonshire, he was in reality quite the reverse; he was fully persuaded that she loved Edwin Mildmay, and thought that perhaps Lisbia's intended journey to Devonshire was but a subterfuge; when in reality, her intention of leaving the castle was to united to Edwin, and return no more to Ravenswood.

"Let her be ever so subtle, she shall not escape me," thought Parrolla; "but I will not put her on her guard, by dropping one word of my suspicions."

On the following day, Lisbia went to pay a visit to Mrs. Durant, and she was prevailed upon by Mrs. Durant to stay and take dinner.

Parrolla called at Mr. Durant's in the afternoon, and said he came for the express purpose of having the pleasure of escorting his cousin Miss Phillimore home.

Lisbia, soon after Parrolla came, took her leave of Mrs. Durant, and wished to go home; but Mrs. Durant said,—

"Stay until Mr. Durant comes home, my dear Miss Phillimore; he will be quite pleased to see you. You must not go yet, especially as you are a going to leave us, and it may be some time before we again see you."

"You must not go yet, Lisbia," said Parrolla; "I came to pay a good long visit to Mr. Durant, and as he is soon expected, I should wish to stay and see him."

"Certainly," said Mrs. Durant, "you must spend the day with us; and if it is late when you leave, you have your cousin for a guard."

Lisbia knew not what to say, nor how to object, but she was miserable; and she felt the greatest objection in staying, and in walking home with her cousin Parrolla.

A heavy foreboding of evil sat on her heart, though for what reason she knew not.

She repented that she had left home, nor would she have done so, if she had known that Parrolla would have followed her to Mrs. Durant's.

Mrs. Durant saw Lisbia was agitated, and that her countenance frequently changed, first pale and then crimson.

"You are not well, my dear Miss Phillimore," said Mrs. Durant. "You are ill, I am sure you are."

"No," said Lisbia, "I am not ill; I once or twice felt rather faint; it was perhaps in consequence of the weather; it has been all day very sultry."

"Yes," said Mrs. Durant. "And I think we shall have a storm; I wish Mr. Durant would come home."

"Your opinion and mine agree," said Lisbia; "therefore as you wish me well, do not persuade me to stay longer."

"If it should begin to rain, I will order the horses to be put in the carriage," said Mrs. Durant, "and you will be home in a quarter of an hour."

"I had much rather walk," said Lisbia; "for some horses are frightened at lightning, and an accident might happen."

After taking her leave of Mrs. Durant, Lisbia departed with Parrolla.

They had walked but a short distance, when dark lurid clouds began to overspread the horizon, emitting flashes of the most vivid lightning, and thunder began to roll in loud peals above them.

Lisbia who was much terrified at thunder and lightning, and had been so from her infancy, seemed ready to faint; Parrolla, with a tenderness of manner Lisbia had never before observed in him, endeavoured to inspire her with fortitude.

"Do not give way to fear," he said, "no harm will happen to us; but I think it will be wisest to go the way by the beach, 'tis much nearer, and instead of being half an hour before we reach the castle we shall not be more than twenty minutes."

The lightning's glare was yet more vivid, and yet more heavily rolled the roaring thunder, and heavy rain drops began to patter down.

They were now close to the cavern, where Lady Mackenzie had taken shelter, and to where Edwin had been decoyed.

"Let us stop here for shelter," said Parrolla.

Lisbia gladly turned into the cavern.

"Even this place is welcome," she said, "a most acceptable shelter now; I would to Heaven that I had stayed for the night at Mrs. Durant's."

"But I do not," said Parrolla; "come, let us go further into the cavern, there we shall see less of the storm. At this moment a more terrific flash than she had yet beheld, caused the sea to look like liquid fire, and the earth as if it was in one blaze. Parrolla took the advantage of the terror Lisbia was in, and he urged her forward. The lightning played through the iron grating, and illumined their path, until they had nearly reached the centre of the cavern, then at intervals, leaving them almost in utter darkness.

"I know this place well," said Parrolla, "and here we can be free from restraint or observation; here we are safe from the storm and every one else. Come, love, and sit down," he said, as he felt about, and tumbled up the straw and dried leaves.

"Never before did I perform the part of a chamberlain," he said; "but, Lisbia, this is your bridal night, and this your bridal bed!"

"What mean you?" said Lisbia, trembling with affright. "Parrolla, what mean you?"

"I mean," replied Parrolla, "that I have put up with your coolness long enough; 'tis that low-bred fellow, the miller's son, that you love! I bridled my anger, and waited for an opportunity—that opportunity is mine, nor shall you escape me; here no earthly power shall save you. Come, be compliable," he continued, "or force shall compel you," and Parrolla pulled Lisbia down on the straw and dried leaves.

"Oh, let me go," cried Lisbia; "let me brave the angry heavens. Better that the fiery bolt should strike me, or the lightning consume my frame, than remain with thee—oh!" she cried, as he still detained her, "have you no fear? Would not your dead mother cry from the grave for pity on her sister's child? Oh! have mercy on me! have mercy on me!"

"Don't think to daunt me, or alter my purpose," cried Parrolla, "by bringing up the dead. This night shall you pass with me;" and he pulled Lisbia down on the straw and leaves he had heaped together. "'Tis useless," he said; "you must submit."

Lisbia did not reply; she fell heavily on the earth, fainting and unconscious.

Notwithstanding the state Lisbia was in, Parrolla, lost to all feeling, was about to satisfy his brutal appetite, when he was startled by hearing a footstep behind him, and whilst he was rising from the ground to discover who or what it might be, he heard a voice cry,—

"Die, d——d Mackenzie! I'd kill the widow Butler, too, but she's dead already."

Parrolla felt that he was wounded, and that mortally; his life's blood gushed fast from him, and in a few moments he breathed his last.

The person who had stabbed Parrolla, and saved Lisbia from being wretched for life, was Lady Mackenzie. She had given her keeper the slip, and secreted herself in her old haunt, the cavern.

In a delusion of mind she believed Parrolla to be Mr. Mackenzie, and Lisbia to be the widow Butler.

The lightning's glare shone through the iron grating at the top of the cavern on the blade of a clasp knife that lay on the ground, with which the smugglers sometimes used to cut their food, and she picked it up, and when another flash came, she directed the knife to the heart of Parrolla, as she cried,—

"Die, d——d Mackenzie!"

Soon as she had done the deed, she ran out of the cavern, rejoicing, shouting, and laughing wildly. It was a laugh that sounded more like a yell than a laugh, as she cried, "Mackenzie's dead! Mackenzie's dead! He can't put me in the madhouse now!"

Long did Lisbia lay in a state of insensibility by the side of the murdered Parrolla. She heard not, nor knew not, what had occurred during her swoon. The first thing that struck her memory was the behaviour of her cousin Parrolla; and she trembled with apprehension, when she recollected the words he had spoken to her. But now all was still; she neither heard nor saw him; the storm had died away, and it was a clear and moonlight night, and some rays of that bright orb fell through the grating at the top of the cavern, so that it was not in utter darkness; there was a faint light, a kind of twilight appearance.

Lisbia arose from the ground, and as she did so, she stumbled over the dead body of Parrolla as she assisted herself to rise. She felt the handle of the knife that was yet sticking in the breast of Parrolla, and when she got out of the tavern, and was standing on the sea beach, she found that her hands were wet, and her garments were saturated with his blood. More dead than alive, Lisbia crawled home, and as soon as the door was opened, which it happened to be by Peter, she fell senseless into the hall.

CHAPTER CV.

In bleeding state I saw him on the earth,
From whence with life he never more sprang up.—SHAKSPEARE.

PETER was much alarmed at the state in which he saw Lisbia; he rang the bell with such violence, that all the servants, alarmed, rushed into the hall, and their surprise at seeing Lisbia in that dreadful state was equal to Peter's. She was taken by Mrs. White, the housekeeper, and some other of the female servants, and laid on her bed, and a physician was immediately sent for. Restoratives were given to Lisbia, and her dress changed by the servants, who were all anxious to hear how their young lady came to be in that gory state, and was not herself in the least wounded; but Lisbia was in no condition to answer any questions; she was so low that she could hardly speak, and fainted a number of times during the night, and the next day she was but little better.

The physician declared that Lisbia was in a very dangerous state, and that her life greatly depended on her being kept quiet. "Nor must she," said the physician, "be allowed to talk; she must be kept in a state of the greatest composure."

Peter and the rest of the servants were surprised on the following day by not seeing their master, and more so by hearing Lisbia say,—

"He is murdered—my cousin Parrolla is murdered, or he has killed himself!" Before the words had died on her lips, a man came running in haste from the castle.

"Mr. Immorf is murdered!" cried the man, "and he lies now in the cavern by the sea-side deluged in blood. I passed that way this morning, and seeing spots of blood, I followed the track into the cavern, where I saw a man lying; but who he was I knew not, for it was too dark in the cavern for me to distinguish his features. I procured a light, and again entered the cavern, when, to my surprise and horror, I saw that the person lying there was young Mr. Immorf; he was lying on his back, and a knife was sticking in his breast that must have penetrated his heart."

"Great God! here is trouble upon trouble, and calamity upon calamity!" said Peter. "This is all owing to the accursed magic-kook, and the portrait with the black cloth hanging over it. Come," continued Peter, "let us go and fetch his body home. I must conduct this dreadful business as well as I can; for there are now none to give orders; Miss Phillimore cannot be spoken with, and Mr. Phillimore is worse than [nobody. Aye!" said Peter, speaking to himself, "well thought of—put the horses in the carriage, my master shall be brought home like himself."

The body of Parrolla was brought to the castle, and as it lay in the splendid coffin, Peter with sorrow looked on the stern countenance of his late lord, for whom he felt the same regard as a parent does for a reprobate child,—when living, he loved, and in death, he lamented him.

Now he was dead, and cut off in the midst of his sins, even whilst his mind was fixed on having dealings with the power of darkness. That was an awful thought to Peter, and made him very unhappy.

Lady Mackenzie was missed by her keeper, and found near the hovel where Maria and her husband had dwelt; there were spots of blood on her clothes, and when the murder of Parrolla became known, it was generally concluded that the mad woman had shed the blood of Parrolla.

But it could not be proved that she did so; and if it was, of course she could not be made accountable for what she did whilst under the influence of insanity; but she was now more restrained than yet she had been. A being looked on now as a dangerous maniac, and she ever after had two keepers instead of one.

Lisbia, after some time, recovered the shock her nervous system had received, and in the course of a week she was able to give orders how the funeral of Parrolla was to be conducted. And as she sat at her window, and saw the pompous caval-cade which attended the burial of the last of the Immorf's wind its funeral way from the castle, she thought how still and mute were those lips which expressed the evil designs, the heart now paralysed, conceived against her.

There was no occasion for lamentation, nor was any show of grief due to the departed. Yet in death there is a solemnity, and that solemnity was deeply felt by Lisbia.

Miserably wicked had been the life of Parrolla, and miserably was his life termi-nated by the hand of a mad woman, and in a rude cavern, whilst he was about to commit a crime, that was death by the law of his country.

Olando now was heir to Ravenswood in right of his mother; but the poor idiot being incapable of governing himself, Lisbia could do no other, he being her brother, than take him under her care, and act as a guardian to him.

And happy it was for Olando that he had such an affectionate sister, for but few persons else would like to have been troubled with him, unless it was to make a property of him.

Lisbia retained all the servants; and Peter, the faithful old servant, was now a man of great consequence in the family.

Lisbia, for the better recovery of her health and spirits, went for some months into Devonshire, and she took with her her brother Olando.

Before she left Cornwall, she gave orders to Peter to have several rooms in the castle newly done up and beautified; and she sent for an upholsterer from London, to whom she gave very extensive orders.

The scenery round Ravenswood Castle was very beautiful; and when the orders that Lisbia had given were completed, it looked a perfect paradise.

When Lisbia returned from Devonshire, she brought Edwin in the carriage with her; for Lisbia was no longer Miss Phillimore, but Mrs. Mildmay; and the dispised miller's son was lord of Ravenswood, Olando not being fit to act for himself.

Rose was married to Mr. Manby, and the families lived at Cornwall in the greatest harmony.

CHAPTER CVI.

Oft in glimmering bower and glades
He met her, and in secret shades.—MILTON.

NEAR Brosely, in Shropshire, stood a neat farmhouse; its white front was adorned by the jessamine and honey-suckle that ran up its walls, and formed a fragrant porch before the house.

Here lived a family, contented and happy in their humble estate; these good people had three children, two girls and one boy.

It was the duty of Ann, the eldest, to help her mother in the dairy, to do the household work, look after the younger children, or do anything she was required to do; never was there so kind, so affectionate a girl as Ann. Whatever she did, she did cheerfully; and a smile always adorned her beautiful countenance,

Ann was at this time sixteen, tall, and her form was symmetry itself, and her raven locks shaded a face of extreme beauty. Her sister Jane was five years old, and her brother John was seven.

The two younger children were put to bed by Ann, and the cloth laid for supper in front of the farm, where Farmer Jenkins, his wife, and daughter usually sat to enjoy their supper on a summer's evening.

"Oh, mother!" said Ann, "I forgot to take my poor grandmother the custard you made for her—I'll run with it now."

"I quite forgot it too!" said her mother, "or I would have sent John with it before he went to bed."

"Never mind," replied Ann; "'tis only across four fields, and I shall soon be there." Ann's bonnet was on in a moment, and her grandmother who was ill, felt revived and better when she saw Ann, and the little present brought her by her granddaughter; for the old woman felt that, though she was old and poor, yet there were those in the world to whom her comfort was no matter of indifference.

Ann stayed some time with her grandmother, when the old woman said,—

"Your company, my sweet Ann, is a comfort to me—I wish I every day could see your pretty face—but 'tis getting late, child, and I fear you will not be home by daylight."

"Never mind, grandmother," said Ann, "if I don't get home by daylight, I shall get home by moonlight; for we have a new moon to-night, and look how beautiful 'tis rising," she said, as she pointed to the window.

After taking an affectionate leave of her grandmother, and promising that either she or her mother would visit her on the following day, Ann departed.

The hay was cut, and its fragrance scented the balmy air, and the nightingale was singing her lovelorn song as Ann in her way passed beneath a tree in which the bird was perched.

"How delightful is the note of that little songster," thought Ann; "how sweet is the air, and how beautiful is the rising moon; how grateful ought we to be to God for these benefits.

"I, above many, ought to be thankful, for God hath prospered my father's labour in the field. He hath been blessed with abundant crops—and all he hath set his hand to hath prospered; and what a blessing," thought Ann, "that we are able to keep my poor grandmother out of the poor-house."

As Ann walked on, she thought she heard a footstep behind her; she started; for Ann was in deep thought, and not aware any one was nigh.

She turned her head, and saw that it was a gentleman who was walking behind her; a stranger, not an inhabitant of that part, Ann was sure, for he was a person she had never seen before.

He advanced to Ann, and said, "I saw you start, I fear I alarmed you."

"Oh no," said Ann, "you have not alarmed me, sir; but I was not at first aware that any person was behind me."

"To have alarmed you would have given me some concern," said the stranger; "but are you not afraid to walk alone in these fields now that it is late in the evening," said the stranger.

"Oh no," replied Ann, "what should I fear?"

"You, indeed, ought to have no cause to fear," said the stranger, "for who could harm beauty and innocence like yours? But if my company is not disagreeable, I will walk with you and see you safe."

The stranger requested to know Ann's name, which she informed him; where she lived, and how many brothers and sisters she had, which Ann, with the greatest simplicity, informed him also.

"There is my father's house," said Ann, pointing to the farm; "I will now, sir, wish you a good night, and I thank you for your company."

"You must not go yet," said the stranger, gently detaining her hand, and pulling her further into the field. I cannot part with you yet; I have something of the utmost consequence to say to you;" and he pressed the hand of Ann as he said, "do not refuse to give me a few moments of your company."

Ann felt inclined to grant the request of the stranger; but she hesitated. "I never saw him before," thought Ann; "it will look bold and forward in me to give my company to a strange gentleman."

The stranger still retained her hand. "Do not refuse me the pleasure of a few moments' conversation," he said; "you cannot have the cruelty to refuse me," and he looked in Ann's face so intreatingly; and his request being seconded by her own wish, she complied; and they continued to walk in the field.

Ann listened to his discourse of love; and though the eyes of the stranger might have appeared as orbs of fire to some, terrific in their lustre, but differently did they appear to Ann; never to her mind had she seen anything so brightly beautiful as the lustre of those eyes of fire, in which the possessor, if he pleased, could throw a tenderness that softened their intense brilliancy.

Ann was charmed with the stranger, and the two hours she passed in his company, appeared to her like two minutes.

But when Ann heard the church clock sound the hour of ten, she started at the unwelcome sound.

"I must go!" she cried, "I fear my father and mother will be uneasy on my account; I am sorry I stayed so long. I was not aware that it was so late."

"I cannot let you go now," said the stranger, "unless you will promise me that you will meet me here the evening after to-morrow."

"I cannot promise," said Ann.

"You must promise," said the stranger; "never will I relinquish this dear hand until you promise me."

"Well, I will come," said Ann.

"You will not disappoint me," said the stranger; "if you do, I will come to the farm and inquire for you."

"Oh no, do not do that!" said Ann, "I should be quite ashamed if you came and asked for me. Don't do that—I will come."

When Ann reached home, her mother was standing at the gate waiting for her.

"How came you to stay so late, Ann?" said her mother; "your father was just a going to set out to look for you."

Ann felt rather at a loss what to say. And she told the first untruth she had ever been guilty of, in point of deceiving her mother.

"I had such a long talk with grandmother." she said; "she was so glad to see me, that she did not like me to come away; I have been talking to nobody but her.

"No," said her mother, "I don't suppose you have; who else should you talk to?"

Ann looked confused; but that was not noticed by her unsuspecting mother.

The thoughts of poor Ann were now wholly taken up with thinking on the stranger; if she heard a footsep. she felt quite in a flutter; she thought it might be him, although he had promised not to come to her dwelling.

On the following day towards evening, Ann was sent to her grandmother's with another custard, for the old woman's supper.

Ann thought as she went across the fields, on the moments she had spent with the stranger, who during the short time she had been in his company, had made an impression on her youthful heart.

As she went through the field to her grandmother's, she did not meet him; but Ann flattered herself that she might meet him in her road back. She loitered, stopped, and looked round the fields as she returned; and when she was in the last field she had to pass through, she saw some one advancing from a distant part of the field, whose figure greatly resembled that of the stranger.

Ann was all of a flutter. "That is him!" she mentally said; "but I will not let him think that I see him. I wished that I might meet him, and now I feel quite flurried; he will think that I came to look for him, and I should not like him to think that."

Ann proceeded with a palpitating heart, but no one approached her ; she ventured to turn her head, and she saw that she was mistaken ; it was not the stranger.

Disappointed and melancholy, Ann reached home ; and when she opened the door and entered the house, Mrs. Jenkins saw that Ann was vexed about something.

"Surely your grandmother is not dead !" she said ; "Ann, what is the matter?"

"Oh, nothing !" replied Ann. "La, mother, how fanciful you are,"

Ann never had answered her mother before so pertly and peevishly, and Mrs. Jenkins was rather surprised at the change in Ann.

The next day was a busy day, for Mrs. Jenkins and Ann were busily employed in making cheese ; nor had they done making the cheese when the hour arrived for Ann to meet the stranger.

Ann knew not what to do ; but at all events she slipped out for

No. 34.

a few moments, and told the stranger that she could not then stop; but that she would meet him the next night instead.

"Do not trifle with me," he said, "if you say you will come, you must come; nor be kept from meeting me by father or mother, or any one. I have selected you; and if you intend to be my bride, you must give up all the world for me."

The stranger took the hand of Ann, and he pressed it to his bosom ; and as his brilliant eyes seemed as if they would pierce her inmost soul, he said,—

"Ann, will you give up all for me? I will resign all for you. Friends, kindred ; all—all, will I give up for you. You, and you alone shall be the mistress of my fate. Leave your home and come with me, and you shall be my wife !"

"No," said Ann, "I will not do that. I cannot stay now, I must go home again."

"You care not what you make me suffer," said the stranger; "to-morrow night I cannot see you, I have an engagement," he said ; but he said that to vex and disappoint Ann, because she would not then stop.

He saw the ascendancy he had gained over her, and a greater ascendancy he intended yet to gain.

He admired Ann, and he liked her better than he had ever before liked a female. He saw that Ann loved him, and it was the intention of the stranger to make Ann the partner of his life; and that she should be the means of lengthening his years, and causing the extension of her own.

"The evening after to-morrow then you will be here?" said the stranger coolly. "Fail not to come,—adieu."

And he waved his hand, and bowed his head whilst he crossed a stile that took him into another field; and in a moment he was lost to the sight of Ann.

Poor Ann was in tears; she found to her sorrow how much the stranger had wormed himself into her affections.

"He is offended !" she mournfully said; "and angry with me for what I cannot help ; how haughty and indifferent he seemed !"

When Ann returned, she had been missed by her mother, who inquired where she had been.

"Only to the door," said Ann.

"Don't say that," said her mother, "I have looked everywhere I could think of for you, but could not find you."

"I must not stir, I suppose," said Ann, sullenly.

On the following day a fair was held at Broseley; and Ann with her father and mother was there.

The young people proposed to have a dance on the green ; a fiddler was in attendance, and the nymphs and rustic swains tripped it on the light fantastic toe, with joy in their faces and content in their hearts, all but poor Ann.

Peter Dobson, the son of a wealthy farmer, had selected Ann for a partner, and the love he bore her, though unknown to any but himself, he found was much increased in consequence of his being in her company that evening; and Peter intended to make proposals to Ann's parents the following day.

Though all was gaiety, and Ann commanded more attention than most of the females present; yet heaviness sat on her heart; she felt she loved, and that all the company, and that all the gaiety in the world, were by no means cheering to her, unless the beloved of her soul was present; music to her was discordant, and but filled her soul with melancholy, and Ann heartily wished to be at home.

CHAPTER CVII.

Again Ann was importuned to go down another dance with Peter Dobson; it was disagreeable to her to do so, and she would have excused herself, but she could not without great rudeness refuse, for Ann had no idea of making insincere but polite excuses. Whilst sitting down to rest after the dance, on a bench, at the back of which there was a hedge row of elder trees, she saw the dark outlines of the stranger's figure pass. Ann passed a miserable evening, but when she met the stranger, all was set to rights again.

Nine months had passed away since Ann first became acquainted with the stranger; he had entirely won her affection, he was then to her as father!—mother!—the supreme whom she worshipped!

The stranger, during every meeting Ann had had with him, was always all love and tenderness; but of late, Ann had observed a change in his manner, a gloominess, abstraction, and melancholy, which it gave her pain to observe, for Ann feared that she had ceased to interest him.

But the stranger assured Ann "that his love for her was unchanged, and that the reason of his melancholy was, a fear of being soon separated from her, and that was eternally."

"Separated!" cried Ann, "wherefore should we be separated?"

"In an evil hour!" cried the stranger, "when my guardian angel slept regardless of his charge, I, from a reprehensible curiosity, pryed into secrets mortals should not dive into, and for so doing in a very short time I must pay the penalty of my crime!"

"And is your doom irrevocably fixed?" inquired Ann; "will not penitence and prayer make an atonement?"

"Repent I cannot," replied the stranger, "nor can I—dare I pray!"

"Oh! what misery is this!" cried Ann. "Why did you not before inform me how you were situated? Why had you the cruelty to win my love, when you knew the destiny that awaited you?"

"I knew my destiny," said the stranger, "and also knew that the evil day might be deferred, could I find one who would serve me; 'tis easy to say I love you, but who, bound down by religious scruples, would say, 'I'll share your fate, and become a victim with you? That, and that alone, would stay my being here."

"If I can serve you, even if it is with my life, I will not hesitate to do it," replied Ann. "Say in what way I can serve you."

"If you would serve me, you must embrace that which I have embraced," said the stranger; "you must enter the service of him whom I serve, and subscribe to the conditions which I have subscribed to. Shall our destinies be united? Shall our fate be the same?"

"And who is he whose conditions you have subscribed to," said Ann, "but whose name you seem afraid to mention? Who is he whose service I must enter?"

"Into the service of that arch chief, who rebelled against his Maker," replied Count Herman, for he it was whose subtlety had gained the heart of the unsuspecting Ann.

Ann turned pale as death, as Count Herman pronounced these words.

"And must I league with the enemy of my Maker?" she said. "Oh, dreadful thought!"

"Ann, you must give up God, or give up me," said Count Herman; "choose—make your own election!"

"I cannot give you up!" cried Ann, in a tremulous voice; "you are all to me, though my eternal perdition is the consequence! Never will I give you up!"

The last words died on the lips of Ann, as fainting she reclined against a tree that grew on the bank on which they were sitting.

Count Herman supported the fainting girl, and, as her head rested on his arm, her long dark ringlets swept the bank, and the moonbeams shone full on her beautiful features, which then were pale and white as statuary marble. And so lovely, innocent, and angelic appeared the countenance of the fainting girl, that he, even he, Count Herman, felt some compassion for his victim, but he then had not time to procure another.

When Ann revived, she was anxious to hear all particulars of the dreaded contract she was about to enter into.

Of these particulars she was informed by Count Herman, who would have persuaded her then to have remained with him; but Ann's mother was ill, and Ann would not be prevailed on to stay that night.

"But six nights from this, at the hour of twelve precisely, you must be introduced to the Demon Zinegratta," said Count Herman.

"I will be punctual," replied Ann.

Ann saw Count Herman on the following day, and on the day after; but still her mother continued to get worse and worse. And the heart of poor Ann was almost broken on account of the situation she was placed in.

The fatal day came! and Count Herman wandered up and down the dwelling of Ann, for he feared that she would not keep her promise.

But Ann found means unperceived to slip out and speak to her lover, whom she assured she would not fail to come; and she desired that he would wait for her at a short distance from her dwelling.

"At the hour of ten," said Ann, "you may depend on seeing me."

"Be punctual," whispered Count Herman, "for if you are not there before the clock has gone twelve, my doom will be irrevocably fixed."

As evening approached, Ann's agitation was excessive. With tears in her eyes she looked at her father and mother, whom she was about to leave for ever; sl. kissed her brother and sister as they lay asleep.

Just as the clock had struck the hour of nine, and Ann was thinking that, in one more little hour, she should bid adieu to home for ever, a heavy storm came on, the wind howled fearfully across the field, the loud thunder and the lightning's vivid glare was that night more awful, than any in that part of the country ever remembered.

Notwithstanding the storm, Ann intended to keep her promise to her lover; but she waited, thinking the storm would subside; finding it did not, as the clock struck eleven, she opened the door, and was hastening from home, when she saw the heavens look like one sheet of vivid fire, and a loud crash of thunder seemed to shake the very foundation of the earth.

Ann, in extreme terror, fell on her knees. "O, God! protect me!" she cried.

Again a more vivid flash descended, and the forked fire struck the kneeling girl, who fell on the earth a lifeless corse.

God did protect her, and saved her, innocent as she was, from every other crime, than the intention of committing the deadly sin which her devotedness to Count Herman induced her to comply with.

Despairingly Count Herman viewed the dreadful storm. Ann was not there, and the crisis of his fate was nigh.

The hour of midnight was come, and, with feelings of dread and horror, he wailed the accomplishment of his fate. The sound of heartrending shrieks were heard mingling with the roaring of the winds; and the hat and black wrapping cloak of Count Herman were seeing lying on the ground, in a woody dell near the house of his intended victim.

THE END.

LONDON: Printed and Published by E. Lloyd, 12, Salisbury-square, Fleet-street.